A Place for Love

Khris Andrews

Copyright © 2024 by Khris Andrews
www.khrisandrews.com
All rights reserved.

This is a work of fiction. Names, characters, places, and incidents are products of the author's imagination or are used fictitiously. Any resemblance to actual events, locales, or persons, living or dead, is entirely coincidental.

A PLACE FOR LOVE

Editing by Celia Killen
Cover Design by Ebook Launch Covers

ISBN: 979-8-9916076-0-5 (ebook)
ISBN: 979-8-9916076-1-2 (paperback)

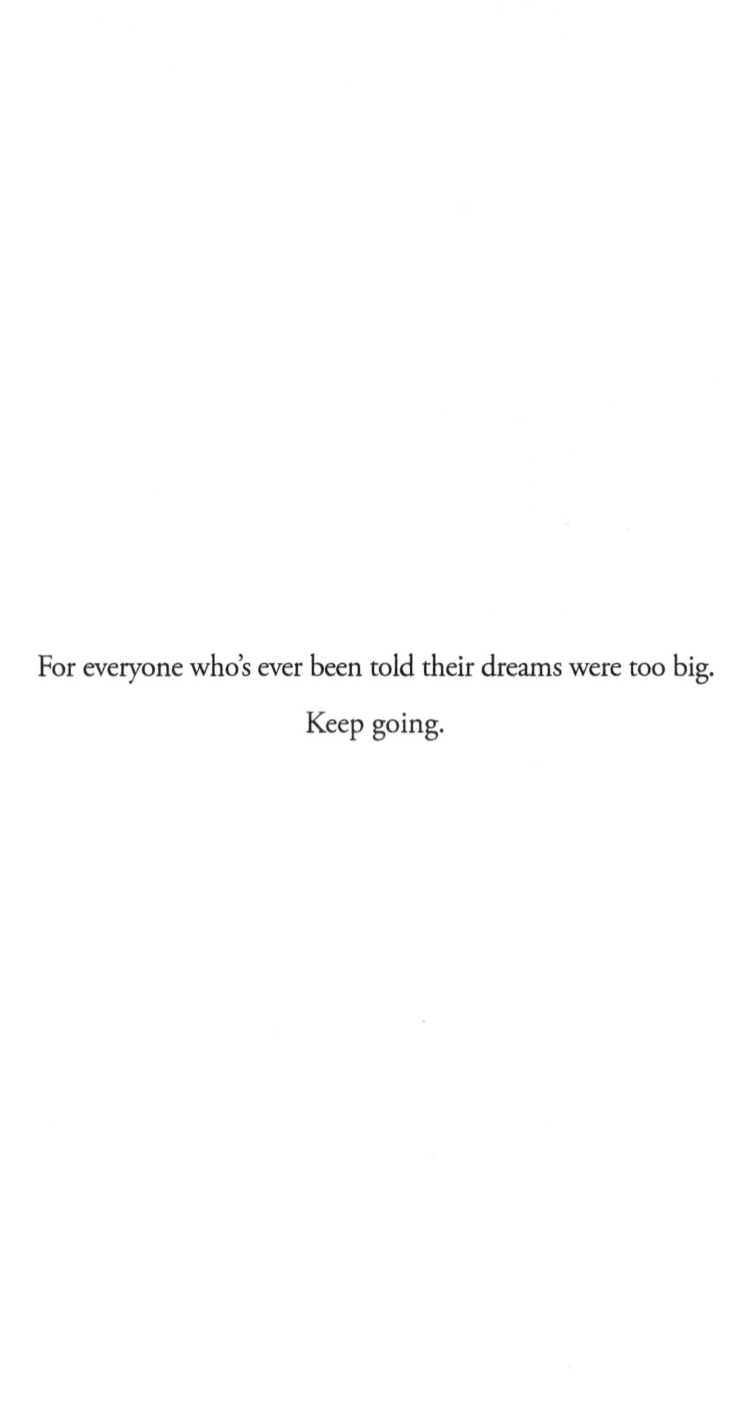

For everyone who's ever been told their dreams were too big.

Keep going.

AUTHOR NOTES:

This love story contains mature themes and topics that may be sensitive to some readers. For a detailed content warning list, please scan the QR code or visit khrisandrews.com/contentwarning/aplaceforlove/

CHAPTER ONE

ELIZA

The kiss cam pans over the frenzied crowd, stopping on a couple making out, and my world shatters.

Drinking a pint of battery acid would be less painful than seeing my boyfriend on the jumbotron, locked in a passionate kiss with one of my best friends. He's cupping her face, a soft stroke of his thumb caressing her cheekbone, and my insides freeze.

The bar's game-night buzz fades into a deafening blanket of white noise, and I'm in a trance, physically incapable of looking away from the large TV hanging above the rows of hard liquor.

The reality around me slowly dissolves. The vintage posters and photos melt into a jumbled mess of colors and the hardwood floor sinks under me, swallowing my chair.

Jared and Caroline are lost in their searing kiss, oblivious to the stadium cheering them on. For me, it's an out-of-body experience. He's now tenderly cradling the back of her head with those hands I'm so familiar with and she's fisting the blue shirt *I* ironed for his trip, while my stomach drops to the sticky wooden floor.

The cold lemonade glass slowly slips from my palms, hitting the worn table with a resounding thud. It brings me back, my surroundings snapping back into focus, but something is off. An eerie silence has settled over the usually bustling sports bar. A stillness now coats every corner of Old Halson's, and only the faint sound of the TV is audible.

Familiar faces are crowded into the faded red leather booths and around tall tables, staring at me, drinks and hot wings forgotten.

I'm mortified and frozen on the wobbly stool, heart beating erratically in my throat. The weight of the situation hits me like a hailstorm of hammers.

Jared and I were talking about getting married. Kids, someday. And I thought Caroline was my friend. My brain scrambles to make sense of what I just saw but doubt and confusion sharpen the betrayal that's slicing my chest open.

And it hurts.

My body doesn't need to wait for my mind to catch up. I focus on my hands as they tremble, a subtle quiver against the smooth wood. The irregular drumming of my heart intensifies, making me dizzy and disoriented. Confusion leads to fear, frost running through my veins. Then the familiar burn of shame spreads through every fiber, making me wish the ground would swallow me whole.

A woman's voice reaches me from a neighboring table. "Was that—"

"Shh!"

"Poor Eliza." The voice is familiar, but I don't have the mental strength to put a face on it.

A callused palm cups my elbow, and I'm reminded I'm not alone. My dazed, tear-filled eyes find Sam, his white eyebrows scrunched in worry and irritation. He dragged me out tonight after his wife found out I'd be alone for a week. They weren't keen on spending time with Jared and jumped at any chance to meet whenever he left town. This was supposed to be a fun night out with a good friend. How did it turn into the end of my life as I've known it for the last eight years?

"Let's get out of here, kid." Sam's voice is low and cautious.

I cling to his words like a lifeline, so I won't crumble in the middle of Old Halson's. It's a small town, so these people are up-to-date on the story of my childhood. I don't want to feed them even more gossip.

I follow him out without a second thought. Not that my brain is capable of any rational thought. It's stuck on the image of my boyfriend on TV, replaying on a loop.

I welcome the chilly April air filling my lungs and cooling my skin. The moment we're out of the bar, gossip erupts behind the closing door, and I half expect the people milling around the main street to bombard me with questions.

"Come on. They'll find out soon enough." Sam points to the passers-by with his chin.

He's right. No one escapes the Silver Lake Falls gossip mill. I should enjoy the lack of whispers and side eyes while I can. I've gone through this once before and the moment the group chats activate, I'll have to avoid most places in town.

Walking in silence to Sam's truck helps me clear my head and I start planning, making lists, anything to keep my mind off the hurt and nausea shredding my insides, and the future I had dreamed about being shattered on live TV.

"Martha's waiting for us," he says, rounding the corner to the back of the red brick building where he usually parks his car. He's sneaking wary glances my way, and guilt gnaws at my insides for making him worry.

"I need to pack," I realize. "And Jared took my car yesterday." I'd given him my precious truck because he kept complaining about the company sending him by train. The car isn't new or expensive, but it was the first one I could afford after saving for years. The first thing I owned, in my name. Humiliation and anger heat the back of my neck.

I mumble as I force myself to put one foot in front of the other, thinking out loud, but Sam interrupts me, his bushy eyebrows drawn together.

"I'll drive you home first. We'll get your stuff. You don't have to stay at your apartment." Sam's fatherly concern tears me up, and I clear my throat to dislodge the embarrassing knot. I can't have a breakdown yet.

Going back home is the last thing I want. There's no way in hell I'll wait five days for him to get home, surrounded by his things, being reminded of the life I worked so hard to build. I wish I could leave it all behind but I'm in no position to give up basic necessities. I couldn't afford it.

"It won't be long," I promise.

Sam pulls up in front of the building and I take a few breaths to get my hands to stop shaking. In and out. I've got this. I've done it before.

"Sure you don't want me to pack you a bag?" I shake my head and he spurs me on with his reassuring smile. "Take all the time you need, kid."

As the front door closes with a soft click behind me, I'm more certain of my decision, terrified as I might be. I can't stay here. The place we've rented for the past five years has too many memories.

Did he ever kiss her when we had parties or movie nights at home? The thought runs like ice shards through my chest. No…I can't torture myself now. I'll find time for hair-splitting later.

Weird how my childhood routine comes in handy now. A habit I couldn't shake, even after eight years of stability. The essentials kit was always packed. Documents, cash, some clothes, and the few precious memories I had.

I pass through the living room, ignoring the evidence of our relationship, all our pictures together, the changes I made so we'd have a home that felt like ours, and head straight for the bedroom. I don't need to pull the switch in the small closet. Jared never tidied up, so I wasn't worried he'd ever find it. On the top shelf, in the back, I shuffle through old sweaters until my fingers graze the worn-out duffel bag.

It's so old and tattered that the zipper almost breaks but I manage to open it. Everything is still inside. I shove in some more underwear and clothes until it's bursting at the seams. In the hiking backpack we never used because Jared is not a fan of the outdoors, I throw the essentials for camping, as a backup.

The silent goodbye to the rest of the apartment doesn't take long. My soul aches for the squeak in the floor near the small open kitchen and the dent in the bathroom door. The little imperfections made this place my real first home.

After one last look, I know there is nothing else I want to take with me. I won't be back. It's a certainty seated deep in my bones.

Leaving the keys under the doormat I'm hit with a painful sense of déjà vu, a laundry basket in my arms, holding what didn't fit in the duffel bag. The moment slides me back through the corridors of time. A little girl stepping out of house after house until I turned eighteen. Each move leaving me worn out, smaller, brittle.

This one? This one might take everything from me.

"That was fast," Sam says, getting out of the truck.

He recognizes my old bag and nods in understanding, going for the laundry basket and placing it in the back seat.

"This all? What about the couch?" Sam rolls his sleeve, ready to move furniture. He thinks he can still do that by himself, at his age.

"I just want to leave, OK?" I pull my jacket tighter around me, nervous to hang around much longer in case Jared materializes next to me. It's stupid, I know, but I can't stop dreading it.

"I'd leave him to sleep on the floor if you asked me," Sam mutters.

"Honestly, I don't want to touch any surface they might have…" Bile fills my mouth. It's awkward enough and I leave him to fill in the blanks.

"Oh," he grimaces in disgust. "Right." Sam pulls at his football-night sweater, visibly uncomfortable. The one Martha made for me is safely tucked in the basket.

"Want to go anywhere else before we head home?"

"Oh, no…" I'm barely hanging on and desperately want to lock myself away. Martha and Sam are better off without my drama.

"Eliza, you know you're always welcome in our home," he says in a soft voice, turning to me, but I can't meet his eyes, or my resolve will crumble. I hate upsetting them.

"I know." I swallow against the dryness in my throat. "I need to be alone right now. Can you take me to Gram's cabin, please?"

Sam sighs but doesn't insist.

"It's not like I'd take you to ours." He laughs for my benefit. "That place is waiting for your magic touch, kid." His abandoned fishing cabin needs more than my DIY skills, but I keep my mouth shut.

"Are you sure it's empty?" Sam makes a U-turn toward the exit for the lakeside road.

"Valerie didn't say anything about reservations for this weekend. Small mercies, I guess," I say, returning a feeble smile.

Gram Miller's cabin is ten minutes out of Silver Lake Falls. She wasn't really my grandma, but the closest thing I had to one. She and her husband took me in when I was sixteen. They were nice, warm people who had already raised their kids, all scattered across the country with families of their own.

Their kindness still overwhelms me. They're the reason I didn't end up on the streets of Portland and now have a place to hide away from Jared.

The night becomes darker as the truck follows the dirt road leading to the lake. Tall pines and oaks eat up the sky as they sway, letting stars shine through from time to time. Deep between the trees, I catch glimpses of other cabins and thin columns of smoke rising from the places more secluded from the road.

Sam parks, the car tires crunching the gravel on the driveway. The sound is loud in the dark cocoon of the trees. The only other sounds are the gentle lapping of the lake and the occasional hoots and howls of night critters.

He grabs the laundry basket and goes right in, as efficient as ever. People don't lock their doors around here. The two sets of keys in existence I leave for guests when they rent the place. The fresh air of the forest and the damp earth around the lake follows us inside, mingling with the strong wood scent.

Sam peers around, making sure he's not about to leave me overnight with a bear chilling in the bathroom.

The tidy living room and the small sage-colored open kitchen I adore are as I left them after Memorial Day weekend. I can't afford to hire somebody to clean after tourists, so I always make sure the cabin is spotless.

I do my best to reassure him. "I'll be alright." I hug him tightly and his eyes get misty.

"If there's any—"

"I'll call you. I promise."

Sam peers at me over his shoulder one last time, a litany of advice restrained behind his tight smile before he softly shuts the door behind him.

Alone for the first time, my shoulders slump, and all the emotions I'd pushed back claw their way out like a pack of rabid raccoons.

My body is on autopilot as my feet take me to the linen closet and I fix the bed in one of the bedrooms. With my hands busy, my mind is free to go through the entire scene again and again.

The heartbreak bleeds into my limbs. My body aches. It reminds me of one winter when a kid shoved me into the freezing lake.

The soft bed molds around me and the darkness of the room hides my shame. The burning sensation behind my eyes becomes intolerable and the air rushes out of my lungs as a wail I can't hold back anymore.

In the solitude, I allow myself to sob uncontrollably and mourn the past eight years of my life. To blame myself for being with him for so long, ignoring the red flags. Jared hardly touched me in the past few months. He stopped showing any little signs of affection. I was starved for touch, but he always found an excuse.

What does that say about me? That I'm stupid or willfully naive. I can't ignore the truth anymore, not when half the town witnessed it, and the other half will find out by tomorrow.

I don't know how long I've been crying before exhaustion settles in my bones and my eyelids grow heavy. Before everything fades to black, I remember it's already Friday and shoot a text to my boss. The idea of going back to work in a couple of hours is ridiculous. I'll probably get an earful from Carl, but I'm too drained to care.

The solid thud of the front door echoes through the cabin. Alarm bells pull me out of my restless sleep, filled with flashes of Jared and Caroline kissing, memories of waiting alone at the curb, laundry basket in my arms, paperwork, dingy offices, and house doors opening over and over again. My mouth is dry and the back of my hand finds strands of hair plastered to my damp forehead.

I slept through the evening again. The room is pitch black, but that's the least of my worries as the distinct shuffling of shoes on the floor and a low grunt reach my bedroom. No one would come here in the middle of the night. My mind races straight to Jared driving back early and figuring out I'd hid here.

I'm not ready to confront him.

My fingers quiver atop the floral comforter and I struggle to steady my breath. I slip from the bed as silently as possible, squeezing the life out of the old pillow I've kept all these years. Leaning against the doorframe, my ears twitch with the effort of listening closely for sounds coming from the living room.

A bag hits the wooden floor, and a deep inhale makes me break out in a cold sweat. Heavy footsteps circle the couch and move toward the kitchen. Jared would've yelled my name by now.

It's a thief. The realization drops to the bottom of my gut like a bag of river stones. I don't have any valuables here, but I don't want the place trashed. My phone is buried somewhere between the sheets, out of battery by now, and I curse myself for not remembering to charge it since I got here.

The intruder turns on the warm light over the kitchen island and it floods the corridor up to the bedroom. It's too late to creep out of the house now, I'm trapped. My palms are clammy and several different plans whiz through my head until I decide against self-preservation. I can't afford to have the cabin ruined. That's the single thing I focus on, stepping gingerly into the small hallway.

The intruder's steps are slow and deliberate. To my horror, they're getting closer as a looming shadow ripples over the wooden panels of the wall. My heart rattles against my ribs.

It's now or never.

Holding my pillow-shield and gulping down air I round the corner to a sight I wasn't expecting. Instead of a petty thief opening the cabinets and pulling the drawers, a frowning, well-dressed man is scanning the rooms, arms crossed over his chest.

If he's a burglar, he's the most put-together one I've ever seen. Not that I've met a lot of them.

His clothes are definitely not from a discount store. They're fitted and show off his broad shoulders and lean frame. His chestnut hair is styled to perfection.

He still hasn't noticed me. The panic slowly makes room for curiosity, and I take another careless step in his direction. The man's stiff posture makes me straighten my back, so I won't look like a creature who's been living in a cave for the past twenty-six years.

A half a beat later his head snaps in my direction and our gazes collide, bringing back the sense of danger I was so stupid to ignore. I panic and throw the pillow at him with a squeal, in what must be the most idiotic blitz attack in the history of self-defense.

The worn-out pillow barely brushes his torso and lands at his feet with a muffled thud.

He's confused for a moment, staring at the soft lump on the floor, but his sharp eyes shift in my direction and then turn analytical, taking me in from head to toe. A deep scowl creasing his forehead tells me he's not pleased with his conclusion.

"Who're you?" he asks in a steely tone.

I gulp in a breath to compose myself and try to find the best way to handle this bizarre encounter. Maybe I'm hallucinating from exhaustion. But the man looming in *my* cabin, who rudely interrupted *my* depression-riddled sleep and scared *me* to death is now scowling in my direction like he found pubes in his fancy hotel bed.

After the last few days, it's enough to make me snap.

"I'm the owner of this house! Who the hell are you? Barging in at this hour asking questions?"

He ignores me and pulls out a phone, while I'm left gaping at him. I give myself a second to check him over again, hoping to spot some clue as to his identity. I've never met such a man before. It's unnerving. His posture projects calm indifference, but his sharp features are tense.

My thoughts fly out of my mouth on their own. "You don't look like a burglar."

"How very judgmental of you," he drawls, still on his phone. Is he joking?

"I'm not judgmental! You broke in in the middle of the night! So, are you a burglar or not?"

"Is this The Millers' Oak Cabin?" He finally graces me with his attention, ignoring my question.

"Yes, it is. Why?" The moment I ask, I get this sinking feeling. Can I be this unlucky?

His eyes roam the cabin, assessing it in a calculated manner that puts me on edge. His gaze falls on my weapon of choice on the floor and he picks it up, twisting the pillow in his hands.

The nicely dressed intruder is stone-faced when his gaze lands back on me. Studying me as if I'm the suspicious one in this situation. He leans against the kitchen island and closes his eyes. A deep inhale expands his chest and stretches the expensive black shirt. After a moment he levels me with a stare that tells me this conversation is taking every ounce of his patience.

"It was rented for me yesterday," he starts in an even tone. "A woman named Valerie set it up."

With a twist of his wrist, he launches the pillow straight at me. In my shocked state, I don't have the good sense to use my hands to catch it, so I get a mouthful of fabric before I scramble and squeeze it defensively to my chest.

Shit. It turns out I *am* this unlucky, but at this point, it doesn't even surprise me. Heat creeps up my neck and my entire face burns with embarrassment in less than two seconds.

I clear my throat of the swelling unease, but the words stick like maple syrup on their way out. "She probably texted me. I've been staying here since Thursday night." I pinch the bridge of my nose to keep the tears at bay. "With my phone off."

I press harder and roll my lips as a last resort because I really don't want to cry in front of the surprise tourist.

"Probably not the smartest decision," I admit, even though last-minute reservations are not a thing around here.

"Obviously," he drags out.

"I've been out of sorts." I'm rooted to the spot, clutching my pillow, disoriented by how quickly my life continues to fall apart.

He breaks the strained silence that's threatening to give me a panic attack, but this time he sounds tired and resigned. "If I *were* a thief my job would've been too easy. The door is unlocked." Then with clear distaste, he asks, "Why?"

"We don't lock our doors here…I thought you were…" *Stop talking, woman!* "Never mind." My body finally jolts into action. I look around for things to pick up, but I've mostly been sleeping, so all my stuff is still packed away in the bedroom.

"In that case, yes…I'll leave you to it." I spin around so fast that I clip my shoulder against the wall. I double over in pain, clutching my throbbing arm, probably giving the impression I'm off my rocker. My hair's a mess, my eyes are puffy and sore. I'm wearing the same long shirt I had on at Old Halson's, creased from sleeping in it for almost two days straight. And no pants.

The embarrassment lights me on fire and I don't know how to get out of his sight fast enough.

"I'm going to pack. My bags are in one of the bedrooms." My voice wavers, dangerously close to breaking. "Won't take long. Sorry again." I can't even look at him.

"Sit down," he says in a gravelly voice.

My knees give at his command, and I sink into the closest chair, goose bumps erupting all over my skin. I blink slowly, shocked at my body's response and the sharp tightness in my belly. I can't help but gape at him.

What just happened?

My gaze is locked onto his slightly parted lips and his eyes widen for the briefest moment before his face hardens and we're stuck in a staring contest once again.

I hold the pillow tighter in a futile attempt to cover myself.

"Were you going to smother me to death with that?" he points to the pillow and I shrug, like it wasn't one of the stupidest things I've ever done.

"The pillow was the only solid object in reach, short of taking the nightstand," I croak out.

"You're not here on holiday." He leaves me no room to deny it. "Are you hiding?" The intruder continues his interrogation, unbothered by my discomfort.

I'm not going to spill my pathetic life story to him, no matter how in control he thinks he is.

"There's a smaller lodge five minutes away. I'll move," I say, evading the question.

"Why didn't you go there in the first place?" Clear suspicion laces his voice.

Damn it, he's persistent.

"You ask too many questions," I shoot back, getting annoyed.

"I want to be prepared if the police come and question me. When a girl ends up dead in the forest it's usually the last known person who talked to her."

I need to give him something so we can get this midnight interrogation over with and I can disappear.

"Well." The truth is, the other place is a dump. No disrespect to the Duntons, but if they're serious about letting me use it, I'd have to put some money into it. Money that I currently don't have. "It's not necessarily ready for visitors, but it's going to be OK for me." I smile at him through the lie, doing my best impression of a totally chill, normal, no-drama human being.

He's shaking his head even before I'm done explaining. Some strands of hair fall over his eyes as he pushes himself off the counter. My pulse quickens.

"I won't be responsible for sending a crazy woman out into the forest at night."

The annoyance rolling of him in waves makes my adrenaline spike and my hand flies instinctively to rub the jagged scar above my temple.

"But—"

"It's the middle of the night. The listing mentions two bedrooms."

With each step closer he comes into sharper focus. The expensive shoes, the effortless grace in the way he moves, and how tall he really is.

"Are you going to kill me in my sleep?" He asks, sounding almost bored.

"What?" I gasp, horrified. I can't tell if he's joking or not. And I want to defuse the tension before mortification chokes me to death. "No! That'd be bad for business," I lamely tell the floor.

When I find the courage to lift my head, the most intimidating stony gray eyes cut through my failed attempt at humor. I couldn't see them clearly when he was sitting on the other side of the room and now I'm stuck speechless again. He's a striking man, a slightly crooked nose the only chip in his polished appearance. Not perfectly aligned, at odds with his curated exterior. I find myself wondering how he got it. I can't imagine him getting into a fistfight.

A heartbeat later the wheels start turning.

"Wait. Are *you* going to murder *me* while I sleep?"

"I'm too tired for this," he says with a groan. "I just want to go to bed."

He takes his phone out again and types something very fast while stepping even closer, his legs almost hitting my knees when he turns the screen. I want to concentrate on what he's showing me, but I'm dazed by a hint of expensive leather and old whiskey cellars. It's a heady scent that makes me imagine men smoking cigars on yachts and driving around with a chauffeur.

"Did you read it?" he asks in a low, exhausted voice.

It shakes me up into checking the phone. It's a message to Valerie.

Arrived at the cabin. The owner is here and will spend the night.

"There. Now I can't make you disappear without incriminating myself," he says in such a business-like manner, it's absurd. It's impossible to read him, irises of solid gray, impenetrable as the thick ice that covers the lake in the middle of winter.

"The direction of your thought process is alarming." I can't help the humor lacing my words.

"I need to rest." He ignores my dig. "Which bedroom?" he asks, swiping through his hair, ruining the GQ look.

He leaves my personal space, and I can finally breathe properly. Leather bags in hand, he zooms past me when I wordlessly point to the left door.

"Wait!" I manage, common sense finally making an appearance. "What's your name?"

He's got that laser-focus glare again, scanning me for a second. "Carter. Rawlings." The sound of the shutting door puts an end to the conversation.

"I'm Eliza," I tell the empty living room.

A few moments pass until I gain control of my body and my brain quiets enough to feel the effects of tonight's surprise. My muscles hurt from how tense I've been for the last half hour, I'm parched, and my head hurts. Some water and food would help, but I've been cooped up in here and keep the fridge empty between rentals. Water will do until tomorrow.

As I drag myself to the kitchen and reach into the cabinet for a glass, I spot a note resting against a familiar jar of herbs—tears well up again. I have to accept I'm a crier now. Gratitude swirls in my chest, as warming as a spring breeze, knowing Martha brought over my favorite tea blend while I've been dead to the world.

On the fridge door, another handwritten yellow Post-it.

Call me if you need anything else.
Or even if you don't. Martha

I open the door to find the fridge fully stocked. Have I been so out of it since Thursday night that I didn't hear them come in, carrying so much food? And why can't I stop crying?!

This is the kind of friends Martha and Sam are. They kept caring for me even after I moved out of the Millers' house eight years ago. Inviting me over and feeding me a week's worth of delicious homemade food. They insisted on taking me out whenever Jared was "busy". I shake the thoughts of his "trips" out of my head because I don't want to start bawling again.

Quietly, I sneak back into my bedroom balancing a bowl of Martha's heavenly mac and cheese and a water bottle. Before I plop in the middle of the bed, I retrieve the laptop from between the folded shirts in the laundry basket. The man's name sounds familiar. I have to look up my mysterious guest, or I'll never be able to sleep with him in the house. He doesn't seem dangerous but there's an edge to him that I've long learned to be careful of.

Hundreds of articles pop up in the search. Financial news bulletins about inheriting the family tech company after his father's death and his decisions as CEO of Rawlings Enterprise. Opening some gossip blogs with pictures of him and various beautiful women at fancy events makes me feel stalkerish so I close them quickly.

The most recent article mentions his absence from the public eye over the past four months. *The company has remained silent on the matter.* Great. Another reason to feel like moose dung. The man needed to get away for some reason and I just crashed his holiday.

At least I can whip up something for breakfast as an apology, in the hope he won't ask for his money back, or even worse, leave a bad review.

On second thought, I move a chair under the doorknob and retrieve an old pepper spray I bought when I was fifteen from the duffel bag. I drift into a fitful sleep, clutching the cold metal of the spray can, a reminder of the last time I felt unsafe.

Chapter Two

CARTER

My body is stiff and it's too damn bright in here. All I crave is a couple more hours of rest. Last night, I fell into an exhaustion-induced sleep the second I touched the bed, plopping directly onto the comforter.

The new setting is a far cry from my New York loft. Wooden walls, a vintage dresser on the other side of the room. An ungodly amount of pillows with intricate embroidered patterns lay scattered around the heavy oak bed. I didn't have the chance to properly take in the room after the debacle with the owner last night. This is what I get for being a good son and a loving brother. They conspired and emotionally blackmailed me into accepting the plan they sprang on me two days ago.

Now I'm stuck in a lake cabin with a crying woman. In the forest, far from where I'm needed the most.

I'd assessed the risks before telling her to stay and might've been worried if she hadn't struck me as pitiful. Dark circles marring the skin under red and swollen eyes. Puffy and chewed lips. Her strawberry blonde hair was a bird's nest, tangled and disheveled. The human equivalent of a cornered fox that's been roughed up by a pack of hound dogs. So sad it made me uncomfortable.

She did ask for my name so it's only going to be a matter of scrolling the search page for a minute. My family and the board have kept the situation under wraps so far. But I doubt she has the gossip press on speed dial, so I'll make sure to buy her silence once she sorts out her living situation. I'm not the most caring person in the world but, unfortunately, my mother raised me better than to throw a crying woman out of the house in the middle of the night.

My phone vibrates on the nightstand.

"Speaking of the devil," I say, once my mom's radiant face pops up on the screen, as regal as ever, ready for a high society brunch or whatever is on her agenda today.

"What a lovely room, sweetheart. Did you sleep well?" She's too chipper for a Sunday morning, but I guess she wants to compensate for the crappy mood I've been sporting since she shared her idea.

"I'm here too!" Jackie takes up the other side of the screen, dressed for her morning yoga.

They're coming on strong with the combined powers of the Rawlings women.

"I wanted to check if you got there in one piece."

"Unfortunately," I sigh.

"Don't be such a grump," my mother chuckles. "This will be good for you."

She sounds confident, but I highly doubt three months stuck in Maine will help me in any way.

Jackie chimes in, grinning, "There is more to life than work."

It takes every bit of willpower not to roll my eyes like a teenager at the overused line. But I let it slide because I had already planned to work remotely the moment I packed my bags. The single upside of leaving New York is that the two of them won't be able to hover over me, making work almost impossible.

"I've been gone long enough, this is unnecessary." I'm worried about the effect my prolonged absence will have on business. Investors are agitated, rumors already coiling in the dark corners of boardrooms and private cigar clubs. I hate still being as useless as I was three months ago.

"Robertson and I have it covered," Jackie's tone is serious. "I won't let you down."

My mother nods along. "You're more important to us, son. The company means nothing if something happens to you again." Her voice breaks a little on the last words and guilt twists my insides.

I know their love is unconditional, but I'm supposed to be the strong one and protect my mother and sister. I'm stuck between a rock and a hard place, keeping them at ease and keeping the family legacy safe.

"The reason I'm even considering doing this is because I trust you," I tell Jackie. "You're the only person I'm comfortable leaving in charge."

Jackie's always been my rock, even back when our father tightened his grip and isolated me. Our bond was indestructible. I know how business-savvy she is, and she wouldn't let our company implode.

"The place has rubbed off on you already." Jackie tries to hide her emotions behind a joke. "You've gone soft."

"The place is certainly…quaint. Not your regular vacation spot, mother."

"I wanted you to enjoy life the way I did when I was little, before"—she waves her hand around the luxurious living room she's walking through—"this happened."

Before my father founded the company and became so rich he forgot where they both came from. I open the large window and take in the lake, sparkling in the morning sun.

"Let me guess. I'm supposed to learn how to enjoy the simple things?" I ask her, unconvinced.

"Exactly!" they both say.

"You can ask the owner to show you around. The Mainers are very nice people," my mother says.

The fresh air wraps around me, cooling my skin.

"I met the owner when I got here."

"Oh, how sweet of them to wait for you so late."

"It was more of a miscommunication. She stayed the night."

"I'm sure she had a perfectly good reason, I hope you weren't rude." My mother gives me that look, meant to be severe.

"You raised a perfect gentleman," I tell her, and she's pleased.

Though I don't understand how the redhead owns and rents this cabin but has nowhere else to go in the time of crisis she's so obviously going through. Unless she's mentally unstable. I should have checked if the bedroom door had a key. Then the intrusive thoughts and suspicion start to slither through my mind.

"Did you have anything to do with it?" The question bursts out.

My mother pales and Jackie is stricken, "Carter—"

"You know I'd never do that to you," my mother says, cutting her off.

I take a deep breath and the crisp air clears my mind.

"Yeah, sorry," I say on an exhale. "It was unexpected, that's all."

"Is she pretty, at least?" Jackie asks.

I laugh at the absurd question. "Definitely not. A dull, countryside mess of a woman." I think about the frightful apparition as I open my bags to change. The wrinkled flannel shirt was an instant red flag. Her face was blotchy. And she appeared to have the same emotional stability as cryptocurrency.

"Carter!" My mother admonishes me as my sister shakes her head disapprovingly. "Everyone has their bad days."

"It might be true, but the last thing I need right now is a charity case."

My mother switches gears. "Did you take your meds today?"

"I'm an adult. I know I have to take them even when you two aren't hovering," I grumble.

I squint at the bottles on the nightstand. With a swipe, they fall into the open drawer. I don't want my temporary roommate to stumble across them.

"I ran into Alicia this morning," Jackie says in a bitter tone and I'm grateful she's not piling on. "I'm surprised by the coincidence," she air quotes the last word.

Alicia's been relentless since she saw me a month ago. I don't care about her excuses and moaning about how she hates hospitals. What I despise, and the main reason I'll never go back to our hookups, is how she used my sister.

"Does she know anything?" That's all that matters when it comes to Alicia.

"Doesn't look like it, she's just sniffing around." A flicker of sadness crosses Jackie's features and I hate that I'm partially to blame. "Don't worry, I won't be fooled again."

"It wasn't your fault, Jackie. She had an agenda all along. It hurt you more than me."

After two years of being joined at the hip, Alicia stopped answering Jackie's calls and avoided her at events. I suspect my sister's lack of good friends is also my fault. She noticed early on that the girls in her school invited her to pajama parties to grill her about me. But she never blamed me.

The clatter of pans and dishes grabs my attention. It's my cue to join…My brain grinds to a stop. I was so tired last night that I didn't even ask her name. Exhaustion made me sloppy. Can't wait to let our security chief, Derrick, know that I didn't notify them about last night *and* I also had no clue about her name. He's going to give me an hour-long lecture about sending his team to their rental as soon as I parked and being an irresponsible principal who's a pain in his ass.

The heavy smell of a full breakfast almost makes me turn around, but I brace myself and follow it to the small kitchen. The morning light showering that corner of the house hits the willowy woman's copper hair like a halo and it takes me a second to notice it's no longer messy. She has it tied neatly at the nape of her slender neck.

"I didn't get your name last night."

She spins sharply, clutching a teacup to her chest that hitches to the rhythm of her startled exhale. She's more put together but her ashen complexion still shows signs of whatever has her hiding in the mountains with her phone off.

"It's…" She clears her throat. "Eliza." Her voice has a raspy pitch I'd normally find seductive. But she's on the verge of crying, which quickly snuffs any temptation.

I hope she doesn't, because it'll be extremely uncomfortable for both of us. I'd rather walk on hot coals than deal with strangers in their most vulnerable moments.

"Well, Eliza, are you expecting company?" I ask, waving my hand over the spread laid out on the kitchen island.

If I'm lucky I'll find some food that won't send me back to the hospital. It can't happen again, so I have to be cautious and follow my plan.

It's the only way I can get back to my normal life without my family breathing down my neck. I just have to stick to the recovery plan and "enjoy" three months in the middle of the woods, hopefully alone.

"Oh, no," Eliza says in a small voice. "It's an apology breakfast, for the mix-up last night. The full Maine experience," she adds with a tilt in her voice. There's a plea to accept her offering in those red-rimmed brown eyes. They stand out eerily, in stark contrast to her pale skin.

"No need." I reach for the fruit and some plain yogurt, bypassing the eggs, sausages, hash browns, and a mountain of pancakes. "I'll accompany you to the lodge you mentioned after I'm done."

Eliza doesn't comment on my choices. She's shuffling on the opposite side. I leave her to break the silence while I enjoy some surprisingly tasty blueberries.

"You were kind enough to let me stay here last night," she starts tentatively, not looking at me. It makes me instantly suspicious. "I have few things anyway; I can move them myself." She keeps adjusting the plates and napkins, still avoiding eye contact.

Now I want to go with her to the other cabin because Eliza is clearly not telling me something. I'm a perfect gentleman, after all. Making sure she won't bother me again is a bonus.

"I'll enjoy the walk." It comes out curt and dismissive, giving her pause. I'm used to cutting through bullshit after dealing with people thinking I was easy prey because I was too young to run the company after my father died.

Eliza fidgets with her apron and tries to come up with something a couple of times before she speaks again.

"The view's not spectacular on that side. You'd be better off visiting the town. There's a great coffee shop I can recommend," she spews in one go, sporting the fakest smile. People trying to charm their way into my graces is nothing new. But she's doing it to get rid of me. Interesting.

"No." I don't negotiate. When I want something, I get it. And now I want to know why she's trying so hard to talk me out of going with her. I'll call it doing my due diligence. She might be hiding something dangerous, and I can't risk it.

"No?" Her mouth is slightly ajar in disbelief that her little customer service grimace didn't persuade me. "It's five minutes away. I'll be fine." The high-pitched inflection at the end makes me wonder if she wants to convince me or herself.

I keep quiet and wait her out. I love using this tactic to make people reveal things they didn't intend to. I let silence work in my favor and enjoy letting them stew. How far is she willing to go to get rid of me?

"You are *very kind*," she continues, but the way she says it makes it clear I'm most certainly not. "I'll ask

Valerie to send some cupcakes for your troubles and we'll leave it at that." Eliza's words are infused with more conviction this time. It's borderline cute.

"Nonsense." I'm enjoying her squirming. "We'll leave in ten." Shutting down any debate, I open my tablet to check today's numbers. In the corner of my eye, her shoulders slump and a defeated exhale deflates her niceness completely, her lips moving in a silent mumble.

I catch the end tail of it and nearly chuckle.

"Or some hay for a stubborn ass."

There's no point in pretending I'm not just plain curious at this point.

CHAPTER THREE

ELIZA

Charity case.

Dull, countryside mess.

The words keep spiraling in my head, and I finish cooking on autopilot. I didn't mean to eavesdrop; I was tiptoeing to the bathroom because I didn't want to disturb him. The words hit me square in the chest when I passed his bedroom. That part of his call rang clearly. Photos I found online of him and the beautiful women flashed in a carousel when feminine laughter chimed through the door. I can imagine the two of them laughing at me.

The tips of my fingers are numb from shame. I'm perfectly aware of my flaws and the two days spent crying in bed didn't do me any favors. Having a stranger stumble on one of the worst times in my life is embarrassing enough without hearing them ridicule my appearance.

Washing some cups to have something to do and clear my head, I focus on planning my next steps. It's more important now than wallowing in Carter's hurtful words. The harsh reality is I don't have a home now. It cuts deep after eight years of finally feeling settled. I didn't think I'd be in this situation again. I refuse to be a burden to the Duntons and can't count on any of my old friends since they were, or became, more Jared's friends than mine. He took over every aspect of my life and I let him, thinking I was so lucky.

"I didn't get your name last night." Carter's voice makes me jump out of my skin, and it's a miracle I don't drop the cup I've been mindlessly washing for the past five minutes.

He's sitting at the little butcher's block kitchen island, looking even better than last night. No dark brown hair is out of place, his fresh shirt hugs his frame. One difference from yesterday's clean-cut image is a slight shadow across his jaw, which unfortunately makes him even more handsome. Carter's eyes are lighter in the sunlight, two dried river stones, and I'm exposed under his scrutiny.

Once I get my heartbeat under control I manage to answer him. "It's Eliza."

My apology breakfast doesn't have the expected result and the hint of disgust in his perusal of the food takes the wind out of my sails. He must be one of those fitness nuts because, in the end, he only places some fruit on his plate.

Carter barely says anything and the frosty politeness makes me itch to get out of here faster. But then he decides to send me into a tailspin when he insists on coming with me. The last thing I want is him following me to Sam's little fishing cabin.

Sam's arthritis made it impossible to spend the night there anymore and so he stopped taking care of the one-bedroom cabin a few years ago. It needs some serious repairs, but I'll figure something out. It'll put a dent in my savings to get an air mattress, but it's cheaper than going to a motel for weeks until I patch the place up. Or maybe I can use a tent for a while.

"Tea?" I push the steaming cup toward Carter.

Grayish blue eyes cut to me, narrowing slightly. Good to know that offering him tea is the equivalent of offending his ancestors.

"I dislike tea." His rejection is flat. "Tastes horrible," he says, going back to leisurely eating his fruits.

Rude.

"Take a sip at least, it's a blend made from local herbs and—"

"No," he says, retrieving a smaller leather bag from the couch.

Yet again I'm left gaping at his back until he pulls out a tablet and I do my best to convince him I can go alone to the other cabin.

Carter's attention is glued to the graphs and numbers filling the screen. My efforts to ditch him fall flat and I have ten minutes to panic and find some excuses when we get there. Even before looking him up, Carter's appearance told me he wasn't your average man, but the Maserati parked outside left no doubt. I don't want him to judge me, especially after he called me a charity case.

When my phone finally charged, I switched it on to a barrage of missed calls and texts this morning. I assured Martha I was still alive and saw that Valerie had indeed left a text after I didn't answer her calls. The ten texts from Jared are ticking bombs in my inbox. It's tens of calls. Someone at the bar must have told him.

He's worried, but not enough to come back Friday night. He always stayed the weekend during his work trips to "rest" or have "informal meetings" with the local companies. I'm such an idiot.

I'm torn between the pain of facing him and listening to his explanations and the hurt of him not bothering to come back home, but there's no time to dwell on it. Carter saunters out of his bedroom and opens the front door, waiting for me.

"Ladies first."

This stretch of lake shore is closer to Silver Lake Falls and peppered with modest-sized old families' cabins, similar to the one I inherited from the Millers, and shabby small fishing cabins like Sam's.

The opposite shore has seen a boom in recent years with rich families from New York or Boston building holiday chalets. It's the kind of place my unwilling companion would fit in. Enjoying the view from enormous lake-facing windows and parking his expensive boat on the private dock.

The walk is silent as I'm still scrambling for ways to cut this short. I don't understand why he insisted on coming to see the place before I bring my bags. Carter moves like he's got all the time in the world, relaxed on the surface, but the sharpness in his eyes keeps me alert. He takes everything in but doesn't say much before we arrive at the old cabin, nestled in the shadows of the dense trees.

I push the rickety gate and the high creak shatters the silence of the crisp morning, scattering some poor birds. The cabin resembles a fading photograph with its weather-worn dull brown exterior.

I move forward, choosing to ignore the rough and gnarled wooden panels left behind by harsh winds and biting winters, when Carter's steps halt behind me.

"See. It's here," I shout, not facing him, waving my arms like a tour guide. "I'll be out of your hair in half an hour. Let's get back so I can get my stuff."

"What is this?" The disbelief in his voice is the first time since he arrived that he's given me anything more than cold indifference.

"It's not so bad." I brush him off with more conviction than I really feel.

"You must be joking," he says, not moving any closer.

"It just needs a bit of cleaning." I peek over my shoulder to assure him and almost trip on a raised plank on the stairs.

Carter's eyebrow arches and a flush of embarrassment warms the back of my neck. I hate my constant state of debilitating stumbling around this man. As if God sent him specifically to shine a bright light on the shitty situation I'm in.

He's so out of place in the small yard, taking in the shabby cabin with his hands in the pockets of his tailored pants.

Who wears business casual in the forest?

"It's not livable," he says with an even tone.

"Don't let the exterior fool you." I amp up the cheeriness until my cheeks hurt. "The interior"—I grunt, pulling and pushing the door—"is much"—another grunt as I internally curse the door that won't budge—"nicer."

The air shifts around me. While I was struggling to open the damn door that insisted on making me look like a moron, Carter has made his way behind me.

He reaches for the doorknob, and I have to tilt my head back to catch the frown darkening his features.

His fingers wrap around the cold brass, sliding over mine, and I'm transfixed by his warm skin and the same overwhelming scent that fills my mind with very inappropriate thoughts. Blood rushes to my cheeks and I'm warm again for a completely different reason.

My body is aware of his every breath, his chest pressing against my back, but I don't have the good sense to move aside.

Carter's glare darts to my fingers and it takes me a moment to snap out of it and release the knob.

A strong yank makes the wooden door groan before Carter pushes the door in and a cloud of dust escapes through the crack.

We both jump back and I nearly lose my footing before two firm hands grab my upper arms and steady me against a solid chest.

I don't have time to register the same heat running through my body before Carter finally speaks again.

"Yes," he drawls. "It looks very inviting."

The obvious sarcasm sobers me, and I step into damage-control mode.

"I'll open some windows." I smile up at him.

"With a bulldozer, you mean."

I don't let his jab stop me from entering and assessing the situation. The last time I went fishing with Sam was two years ago, and the signs of neglect are obvious.

The small living room is dark, dusty gray windows blocking the light. The kitchenette in the corner has seen better days… thirty years ago. I don't even want to check the small bathroom. I hope Carter won't get any ideas about opening the doors.

"You can't stay here," he says sternly.

"I'll dust it off. Polish the floors a bit." I'm a freaking bubble of optimism, my cheeks in pain from the strained smile I have plastered on my face.

"Dust it off?" He scoffs. "The place will fall on us if the wind picks up."

"The structure is fine." I brush him off. "You have to look past the—"

"The health hazard, probably rat infested, jewel this place is?" he asks, coming closer.

His disdain makes my scalp prickle and I get the urge to defend Sam's place. He loved and cared for it for over forty years.

"The roof is good and only a few of the windows are broken. It's summer anyways."

Why am I trying so hard to convince this man I can live here? I don't need his permission. I want to get him out, so I don't have to watch him turn his nose up at everything. He looks ready to take water samples from the tap and send them for testing. He's probably a control freak who micromanages his poor employees.

He takes up too much space in this cramped cabin. Combined with the dusty air, it's a struggle to breathe. Stepping outside loosens the claws constricting my lungs.

Carter follows me, taking his sweet time, strolling out. Unfortunately, he is not done and rounds the house, checking the shabby exterior like he's appraising it for sale.

"Now that you know what to tell the police, we can go," I say, to get his attention away from the missing roof tiles.

He ignores me until he reaches the other side and Sam's large blue plastic container catches his eye.

I'm about to tell him that it's where I keep the bodies of my bad tenants, when he reaches for the lid and cracks it open to peer inside.

"No, don't!" I cry out a second too late.

Carter's pale skin is already a worrisome shade of green by the time I reach his side and he's bent over, mouth-breathing hard.

Worry changes into amusement at the sight of him struggling to hold it together and not throw up on his expensive shoes. I bite the inside of my cheek, so I don't laugh in the poor man's face.

"Let that be a lesson about sticking your nose in other people's stuff." My eyes water from keeping myself from laughing, but I reach out and start rubbing soothing circles on his back.

No matter how annoying I find him, I'm guessing it's the first time in his coddled life he's come across this type of smell. It's bad enough to make a grown man tear up.

"What. The hell. Is. That?" He punctures each word with deep inhales and exhales, color returning to his cheeks.

"That's Sam's old chum storage. Nobody's cleaned it since he last went fishing."

"Somebody needs to burn it," he says miserably, his poise and arrogance lost.

I can't help but burst out laughing.

"Why do you insist on living here? Go back to town or ask your family or friends for help." He straightens, irritated with my stubbornness.

The humor and lightness evaporate, and I know he can spot it but I'm too tired to hide. I can't go back to the apartment. And I refuse to spend the little savings I have on a motel. I'll be out of a job very soon.

"I'm not going back to town," I say with determination. "I'm fine here. By myself."

I can't go to Martha and her husband after everything they've done for me already. They'll worry and get mad on my behalf. They'll cook and try to talk it out and I can't yet. It hurts too much. I'm too humiliated.

Carter glances back at the house, a hint of displeasure flashing over his face, and then his serious gray eyes land back on me with an intensity that makes me feel exposed.

"I don't understand why you want to live here."

"Look. Long story short, I had to move out of my place. I own the Old Miller cabin and this one belongs to good friends who said I could use it." It's stretching the truth, but he doesn't have to know.

"Some friends." At my incredulous wince, he continues, "If they were good friends, they wouldn't suggest you live here."

Exasperated, I'm close to stomping my feet.

"I don't want to explain it to you. You rented out the cabin, not the rights to my life story."

A buzzing breaks the glaring contest. I extract my phone from my back pocket and freeze, staring at Jared's number until the phone stops vibrating in my hand.

Carter's eyes slide from the phone to my face but he doesn't say anything. Hands planted on his hips, he inhales deeply and, in the daylight, I notice the lines of muscles contracting where his light-blue shirt stretches over his torso. It looks firm and safe, the kind of place you rest your head when you have a bad day.

You're losing it, Eliza.

"Here's what's going to happen," he says, and it's obvious from his tone that he's made a decision he's not pleased with. "We share the lake house. You make me a light breakfast and show me around as payment, until you get your life in order, and I can continue my stay in peace."

I gape at him, blinking slowly as I do my best to make sense of what he said. It's the last thing I expected to come out of his mouth. It's one thing to not throw me out in the middle of the night, but offering to share the place—

"I can't do that," I argue, shocked. "You…" I babble. "We're strangers and you rented the cabin for yourself."

It's absurd. He's been eyeing me with the same disgust reserved for a fly on his gourmet lunch ever since he arrived.

"If you come here, I'll call the police on you." He crosses his arms, and tension ripples through the tendons.

"You wouldn't dare!" I splutter.

"I'd have no qualms about it."

"Fine, I'll go somewhere else," I bluff, to get him off my back.

"Great, let's go. I'll drive you there." His tone is mocking. The man can see right through me.

"You can't. They don't like strangers," I stammer. "I—"

"I'm not doing this because I'm nice." Carter cuts me off. "I'm used to having help in the house. Consider it a part-time job until you do something about this." He waves his hand dismissively toward the little house.

I stare at him in disbelief. He wants me to be his cook. I'm not surprised he has help where he lives but to ask the first person he meets here is another level of audacity.

"You want me to work for you?"

"It's a fair deal," he says in a detached tone. I can picture him in a boardroom discussing multi-million-dollar contracts without batting an eye. "A non-leaking roof over your head in exchange for basic cooking skills and showing me what this wonderful area has to offer."

The way he keeps dismissing the town makes me wonder why he chose to spend his holiday here.

But he does have a point and I find myself contemplating the offer. What's the alternative? Sleep in a tent here on a hard floor and wake up like Snow White with forest creatures around me. Or accept Sam's offer. Not an option. It sounds whiny and ungrateful, but I'd rather cook breakfast for a spoiled icy stranger than bear my soul in front of my oldest friends and burden them with my problems.

Carter is arrogant and cold, too put together and attractive. Best case scenario he ignores me. The worst that could happen is he throws some polite insults my way. I've lived through harder times.

"Yeah, sure. What could go wrong?"

I can almost hear the ominous sounds coming from the forest behind us. The spirits mocking my naivety.

Chapter Four

ELIZA

On our way back, I already regret accepting his offer. He moves with purpose, not once stopping to admire the view. I hate silence when I'm not alone. It makes me nervous. I'm desperate to ask him questions but there's an aura about Carter like an electric fence. I'm afraid it will zap me to a crisp if I get too close.

The longer we walk without talking, the higher the itchy bubbles of restlessness rise inside me. I cave after thirty more seconds.

"You know what you want to visit while you're here?"

Carter doesn't even spare me a glance. "I'll be doing something more productive most of the time."

"But you said—"

"Is there anything you want?" The coldness in his voice takes me aback.

"I gathered I could keep you entertained."

"Don't feel obliged to do so," he says in a clipped tone.

OK, so I guess the invitation to stay does not include having me in his sight too often. The rejection stings, but apparently money doesn't come with small-talk skills and manners. Or maybe Carter doesn't bother to use them with me. I'll be just the help.

As soon as we're back, I throw a thank you his way and make myself busy checking everything is dusted, and the shared bathroom is stocked with my favorite local lavender body wash and herbal shampoo. The wildflowers I painted on the white ceramic still make me smile remembering the days I spent watching YouTube videos, learning how to tile the bathroom by myself. I poured my soul and any time and money I could afford into this cabin after Gramps died, a short six months after his wife. They were the last and best foster family I stayed with. Even though they were old and had grown kids with families of their own, the Millers did their best to care for a scared sixteen-year-old. They were patient and understanding and brought me here whenever I got overwhelmed or when Jim wanted to hide some new tools from his wife in the back shed.

The Millers even encouraged me to take their last name and leave the past behind. They wanted me to be a part of the family, even if they were too old to adopt me.

They left me the small cabin because I was the only one of their kids, blood or foster, who never left Silver Lake Falls. Now I wish I'd stayed with them a bit longer. I was so young when I met Jared. After my eighteenth birthday, I moved in with him without a second thought. And now I have to live with the consequences.

After going through every task I could think of to keep myself busy and out of the way of the man with the personality of a constipated porcupine, I return to the kitchen to find Carter eating a lunch he prepared himself.

This man makes the little rustic kitchen look even better.

"How come you're not staying at one of the fancy hotels around here?" I blurt out. The question has been churning in the back of my mind.

"Is it wise to ask your guest why he didn't choose another rental?"

The pulsing headache I always got when Jared evaded a question makes its reappearance.

"You seem more of a seven-star-hotel tourist than a family-cabin-in-the-middle-of-the-woods type of person."

"What gave it away? The Maserati outside?" He tuts. "Here you go judging people again."

"It's a valid question." I defend myself. "It's great to have a tenant for three months, but it's odd."

Carter eats with such deliberation and control, cutting the food into precise bites. Where do you learn that?

"Want to join me?"

"Oh, no, I already ate," I answer quickly, afraid he assumes I'm staring because I wanted to eat his food.

His brows crease but he doesn't push it. Probably more of a good manners thing than a sincere offer.

The silence is my cue to retreat to my bedroom.

"My mother chose it." He takes a sip of water. "I can't say no to her."

I'm surprised he's willing to share such private details. So the man has a heart. Despite myself, I find it endearing he cares enough to want his mother happy.

Carter is pensive, tapping his index finger on the dull surface of the island. "This place looks better than the pictures."

"Yeah. I didn't have time to take other photos and don't know how to go about a website. I suck at marketing and online stuff." I keep talking. "I love to do home improvements. I'm not an interior designer, but I pretend I'm on one of those fixer-upper shows on TV…"

My laugh freezes on its way out when I notice him staring at me. I guess our little exchange was not an invitation to chat. I know I talk too much about things people don't care about. Jared enjoyed reminding me constantly.

"Yeah, never mind. I'll leave you to it," I say, my ears warming. I've already lost count of the times this has happened in his presence. It's ridiculous.

I'm almost at the door, with no clear destination in mind, when Carter surprises me.

"That's what you want to do with the other cabin?"

I nod, not trusting myself not to start blabbering again about the ideas I have for the place. As soon as I figure out how to do it without ending up broke.

"It will turn out nice then."

The compliment blooms inside me, warming my cheeks, until he continues.

"How long will it take to get it ready?"

Right. It was only a segue into asking me how long I planned to disrupt his solitude.

I want to tell him I'll work as fast as possible, even though I haven't talked to Martha yet and maybe they were kidding.

I open my mouth to assure him it won't take long but a knock at the door robs me of my voice and fills me with dread.

I can't ask Carter to open the door. I'd have to share the embarrassing details of my life.

He keeps looking at me expectantly, forcing me to move toward the door. His eyes are boring in the back of my head. My hesitation made him suspicious, and peering discreetly through the curtains didn't help my case.

A heavy sigh of relief leaves my lungs when I spot Jenna and Amy on the porch, shooting furtive glances at the luxury car parked in the driveway. My mood lifts and I yank the door open.

"We were so worried about you!" Both women jump on me, hugging me tightly.

I needed this. I'm so happy they're here, I get a bit choked up.

"Everything's fine," I breathe out into Jenna's shoulder, and she pulls me closer.

Amy leans back and gives me a small smile. "Why didn't you call us? You could've crashed at my place." She looks around, pointing at the forest. "This is too secluded."

"Good point," Jenna chirps. "You could come back into town, and we'll have a man-bashing shots night to get it out of your system."

She's forgotten I don't drink, but I appreciate her offer. "Don't tempt me with an awful hangover," I chuckle and wave them in. "Come on. Give it to me straight. What's been going on?"

"Everyone knows what happened." Amy confirms what I feared, pity painting her blue eyes. News spreads fast in Silver Lake Falls.

"We didn't know what you'd do, all alone and desperate," Jenna says, a hint of condescension lacing her words. It stirs something unpleasant in my gut.

"Desperate" had such a harsh ring to it. It took me two nights of crying myself to sleep to cope with my new reality. My boyfriend is a cheater and one of my best friends a backstabbing excuse of a woman. But I wasn't going to do something stupid about it. I've suffered through worse and never gave up. Also, I'm not technically alone. I have unwilling company. A brooding, handsome New Yorker who retreated to his bedroom seconds before I opened the front door.

I hope he's busy sorting his expensive clothes by color or checking the stock market. Or whatever Carter gets up to when he's alone. I don't want him to hear the inevitable details.

"I can't imagine finding out this way." Jenna plops on the couch, shaking her head.

I take the time to make tea and compose myself before I dive into it with them.

"I was shocked and blindsided," I admit, once I place the tray on the table.

"You two have such a strong relationship. After you've calmed down, think about that." Amy looks to Jenna for confirmation.

They've already discussed it. They're always on the same page.

I'm confused. "What do you mean? What's there to talk about?"

"You should forgive him. Nothing has to change, you know."

Amy's conviction gives me pause. Am I wrong for wanting nothing to do with Jared?

"Men will be men. They get bored after some years. The important thing is you're the one he's coming home to," Jenna says, like Jared did an oopsy and forgot to put his dirty socks in the hamper. Which he always did.

They can't be serious. I know I ignored a lot for the chance at a family someday, but this?

"Cheating isn't something I can overlook. I wonder how long it's been going on, right under my nose..." I say, staring into the hot cup of tea.

Their silence makes me raise my gaze in time to catch Amy and Jenna exchanging a look that increases my heartbeat, my pulse drumming in my ears. Unease settles deep in my bones.

"Well...he made us swear not to tell you," Amy says with a grimace.

My shocked expression compels her to continue. "Because he loves you so much and wants to have a family with you—"

"How long?" My words are brittle, and I push the question out through the pain.

The two lean back, clearly worried they might have to deal with a meltdown.

"You have to understand, they're just having fun. It's nothing serious."

"How long?" I already know the answer will shatter me completely.

They have another one of their wordless conversations that always excluded me.

Jenna rips the Band-Aid. "About two years. But again, it's not like—"

The rest of their joint explanation and excuses dissolve in the ringing in my ears.

They knew.

I was an addition to their tight group but after years of working together, I thought that we were friends. That they cared about me enough not to cover up something so vile. I was always there for them when they needed me. If they had a bad breakup, wanted food for a party. Covered their work when they were tired or sick. I supported them and cried with them when times were tough. And for the past two years, Amy and Jenna have been lying to my face, helping Jared and Caroline hide their affair.

Two fucking years.

Those work trips Jared and Caroline went on together. It dawns on me how attentive and hungry for me he always was when he returned, up until the past months. I'd be giddy that he missed me so much. But it was nothing more than guilt disguised with fake touches. Jared used sex to hide the truth.

They're not chatting anymore and when the silence draws me back, they're staring expectantly.

"What?" I'm still off-kilter.

"We have to talk about the Maserati in the room." Amy laughs.

"What's up with that? Don't tell me your long-lost parents have some deep pockets and they've come back for you," Jenna says, like my childhood story is the funniest thing in the world.

It's a running joke in our circle. Especially when they've had too much to drink. The game is "Reasons why Eliza's parents abandoned her".

Maybe there's a thirty-day return policy for ginger babies.
What if she was an affair baby?
Maybe she fell off the back of a truck.

It's not a subject I talk about if I can help it and they know it. The corners of my eyes burn from unshed tears I'm fighting to keep at bay.

I open my mouth but no words come out. I don't know how to explain why I'm staying here and who Carter is without feeding the rumor mill.

Jenna giggles. "Come on, don't be so sensitive, we're just lightening the mood."

"Yeah, it's uncomfortable seeing someone so miserable," Amy whines.

Carter's bedroom door slams hard and it steals the women's attention, giving me a moment to rub away the prickling tears with the heels of my palms.

The girls' jaws drop and they gawk at him shamelessly. The truth is that on a normal day, I would've admired him too. The air of confidence following him is magnetic. But now I'm trapped in the storm rumbling under his dark eyebrows until he zeroes in on the spot where I'm mechanically rubbing my old scar.

How much did he hear?

He lowers his head in a curt nod on his way to the kitchen and both women follow his movements, as graceful as a couple of hypnotized geese twisting their necks.

"He's staying here?" Amy asks greedily for details and I'm unable to do anything else but nod.

"Did he hire you as his maid?" Jenna whisper-yells. "A man like *that* is clearly used to having help at his beck and call."

The familiar rush of shame crawls up my chest and neck again. It *was* our agreement, but the way she said it delivered another blow to my fragile state of mind. There's a loud clang in the kitchen as Carter places a glass on the counter with too much force.

Amy and Jenna continue, ignorant of the change of temperature in the other room, and I don't know how to stop them.

"You have to introduce us." They both giggle.

A low hum reverberates through the small space, and I know he is listening. I'm mortified and my knee bounces uncontrollably.

"Maybe throw a party so we can get to know him better," Jenna says suggestively, wiggling her thin eyebrows my way.

Carter comes back slowly and stops next to the armchair I'm trapped in.

"We'll have to cut this short, I'm afraid," he tells them, with zero remorse in his tone. "Eliza and I have urgent business to attend to, and I have to steal her away." His hand lands on my shoulder, making me jolt. He's looking at me to play along and I can't for the life of me understand what he's doing.

Their focus keeps bouncing between us, eyebrows hiked up to their hairlines. My internal temperature rises to new highs by the second and I'm close to combustion. The man who ignores me like I'm a house plant thinks I'm so pathetic he has to jump in and help me save face in front of my friends.

"Can we assist you in any way?" Jenna tries to get his attention once she snaps out of her stupor.

"I doubt you'd have the qualifications," Carter says in a posh tone that grates on my nerves.

His reply silences her, and they rise in a huff. I don't know how much time passes before they finally leave with promises of coffees and girls' nights I did not quite register.

"Thank you," I tell the floor once they're gone, struggling to keep up a frail protective wall. "You didn't need to pretend I can help you."

"I don't care what they think. The way they were talking down to you is unacceptable."

That's rich coming from him.

"You mean, like you do?" I don't know where I got the nerve to talk back to him and it takes me by surprise. Another shock is the slight twitch of the corner of his lips.

Carter ignores my question but he's not done with me.

"We *do* have urgent business to attend to." His voice is slightly amused, and I don't like it at all.

I reject Jared's call once again while I stare into the black box Carter placed in front of me. It's filled with cables, small plastic accessories, a flat metal square, and a metal contraption similar to a tripod.

Jared texts again.

> *We need to talk, baby.*
> *Answer the phone, please.*
> *I only love you, you're the woman I want to spend my life with.*
> *Fine. I'll let you mope at the cabin until I come back.*

Now I wonder if Amy and Jenna came here on his behalf and not because they actually cared about me.

The scar near my temple itches. I don't know if I'm strong enough to resist his attempts to convince me. To not let him pressure me back to the safety of a shared home. To tell him to leave me alone forever. The alternative, cutting myself out of his life, is equally terrifying.

Rummaging through the box for the user manual helps me take my mind off the visit and even if I don't want to admit it, I'm grateful for something to do.

"I found the perfect place to mount the dish," Carter says after checking the cabin, inspecting the roof.

As I suspected, he is a control freak. The man has brought his own fancy kit to connect with the famous Rawlings' satellite internet, even though the cabin has Wi-Fi.

I hate being bad at things and this expensive equipment is testing my patience, along with Carter who's watching me unhurriedly.

"I was never a fan of puzzles," I confess, relieved when I find the manual at the bottom. "Don't you have people to set this up? What if I break something?"

"Nonsense. We created it to be used by anyone, anywhere in the world."

"Then I must be the dumbest person alive because I can't manage it."

The sharp edge of his glare dulls, and he moves to the chair next to me on the wraparound porch.

"You're not concentrating. Your mind is elsewhere."

Carter takes each piece and shows me how they work without needing the manual. The modulation of his voice, and the way he explains how they fit together so it makes sense is soothing. I could listen to him talk for hours.

"Do you have a ladder here?" he asks, once the dish is complete.

"No way! I don't have any liability insurance for this place."

"I won't fall." He sounds offended.

"When was the last time you climbed up a ladder?"

"Some time ago," he lies through his teeth.

I don't budge. The last thing I need is to scrape Carter off the ground. "I'll do it."

"Out of the question."

"I won't drop your precious—"

"It's not that." He avoids looking at me. "I'm being a gentleman."

City boy manages to mount the eyesore on my roof without breaking his bones. I might have stolen a glimpse or two when his back and legs tensed as he worked. For safety reasons, of course.

"Now you're connected with civilization," he sounds off.

A layer of weariness softens his posture, but I don't want him to bite my head off, so I don't ask if he's OK. "Let me get you something to drink," I offer instead.

Back inside, the knots around my middle loosen as the heaviness from this morning is more bearable.

He's at the island, spinning his water glass in place. Something is clearly on his mind.

"Have you been friends for long? With those women?" he asks, a hint of hesitation hidden in his casual tone.

Mr. Broody wants to talk about me of all things. This morning, he didn't want my company, but I'm not going to call him out on it. I might as well tell him. This is a small town and people tend to talk about everybody's business. He'll surely be filled in by one of the town's busybodies once they find out he's staying at my cabin.

Let's get it over with. His opinion about me can't get any worse.

"Do you mind if I put on some tea before I tell you about this mess?"

I rarely drink alcohol and I need something to soothe the heartache and shame churning deep in my body. Carter doesn't say anything the whole time I prepare the brew. But I can feel his gaze following me. Occasionally, I steal glances at the man resting his lean arms on the counter, long fingers intertwined.

I can't remember the last time a man watched me so intently. It stirs old parts of myself I laid to rest a long time ago. When I realized Jared was not the type of partner to appreciate them.

The smell of chamomile and cinnamon dulls the restlessness.

I place the second cup in front of him, but he doesn't reach for it, scanning the steamy mug, eyes traveling up my arms and resting with an expectant heaviness on my face.

"We work together. Amy and Jenna, you saw today—"

"Delightful women," he drawls.

"And my boyfriend." I pause on the word. "I mean ex-boyfriend." I brace myself with a deep inhale. "And the woman I found out he's been cheating on me with for the past two years." I get physically ill thinking about it. "That's why I came here."

He doesn't say a word for a few seconds before voicing his opinion.

"What a piece of garbage." He leans back in the chair. "Do you want him gone? I have a military contractor on retainer."

I burst out laughing. "Do you offer this kind of service to every scorned woman you meet?"

"I can add the home-wrecker to the hit list," he says with the air of someone taking down your lunch order.

"Caroline"—her name tastes like ash—"is their friend. We got close after a while. I thought she was my friend too, especially after she helped Jared land a job in her department." He's a natural, charming, sweet talker. It was perfect for him. "They had to travel to business fairs with the sales department. I guess that's how it started."

Fidgeting with my cup is a better idea than making eye contact.

"They had these inside jokes after a while, and they'd laugh without letting me in on it. It was always, 'You wouldn't get it' or 'You had to be there'." I make a poor attempt at mimicking Jared and Caroline.

"Didn't it piss you off?" Carter asks, confused. Of course, he'd go scorched-earth and annihilate anyone messing with him.

But I don't know how to answer. An uncomfortable sensation roiled through me every time they did that. Same as the indigestion I get if I eat something too spicy. It was quickly replaced by guilt about my reaction. Being angry meant something was wrong with our relationship, that it was damaged, and I couldn't let that thought poison my day-to-day life.

"I thought she had a thing for a high school classmate of his." I change the conversation not too smoothly, but Carter doesn't comment on it. "I encouraged her to go for it."

A humorless laugh escapes me.

"And you had no idea about their affair."

"Obviously." Defensiveness masked as outrage pinches my voice. "I was blind, not in denial." That's stretching the truth. "Or maybe I was and don't want to admit I was so focused on not ending up alone, that I completely missed the signs."

"Being single is not the end of the world. It gives you control over your life, your time."

He doesn't understand what I mean when I tell him I don't want to be alone. He at least has a mother and probably other family. I don't want to tell him what it means to me.

Instead, I grab the opportunity to find out more about him, since he's surprisingly open today.

"It sounds lonely. Not having somebody to consider in your plans, in your life. Somebody to miss you when you're not with them."

"I'm not alone when I don't want to be," he says, the innuendo more than clear, and I remember the women in the articles.

"I'm talking more about emotional connection and security than casual sex. I want someone I'm safe with, somebody I can build a family with."

His smirk is condescending, "You mean marriage and kids and the white picket fence?"

"Yes, kids are part of my perfect future, either by blood or not, but more than that..." How can I explain this visceral hunger for belonging and intimacy, so haunting it becomes an ache sometimes?

Even after eight years, the ache never subsided. I knew in my bones that Jared wasn't my safe space, my forever home.

The swaying trees outside catch my eye and the soothing dance of the branches quiets my mind enough to articulate the messy emotion hiding behind the surface.

"I'm far from perfect. Inside or out. I want to be able to be my whole self with somebody. A man who'd take it all and love me because of it. I know now that Jared didn't allow it and I had to hide who I am. To look the way he liked, to act the way our friends expected me to."

Carter doesn't say anything, and I realize I might have shared too much and rest the already cold teacup against my reddening cheek. I wanted to be completely honest for a change. It's hard to open my soul to people who knew about my past and would look at me with pity. Who already think I'm fragile. The stranger before me is the closest thing to sending my thoughts into the void.

"Sorry, TMI from the crazy woman in the woods," I joke, but he's still as a statue, his Adam's apple bobbing and his eyes burning with an intensity I don't know how to decipher.

"What if it never happens, the way you want it?" The slight waver in his voice lodges in my airways.

The question comes off as loaded, with a lot of missing pieces, but I don't have the courage to ask him about it. This thread of connection is too fragile.

CHAPTER FIVE

ELIZA

Monday morning rolls in, as inevitable as the thunder after lightning, filling my insides with anxiety. I desperately need the paycheck, but I can't go back to work and bump into them daily. On the other hand, the town is too small to find another job with the same salary. I have some savings but not enough and I should be smart about it. Have a safety net.

When I inherited the cabin four years ago, Jared wanted nothing to do with it and said he didn't want to live in the forest. He resented me for not selling it so he could get a brand-new car.

What do you know about renovation and decorating?

I did my best with minor updates and pieces I reconditioned from the flea market and rented the place out through Valerie, a real estate agent I knew from billboards in town.

Jared scoffed and pouted for every bit of time I put in getting it ready and couldn't care less about the few tourists that came my way.

You're wasting your time for scraps.

I saved all the little money I made from the rental to surprise him with when I had enough for a deposit, so we could buy our dream house and start a family, even if he brushed me off whenever I wanted to show him a listing.

The thought of spending my savings makes me physically sick. Without a second thought, I know what's going to happen. I slip back into the old survival mechanism.

The sheets are as comfortable as sleeping on sandpaper. It's pointless to force myself to stay in bed so I start cooking breakfast for my grumpy roommate. It gives me enough time to whip up something different from yesterday.

Carter's reaction is lackluster at best.

Oatmeal and nuts. He doesn't touch the tea again. I'll get to him eventually.

"You're not eating?" he asks.

The lie comes easy. "I'll get something on my way to work."

"Hm." Carter leans back, crossing his arms, and I'm forced to look away from his intense stare.

I tune him out, miserable about how fast my life went south. I had a boyfriend who hinted at marriage and a good job. After I left the Millers, I swore I'd never be alone and penniless again. But here I am, after working so hard.

After a string of minimum-wage jobs, I managed to get my first office job at the paper company. It took so long to compensate for the lack of a college degree.

I remember the day I graduated from the online courses two years ago. Despite Jared's constant grumbling whenever I had to study.

"Why does a girl like you need a college degree? Just be grateful for the job you have."

"I could get paid more, get a promotion."

"Why would you need more money? I make enough to take care of you."

In hindsight, it meant he could control me. The pay raise and added responsibility were such a step up, that I wanted to celebrate them with him. His reaction is burnt into my brain forever.

"Congrats, you showed me, you can." Jared rolled his eyes.

"This is good for both of us," I argued.

"I hope it won't affect your work around the house. I'd hate to start looking for a real woman who can take care of her man."

His phone rang and he rushed out to go fishing with his buddies, leaving me sobbing into a cupcake with Quinn bringing me pity smoothies for free.

"You're awfully quiet this morning."

Carter's voice draws me out of the sad memory, and it takes me a moment to catch the meaning of his words.

"Thinking about work."

"Is it stressful?"

"Oh, no, I like it."

It might be a slight exaggeration. It pays well and I sit at a computer. Not bad, right?

He's on his tablet and I don't go into details about how I'm about to blow up my life even more.

"You don't have a car." He says matter of factly, not looking away from his device.

"Yeah." I'm confused. "I do, I mean. Jared took it to—you know."

"To go and cheat on you with your supposed friend." His tone is even and clinical, like a coroner examining the carcass of my relationship.

Fury bubbles under my skin so fast I see black spots.

"Will somebody pick you up?"

The question comes out of left field and cuts the wind in my sails.

"No, I'll walk to the main road and take the bus. You might not be aware, but there are these big cars with more than two seats. People use them to get around."

He levels me with a blank stare, not amused.

"We leave in ten minutes. I have some business in town," Carter says, like I'm one of his employees. Theoretically, I suppose I am, but still.

"What's with you and ordering me around? I don't need your pity drive."

His eyes widen then narrow dangerously. "I'll go either way. It's your choice if you'd rather traipse through the woods to work."

He goes back to ignoring me and I'm left boiling with anger. Furious at him for his aggravating logic and attitude. But also at myself because I know I'll accept his help yet again and it's eating me inside. His voice echoes on repeat in my head. *Charity case.* No matter how hard I try to hide them from him, he's got a sadistic talent for digging up all my problems.

Mercifully, Carter refrains from being an arrogant ass during the ten-minute drive. It gives me the chance to catalog the interior of his rental to keep my mind from spiraling. I've always admired the expensive cars cruising through town or parked at the marina when the owner of one of the yachts comes in for the season. But I've never actually been inside one until now.

Nestled in the leather seat I leave as much distance between us as humanly possible. In an enclosed space, Carter's presence is overwhelming. His smell and the heat of his skin when he uses the armrest fuel the rapid thrum of my heart. I'm not scared of him. Rather drawn in, like Martha to the yarn discount bin.

"Please stop here," I plead when we're too close to the office.

"Don't you—" He points into the distance, where the GPS shows the red pin.

"Thanks," I yell over my shoulder while I dash out of the car. I want to avoid unwanted attention. That won't happen if a Maserati drops me off in front of the building.

This end of Main Street is less historic and whimsical than the opposite end that plunges into the harbor area. It has a more utilitarian feel, built to house new businesses, low-rise residential buildings similar to the one I lived in until three days ago, and less traditional seaside places. I zoom past Quinn's coffee shop, the tendrils of panic tightening around my lungs with each step I take.

The gray building looms on the other side and my knuckles are white from gripping my bag. I force air in and out in slow succession while I stare at the weather-washed Vista Pine Paper Company sign over the entrance.

Working in the Supply Chain Department is not the most exciting job, but it pays the bills. Brain-numbing, but safe. And I'm about to walk away from it.

I'm frozen in place. The prospect of handing in my resignation and facing coworkers doesn't make my legs move. They'll pity me or laugh at me for being so blind and naive. I got cheated on with somebody prettier, funnier, so sure of herself. Who's Eliza to compete with her?

It's not until a car horn makes me jump out of my skin that I practically throw myself across the street, so I won't change my mind.

The access card trembles in my hand as I swipe it three times before the beep of the door pushes me forward on wobbly legs. I take hesitant, slow steps like I'm walking through a land mine. I want to avoid running into people I know but I can't concentrate with the erratic pulse whooshing in my ears.

The stairs are a better idea than risking getting trapped in the elevator with any of the people working here or, God forbid, Amy or Jenna.

Anxiety propels me up the stairs but my leg muscles cramp and I'm panting by the fourth floor. In the darkness of the stairwell, I stop to catch my breath against the metal door. I don't get much of a reprieve when a burst of laughter follows the sound of the door creaking open some floors below. The Customer Service team is like clockwork with their smoke break. They're nice people but worse gossipers than my so-called friends and I don't want to get on their radar.

I slip through the door, holding it steady with increasingly sweaty palms. A few more steps and I'm facing my manager's door. Luckily his office is in the hallway to the elevators and not in the open space that takes up half the floor.

CARL DAVIS
Supply Chain Manager

The department manager's name catches your eye in bold letters on a plaque he had made himself. No other manager has their name on the door. I guess it gives him a rush of power he doesn't hesitate to use any chance he gets.

Nervous and shaky, I knock and wait, swaying on the balls of my feet. He always makes you wait a couple of seconds, but this time an eternity passes as I frantically look out for people who might pass by.

"Come in!" He barks the order, pretending I'm interrupting his workflow. But I know better, since *last minute/oh, I forgot about this/ you're the best at it* reports often land on my desk.

A sleazy grin splits his face when he notices it's me and I pretend not to register the inappropriate once-over he gives me.

"Mornin', sweet Eliza," he coos in a sickening sugary voice.

I guess this is him being comforting. Gross. He's always been lewd, but he must know what happened already because he's upping the ante.

"Morning, Carl. Can we talk for a minute?" I close the door behind me, but his expression changes to a mixture of interest and something slimy. Maybe it wasn't the best idea.

"We can talk all you want. I'll always make time for you. Even after hours." He quirks his eyebrows, resembling two large caterpillars.

His innuendos always made me feel like I'd taken a roll in a pigsty, and I fight a shudder.

Just rip the Band-Aid, Eliza. Say it.

"I quit."

The folds in his cheeks tremble as his face morphs in confusion and he drops the sleazy smirk. "Why? I mean—" He fumbles, dropping his mask.

The way his expression changes would be funny if it didn't terrify me.

"Let's cut to the chase. I know about Jared and Caroline. I sympathize." The mock sadness with the palm-on-his-bosom act is not convincing. "But I can move you to another floor. Change your department."

"I can't." My voice trembles and I hate it.

I don't want to look weak in front of him because I know he'll take advantage of it.

"Don't be stupid, girl," he says, shaking his head, his voice rising an octave.

Tears fill my eyes. I don't want to be in the same building with these people. I'll never escape the rumors; it would be impossible to avoid Jared and Caroline.

"I have every right to quit." I stand my ground with the last ounce of nerve I own. "I have enough days off to cover the two weeks' notice."

"What did you say?" Carl leaps to his feet, slamming his palms on the cheap plywood desk and I jump back.

Beads of sweat slide down his forehead to the rhythm of his heavy wheeze. This side of Carl has my pulse spiking, my heart frantic like a little bird squished in his meaty fist.

The door stops my retreat when I take another step back, my fingers reaching for that raised white line near my left eyebrow.

"I—" There is not enough air in this room and I'm grateful Carl is too sluggish to walk around the desk and get closer.

He changes gears again and the benevolent boss mask is back on when I fumble for the doorknob. I can't be here another second.

"A single woman, with no family or connections needs every penny. I can withhold your last paycheck," Carl says.

"You wouldn't! It's not legal!" I croak, panic struck.

"One dinner at my place. I'm not asking for much."

My knees almost give and I'm blinded by tears. With my last ounce of will I dash out, running to the exit, any precaution forgotten.

"Eliza!" Somebody is calling my name, but I can't stop.

Fuck. I forgot about the stairs. The elevator doors open in slow motion and I nearly ram into a wall of people getting off at this floor.

Their words register as muffled mumbles while the doors close, and I lean against the floor-to-ceiling mirror. Shallow breaths fog the cold surface, but I shake off the dark spots at the edge of my vision when my phone chimes in my pocket.

Chapter Six

CARTER

Eliza's absence releases the pressure knotting the muscles in my shoulders. Whenever we're in the same room I'm aware of her every move, my mind trying to make sense of her, always on alert. I'm used to knowing everything about the people around me and her unexpected appearance in my life unsettles me.

She invades my senses in a manner no other woman has. I wake up to the sounds of her showering, the noise of the water pelting the tiles not enough to drown out that content hum she lets out when the hot water hits her skin. It travels through the hallway and under the door. It swirls hot in my lower abdomen. I wish her presence wasn't so loud. None of the women I spend the night with stay over to disrupt my mornings.

Maybe it wasn't the best decision to have her here, but the idea of Eliza spending the night in a dump didn't sit well with me.

Even if her presence still irks me, something shifted when she told me about her long-time cheater boyfriend.

The deceit, the betrayal.

I knew how those taste.

Asking her to cook was unnecessary, but I couldn't think of another way to put her at ease. Most of the things she's made are not on the list and I'm not about to share the details with her. She asks too many questions.

She's a distraction and I'm relieved that today I can work in peace.

The cabin has a perfect corner with a worktop and a chair. The large windows overlook the placid lake, surrounded by gentle swaying reeds. The green mountains rolling down on the other side are a barrier to the outside world.

I guess it's not the most horrible place to be sentenced for "recovery".

"You will take three more months off." My mother raises her voice.

"This is absurd. You can't ask me to play Boy Scout while the company is in danger!"

"Carter," she said tenderly, cupping my face. "I need… NEED…you understand me. Need to know that you are— I can't sleep since—" She sighs and the exhaustion on her face lands like a gut punch.

After what happened four months ago, I couldn't put my mother through more stress.

That didn't stop me from taking my calendar from the office. We might be the biggest tech company in the USA, but I crave the satisfaction of scratching an itch when I cross out important projects.

I put the calendar on the wall next to my new "office" so I can cross off the days and have a physical reminder of how much time I have left before returning to my life. The first Monday after my mother's imposed holiday is circled in red: BACK TO THE OFFICE!!!

My mother is lucky I love her so much because I wouldn't submit myself to this otherwise.

The satellite Internet connects instantly and I'm ready to dive in.

"What the—"

Somebody's going to get fired. Why the fuck am I locked out of all my accounts? I'm murderous when my calls to my assistant, IT Director, and Security Chief get blocked.

This is not a coincidence and when the next person on my list answers it confirms my suspicion.

"I was wondering how long it would take you," he says, skipping the pleasantries. Joseph Robertson, the company COO, my father's right-hand man ever since the business took off.

"What is going on with my access?"

"So nice to hear from you. How's the air in Maine?" His hoarse voice grates my eardrums. He's puffing those awful cigars.

"Cut the bullshit. I'm in no mood for your games." I'm too harsh to the only man who openly disapproved of my father's ways, but it smells of a hostile takeover.

"You're still on your sabbatical, Carter. You promised your mother."

I used to be grateful for his unwavering calm when I was thrust into the CEO role, but right now, the even and warm inflection fuels my anger.

"It's not a matter that concerns you, Joseph. I'm still the majority stakeholder, you can't lock me out. I have a business to run."

Joseph had been pestering me to take it easy. Especially after my father's death when I refused to take time off. It has always been a heated topic between us the past three years.

The last thing I remember from our most recent fight was his exasperated plea.

"You have to ease up. Life's not happening between these office windows, son!"

Next time I saw him he looked ten years older, holding my mother's hand in my hospital room.

It's been four months, and I'm antsy to get back. The market has noticed my absence at the head of the company. Especially since that asshole reporter, Fred Pierson, is making too much noise. The price of our stocks decreased slightly for the first time in the last thirty years.

"Your mother knows you haven't kept your end of the deal while you were recovering," Joseph says on a deep inhale from his cigar.

"Because you told her." I'm beyond pissed.

"I can't lie to her, son." The tenderness in his voice whenever he talks about my mother has always disarmed me.

"Jackie's in on this too, right? Mother couldn't have pulled it off alone."

"They called an emergency meeting with the board and voted."

My mother and sister together had more power. I never thought they would use it to sideline me.

"We want what's best for you. Even if you can't see it now."

"What's best for me is to make sure the company my family built doesn't turn to ashes!"

The only time I've felt this powerless was when I came back, tail between my legs, after not finding Laura at Harvard. The heartbreak, the fury, blindsided and unable to do anything about it. My father cruelly turned it into a teachable moment that shaped my future as the head of the company.

"Lesson number one," he said. *"Don't let your guard down. Lesson number two, always be ten steps ahead."*

I'm always scouting for the weak spots, analyzing the risks, and being ahead of our competition.

"Arrogance will be your undoing, son." Joseph brings me back to the call. "Over 300,000 people work for you. Hand-picked. The best in the industry. You think we're going to run around like a bunch of headless chickens without you for a few months?"

"Do you mean I'm useless?" A sense of worthlessness gnaws at my insides, drilling a hole in my stomach.

"No, son. I mean that you being on top of your game is what's best for the company. If something happened to you it would impact all these people you're responsible for." His loud exhale makes the connection crackle. "Your ten-year business plan is our Bible. We know what we have to do, OK?"

The call doesn't get me closer to fixing this. I never imagined my mother would stoop so low.

"I'm doing this because I love you," the always impeccable Clara Rawlings answers on the first ring, sitting in her office.

"Yeah, you sound just like father."

Her gasp dampens my frustration. It's not fair to her. She's his complete opposite.

"Listen to me, Carter," she says in a stern voice and I'm six again after breaking one of her thousand-dollar vases. "I will not allow you to scare us like that ever again, even if it means restraining you." She lifts her chin, not backing down.

"That doesn't sound too relaxing," I mumble.

"It's up to you. You either mope for three months or find something to enjoy. I don't care, as long as you take a break."

"I never moped more than two weeks," I say, defeated.

"Good. Then it's settled." She sounds victorious, leaning back in her leather chair.

I sigh. "This place isn't so bad."

Her smile lights up her eyes and it makes her look younger.

"It reminded me of where I lived when I was little. I told you about my brother who still lives in the area. I thought it would do you good to get back to my family's roots for a while."

"The mysterious uncle I've never met? What a fun reunion."

"Kenneth is a good man. He's excited to meet you."

"Why hasn't he visited if he wants to meet me so much?"

My mother's face contorts with regret and apologies.

"Let me guess, father dearest didn't approve."

Why am I not surprised? Family ties were not relevant in my father's eyes. Sometimes I felt he'd leave me behind without a second thought if I weren't his heir.

I've done more rehab and check-ups than necessary, but it still wasn't enough for my mother. The only reason I'm willing to follow her insane timeline for going back to work is because my father passed away three years ago and she's afraid she'll lose me too. I see it in the way she looks at me like she did when I was lying in the hospital bed four months ago.

I can't bear to break her heart or be the reason she goes through months of sleepless nights again. Losing my father almost killed her too and I won't let her shatter again.

Still, she can't expect me to put my life on hold. This has been my path since the day I was born. My father trained me relentlessly to take over the family business. This is my sole focus and my purpose.

I didn't leave or rebel even after the horrible graduation gift he gave me. My mother begged me to stay. I loved her but she was blind to the real him. He didn't do it to protect me. But to control me so I'd never step outside of the lines he drew.

He was prospecting the field for a suitable wife to birth the next heir, right before he died. I had no choice in the matter, and I couldn't get out of it if I wanted to inherit the company. What was the alternative? His dreams were my dreams, his goals my own.

Thankfully, the company is in good hands in my absence. Jackie was always a willing student. Passionate about finances and tech, even though our father never saw her as more than a future socialite wife. I didn't understand this side of him. He allowed her to shadow us just so she'd stop pestering him.

This is something I can control. The breath out every time my feet hit the narrow uneven path along the lake shore. The rhythm I set under the shadow of the pines bordering the way. I burn through my frustration with each mile. After months of slowly regaining my strength and endurance, I'm back to my running routine. And I don't intend to slip up.

A sense of satisfaction drives me for the last yards to the cabin. I'm drenched in sweat, my T-shirt and running shorts clinging like a second skin.

Eliza is already back, with her laptop on the couch, biting her nails. I hate that habit on people. She didn't hear me and it gives me a few seconds to notice the delicate slopes of her profile.

"Why are you here?" It comes out harsher than I meant. It's the default mood I can't shake off.

She jumps in her seat but instead of answering, her mouth forms a silent "Oh". Her eyes travel along my body and it's amusing to witness her reaction. It gives my ego a boost it badly needs. Dating wasn't a priority during recovery.

I clear my throat and she shakes out of her trance. The top of her ears redden and the way her neck contracts when she swallows uncomfortably hypnotizes me for a moment. I get the surprising urge to trace the movement with my thumb and press on her pulse point to feel it thumping against my skin.

"It's been a short day." Her voice is low, bordering on husky, and for the first time in months my lower abdomen twinges so lightly I could have missed it. It's a relief that comes at the worst time. I don't want to get hard for this messy woman. So I turn on my heels with a curt nod and head straight to the bathroom for a shower.

Eliza's voice stops me. "Where did you go running?"

"It doesn't concern you."

She's stuck on a silent word that fizzles out, then her arched eyebrows knit together making her nose scrunch.

"I get that you're a private person. You don't have to repeat it like I'm a toddler." She tucks her hair behind her ear, her mouth a hard line. "I thought you'd want to know how to avoid bears around here. But suit yourself." She turns back to the laptop and hate-types, hitting the keys with unnecessary force.

"Bears? Really?" I ask incredulously.

"Feel free to Google it. Or don't. The cabin's been paid for three months, so I don't care." She doesn't look at me and I deserve her cold shoulder. It's not her fault my body remembered I haven't had sex in months.

This version of her is quite entertaining. Not afraid to say what's on her mind. Feisty.

The last hours did nothing to improve my mood. The jog was a temporary fix for my current problem. What am I supposed to do out here?

"You don't need to wash them."

Eliza reaches for the dishes I've been scrubbing mindlessly in the sink and I frown.

"Men don't like doing this kind of thing," she tries again. "It's no problem, I can—"

The words are out before I can stop to think better of it. "You couldn't possibly imagine what a man like me likes."

She's red in the face and lost for words.

"What kind of man were you living with before, anyway?" I snap at her, unable to temper my annoyance.

"I just wanted to help," she stammers.

"Of course." I can't help the sarcasm dripping off my words. "I'm not an invalid. Don't need you or anybody babying me." I know she's not the true source of my issues, but I can't stop.

"I'm not doubting your ability to do the dishes," Eliza says, looking at me, worried. "We have a deal, remember? I stay here and help you, in exchange?"

She's holding up her end of the bargain and I'm taking my frustration out on her.

"I want to be decent here and you're making it very hard," she presses on calmly.

My aggravation balloons. "Don't bother. I got it covered."

She keeps staring at me with those big brown eyes and I need space. "You can go."

Eliza turns on her heels and heads for the bedroom without another word and I hate myself. I deflate, the anger pouring out leaving me empty, tired, and guilt-ridden.

Her being a decent person irrationally gets on my nerves.

At dinner, she doesn't come out. I'm too proud to go knocking at her door, despite the nagging inkling she hasn't eaten anything today.

She's probably waiting for me to go to bed so she can have her dinner in peace.

CHAPTER SEVEN

ELIZA

With each scroll through the jobs listed in the area, my insides clench harder. The need to be financially stable is deeply rooted in my bones after growing up in the system. Every day without a job makes me slowly slide into survival mode. Back to when I was little and some of the families didn't bother to feed their foster kids. I've learned to get by with almost nothing whenever my life is unstable. It's the one thing I can control when everything else is off the rails.

All kinds of dark scenarios play through my head and before I drive myself crazy I decide it would be more productive to catch the bus to the store, chipping away at the list of necessities and deciding what I can do without. It's also a good reason to stay out of Carter's way.

Some of the money from the rental will go into getting him groceries. I'm going to keep my end of the deal whether he likes it or not. The rest goes into saving as much as I can. Who knows when I'll be able to get another job?

I'll use every penny to make the small cabin livable. There's no way in hell I can continue to be roommates with Carter for much longer.

For one, I can better manage on my own, and adapt my spending so I can survive. Plus, it's mentally exhausting to constantly pretend I'm not spiraling out of control. It's becoming increasingly difficult to share the space with him. He's incredibly attractive and the way he looks at me stirs something inside me that I don't want to explore.

Luckily, he's a massive dick.

Rounding the aisle, I bump into the person I least want to see right now besides Jared. His mother.

"Oh, Eliza." She looks like she hates this encounter more than I do. "How have you been?"

"How have I been?" I can't avoid the slight pitch in my voice.

Mary checks the price on a nearby shelf with an uncomfortable grimace, afraid I'll make a scene. She knows, I'm sure. And that's her reaction. I didn't expect much from her. To say she barely tolerated me is an understatement. She never missed an opportunity to express her disapproval. In her book, I'm unreliable because I have no family, no roots. My food was bad. My house never met her standards of cleanliness.

"Please, Eliza. Don't embarrass yourself." The dismissive pitch of her voice flips a switch in me.

"What?" I can't believe my ears. "Why should I be the one embarrassed? I'm not the one who cheated."

"Maybe he wouldn't have if you were what my son needs," she spits through her teeth.

She grabs a pack of rice and throws it in the cart, turning her back on me and stomping toward the checkout, leaving me stunned.

The self-doubt begins to creep back in. *I wasn't good enough.* A recurring tune following me since I was old enough to understand that my parents abandoned me. It's a deep-seated fear I haven't shared with anyone.

It's shameful.

It's a burden.

Going back to my ass of a roommate is the last thing I want. I know exactly who's expecting a long overdue visit and so I give her a call.

"I'm at the store. Can I come over?"

"Oh, sweetheart. I've been so worried." Martha's motherly voice is a balm traveling through my system. "The pecan pie is fresh out of the oven. It'll cool by the time you get here."

I was left unsupervised most of my childhood and craved the feeling of being taken care of and having someone to care enough to make decisions and steer me in the right direction.

In my darkest moments, I used to pick myself apart in the mirror wondering how my parents looked. Did my father have the same brown eyes? Do I have my mother's strawberry blonde hair? Not knowing hurts as bad as not having them by my side to lean on.

Gram Miller is gone and the only people I can talk to now are Martha and Sam, my foster parents' neighbors. I loved to help them with their home and garden when I lived next door.

"I'm so happy you're here!" Martha's embrace is so strong it has the power to glue me back together.

"Sorry it took so long to drop by. I'm a mess."

"Hush, child. You're in a bit of a mess, but you— look at me." She gently grabs my chin and tilts it up. "You will be alright. It will pass."

A feeble smile is all I can give her.

"Now, go rest and I'll bring you something to eat."

The interior of their home, with its flowery wallpaper, reminds me of the two years I got to spend at the Miller's house. Their knickknacks collected over a lifetime are scattered around the solid wood furniture and pictures of Martha and Sam hang in every room.

My favorite piece is the vintage stove where I learned how to cook. Martha is a great teacher and the closest connection to the best foster parents I ever had.

Gramps' children sold the house after he died. The five siblings lived with their families, scattered between the East and West Coasts, and none of them planned to return. I got the cabin from their parents and the sale of their house happened so fast. I couldn't afford to buy the first place that was a real home, even if I wanted to.

A nice young family with twins lives there now. Their giggles fill the street whenever I visit Martha and Sam. Each time my heart twists. With joy for those kids who have loving parents and will grow up in a lovely home. And with a sense of longing bleeding into my bones for the things I missed out on. My parents didn't love me enough to give me that kind of life. Instead of being cradled in my mother's love, I was raised by strangers with no fondness in their hearts for an urchin.

Melting on Martha's worn-out couch after she stuffed me with food takes the edge off my anxiety.

"I was hoping you'd leave him."

"You know it's hard for me to let people go," I say, leaning back on the soft couch. "He showed me I wasn't enough, but I stayed. I thought it was the best I could do." I'm mourning the shattered dream of a family more than the relationship with Jared.

Is it normal? Shouldn't I miss him?

Martha beams at me. "That's why I'm so proud of you now."

"I did it because I saw him with my own eyes. I'm relieved the decision was taken for me. Isn't that pathetic?"

"You packed your bags and left. Some people never do, even in the face of undeniable proof that the other person is not good for them."

"I feel stupid for not seeing it sooner," I admit in a whisper. "I never won. No matter how hard I tried."

Martha's crumpled face adds to my shame. Her distress is palpable because I never shared this side of my relationship with Jared. I knew he wasn't her favorite person and there was no point in making him look worse.

She reaches out to comfort me. "It's not your—"

"Does it mean there is something wrong with me? Jared's mom thinks so. Am I not good enough?"

My own mother thought so and gave me up just days after I was born. My lip wobbles and I can't unsay the words which bring Martha closer, squeezing me to her side. She mumbles into my hair and her reaction is so on-brand.

"That bitch. She's about as useful in this world as a moose in a knitting circle."

She leans away and holds me by my slumped shoulders.

"It means he's not it for you. The one who loves and cherishes you as you deserve," she says in a serious tone. "Don't let what happened with Jared make you doubt yourself."

"Alright," I say, my smile a bit unsteady.

"Now. I've been sitting on this for a while. But since the great douche is finally out of the picture…" Martha rises to her feet with a slap on her knees. She rummages through a drawer behind me and returns with a thick folder in her hands and a satisfied grin.

"I want to make this official," she says, pulling out a stack of papers, and I wait with bated breath. "My only requirement is that you get Sam out of my hair from time to time. I love the man to death, but it's healthier for everyone involved if he spends some hours fishing once in a while."

I skim the first page of the document and it dawns on me it's the deed to Sam's shabby cabin. This is not an inside joke anymore and my mind shifts into overdrive.

"You know that's not why I came, right?" I say, with a hint of panic.

Martha's eyes crinkle at the corners and a warm smile tempers my worry.

"We don't have kids and I don't want it to go to that awful cousin on Sam's side. We haven't spoken to her in twenty years." The disgust on her face makes me giggle. She smirks, flipping the pages until she reaches the last one and points to the dotted line. "You're the closest thing we have to a daughter. Your name belongs here."

A rush of affection pushes me into Martha's arms, and I hold on tight.

"I'll forever be grateful to have you two in my life."

She dabs at the wet spots under her eyes and clears her voice, removing invisible lint from her green-striped pants, giving us both time to pull ourselves together.

"I promise it will be the prettiest fishing cabin." I sniffle while signing my name. "I'll get Sam a recliner for his afternoon nap and a small fridge outside for his beers."

"I know you will," Martha says through her watery grin. "We trust you with it because you're so talented."

"Don't exaggerate—"

"I know it's just a hobby for you. But you did so well with the Miller cabin." She stops my protests and continues. "Which brings me to the next order of business." She pulls out a smaller envelope from the file and the confusion on my face must be obvious. "I know why you had to quit."

"How did you find out so fast?" I screech, bewildered.

"Oh please. I knew by lunch. I hope the creep didn't give you any grief."

I can't look at her and I'm nauseous remembering how Carl acted.

"Eliza—" Her warmth is my undoing.

No chance to hide anything from her. It's why I chose to share the space with Carter, the embodiment of a metal ice scraper in sub-zero temperatures, rather than come here.

"He threatened to hold my last paycheck," I tell her with a sigh.

Martha's eyes bulge. "That good for nothing…I'll call his mom, she'll set him straight."

"Please, no!" I grip her arm, holding her in place. "I'll fix it, but I don't want to make waves. Especially now." I'm not strong enough to deal with the fallout of ending my relationship and quitting my job. I'm unsteady as an old house about to crumble.

"Fine," she says, her tone making it obvious she disagrees. "Then this comes at the best time."

The envelope she places on the cherrywood table looks full.

"Martha—" I have an inkling about what's in there and my ears burn.

"I've already had a chat with Thomas," she cuts me off. "He's found some reclaimed wood and has some extra materials returned from his nephew's construction projects. The boy has his own crew and won't rip you off."

Why doesn't it surprise me that Thomas, the grumpy old man running the hardware store in town, wants to come to my rescue again? He's such a good soul, hiding behind those scowls and grunts he calls conversations.

"I can't accept it," I falter. The lump in my throat is a dry sponge I can't swallow. *Charity case.* "I don't want to ask for any more favors."

"I know this town has failed you over the years, but you're one of our own and we help each other. There's no shame in relying on your neighbor to help keep your head above water."

"What if I can't pay you back?"

"Oh, sweet child. Nobody's keeping score."

She gently lays her tender hand over mine, stopping me from cracking my knuckles.

"We won't abandon you, OK? You'll be back on your feet in no time."

Her optimism kindles my own like a candle in the dark galleries of a mine and I wonder if I can keep it burning until I safely reach the surface.

"It's not much." She pushes the money forward. "It was in my will for you if you were still with Jared when I kicked the bucket. At least now I have something to be excited for besides Saturday's knitting club."

She claps and I giggle at the visions of fixing the cabin, living on my own, and having the freedom to live as myself, without being forced to fit Jared's mold.

The thought is also frightening. The Miller's cabin was in better shape. What if I can't fix it and waste everybody's time and Martha's money?

Jared didn't care when I asked him about the color he'd prefer for the walls and rolled his eyes when I restored an old chic coffee table I found at a yard sale.

"There will be no one to tell you what you can do with it," Martha says, reading me as always. "The boy has no clue what he's lost."

Her words make me uncomfortable. "I don't think—"

"Didn't you fix the couch by yourself?"

Jared blew a gasket when he came home early one time from his business trip and found me reupholstering the couch. It was the first time I did something so big, and it took a while longer than planned. I wanted to surprise him.

"All of Main Street could hear his screams."

My skin crawls at the memory. Jared yelled at me for ruining the couch.

You know nothing about fixing furniture. YouTube does not make you an expert.

"Because he's an idiot. A good man would've rolled up his sleeves and helped you finish."

He didn't. So I did my best to finish faster. Blinded by tears, I almost chopped my finger off. He never said anything about it, even with all the afternoons he spent plopped on the couch watching TV.

Martha pats my knee. "You don't get to be my age and not learn a thing or two about life. It's OK to start wanting different things along the way. You grow, you change, and that's the beauty of it."

"What if what I want is foolish?" Could I turn my hobby into something more?

"You'll find your spark, dear," she says knowingly.

"My spark?"

"Yes. The thing that makes you jump out of bed in the morning. That drives you."

Her words settle over me and I soak them in.

"Now." Her squint means trouble. "Want to tell me about that mysterious roommate of yours?"

Martha's motherly goodbye hug still lingers comfortingly on the surface of my skin when my back pocket vibrates again and I reject Jared's call.

Back at the cabin, I look for a distraction and to give myself and Carter some space. Avoiding the charged air seems safest so I go straight to the shed in the back.

The smell of wood shavings and paint reminds me of sitting next to Sam while he worked on his orders. It makes me feel less alone. The shed doesn't compare to his generous garage where he kept his carpenter's tools, but it is my own space and holds everything I could afford and some hand-me-downs from him.

I love the process of scraping the worn varnish from old wooden parts. It gives me such satisfaction when the piece is clean and ready for its next step. It's when I can visualize clearly how I want to transform it.

This old nightstand is a bit of a headache. I'm halfway through cleaning the dreadful black paint sprayed over the original color.

Under the painting, I discovered beautiful rich maple wood, and I don't have the heart to paint over it. I'll probably only change the legs and the knob to fit the modern cottage vibes I settled on for my new home during the bus ride back.

I continue until my stiff back and the evening chill makes me stretch out in the chair, exposing my midriff to the pricking cold.

"Should you be handling sharp objects?" Carter's voice booms in the dark.

I nearly topple over and drop the paint scraper.

He casts a curious glance and inches closer, stretching his neck to get a better view but I scurry out, shutting the two shed doors behind me.

Sam is the only one allowed back here. I don't want to let a stranger in my space, especially him. I'm still overwhelmed by Carl's blackmail, meeting Jared's mom, and Martha's surprise. I can't handle his snark.

Carter looks back and then straight at me.

"Do you need anything?" I bite out.

Obvious interest is battling with his ego. "For your information, I'm not trained to sew back hacked fingers."

I roll my eyes at him. "I've been doing this for years. And if something happens and you're too scared, I can save them in a bucket of ice myself."

"I'm not scared! It's not advisable to use dangerous tools in your state of mind."

"How—" I falter. "It's none of your business anyways."

"It might be if you have to cook with a missing thumb. You barely manage it with your hand intact."

"What the hell!" Did he just say I'm a bad cook? "Who pissed in your porridge?"

"You might have, considering the way it tasted."

I stare at him, mouth agape at his bluntness, when the shadow of a smirk crosses his lips.

"You awful—"

"Eliza," he stops me. The deep timbre of his voice makes my name sound more sensual than it has any right to. "You're too easy to rattle." Carter shakes his head and leaves me confused about what just happened.

How can a man who has known me for less than a week sense that I'm off, when Jared didn't even notice I'd stop eating for days after a big fight?

When I'm lying in my bed, rewinding our interaction, it hits me. Carter managed to annoy me out of getting stuck in my head and obsessing about the past couple of days.

Did he do it on purpose?

Chapter Eight

ELIZA

A girl of a certain age needs her morning routine to function like a human being. So far, I've had enough time before Carter's shadow darkens my kitchen. But my good luck ran out this morning. Before I reach the doorknob, Carter stumbles out of the bathroom, startling me to death.

Hair tousled, sleepy, dusty jaw, he smells like a warm morning embrace. How does one wake up looking so edible? I've tossed and turned every night since I've been here. I'm so tired that the comfort of his arms calls to me and I let myself imagine for a second what it would be like to sleep next to him.

I'm still in REM asleep. There is no other explanation for the way my mind wanders unchecked.

His eyes roam over my body and I get self-conscious about the flimsy tank top and shorts.

Carter swallows and I'm compelled to press my lips against his Adam's apple. My brain's gone haywire from these sleepless nights. Also, I haven't had any good sex for the past year, which might explain the surprising urge to taste his skin.

"'Scuse me," I manage to rasp out and his head snaps back, wide stormy eyes full of surprise.

Carter shakes himself out of his stupor and drags a palm over his stubbled jaw, clearing his throat. His entire demeanor changes and the warmth is replaced by his usual chilly aura.

"I know this house is small, but it would be lovely if you didn't invade my space so often."

What is wrong with this man? I'm getting whiplash from his mood swings.

"I was just going to the bathroom, not cornering you in the shower."

The comeback freezes him for a second and the faintest pink dusts Carter's cheekbones before he scowls.

"Speaking about the shower. Could you be any louder?" He crosses his arms and I involuntarily follow the coil of his muscles. Then I remember his question.

"What's your problem now?" I ask, exasperated.

"I wake up to the sounds of a drowning puppy. It's aggravating."

I grit my teeth. "If it bothers you so much, I'll gladly go to the other cabin." At this point, I'd take a bath in the cold lake rather than listen to him complain about me breathing too loudly.

Before he gets to say anything, I squeeze past and slam the door instead of threatening him with my shower rendition of "I Will Always Love You." I bite my tongue because I'm in no position to give his money back if he decides to leave.

Confrontations also make me break out in hives. Even if he weren't paying me, I'd probably find somewhere else to shower instead of telling him to get some earplugs.

Carter sits at the small butcher's block kitchen island, overdressed again. I steal glances at the light gray buttoned shirt and black crease-front trousers while making another attempt at a breakfast his majesty would enjoy.

I can't help but find it suspicious his mom sent him here. Old habits die hard, and I can't squash the doubts.

"Did your mom find the cabin online?"

Carter peels his eyes off his tablet with a sigh but decides to be civil this time.

"I doubt she has the time to research places in the middle of nowhere where she can exile her only son."

He sounds dejected, a grown man pouting like a teenager sent to his room by his mom. It's hilarious, but the issue still bothers me.

"I still find it odd a person like you would stay in this type of rental."

"A person like me?" Carter raises an eyebrow and I feel foolish and classless for pointing out he's rich.

He obviously is. Carter moves with the confidence of a man who has everything. Who grew up surrounded by the finest things. Who knows the difference between types of wine and spoke French with his grandparents.

Jared once said nobody wants to rent a cabin filled with junk because I kept adding refurbished pieces. I thought the place looked nice, but that was before having Carter in the same space.

"What I meant..." I fumble. Embarrassment flushes my cheeks, and I don't know how to get out of the hole I dug myself into.

Carter pins me with his stare, a hint of amusement crossing his features.

"Someone in her team probably sent her a shortlist of places near my uncle." He decides to overlook my blunder and I jump at the change of topic.

"Oh, you have family around here?" Maybe he'll decide to spend more time with them, and I won't have to stew in this uncomfortable mishmash of embarrassment and secrets.

Carter's eyebrows slant and his lips press into a thin line while he rolls the watch on his wrist.

"Apparently. I don't know them." He taps the screen and gets back to what he was doing.

I want to ask him more but the way he focuses on his tablet suggests the topic is closed.

"I hope you'll enjoy staying here, despite my unwelcome presence," I say in the wake of his silence.

"It will do." It's all I get from him, and he doesn't spare me a glance again. This stillness fuels my restlessness. I can't sit in absolute silence in the same room with another person.

So, I study his sharp features that don't give anything away. What would happen to his face if he genuinely smiled? The slight twitch of his lips changes Carter's features whenever he crosses out another day on the calendar he pitched near his laptop.

After he pushes his food around and eats some toast with egg whites, he picks up a red marker and does the same thing.

"Who gets this happy about a holiday going by quickly?"

"You wouldn't understand. I have better things to do than admire the sunset on your porch."

"Wow. Boring and condescending." My mouth clams up a second too late. What on earth possessed me to say that? Carter damaged my filters.

"Boring," he says, taken aback. "Aren't you a little mouthy today?"

"I'm sorry," I stammer.

Carter plays with the red marker and tilts his head, scanning me from head to toe.

"You're more entertaining when you say what's on your mind."

"Well." I clear my throat. "The cabin doesn't come with a circus monkey." I cross my arms defensively and shuffle away before I say any more things I shouldn't.

Something in his jab scraped over the truth I'd looked past for so many years. Always careful of what I said, I hated offending anyone, and mostly held my tongue with Jared.

Carter doesn't get angry when I talk back. I let it go for now because I have more urgent things to do. I grab my laptop and plop on the couch. My CV needs some dusting off.

I'm struggling to put into words the skills I have when Carter's voice makes me fall into his calculating gaze.

"Don't you have a job to go to?"

It was inevitable he would notice. I was just hoping he wouldn't bring it up.

"I quit," I mumble, collecting invisible lint from the arm of the couch.

"Please use your whole mouth to speak."

"I can't go back to the office. So I resigned." I exhale and prepare to get it over with.

His raised eyebrow demands I elaborate.

"They're"—I enunciate—"there."

"And? Is that supposed to make you quit?" He puffs, shaking his head. "You got kicked out of your house and job. What a shit week you've had. I bet your family is very proud of you." He lowers into his chair at the little desk and slides an ankle over his knee. "That's why you don't want to move back in with your parents? Because you're embarrassed? So you're hiding in the woods like a coward?"

Carter rests in the reclaimed chair I worked on for weeks with the posture of a king scolding his subject.

The practiced smile slips into place to hide my shock and hurt. But no matter how hard I try to play it off, my vision blurs.

"There is no family for me to fall back on. I'm a foster child."

Carter's smugness drops and a soft swell of pity I'm too familiar with rounds his eyes. I don't want it from him.

"It'll be alright. I'll make it work. Some friends are helping." I don't know who the pep talk is for, but I'd say anything to wipe that *oh, poor Eliza* grimace off his face.

"Eliza—"

"You didn't know. It's in the past. Let's not—" I suck in a breath to smother the shift in my voice.

Carter reaches me in a few long strides and stops so close my brain screams at me to put some distance between us, but he cups my shoulders and I'm trapped, staring into the silver whirlpools circling his pupils.

His grip is firm but not constricting, easy to shake off if I wanted to. It's the smart thing to do, but it's so warm and I'm so touch-starved that I find it comforting.

We face each other in an unbearable silence, our gazes searching.

This is pity. Nothing else.

So I slide from under his palms because all I want is to seek the warmth of his embrace until he closes around me like a cocoon.

Chapter Nine

CARTER

The people on the cybersecurity team at Rawlings Enterprise are the best in the Northern Hemisphere and I hate them today. I'm glad they're top of the industry, but the entire department is another failed log-in attempt away from being fired. My shots at bypassing the ban on my accounts are stonewalled and I'm getting increasingly agitated.

> CARTER: I'll give you that 1924 Macallan from the BlackGold auction.

> JOE: I need to be alive to drink it. Your mother will cut my brakes.

> CARTER: You're overreacting. She doesn't have to know.

> JOE: You're right. She'll take me to my favorite steak place and poison my wine. Like a lady.

I don't even call Jackie or my mother. If they hatched this plan, I can't change their minds. The floor creaks under my feet as I spiral around like a kid on a sugar rush. My early morning is spent calling and texting whoever I could bribe or threaten to give me access.

CARTER: I'll fire you.

DERRICK: Your sister changed my employment contract. It needs to be a board decision.

I didn't want to ask Logan. We've been friends since we got stuck socializing during my father's private meetings in Joseph's home office. Logan joined the army, spent years abroad, and returned to build an impressive military consultancy firm. The problem is I don't trust his hackers around our systems.

The ball of anxiety swirling in my chest grows with each call. I understand they think it's for my benefit, but it still stings that Jackie and my mother broke our pact. After my father died, we vowed to never combine our shares to hurt or push out one of the three of us.

After I burn through all my options, I brace to face Eliza after our bathroom run-in. She caught me off guard and those pajamas hardly covered anything.

I might have overreacted about the shower. To be honest, those sounds are a good distraction from my constant state of frustration.

I do my best not to picture other activities that could pull those noises out of Eliza when I find her singing along to a melody in her head, lips barely moving. The black leggings hug every line of her lean legs. I might find it sexy until her hideous fuzzy cat slippers catch my eye.

It's not as bad as I thought to have her here. The breakfast is still not what I can eat, but I don't want to tell her because I'm sure she'll ask a lot of questions and I'm tired of the disappointed twinge in her eyes when I end conversations I don't want to have.

Then I put my foot in my mouth in the worst possible way and when she told me she doesn't have a family I wanted to run into the lake behind us and hug a rock.

I feel like shit.

"Look. I—"

She brushes it off, but I can't miss the veil of sadness wrapping around her.

An invisible pull brings me near her without second-guessing myself. She's so close I can see the freckles scattered over her nose.

"It's not. I—" My pulse quickens when her lower lip quivers and I'm lost for words.

"I have to go," she chokes out, and I can tell her throat is closing. Eliza's eyes shine, holding back tears.

Near the front door, she stops and squares her shoulders.

"I'm not a charity case," she says with a sharpness that stings like a paper cut.

Fuck. The video call on Sunday. I don't even know why I said it.

Now that I know she was in the system it's even worse. How many times did she hear it growing up? My stomach clenches. I rush out the back door, grateful for the biting morning air, and swipe a hand through my hair in frustration.

Maybe I inherited more from my father than I'm willing to admit.

The sting of the slap still burned my cheek, my report card shredded on the carpet.

"If you're not above them, you're nothing."

My phone rings and I leap at the chance to do anything else than be consumed by guilt.

"Miss getting your ass handed to you already?" I rib Adam.

"Just because you and Logan shared a diaper and sparred before walking, doesn't mean you're better," Adam huffs.

"The board in the gym says I am." I chuckle.

"Pierre from R&D is the only one making noise in-house." Adam gets to the point since there's nothing he can say to contradict me. "She's telling the poor souls who use the fourth-floor employee lounge that you two had a monthly date and you have been avoiding her since January."

"We did not go on dates," I snap at him. Employees are off-limits. Company and personal policy. "They were meetings."

"Don't have to explain it to me, I'm not HR," he says suggestively.

"You don't work there at all, yet you know more about what's going on than anybody else."

"My charm is a master's key." He's grinning through the phone, annoying me with his good mood.

"Or it's your ability to blackmail people. Luckily, you're on my payroll and there's a signed NDA with your name on it."

"I'd feel offended you didn't mention I'm your best friend and I'd rather gouge my eyes out than sell your secrets, but you're in distress, so I'll overlook it."

"How generous of you," I deadpan.

"On the other hand…" Adam jumps back into business mode. "UniCore is acting pretty confident about the next Pentagon bid since it's a month away and you're nowhere in sight."

I start pacing again, my steps taking me to Eliza's off-limits shed.

That bid is worth billions and I'm sidelined, even though physically, I'm perfectly capable of resuming my responsibilities. I don't know how Joseph expects me to relax.

"I wouldn't worry. Your sis—" He catches himself. "Your team has the pitch covered."

As always, I pretend not to notice how he trips on any mention of Jackie. Nothing good would come of it.

"UniCore has Senator Jackson in their pocket. He has a lot of sway in the commission."

Adam chuckles and I bet the smug bastard couldn't wait to serve me this tidbit. "Let's just say it wouldn't matter. Their satellite tracking system has missed the mark during the latest tests. Substantially."

I don't even want to know how he found out. It's a fine line between gossip and corporate espionage.

"They're confident you guys won't have anything to show because you're the one running the show and you're MIA."

I sigh, and the grip on my lungs loosens slightly. "I appreciate you not freezing me out."

"You should take it easy," he stresses. "But I never agreed to keep you in the dark." That probably meant also avoiding my mother like the plague. "I know it makes things worse for you."

Adam knows me too well.

He's the one who saw me and had my back at the lowest point of my life. Or what I thought was my lowest, until four months ago. Somehow my mind drifts back to the wide-eyed copper-haired woman who left the house in tears. Does she have an Adam in her life? With no family, a painful breakup, and garbage for friends, is there someone she can turn to? If there were, wouldn't she have crashed at their place rather than planning to live in a run-down cabin?

I'm not necessarily cruel. I put people in their place when they need a reminder. But she didn't deserve to be talked to in that manner.

"What's wrong? You're more taciturn than ever."

I'll never hear the end of it if I tell him what's bothering me. I might want to pretend I'm making a fuss over nothing, and her problems don't concern me. Tell myself she's a stranger and I'm practically doing her a favor already. But…

"I might have hurt somebody's feelings."

There's a deafening silence on the other end. I should end the call and pretend I never said anything.

"Let me get this straight. You have feelings because of somebody else's feelings?" Adams asks in the worst mock therapist's voice. "First of all, how does it make you feel? Secondly, what's the name of the squirrel that used to jump in the campus pool?"

"Be serious."

"I'm dead serious. I have to check if you're the real Carter."

This was a colossal mistake. "Hilarious as always."

"Spill, what did you do?" His tone is chipper. The bastard is enjoying this too much. "Is it worse than the time you gave your half-eaten sandwich to Prof. Alfson because you thought he was homeless?"

I give him the short version and it sours my mood even more. The talk about loneliness and her dreams for a family takes on a different meaning now.

"Did you apologize, like a big boy?"

"I tried to, but it's more than accidentally stepping on her toes. I made a bad situation worse. She probably thinks I'm a dick."

"And you care…" Adam pauses for dramatic effect. "Because?"

That's a good question. I don't give myself time to dissect this lingering bitter aftertaste of our last conversation. I learned early on to keep a certain distance in business and my relationships. My father's words are still ringing in my ears. *"You don't need friends, you need allies. Power, money or blackmail will get anyone on your side."*

Still, there's something about Eliza's vulnerability tugging at my chest uncomfortably. For better or worse I always had mother and Jackie on my side. Can't imagine being on your own like that.

"One more thing," I ask Adam before hanging up. "Do something about Pierson. His latest article toes the line of macabre. He's one deadline away from writing that they're keeping me in a cryo-crypt in the Rawlings Enterprise's secret underground tunnels."

I pace around the cabin, waiting for her at the small dock over the lake, but she doesn't show up until late at night when I'm lying in bed tracing the shapes of the trees in the shadows on the walls. After her efforts to avoid me today, it might be safer to talk to her tomorrow.

Friday morning the sound of pots on the stove fills the cabin and I can only hope she doesn't sprinkle rat poison over my food. I didn't expect her to cook today after the way she left. Frankly, I could care less if she kept her end of the deal. I wouldn't wish a night in that slum of a cabin on even my worst enemy. Well, most of them.

Who am I kidding? I couldn't stomach the idea of leaving Eliza in that safety hazard.

"You don't have to cook breakfast every morning."

Eliza peers at me over her shoulder and for the first time in a week, I'm not able to ignore her presence. Those amber eyes pick me apart and it's unsettling.

"That's the deal," she says casually, but her movements are rigid and terse.

"I know." I'm uncomfortable, fighting the urge to pick at my ill-fitting skin. "I won't sue you if you don't." It's a bad joke even for me.

She shakes her head slowly. A subtle crease forms between her eyebrows while she inhales deeply.

"If it's because of what I told you yesterday," she exhales disappointed. "It was a long time ago; I don't need anyone's pity." Eliza looks straight at me and unlike other times since we've been here, her gaze doesn't waver. A determined glint in her eyes warns me to tread carefully.

The stupid *charity case* comment floats between us like the poisonous tendrils of a jellyfish. Neither of us dares approach it. This morning is not off to the start I hoped for.

"No. It—"

"Eat your breakfast before it goes cold." She cuts me off and removes the cover from the tray.

I stare at the much smaller spread and I'm lost for words. I never reveal too much. It took years for a relentless Jackie to find out the details of what happened after Harvard. There's never been anyone to pick up things about me so quickly. With no context. While I've been the worst version of myself, and she was going through a heartbreak and her life was turned upside down.

Eliza read me and I didn't even realize. This is more than our bargain. She did it for me.

The bowl with yogurt and fresh berries has the same flowery pattern as the plate with egg whites and vegetables on whole-grain bread.

And there's the tea again. I hold the stripped cup to gather my thoughts and take a sip as a reflex. The liquid doesn't taste like a wrestler's bathwater. The delicious warm brew coats my insides, and my shoulders drop the tension that's been pulling at my muscles for the past few weeks.

But it's the small quirk of the corner of her mouth that is enough to make me drink a barrel of her tea if it means we can go back to our usual mornings.

"This tea isn't store-bought." I point to the jar on the counter.

She sways from one foot to the other, uncertain and confused that I've said something inoffensive. I'd rather have a root canal without anesthesia than get that reaction. We're not friends, she doesn't have to like me, but there's no point in being an asshole.

"It's from my friend's garden. She lived next door to my last family, and I helped her tend the herb patch." She smiles, probably imagining the place. "She taught me how to dry them and make tea blends. I give my friends a custom mix each Christmas…" She pauses as a wave of sadness crosses her face. "This year there will be four bags less to worry about." Her voice is low, talking mostly to herself.

She shakes her head to banish the intrusive thoughts and inhales the wispy steam of her cup, her long lashes drifting down. Today she braided her hair to one side, giving me the perfect view of her delicate neck, contracting with every swallow.

"This one is my favorite. Lemon grass, ginger, chamomile…" She names the ingredients animatedly until she remembers who she's talking to, and her voice dissipates into silence.

I'm bracing to make a real apology. It's not some=thing that comes easy. My father always said only weak men apologized and the Rawlings were never wrong. I'm so out of practice I jump right into it, without warning.

"I know it's not an excuse," I huff. "I'm going through a rough time, and it has turned me into a person who talks out of his ass."

Eliza's snort loosens the knot of anxiety a little more and I keep going.

"I had no right to tell you those things. Completely out of line." I knock on the wooden surface, unsatisfied because it's not enough. "You must think I'm a rich New Yorker who doesn't realize how real life works."

I lock my gaze with hers because I want Eliza to know I mean it. The banter is all fun and games, but the low blow about the mess in her life…My mother would be appalled.

That adorable blush finds its way up her neck and catches her cheeks. She rolls her lips and the hesitation in her demeanor is completely called for. It's irritating, nonetheless. She hugs her willowy frame, trying to comfort herself. The gesture speaks of something so lonely. The uncomfortable pull to my insides doesn't let up.

I round the island to her side, where she is sitting on the barstool, and she has to look up at me. This is not a performative apology. I'm uncomfortable seeing her hurt for some reason, and I can't explain why, but I need her to know. I'm not making fun of her situation.

I didn't realize how close I'd got until her breath hitches slightly, brushing my neck. It rattles something inside me, but I have to stay on track.

"I do, but I got so used to the way people in my world get their problems fixed. I didn't pause to consider you have nothing in common with them."

"Uh, obviously." The blush spreading from her cheeks to her ears unsettles me this time. I didn't mean to point out she's not well off.

I'm out of practice with apologies, but this comes so easily. I place my hand over hers in a gesture of reassurance, taking us both by surprise. Those warm eyes widen, two pools of molten bronze. She's so close I can smell the lavender from the shower gel I'll never admit I used a couple of times and taste the sweet tea in her breath.

"I'm not talking money, OK?" I add hastily. "You're a nice person, a thing I can't say about most of my acquaintances."

I want her to tell me she understands so we can get back to being the most unlikely roommates and she can pester me with questions while I rile her up.

Before Eliza has the chance to answer, the sound of the driveway's gravel crunching under the wheels of a car stiffens her back, horror blooming on her face.

CHAPTER TEN

ELIZA

The familiar deep rumble of my truck freezes the blood in my veins when the old brakes grind to a stop, piercing the heavy silence of the cabin.

So many things happened this week, my mind managed to skip over some important details. Including the fact that Jared was supposed to come back Wednesday night. He's been home for two days already. It took him two whole days to come and talk to me. That's how much respect and consideration this man thinks I deserve after eight years together.

I bolt to the door and catch Jared slamming the truck's door through the peephole. Panic bubbles inside me and I lock the door. I'm not ready to talk about it. About Caroline. To listen to his excuses. Or to have him confirm my worst fear. That I mean nothing to him.

"Come on, babe," Jared yells through the door. "Open up. Give your man a proper welcome!" The tension lacing his words makes my skin crawl. His outbursts always made me shrink, but now it's worse. "Eliza!" he yells, and the bangs reverberate in my ribcage. "Open the damn door, or I'll open it for you. Stop being dramatic."

Carter's still by the island, looking angrier by the second.

"You're only making things harder for yourself. If you come home with me now, I'll be a forgiving boyfriend," he chuckles and I'm too shocked to grow a backbone and tell the cheater to fuck off. I lean against the door, frozen, a dark mist dancing over my vision.

There's a shift in the air and I sense Carter slowly approaching. He's getting bigger and angrier with each step. This is the moment he's had enough of my drama. He's coming to kick me out. The trembling in my limbs is uncontrollable. Each bang on the door brings Carter closer until his hand shoots out. Instead of reaching for the doorknob he slides his large palm under the back of my head and pulls me to his chest. The deafening thrumming vibrating in my head could be his heartbeat. But it's mine.

Bending his head, his lips move against my hair.

"Go in the bedroom. Don't come out," he says in a soothing voice. In complete contrast to the angry set of his jaw.

I can't say anything, knees trembling so badly, I can barely stay upright.

"Eliza, do you hear me?" The familiar irritation in Jared's question makes my stomach drop.

I nod and rush to the only place that feels safe. Sliding down the wall in Carter's bedroom, my lungs fight for air.

Jared's pounding stops for a moment as Carter steps outside and closes the door behind him. Carter's words are muffled, but my ex-boyfriend bellows again. I'll never be able to look Carter in the eye. There's a high chance I'll die of mortification.

"Who the hell are you?"

I creep toward the hallway where Carter's low, dangerously calm voice carries. I catch some parts of his answers.

"Are you keeping my girlfriend from me?"

My roommate's answer is short and hushed.

"I'm going to call the police for kidnap!" Jared pushes back.

Carter's voice rises dangerously. "Go ahead, if you want to end up in jail for trespassing. Isn't that her truck?"

"What?! How do you—"

"Keys. Now. Or do you want to add theft to the list?"

"But…you can't," he stutters before yelling again. "Eliza! Come out! Who's this clown?"

"Maybe I'll call the police since you don't understand simple instructions."

"Not man enough to fight me yourself?" Jared mocks him and I shrivel with embarrassment.

"You're not worth a trip to the police station," Carter chuckles humorlessly. "Move."

"Fuck you, city boy. You about done warming the bed for me?" A hurt gasp dies in my throat. Who is this man?

The next moment, heavy steady footsteps thunder on the gravel and hurried shuffle ones follow.

"OK! OK!" Jared pleads. "Keep the damn junk."

The metallic clink of the keys hitting the gravel is followed by Jared's parting yells.

"Eliza! I know you can hear me! This is not over! I love you."

"Leave." The hairs on the back of my neck prickle from the sheer force of Carter's command.

I hold my breath waiting to see if Jared tries anything stupid. A sigh of relief whooshes out when the front door closes gently, and the sound of Carter's leather shoes approaches the bedroom.

He finds me gathered in a ball and frowns.

"I'm s-s-sorry," I manage to say in a shuttered exhale. "I—" There's not enough air to speak and my eyes sting.

Carter crouches in front of me and wordlessly wraps his palm gently around my wrist and plants my palm on his chest.

"Count to five in," he inhales deeply, warm fingers still anchoring me to him. "And five out," he says firmly after a long exhale.

Tears fill my vision and it's impossible to keep the panic at bay.

"Eliza, just breathe with me. Let's do it together."

My name on his lips helps me focus on what he's asking me to do. Breathing. I should be able to do that, right? I take a deep breath in to check.

"Good girl," he says, and I heat up under his praise. "Now let it out slowly."

Breathing in sync slowly grounds me. When my heartbeat slows to a steady thump and the fog drowning my mind lifts, I'm hit with the awareness of how close we are, my fingers clutching his crisp shirt.

"Better?"

"Yeah," I rasp out. "Thank you."

Carter must register the closeness too because he quickly springs up. "I'll give you a minute. Come have some water when you're ready," he says evenly before leaving me in a room that smells like him.

I almost don't want to leave.

Carter went for a jog this morning and skipped breakfast. It's the first time since he got here, and you don't have to be a genius to know he's avoiding me. Of course this mess is unpleasant for him.

I'm not sure what I'm supposed to do either. The comfortable life I thought I had is gone. I'm in unknown territory.

I'm so lost in my thoughts the loud knock paralyzes me. Has Jared returned to yell some sense into me? I'm alone and scared of what he might say, or even worse, what I might do.

A big surprise is swaying on the balls of her feet on my porch with a coffee cup in one hand and a paper bag in the other.

"Hi! I know we've never hung out outside the coffee shop but the whole town is talking about you, and I was worried. Is that alright?" She rushes the words out.

Quinn owns and runs my favorite coffee shop. She's a cute blonde with no filter. We started chatting a couple of years ago when I went in for my sadness-relief—her perfectly thickened hot chocolate. It became my way of decompressing before heading back home.

"I found out from the town's gossip mill where you live now. I come in peace with caramel coffee and cake." She grins at me, shaking the bag again, and I snap out of my shock.

"You're so sweet, you didn't have to."

"I know," she says simply. "You going to let me in or what?"

Quinn makes herself comfortable on the couch and I take her lead. That ugly suspicion is showing its head again. Is she here to dig for gossip?

"I had a feeling something was wrong when you didn't pick up your coffees on two Fridays in a row."

It had become such a regular thing for me to bring coffees to the office that Quinn would have them ready so I wouldn't be late for work. Now that I think about it, the girls never thanked me or offered to get it once in a while.

"I'll be getting coffee for one, for the foreseeable future." I wait for her to ask about the juicy details. To confirm the wild stories in the aftermath of the night at the bar. That the people living in quiet Silver Lake Falls are having a field day with this. But Quinn surprises me.

"Can I be honest?"

"Of—"

"It's better this way," she prattles on. "I noticed some things that really bothered me when you came in." Quinn leans forward. "If you had an argument with him, those airheads never defended you. They sided with him." She uses her fingers to keep score of their offenses. "If he made fun of you, they laughed like a bunch of hyenas." Finally, she looks me dead in the eyes and with a straight face says, "And the dude was not funny."

I blink slowly. Martha was the only other friend who disapproved of Jared, but at least she voiced her opinion loud and clear like a foghorn.

Quinn has hit the mark though.

"You never said anything before," I say cautiously.

Quinn rolls her eyes. "Relationship mess avoidance 101."

My confusion must be clear because she continues.

"You were still together, no matter how many times you drowned your sorrows in hot chocolate. I know better than to be vocal about it. However the winds blew, I'd get the short end of it. You'd stop coming by and I'd lose a friendship with a cool girl. This town is too small to afford that." She gives me another dazzling smile and the wave of gratitude chokes me. I can't afford it either.

"So, you see. Now I can say how much I hated the way that jerk and the chicken-head trio treated you."

A bubble of laughter bursts out and lifts the heaviness slumping my shoulders. Her nonsensical attitude gives me a small boost of confidence to look at things as they truly are.

"I didn't mind it because I loved him and was happy he got along with my friends at first."

"I'm sorry."

"Yeah, so am I." He was so good at making me forget those moments. "I forgave him so easily. It's stupid."

"What are you going to do about the job? Are you OK? Can I help you with anything?"

The question earns a long-suffering groan from somewhere deep inside me. Everybody is in everyone's business around here but come on!

Quinn cringes, "I didn't mean to come on so strong. It sucks, doesn't it?"

"Oh, no. I'm fine," I wave her off. *What's the market value for a kidney?* "I'm sure I'll find something soon," I say with too much confidence for somebody who's been desperately applying to every listing in a 20-mile radius.

The front door bursts open and my grumpy roommate comes to a halt, sweating and panting. The sight of a disheveled Carter, so different from the proper and collected version I usually get, stirs something low in my belly.

"What the fu—" Quinn gasps, jumping to her feet and clutching a coffee stirrer. "Who're you?"

"What's with women around here and their impractical weapons?" Carter says in a cool tone, sounding bored.

But Quinn is in full protective mode, even though we're the same height and Carter towers over her. He's got that calculating glint in his eyes, assessing Quinn's level of threat. He's not worried.

"I'm somebody who's tired of unannounced visitors," he deadpans, and the reproach fills me with shame. He was a gentleman about my ex, but it's piling up. My stay here is bothersome enough without the drama.

"I'm sorry—" I begin reflexively, but Quinn cuts me off.

"Listen here, mister." Against all odds, she is staring him down. "Proper manners are to identify yourself when you barge in on two ladies."

Carter snorts. And it's the weirdest reaction. It's not something I thought he was physically capable of. And I'm too entertained to say anything.

"Proper manners dictate you shouldn't threaten me with a coffee stirrer in the place I currently live in." He veers back to his usual attitude.

Quinn's head snaps toward me, big green eyes round with surprise.

"Wow. That was fast. I mean…" She clears her throat. "Don't get me wrong, good for you." She scans Carter from head to toe and nods approvingly. "But here I was, worrying for you."

"Oh, no! That's not what's happening," I hastily jump in, looking at Carter apologetically.

He's taken aback for a moment before raising an amused eyebrow in my direction.

"I'll move soon. It's temporary. Carter's staying the summer."

Quinn's light eyebrows pinch adorably and her lips purse around the weapon of choice she's now chewing on.

"Hm. Too bad," she says, plopping back on the couch, unfazed by the death glare coming from Carter. "Anyway. Penelope came by yesterday asking for you. Since you didn't show up this week."

"I'm sorry. I'm so—" My head drops on the back of the couch.

"No sweetie, she's not upset you missed it. Just worried." Quinn tilts her head and softens her features. "She likes having you there."

For someone who always thinks people at most tolerate her, it means more than anything.

"Missed what?"

I didn't expect Carter to linger. But he's rounding the small island toward the cabinets.

"Uh," I stammer for a moment. "It's something I do at the library."

While gulping water, his Adam's apple bobs hypnotically. Those gray eyes bore into me, expectantly. He actually wants to know the details. That's unnerving.

"Twice a month local kids and others from the neighboring towns come to the library for story time. I read to them, not a big deal." I look at my toes. I don't know why. I'm embarrassed since Jared always scoffed. *"Waste of time."*

"Adorable," he says quietly, talking to himself. His tone is not laced with his usual disdain, and I dare to take a peek. He's staring into the water glass like he's doing a tea leaf reading.

"What did you say, Mr. Etiquette?" Quinn needles him while grinning at me.

"The kids must find it adorable," Carter mumbles. I don't know if the kids or the reading part displease him so profoundly, but I don't get a chance to find out before he heads straight for his bedroom without another word.

The next day I invite him to explore the surroundings while I forage for some herbs for my teas. I hope to find some freshly bloomed clover blossoms and raspberry leaves.

"No. Thank you."

He's as friendly as a water snake, but I press on. "You're in a beautiful area. Do you plan to spend three months cooped up here, staring at your screens?"

"I can walk out on the back porch and get some fresh air." Carter's distracted monotone matches his blank expression.

"I'll start singing in the shower," I say sweetly to get a reaction from him.

"I have some earplugs in my emergency kit."

"I'll call the mayor and he'll come and pester you. He's relentless. You'll get invited to every pothole repair reveal ceremony."

"He'll find himself in possession of a big enough check to forget I even exist."

"I'll—" His mocking eyebrow makes me play dirty. "I'll call your mother."

It's the first time his apathetic facade cracks and he narrows his eyes.

"You can't get to her," he sneers.

"Wanna bet?"

I count the loud thud of the poor tablet against the table and his next grumble as a win.

CHAPTER ELEVEN

CARTER

Mornings have been too quiet. The glitch in the routine unbalancing my day. It's complete silence. No sound of running water. No out-of-tune hums. No little moans of contentment fueling the fantasies I have no business replaying in my head late at night.

Today I was expecting things to get back to normal, but the house is eerily silent again and it's too late for Eliza to be still in her room at this hour. I have to check on her. I tell myself it's because she makes a great breakfast now and she has to stick to our deal.

But I falter in front of her door. A faint pained moan and the rustle of sheets stop me in my tracks. I knock louder than I intended, and the sound bounces with too much force around the quiet hallway.

"Sorry. Can't help with food today," she says in a tiny voice I strain to make out.

"You alright?" I find myself asking through the door, slight panic pecking at my lungs.

"Yeah. I just need a minute," she croaks.

Her feet drag on the floor and when she opens the door Eliza looks worse than the night I met her, gently rocking side to side.

"What do you want to eat?" she says, her voice hoarse, swaying on her feet. "I have no inspiration today."

"Hell, no! Go back to bed." I gently spin her around and guide her to bed in the stuffy and dark room.

I follow Eliza's shivering back until she collapses on the rumpled sheets. My hand hesitates above her forehead for a split second. What if I get something from her?

But she looks so miserable and small, dark shadows under her eyes. Her pale skin is clammy, and she pulls her knees up, holding her stomach.

I can't help it. I brush her sweaty forehead with my fingers and a tremor runs through her entire body.

She's burning up and looks so fragile it pushes me to do something, anything, to make it better.

"Go away," she commands me in a barely audible voice. "I'm gross. I'm gonna be sick again," Eliza heaves and I conceal my discomfort for her sake.

"Nonsense. You remind me of my pet iguana," I say pulling the sheet to her chin. "He used to regurgitate his food and then eat it. It was fascinating."

The glare she gives me would be withering if she could hold her eyes open.

"That's until my father found out and disposed of it."

"So, you're telling me," she grunts, holding her midsection tighter, "I remind you of a dead puking iguana?"

"If the shoe fits."

She's groggy and the fact she does not fight back worries me.

"Stupid beans," she mutters, burrowing her face in the pillow.

"What?"

She's mumbling something I can't catch, so I don't press and make myself useful. I give her some water and place a bucket next to the nightstand.

"Just in case," I tell her, rushing out of the room. I can't miss the sadness crumpling her face when she realizes I'm leaving and my insides twist into uncomfortable knots.

The little old lady with the purple perm at the local drugstore was more helpful than I could have hoped for. I described Eliza's symptoms and she sent me on my way with a bag full of meds. The quirky pharmacist even gave me specific instructions for what *my wife* should eat in the next few days.

I was in such a hurry to get back I let it slide.

"She'll be as good as new if you take care of her properly," the pharmacist said sympathetically.

I give Eliza the pills, but she's so tired and sick she can't hold the glass of water and I rush to cup her hands around it.

Her big coffee eyes hold so much dismay, it's unsettling.

"Why are you so nice to me?" she asks in a small voice, like she can't believe I'm back at her side taking care of her.

"It would take forever to pack if you kicked the bucket," I say and drag a chair closer so I can dab her forehead with a wet towel. "I did a really good job at lining up those shirts."

She nods to herself like what I said made perfect sense, but I don't want her to think the worst of me this time.

"It's nothing. I'd bet my company you'd do the same for me. Who would let somebody suffer through this?"

"Some people would," she whispers, but I'm not sure her words are meant for me. Eliza's glassy eyes are out of focus, her mind far away.

"Who?" I fight to keep my composure and light tone. I have a sinking feeling some stories in Eliza's past will gut me.

A soft groan as she tosses is her only reply.

"Your ex?" I ask her, already plotting his disappearance, but Eliza shakes her head.

The next question gets lodged in my dry throat and I swallow hard before voicing my suspicion, "Foster parents?"

"Sleep it off," Eliza murmurs, her eyelids swollen and heavy. "One time I was hallucinating so bad from a fever I thought my parents were sitting on the edge of the bed holding my hand. It was stupid. I have no idea what they look like," she sounds detached.

A hot pulsing rage is at odds with the need to cradle this delicate woman who's been through so much. But I sit as still as I can, watching her breathing becoming more even. The hard lines around her eyes and mouth mellow while her body relaxes, and she sinks into a deep sleep.

That's where the midday warmth finds me, and I finally move to open a window and give Eliza her treatment.

"I'll pay you back," she says as soon as she's alert. "Don't worry."

I'm offended this is her first thought. I've noticed already she hates asking for help. The aftermath of my regrettable choice of words gives me a hint as to why that is. I won't push the subject now when she's so frail.

"What made you sick?"

She scoots lower, covering herself instead of giving an answer.

"I have to know," I plead with her. What if it's something from the fridge?

"It's nothing," Eliza's faint voice is muffled under the sheets.

"It is if I eat it by accident. I can't get this sick." I'm miles away from a decent hospital if I had complications.

"Oh, no. It's nothing from your food."

The statement gives me pause. "My food? We live in the same house."

What is she talking about? It's true, we haven't eaten together. I thought she wanted to enjoy her meals in peace. Away from me.

"Not everybody can afford—" she begins, but stops herself.

What the hell? What is she eating?

I let her rest and call my doctor. He'll know if I need to do something more for her.

"Any symptoms?" He sounds worried.

"I'm fine. We'd be having this conversation in my suite at the hospital if I felt the way she looks."

"The pharmacist is correct. The treatment will have her in better shape in a couple of days," he rustles his charts over the background noise of medical equipment. "The most important part is to keep her hydrated, rested, and on certain foods. I'll send you a list."

Before I hang up, he doesn't miss the opportunity to pester me, "Don't forget about the tests next month."

The following days Eliza reluctantly accepts my help. Probably because she can barely make it to the bathroom without collapsing. My offer to get her into the shower is met with a hard no so I'm left pacing outside while she sounds like she's on the brink of death.

"I'll be honest," she says, munching on the limited edition whole-grain crackers made by Quinn, who interrogated me the moment I made the stupid decision to answer Eliza's phone when I saw the caller. She scolded me quite rudely when I told her the stores didn't have any. "You taking care of me is weird."

"My calendar is wide open," is the single sliver of truth I'm open to sharing, because taking care of Eliza came too effortlessly to admit.

What a terrifying thought.

Her *Good mornings* come on the crest of that slightly husky voice when she's still sleepy. The two words make the hairs on the back of my neck stand up.

"No, I ate before you woke up." This thing again. Her feverish ramblings made me pay closer attention to a certain pattern.

There's always food for me but she never makes a plate for herself. She always has an answer on the tip of her tongue when I ask her. Thinking back on her reaction when I was an idiot and made fun of her for losing so much, I can't help but wonder. Is she broke? A Rawlings always pays on time, and I don't suspect my mother of being forgetful.

She's frowning at the phone and a nagging thought makes me blurt out, "Your ex?"

"Don't worry. This won't ruin the rest of your holiday. He might try to talk to me again, but I'll work as fast as possible to finish the other cabin." She's absentmindedly braiding a strand of her light strawberry hair.

"What is even there to finish? It needs to be demolished. Also, I'm not a fan of him coming there instead." I tap the countertop so I can catch her eye. "Where you'll be alone."

"I had somebody appraise Sam's place. I'll have to strip it myself so I can stick to the budget," she says more to herself. "You don't have to get rid of everything that looks broken, you know? It just needs a bit of love."

I don't miss her poor attempt at evasion and my body tenses. Maybe she wants to fix her relationship too. Does she see potential in going back to that asshole? I dated for social events and casual sex. Fixing broken trust or houses is a waste of time.

"I'm on sabbatical." I don't know why I tell her this. "Not a holiday."

"You didn't take time off voluntarily."

"How perceptive of you." I'd rather be joking with her and having her roll those pretty eyes at me than telling her the truth. After rehabilitation, my mother said she would stop talking to me if I didn't take a break and reconsider my life.

"Why would you do math so bright and early?" she asks with a grimace, squinting at the Sudoku on my tablet.

"It's not math. It helps me concentrate." It sharpens the focus I need before I dive into the industry updates and reports every morning.

She wrinkles her nose. "It looks headache-inducing." Eliza keeps tilting her head as if maybe a different perspective will help her make sense of it.

Up close I stare at her pouty mouth, scrunched in concentration when she nicks her lower lip. The image lights up my insides so abruptly a shudder rips through me, my senses on alert.

"Are you any good at it?" Luckily, she's still focused on the tablet and doesn't notice I have to shift my position on the bar stool.

I can't suppress the twist of my lips, and she gives me a side eye and groans.

"I'm competitive, what can I say? Top 1% of people who play online."

"You want to show the world you're better. Nobody would know if you did it the old-fashioned way."

"I don't have to try very hard," I smirk. "It comes naturally."

She bursts out laughing and the soft sound takes me by surprise. But it's not as shocking as another jolt to my lower abdomen.

"Do you want me to leave you something for lunch?" she asks, leaving my side. "It will take a while at the store."

"I'll survive. Going on a shopping spree?"

"I guess going on a supplies run counts as shopping therapy for me," she huffs another gentle laugh, bending to get her shoes, and for some reason, I don't want her to leave yet.

"Do you need a hand?"

Eliza snaps her head up and her eyebrows press together.

"Um, thanks," she says, tucking a strand behind her ear. "I'll just make a list with Thomas for the renovations and get some paint for the fence here." Eliza tilts her head and bites her lip nervously. "Do you mind? I can paint when you're away or something."

"I can do it for you." Why did I say that? Her eyes become round with wonder, and I never thought I could shock somebody into silence by offering to help.

"Do you know how to paint a fence?" she asks hesitantly.

"Of course I do." I have no idea what I'm talking about. "I have nothing better to do anyway."

The more she insists I shouldn't, the more intent I am to start. To prove to her I'm capable of painting a damn fence.

But first, I'll stock the pantry and fridge while she's gone. I wonder what she likes to eat. Only because I hate wasting ingredients. I'm nothing if not efficient.

CHAPTER TWELVE

ELIZA

My head is still spinning from hours of watching Sam and Thomas arguing over every bolt, pipe, and wire on the list. The learning curve for the electrical and plumbing part of renovating a house is more of an off-the-rail rollercoaster and I can't wait to arrive at the decorating stage.

Worry still manages to dampen my excitement. I'll have to get creative and hunt for junkyard furniture I can recondition. Even with Sam's experience and Thomas's help with the returned and discounted construction materials, the total adds up to most of the money Martha gave me.

"What the—" A divine smell makes my stomach rumble ungraciously after I close the front door behind me.

Carter is in the kitchen.

Cooking.

I knew he tended to himself while I was not here, but it's a sight to behold. He's moving with the ease of somebody who knows his way around a kitchen.

A small towel drapes over his shoulder, and I take in his tall frame. The tailored trousers hug his behind, and I can't stop staring at him.

He must have said something while I was lost in my head because I'm met with an expectant arch of his eyebrows.

"Have a seat. Dinner is ready."

"Oh," I manage to say, my face flaring with embarrassment. "I'm too tired for dinner. I'd better call it a night."

His food is off-limits. It's something so ingrained in me after years of "tough love" from some of my former guardians. It took me years to accept a dinner invitation from the Duntons.

Carter slides the pan off the cooker and calmly wipes his hands. "Are you on a diet?"

"No." I might have lost a pound or two, with the stress of the past weeks. The question brings back the taunts at school and my fists curl involuntarily. *She's too skinny. Look at her. Do they keep you in chains, behind the house? The laughter.*

"Are you on a medical regime?" Carter's voice is even and soothing.

"No," I mumble.

"Then sit." He's unwavering and places the plate in front of me when I reach the kitchen island.

He caught on to the meal skipping. I can see it in his eyes. The challenge to give him more excuses and refuse to eat with him. He must expect me to be grateful because I'm a charity case.

"It looks and smells delicious."

"So does *your* cooking. Why aren't you eating it?"

The turn in conversation makes me uncomfortable and I wring my hands mindlessly.

"Are you micro-poisoning me?" he asks, with a hint of amusement that does nothing to calm my anxiety.

"What? No. No!" My cheeks must be incandescent at this point. The ginger curse. "It's…I…" How do I tell him it's a time-tested survival mechanism? That if I don't ration my food I feel out of control. That I got sick because my emergency stash of canned beans went bad. That his attempts to help put me on edge.

"Is it a financial issue?" The question is straight to the point, without judgment.

"I'm not comfortable explaining it to you." It's all I manage to say.

"Tell me if I'm not paying enough for the cabin."

"No, it's more than enough." I focus on a scratch on the wood. Sam would say it's ridiculous, I'm not a kid anymore, at the mercy of my foster parents who'd throw perfectly good food away or give it to the pigs to teach me a lesson. But I couldn't sleep at night if I didn't protect myself the way I know how. Eight years of a "stable" life with Jared didn't help cure this wound. I wonder if it will ever close.

The stool creaks under Carter's weight and his long fingers pick up the fork. I sense him staring at me and I start to eat for something to do. It's indecently delicious and I can't help the hum of appreciation as the aromas twirl around my tongue.

At last, he takes a bite.

"Are you allergic to anything?"

"No, why?"

"I…" He pauses to consider his next words. "I've never shared food I made with anyone other than my sister." He shrugs dismissively while I'm internally melting into a puddle knowing I'm the second person in the world he decided to share his food with.

Carter gazes straight into my eyes and considers his words for a moment. "It's pleasant."

For me, homemade meals are a sign of care. The kinds with no strings attached. It was hard enough to accept being nursed back to health. Not quite lucid the first day, I didn't know how to take it. Especially since Carter isn't the Florence Nightingale type.

But this. I hated being more indebted to him. I'm confused and too warm for comfort. "What about your girlfriends?"

Carter stills. "No need to cook for them at home."

"Why? You clearly know what you're doing." I press on because curiosity and suspicion in equal measure won't let me drop the subject.

A cocky smile lights up his features. "Not that type of girlfriend." He taps the glass of water and says, "And I'm not that kind of boyfriend."

The way his eyes bore into mine is intended to drive a point home and the topic is closed. Whatever. His personal life is not my business. I don't care what he does with those gorgeous women I saw in the articles.

"I'm still confused about those women who came by."

The abrupt change in topic gives me whiplash. His attempt at conversation sounds more like a yearly performance evaluation, but I play along to keep him talking.

"They struck me as gossipy," Carter continues.

The smell gets to me, and I take another delicious bite.

"I was happy to be included. I listened to their never-ending dramas, baked elaborate cakes for their birthdays, cooked trays of food when I was invited to their house parties."

"They were using you."

"I guess that is why they kept me around." I burst into a fit of angry laughter. "I baked my own birthday cake for the last eight years."

"And you continued to be there for them?" he asks incredulously.

"I know why I did it. I don't need a therapist to put two and two together. I suppose everybody who knows my history at least suspects it."

The carrot I'm chasing around the plate gets impaled with too much force and almost rolls on the table.

"I'm no fairy tale princess with a golden heart. I'm just scared." That I'm not enough. I wasn't for my mother. She taught me that people close to me will leave if I don't twist myself into whatever they need me to be.

He looks at me like I'm his morning sudoku. "You might be underestimating yourself," he finally says, and that simple statement blows a fuse in my mental circuit.

In the lull in conversation, I notice the flawless way Carter eats, and I can't help but sneak glances. Elbows off the table, no clinking with the fork and knife. He places the water glass silently in the same place after taking a sip. The bites are the perfect size when he closes his lips over the fork. I imagine him as a little boy sitting at the end of the family's formal dining table with a severe woman looking over his shoulder, ready to scold him if he used the wrong spoon.

"Is there anything you want to ask?" He carefully places his cutlery on his plate, giving me his undivided attention.

Any situation when I might annoy somebody puts me on edge, but there's no impatient sigh. The lines of his face are not tense and his eyes are warm and inviting. Jared always made me feel like I asked stupid questions so I got used to keeping my curiosity in check around him and our friends.

But Carter's patience and rare instance of openness put me at ease.

"Did you have a governess?"

His lips twitch and I regret letting curiosity get the better of me. He'll shut me down, as he's done before, keeping his private life away from the weird woman he stumbled upon in the woods.

"More of a high society coach," he says with a hint of amusement, surprising me. "I couldn't embarrass my father at the events he dragged me to."

This extra glimpse into his life startles both of us.

"It must be nice to have this figured out," I encourage him. The sturdier the wall he builds around himself, the more I want to scrape at it until I get a peek at the other side. "I'd probably have an anxiety attack if I ever attended a fancy party. Always afraid to do or say the wrong thing," I tell him, focused on taking in any small tell to help me figure out Carter Rawlings.

He already knows enough about me, but I can't help giving him more ammunition if it means he won't clam up again. I'm not a threat if people think less of me. It tempers any conflict before it escalates.

He's still silent, and the intensity of his searching gaze makes me squirm in my seat. My skin itches uncomfortably when I'm under scrutiny and he's had time to catalog every flaw by now.

"The only reason you wouldn't fit in is because you don't see the world in the same way as them. You're too caring and genuine," he says casually, raising his fork. He goes back to his aristocratic eating, while I don't know how to digest his statement that sounded like a compliment.

Carter's olive branch binds us to a tentative truce and we each go about our days.

I desperately send job applications and spend the rest of the time sorting through the fishing cabin with Sam. I have a sneaking suspicion he's been hiding his hoarding tendencies here, far from Martha's cleaning-obsessed radar.

Carter goes on his jog in the mornings after breakfast and I do my best not to be in the house when he barges in, his running clothes sticking to every muscle and ridge of his body.

There's no point in denying I find the man attractive. Too bad about his personality that sometimes irritates me to the point I want to smother him. Preferably with my lips. It's useless to entertain this idea anyway. I'm still shaken about Jared and haven't even talked to him yet. My life is a mess and I'm about to start renovating my future little home.

Not to mention I'm far from Carter's type. I might have searched his name again and taken a better look at the gossip articles. I'd stand a chance if we were stranded in this cabin for the rest of our lives after an apocalypse.

Today he insisted…No. He *demanded* we go grocery shopping together.

"I'm driving," Carter tells me over his shoulder while grabbing his keys. He opens the front door and waves for me to pass.

I stare at him, speechless at the audacity to boss me around.

"I know you have no way of knowing this, but this is the way a gentleman opens the door so you can go first. So if you could hurry, please."

I'm fond of any activity that gives me time away from him. Going to the supermarket today isn't going to be one of those times.

"It's too late to deal with your insanity. Everybody shops around this time," I grumble and walk out.

"It's called manners," he says in that posh nasal tone he uses to drive me up the wall. And I stop in my tracks, a legion of fire ants marching under my skin. Until Carter places his hand gently on my lower back and opens the passenger door.

"It's what you should expect," he whispers in my ear, and his breath dances along the side of my neck. I'm thankful for the cardigan I grabbed on my way out. My thin top can't hide the effect of his proximity.

He's at my door in the blink of an eye after he parks. This is how he was raised. The boy who had a *high society coach*.

I'm nothing special, just a small-town girl who gets turned on by basic manners.

I'm about to pull out the shopping list when a painfully familiar voice echoes through the aisles.

"Eliza!" I hear the metallic grind of his cart and turn on my heels in the opposite direction. Black fog tunnels my vision as the faraway sound of my name tells me I'm safe for now.

I spot a small space between a fridge and a shelf, and I slip in there instinctively, my pulse thundering in my ears.

"Are you also a fugitive?" Carter's low voice alarms me and I bump my head against the cold metal. I want to smack that annoying smirk off his face.

"What? No! Just—" I forgot about Carter the moment Jared called my name. Rising on my toes I take a peek over his shoulders. Damn it. Jared is getting closer. "Cover me!"

I pull him closer, as a protective wall, and Carter ends up crowding me against the shelf. He's stiff, but his arms and back muscles slowly relax. I now realize I can feel everything. The light pressure of his body works like a heat pad, and I melt into him.

My eyes travel from the last button of his dark shirt to the bump of his Adam's apple, following its movements. His chin is not as clean-shaven as the night he stormed into my life.

"Stop looking at me like that," he demands, his voice a harsh whisper.

Carter's rumble makes my heart drum frantically. He must feel it given the way our chests are pressed together.

I muster the courage to look up at him and he's pining me to the metallic wall with eyes dark as old silver. "Like what?" I gulp.

His hand grazes my arm and I think he might cup my face, but he threads his fingers through my hair, lightly touching the tender spot.

"You should put some ice on it."

His non-answer is a cold bucket of ice on my scorching skin and the cherry on top of my humiliation just found us and is clearing his throat. Loudly.

"Can I help you?" Carter swivels his head toward Jared, keeping me out of sight.

"I want to speak to my girl, dick. Move."

"You've found your courage now that you're in public." Carter lowers his hand, and it lands on my waist, my lower belly catching fire when he presses his thumb on my hipbone to get my attention. "What do you want to do?" he asks quietly so only I can hear him.

My heart is still beating furiously, but I take a deep breath to settle my fears. I can't run away whenever I bump into Jared. This town is small. I can lean on Carter's steady presence while I face my ex. He's a gentleman and won't let anything happen to me.

The shape of his palm still burns through my clothes when I sidestep Carter with more confidence than I actually feel.

"There's nothing to talk about." I level Jared with a glare. I don't want to give him the satisfaction of a reaction. He thrives on that shit. "And it's *ex*-girlfriend."

"It was a joke for the cameras. Don't be such a bore." Jared smirks and comes in for a hug. A low noise somewhere behind makes him lower his hands and shove them in his pockets awkwardly.

Too bad for him, Amy and Jenna spilled the clams.

"The joke on me, you mean. The running joke between you and Caroline over the past two years." My voice is shaky, no matter how hard I hold onto my mask.

Jared's eyes widen, the wheels in his head turning.

"You're overreacting, as usual," he says lazily, in that chiding tone he used to guilt trip me with.

"The gaslighting won't work this time."

He shuffles from one foot to the other, dragging a hand over his short hair. He's not used to me standing my ground. I usually fold so easily, and I'm afraid I won't be strong enough to resist if I stay here a second longer.

"Come on baby, how much longer you gonna give me the cold shoulder? It's been three weeks. I miss you."

A burst of unexpected anger straightens my spine. I get a violent urge to grab the baguette off the shelf and smack him with it and I somehow restrain myself.

"You cheated! There's no going back!"

"Are you going to give up after all these years? I love you. Let's get married. Don't let a mistake ruin what we have." Those blue eyes brim with sincerity. He's scared. They remind me of the boy I fell in love with. "Baby, you know I'm the best for you. Trust fund bro here won't even remember your name after you spread your—"

Carter's punch comes down in a flash, landing with a sickening crunch. I can't move, staring at Jared's bloody nose while he rolls on the supermarket floor.

"I warned you." The dangerous vibration in Carter's voice surprises me more than the punch.

He doesn't say anything more, grabs my hand and storms out. The pounding in my chest is all-consuming and it's a good thing he's dragging me through the parking lot because my knees are shaking.

I'm panting by the time we reach his Maserati and I'm unsteady on my feet.

"The food—" I don't know why but it's the first thing to come out of my mouth.

"It's take-out night," he says gruffly and opens the passenger door.

The silent ride back gives me time to pull myself together. Violence has always been a part of my life growing up, but tonight it was too much at once.

Carter's hiss when I put the ice bag over his knuckles makes me cringe. "Why did you do it? What if he reports you to the police?"

"Nothing's going to happen to me," he scoffs with the self-assurance of someone who has an expensive lawyer on retainer. "The way he talked about you was unacceptable."

It's not like I haven't been called worse. "They're just words."

His reply is stern. "That you shouldn't accept from anyone."

His anger visibly subsides by the time the food arrives. "Feast" is a better way to describe it. What's laid out on the table is enough to feed a small village.

"I didn't know what you liked," Carter shrugs.

I don't question him. I've noticed food makes him more mellow, so I have a good chance to find out more about my taciturn roommate.

"You suffer from a serious case of small-town dried-up dating pool," he says, looking through the food containers.

"We can't all live in the *big city*, dating a new academically inclined supermodel every Friday."

"You think I date a lot?" The corner of his mouth lifts, while he scoops the perfect bite with the cheap chopsticks.

"Yeah, obviously. Stop fishing for compliments." I poke around for a piece of sweet and sour chicken with my trusted fork.

"Don't know about that. They sound good coming from you."

Carter's eyes rest on my face and trail down to my mouth. He couldn't be attracted to me. It makes no sense. What I overheard the first morning still rings in my ears. *Dull. Mess.*

"Then I must take a vow of silence. We can't risk your head getting bigger."

When we clean up I'm struck again by the way he moves through the space like no other man. Each movement is the embodiment of sheer efficiency.

I've learned this trait also extends to the way he communicates. He doesn't say anything unnecessary to fill the space with words. Something I do whenever I'm uncomfortable. Or excited about something. Or bored. But I've trained myself to reel in my impulses, so I don't annoy the people around me.

I place the glasses in the sink, hip-bumping him to move. Instead, I end up plastered to his side.

"I'll take care of those." Carter is unmoving, the cloudy gray in his eyes swirling dangerously. He's searching for something in my expression, and I'm pulled toward him again, against my better judgment.

The tension in the air is close to a breaking point, our breathing shallow and I'm frozen in place, my body humming with anticipation. There's a resolution in the lines of his face before Carter lowers his gaze to my lips and time stills around me.

A loud ring breaks the silence, and the walls go up again. He takes a big step away, answering the phone.

"No, I'm not doing anything important. Do you have any updates?" His voice trails until he reaches the back porch. I'm released from the spell keeping me in place by the creak of the outdoor furniture, a dull ache in my belly replacing the dimming heat.

CHAPTER THIRTEEN

ELIZA

The phone nearly slips from my shoulder, and I press my cheek harder against the screen.

"I'm on my way." It's not a lie, more of a different interpretation of distance and time.

"Finn's already here," Martha whispers in a giddy voice. "He thought you were staying with us."

Not paying too much attention to what she's saying, I pray to all the deities out there I didn't burn this batch. "Um, OK."

I hope the Duntons and Finn won't notice I baked these cookies dead on my feet. The tension crackling whenever Carter and I gravitated too close had me bouncing off the walls all night. I'm frustrated to no end I don't have the guts to confront him about what happened. Or almost happened.

The phone lands in my open bag with a worrisome crack and I twirl like a tornado so I can leave before Carter returns from his run.

"You're a bit too hot," I tell the cookies because I've completely lost it. "It's fine. I'll drive with the windows down."

The thud of the front door mocks my best-laid plans and the man I've been hoping to avoid halts to a stop in front of the kitchen. His grimace, assessing the mess, propels me into damage-control mode.

"I'll clean it, don't worry." I cut him off before he gets to say anything. I throw the dirty bowl and the spoon in the sink. "Pretend you don't see this" —I gesture to the messy surfaces and the ingredients scattered all over the island—"until I get back. They're for…"

The words dim into silence on my lips when Carter steps closer. My sleep-deprived brain is not equipped to handle the heat radiating from him. This man has zero regard for the frail thread holding my sanity together and bends over the tray, lightly grazing my waist with his fingers.

"Mmm, I wish I could take a bite."

My mouth is dry, my pulse erratic. The content noise he makes smelling the cookies goes straight to my core. I've never been so aware of someone's body. How I have to crane my neck to look into his eyes, sparkling with mischief. The movement of his hand swiping his burnt chestnut hair reverberates through the air, bouncing back against my skin. The way he smells after a run, of forest and salt, is intoxicating.

I'm in so much trouble.

Carter's going to bite my head off. I peek inside the bag with dread. The items caught my eye on my way to the coffee shop and for whatever reason I thought it would be a good idea to buy them.

"I've missed this place." I sit at my usual little red table and Quinn brings me an iced coffee.

"I got some new plants since you've been hiding away with your hot roommate," she says louder than necessary, drawing the attention of the two other people here, and pointing to the different potted miniature lavender shrubs. They're scattered along the heavy wooden beam lining the whitewashed brick wall.

"I'm not hiding," I hiss through my teeth and swat her arm. "Keep it down."

Breathe in. The heavy aroma of coffee and baked goods settles in my soul. *Breathe out.* "I'm dealing with stuff."

Quinn crosses her legs and wraps her fingers around her knee.

"You might want to deal with stuff," she says, putting a spin on the word, "out in public too." The blonde menace levels me with what I can assume is her *giving serious advice* expression. "Some people went straight into true crime podcast mode."

"I'm up and about," I defend myself. Going to Thomas's store and the Duntons' must count for something. Even if I make sure there's no human being in a ten-yard radius before I step out of the pickup truck. "I'm here!"

"Did some post-breakup shopping on your way here?" She points to the paper bag with her chin. "I'd so come with you and splurge."

"No." Staring into the glass is my safest bet because Quinn has the determination of a hound on a trail.

"Who's the bag for, Eliza?" she asks with the most infuriating satisfied grin. Those dimples of hers mocking my poor decision-making.

If I don't tell her she'll keep pestering me and it will become even more embarrassing.

Telling the truth is the only option so I brace my elbows on the table and confess. "It's for Carter," I sigh.

She waves her hand for me to continue, obviously not satisfied with the lack of details.

"The man has no casual wear, besides what he wears for jogging," I lay out my argument. "He only has slacks and different textured pants! He might have some emergency jeans."

Quinn nods in understanding. "Not surprising, considering who he is."

I bury my face in my hands, feeling foolish.

"Continue. I'm dying to see where this is going."

"I got him sweatpants," I tell her in a muffled whisper through my fingers. "Gray."

He's going to throw them in the backyard fire pit. Or worse. Strangle me with soft cotton leisure pants. What a way to die. "He'll hate them and say I'm ridiculous for gifting the equivalent of store-brand toilet paper to a man who probably wipes his ass with silk."

Quinn clears her throat and I peer at her through my fingers. Her eyes are big and glassy, with a small palm resting on her chest. She makes me nervous.

"If you get that annoyingly hot man in gray sweatpants and get a picture…" She pauses for a beat and considers her offer. "I'll give you free coffee for—"

I burst out laughing. She's being the kind of ridiculous I longed for as a teenager. I love it and for the first time, I don't have to put a lid on it.

"Listen, Eliza!" She hovers over the small table. "Eliza! For a year!"

The blonde nutjob pats her apron and fishes out her notepad. "I'll put it in writing. No joke."

Tears fill my eyes, "I promise you. If I don't die by pantsicide, I'll treat you to the experience." I swipe the fallen tear, shaking. "Expect a text. You'd better rush and gawk at him live, in all his glory." I can barely finish my sentence between bouts of laughter.

We're now giggling like two teenagers, and I've never felt so light and unbothered.

Driving back to the cabin I glance at the shopping bag sitting innocently on the passenger seat and continue to have doubts. This is stupid. It's just pants. I'll give them to Carter, and he can wear them or not.

Though I hope he will.

I find him reading on the back porch, laid back on the chair, long legs propped on the banister. He could be a model for Reader's Digest, lifestyle edition.

"Yes?"

His low voice snaps me out of the trance and the courage to give him what I bought dissipates in the evening breeze.

My silence must annoy him, and he plops the open book on the table.

"What is it, Eliza?"

He says my name in his deep upper-class voice, sending tingles swarming under my skin, and in a moment of complete insanity I hold out the bag with my death sentence in it.

He doesn't reach out to take it.

"It's for you," I manage to squeeze out. "I noticed… umm…I mean I saw them at the store…and umm… thought you might need them."

Well, that wasn't embarrassing at all. I did great. Except he's still in his chair figuring out what's wrong with me.

I give it one more go before I make myself lost in the wilderness and only come out when the locals leave offerings for the mythical wood lady. I hope it will be chocolate and fluffy socks.

This will work better if I stare at my nails. Less distracting.

"You don't have to wear them if you hate them. I know they're not the designer pants you're used to. You're going to stay some time here and I thought it might be more comfortable to—"

Large warm hands cover mine and he slowly slides the bag's handles from the death grip of my fingers.

"Thank you. It's very kind of you."

His words caress the top of my head and I look up to see amusement dancing in his grayish-blue eyes. They're lighter today, resembling the feathers of a Gnatcatcher glinting in the summer sun.

My mouth is bone dry. I fear dust will come out instead of my reply. "You're welcome."

He smiles and I'm lost for words. Carter grabs his book and returns inside, leaving me behind in the chilly spring late evening.

I don't know how long I've been here, cooling off, when the back door creaks open and Carter's head pops out. "I'm cooking. Care to keep me company?"

Perched on the seat of the kitchen island, I'm at a loss for what to do with myself to stop from staring at him. I either made the biggest mistake of my life and he'll drive me crazy, or I should be given the Nobel Prize.

Humanity will forever be grateful for my success in making Carter wear gray sweatpants and the black T-shirt I also got.

It will be written in my obituary. My great service to humankind.

The tailor-made clothes make him look delicious, but this casual Carter makes my pulse spike. His muscles tense when he stirs the pan above the flames, and you'd think I've never seen a man's forearm before.

He lowers the intensity of the stove and looks straight at me with the air of a man waiting for an answer.

"Did you say something?" I play it cool, but my traitorous face is at 75% tomato by now.

He crosses his arms over that solid chest and like a brainless puppet, I follow the movement, noticing the details of his wide frame. The chiseled cords rippling with the slow rise and fall of his torso. His aggravated look is my cue to switch on coherent-Eliza mode.

"Yes?"

"Can you get started with the salad? I'm almost done with the meat."

I only nod because the rich velvety tone of his voice lands differently than usual. It unsettles me. I have to keep my head on straight and not let myself be swept up by a silly schoolgirl crush.

"It's one of the nicest gifts I ever got," he says, pouring water in my glass.

I can't help but laugh. "I highly doubt it."

"I'm serious. It's in the top ten most thoughtful gifts." Carter lifts his palm, to stop me from cutting him off. "Yeah. I surely got expensive gifts. Rare collectibles. Custom-made. The type that showed how rich the giver is," he continues, a genuine warmth relaxing his features. "But no one goes about their day and thinks, *Oh, Carter would love or need this.*"

I gulp, taken aback by his sincerity. "You're welcome."

Carter chases a piece of asparagus around, mulling over something. "I didn't pack for comfort because I hated the idea of coming here. I wanted to not enjoy it."

"And now?" I ask, without a clear idea of what I'm hoping for.

His mouth quirks and I don't know how I'm supposed to ignore how handsome he is.

"Now, my wardrobe could use an update, plus some work boots. Do you know any places in town?"

"Maybe hiking ones if you're adventurous."

"You didn't think I was letting you have all the fun? When's demo day?"

The small fishing cabin looks better in the May mid-morning sunlight without Sam's hoarded treasures.

"I can't believe you convinced this guy to do manual labor," Sam says, scratching his overgrown salt and pepper beard. He's leaning on the beech tree, unsure what to make of Carter.

"I didn't."

He comes closer to the broken bathroom door we laid over two sawhorses, acting as a makeshift table. "He's not what I expected."

We're both watching Carter check the place, knocking on different parts of the walls for some reason. I hadn't expected him at all but he still barged in and commanded my attention.

Carter joins us in the shade and looks entirely too confident for a man who has never even seen a sledgehammer up close.

"Where do we start?"

I jump into action and point out the foreman's notes on the cabin plan.

Waving over the little red Xs, I explain, "Finn said to begin with the interior walls, so we can check the bones."

"Don't get why you didn't let the man tear them down." Sam turns a bucket and sits. His arthritis is flaring, but he wanted to be here for moral support. And to keep an eye on Carter, even if he doesn't want to admit it.

"He wanted to do it in his free time so he wouldn't charge me," I sigh impatiently. We've been over this already. "Besides"—I glance at Carter who is laser-focused on the plan—"the place is small, it shouldn't take long."

"Finn would make it quicker," Sam says, nudging me. "I might be old, but I see how he looks at you."

The air around us cools by a couple of degrees when Carter's head snaps toward Sam and those quicksilvers turn to slits. "Are you sure he'll not take advantage of Eliza?"

"I vouch for him." Sam waves him off. "We worked together on houses before I retired."

A muscle in Carter's jaw ticks. "What's the first step?" he grumbles.

Why is he being so weird?

"We need to pull out the kitchen cabinets and the shiplap. I want to reuse it, so be careful not to snap it. Then move the furniture outside. Intact," I point out for Carter's benefit. "Last chance to bail," I warn the two men.

Sam rises and rolls his sleeves, nodding Carter along. "Do you know what a pry bar is?"

It doesn't take them long. Carter listens and follows Sam's patient instructions without complaint. I would've gotten the smaller pieces of furniture out faster if I hadn't stopped so many times to stare at the two men. Mr. CEO in jeans and a tight black T-shirt pulling cabinets off the walls is unfairly hot.

I have no idea what to do with this realization. He's pulled back his pointy spikes the past couple of weeks, but it feels like we're dancing dangerously on a tightrope. In unguarded moments or during our dinners I almost forget who he is. That the realities of our lives couldn't be more different.

"Gonna get some roast beef sandwiches from Sadie's. You want anything?" Sam asks me.

"Not hungry is not an option." Carter's raised voice carries to the front yard.

Sam grins into his overalls. "I like the man. Bring him over next time."

"Don't get too attached, he's leaving in two months," I tell him, heading toward the living room.

"There's nothing a grown man loves more than to be talked about like he's an elderly pet, one paw in the grave," Carter grumbles.

"It's the truth. You're going to be pen pals? Write him about your busy week or how your stocks went up?"

"You've been doing your homework," he says, sounding pleased.

I did. It was a much-needed reality check. My mind is playing a dangerous game of *what else can Carter do to turn you on* whenever I'm near him.

"Had to be sure you weren't on the Most Wanted list."

"So. What's the plan here?" He waves his hand around the dusty place.

"I'm going to turn it into my perfect tiny home. It's faster, cheaper and it's all I need for myself."

Carter, who up to today hasn't used the words "tiny" and "house" in the same breath, hums unconvinced.

"What?" I snap defensively. "Maybe I'll meet my soulmate and build a bigger house together. Or I'll grow old alone here and get a parrot to keep me company," I say, lifting the sledgehammer I borrowed from Finn.

My foreman is cute. He's the type of man who would feel like cool aloe on my bruised heart. His interest is obvious, but he's not been overly flirty with Sam or Thomas hovering all the time, two nosy helicopter wingmen. He's got the two men in the back of his pocket, rooting for him for the past few weeks.

Before I take a swing at the first wall my phone pings with a text.

CARL: It's not too late to change your mind.

I'm still figuring out how to get my last paycheck without landing in the middle of another town drama. What's so wrong with me that most people abandon me or make me feel worthless?

The first blow makes a large hole, clouds of dust swirling around me. I lift the hammer again and my tense muscles strain, a headache blooming in the back of my head, my heart pounding in my ears. I swing again and again, my arms screaming in protest. Every hole in the drywall brings me closer to spilling the tears of frustration prickling behind my eyes.

I'm not sad. It's a collision of dark particles twisting into a tornado inside my chest.

"Remind me not to make you angry." Carter scans me with a strange expression. Surprised I'm capable of tearing these walls down by myself.

"I'm not. I'm sweating out my frustration." I never get angry because I had to be grateful and keep my mouth shut. "Can you take the debris outside?"

"Isn't this fun? I'm paying you and still doing hard work."

"Isn't this a rich guy thing? Paying some fancy trainer to make you suffer? At least I'm not yelling at you."

"Maybe you should."

"I'm not the type."

After taking a break to enjoy Sadie's famous sandwich I start to sort through the pieces of furniture I want to keep and fix.

"What are you going to do with them? They're old"—he picks up a banged-up wooden stool—"and some are broken."

"I'll fix them. Give them a new purpose so they don't end up in landfill."

"Why? Isn't it easier to get new ones? Do something else with your time?"

Living in the smallest, darkest, dampest rooms or corners, I had little stuff of my own. "It's part habit, part hobby. I mostly got old and broken furniture. I had to improvise."

"Where did you learn to fix them?"

"I started small. A little glue. A lick of paint. When I moved in with the Millers, I'd always linger around Sam's garage next door. He's a carpenter and taught me a lot." I also loved TV shows about home improvements and picked up a few tricks. It's still my comfort activity when I'm upset.

For the first time, Carter looks unsure. He opens and closes his mouth a couple of times.

"How did you end up in foster care?"

The question leaves me stunned. I know people have this morbid curiosity after they find out, but this is the point of no return. If I tell him about it he'll see me the way the whole town does. Like I'm damaged goods.

Maybe it would be for the best and he'll take a step back and stop overwhelming me.

"I don't remember what happened when I was a toddler. I only know what my social worker told me." And what most of the families reminded me constantly. "I was put up for adoption after I was born, got lucky enough and another family wanted me." And everything changed after that. "They returned me after two years."

"Returned?" Carter asks, horrified.

"Yeah…like a present you don't want." I laugh humorlessly.

"Did anyone else—"

"No. I bounced from one foster home to another until I was too old to have another chance. People want to adopt babies." I never spent more than three years in one place, moving around Maine. "There was something about me that meant not even a government check could convince them to keep me. The Millers were the last family to take me in before I turned eighteen. Moved me to Silver Lake Falls where I've been living for the past ten years."

"Did they kick you out?"

The question is not surprising. That's what usually happens when the checks stop coming.

"Oh, no! They wanted me to stay. Get a college degree. But—" I shake my head, disappointed in myself. "I had other plans." Jared convinced me to get a job first and a degree later.

He's pensive, mindlessly dusting off the small China hutch. I knew it. The mention of my history tends to put a damper on conversations.

"Aren't you angry about it?"

What's with him and anger?

"No, I left it in the past," I repeat the feel-good line I feed people. "I choose to focus on the good things."

"You just pretend your childhood didn't happen?"

"Not everybody has a soft cushioned great time. So yeah, I'd rather not rehash it."

Carter stews over his words for a moment. "I had reasons for anger growing up. My father being the main source. But I let it fuel me. I thrived feeding on it."

"That sounds *way* healthier than ignoring it," I say sarcastically.

"What I mean is anyone would be angry. You are lying to yourself by denying it. This Little Miss Sunshine act is rather pathetic if you ask me—the wounded girl who's so nice and lets people walk all over her."

A wave of heat swells in my belly. Flames lick my chest, neck, and slowly rise to scorch my cheeks and pinch the tips of my ears.

Carter's the embodiment of infinite patience, eyebrow raised, resting on his pry bar. Infuriating. He huffs a patronizing sigh and turns around.

"What. The. Hell!" My high-pitched scream rolls through the trees like a sound wave, chasing away some birds, who squeak in indignation. "What kind of person…" I splutter. "You can't go around telling people…"

The vein on the side of my neck is throbbing, ready to pop.

"I'm not an act. I'm somebody who tries to make the best of a shitty situation." Another gulp of air. "And either way I don't have to explain myself to you… you arrogant…prick. Silver spoon trust fund nepo baby!"

He just waits me out until I finish my rant, almost panting.

"So, you *are* the type. Better?"

I wordlessly blink at him, mimicking an owl, spent.

He casually gets back to work, a shadow of a smirk passing the left corner of his mouth.

What just happened? Weirdly, I'm lighter and the headache has subsided. The wave of acid in my stomach has simmered down and my eyes don't burn with unshed tears.

I'd be annoyed with him for the stunt, but…I feel so good. And safe. I never felt safe enough to let it out. My defense mechanisms must be broken. Because the alternative is I trust him and that's another can of worms I don't want to open.

He'll disappear back to New York and whatever this is will end.

I've been shut tightly in my cocoon for so long, I forgot who the real me even is. Being a people pleaser to the point I let people walk all over me.

Carter forces me to step outside my self-woven pod. It's uncomfortable, but I'm more alive than I've been in years.

Chapter Fourteen

CARTER

Revealing so much of myself to Eliza is beginning to be a problem because it's shaping up to be a compulsion growing to worrisome proportions. I'm keen on having her undivided attention. I bask in the warmth of her laughter. The sound unlocks a section of my brain that shoots a bizarre concoction into my bloodstream.

It's a double-edged shovel, digging myself a deeper hole. I know she shouldn't be at the forefront of my brain when I wake up in the morning with a hard-on and no other release than a quick jack-off in the small shower. It takes the edge off, but then she looks at me with those pretty hazels when the morning light showers the kitchen through the leaves. It takes all my self-control not to do something stupid, like kiss her.

Eliza doesn't even try to seduce me, there's a gravitational pull bringing us too close and it's becoming harder to keep my distance.

The mental list of reasons I'm not supposed to cross the line is circling my head with the cadence of a mantra. *I don't know if I can trust her. She just ended an eight-year relationship. She's not the casual type.*

I start my morning bombarding Jackie and Joseph with texts I get useless answers to. Eliza's morning routine includes pestering me with random questions. I can't ignore her because she keeps hovering or staring and I'm a gentleman.

"What's your biggest fear?" is the debut of today's game of twenty-one questions.

"What are you, twelve?"

"Come on, humor me." She points to the plate. "I agreed to eat your weird omelet. You owe me."

An offended exhale buys me some time. "A Michelin star chef shared that recipe with me."

"Then he's weird too. Quit stalling,"

I don't know why I don't just leave and check in at the Steamship Inn near the harbor.

"Becoming my father." I breath out the bitter truth before I have time to mull the answer over in my head.

Eliza blinks like a chocolate-brown-eyed owl. "Wow. That's deep," she finally says, while I'm tense as a taut wire. "I was expecting spiders or something."

The enormity of the confession I blurted out hits me. The bubble of laughter is uncontrollable. Her face does that thing when she looks at me with such wonder it shifts something in my chest.

"Your laugh is very warm," she says, looking at her plate.

I clear my throat and get back to the article to get my mind off this moment of temporary insanity. Some reporters were asking where the face of the company was. "The young and promising CEO Carter Rawlings was MIA from yesterday's Global Technology Forum." Jackie did a spectacular job. I watched the video at least ten times. The camera loves her. Stepping in for me allowed her to show off her natural charm and sharp mind.

But the media keeps asking questions and they'll become more insistent. I have to convince my mother and sister that staying two more months is unnecessary.

"Why don't you want to be like him?"

Few people know the reality of being Angus Rawlings' son. After his rapid ascension into the top ten richest people stratosphere, many wanted to dig up dirt on us. So my father kept everyone on a short leash, including his children. He'd be horrified by our breakfast conversations.

Maybe the need to go against him drives me to answer her.

"The company was his sole focus. We, his family, were just pawns in his grand scheme. Each time I witnessed my mother's disappointment over another missed dinner or my sister's gloom on her birthday, I wondered if we were really a family. Nothing else mattered to him."

"It reminds me of someone who crosses the days in the calendar, hoping he can go back to the office faster," she says with humorous reproach.

It's true, I'm not subtle about my desire to return.

"It's different. I chose not to have a family, so I won't hurt them. At least there's no one to disappoint."

"Other than yourself." And with that blow, she casually twists in her chair to finish the dishes. "Damn, I'll be late for the interview," she scoffs. "Another dream job."

Her sarcasm gets zero reaction. She doesn't notice I'm speechless as she's already half out the door yelling, "Hot cocoa by the dock tonight. Clear skies, lots of stars and all that."

The words are stuck in my head. There is no one because I refused to let anyone in. Again. Or hurt my family like my father did. It's a decision that comes with the cutting loneliness of not having a true partner to share normal, domestic bits of bliss. Around whom I'd be comfortable enough to be open.

I'd never admit it out loud, but I look forward to dinners with Eliza and finding new ways to annoy her. The instant gratification from the little moans she makes because she enjoys what I cook. Or the silly quests she drags me into the forest for. But how would such a connection survive in the real world? When responsibilities and stress pull me away. Could I bear to see my mother's suffering on the face of someone like Eliza? Sensing her drift apart into separate bedrooms and scheduled family meals. It's another chant to add to my mental self-restraint mantra.

I don't want to hurt her.

An entire week passes without me sharing another deep-hidden secret. I count it as a win. The only one since I'm getting nowhere with getting access back to my accounts. It's unnerving to witness projects unfold as an outsider, from the media and the occasional juicy bits from Adam.

Speaking of juicy bits, Eliza's truck of horrors is back earlier than expected. The booming slam of the driver's door is nothing new. She's one more creative wire contraption closer to me making her so-called car disappear. I'll fake a lottery ticket or ask Logan to come up with a long-lost relative's last will.

What's odd is that she doesn't come in. I follow her rigid silhouette through the lacy curtains until she reaches the uncut stack of firewood and grabs the axe. There's no good reason for her to chop wood but she's determined and the first swing of the ax lodges in the stump.

The tension in her body pulls me outside where I'm met with the sight of a disheveled Eliza frantically splitting logs. Her long copper hair is in disarray, flying around her face, caught in the hard set of her lips.

"Doing your workout?" I test the waters, but her focus is on the tree stump. Swinging and mechanically replacing the pieces of wood without saying a word.

"It's for the fire pit tonight." *Chop. Chop.* "Go inside. I'll come in a minute," Eliza says with forced evenness in a scratchy voice.

The pile of firewood already stacked neatly in the rack near the shed calls out her bullshit. If my self-preservation instinct decided to do its job, I'd let her be.

"Eliza." *Chop. Chop.* I cautiously inch closer and a chip of wood narrowly misses my chin. "I'm going to reach for the ax and remind you about my family's propensity for revenge and inflicting financial ruin. Let's stop swinging."

She stills but doesn't let go of the tool, so I reach for the back of her hand and slide my palm until I grab the rough handle of the ax and toss it out of reach.

As natural as breathing, my arms automatically go around her trembling body and hold Eliza against me. "You OK?"

"My engagement ring," she wails.

"You were engaged?" The mix of surprise and disappointment goes over her head as she keeps looking at the ground.

Her lips are glued shut in a brave attempt to stop a sob, but it's a lost battle when she tries to speak.

"He gave it to her." Eliza gets the words out between whimpers.

It doesn't take a genius to figure out what happened. Jared jumped boats faster than a rat with a water allergy and I'm secretly relieved he'll be out of the picture.

"Everybody's congratulating them. His parents, our friends," she sniffs. "Like I didn't exist the last eight years. Like I'm a speck of dirt they brushed off," her voice is faint, and her unfocused gaze roams the lake.

Her tears stir something I can't name behind my ribs. I help her sit on the back porch stairs, but she keeps staring at the still surface of the water, reflecting the green belt of trees around it.

Eliza pulls out her phone and shows me Caroline's post. The picture shows her holding the back of her hand to the camera so you can't miss the ring. Jared holds a sonogram over her still-flat belly.

Some blessings take you by surprise, but there's nothing better than having the right person by your side. My soulmate. My fiancé.

Nauseating.

"His mother never accepted me, because I'm a *stray*. She called me that to my face," Eliza says through a watery laugh. "I bent over backward to make her like me. Now she calls Caroline the daughter she never had!"

Her knee bounces restlessly and she reaches for the faint line over her temple, rubbing it absentmindedly.

"We were together for eight years," Eliza shrieks. "And she still got my name wrong!"

"You shouldn't have to beg for their love. You're lucky. The trash took itself out."

Finally, I get her attention, her eyebrows slumped, wet lashes brimming with tears.

"Better to be alone than surrounded by people who don't appreciate you."

Her lower lip wobbles and she's trying so hard to keep it in.

"I'm s-s-orry," she snivels. "I showed him that ring last year."

Eliza's body is shuddering under the weight of her suppressed sobs. She curls into herself tighter and it creates an uncomfortable twist as I feel awash in her hurt.

My body is guided by a strange force, and I settle behind her on the wooden step.

"Let it out," I whisper into her ear, as I pull her against my chest, wrapping my palms around her dainty wrists. Her pulse thrums under my fingertips, spiking my heartbeat.

"You don't have to be nice to me." She rests her head on my shoulder and tilts her face up. I have to squash another urge to wipe her tears away.

"Shh. Cry it out. Don't apologize." I hold on a little tighter and rub her arms, hoping I can soothe her pain.

When her breathing steadies I dry her tears with my handkerchief.

"You can keep it."

Eliza sniffles. "Who the hell carries monogrammed handkerchiefs? Are you eighty?"

"I got my first set for my fifth birthday."

Her unwarranted outraged expression is amusing.

"You've already seen me bawling more than some people who've known me since I was little."

For some unknown reason, satisfaction coats my insides, knowing she lets herself be vulnerable around me.

"Your secret is safe with me." I try to lighten the moment.

I know it's a promise I won't break when hope and apprehension battle in the strained lines around her watery smile.

I'm not a person people seek for comfort. I don't know what I'm doing, but witnessing Eliza take hit after hit makes me do the most uncharacteristic things.

That's how I find myself inside Quinn's coffee shop on a Wednesday morning.

This is after I spent more than an hour at an arts and crafts store with the pinkest Victorian front on the East Coast. The truth is that the rows of brick and classic coastal fronts have a certain charm when you've spent your entire life between glass and steel towers.

I wanted to buy some new pencils for her sketches. Did I get the woman, who wouldn't accept dinner or help, a limited edition art and graphic wooden box set worth more than the three months' rent for her cabin? I did.

It's over the top but it might distract her from obsessively checking Jared and Caroline's profiles. Even if it means she'll yell at me, and I'll have to resort to some creative mental gymnastics to convince her to accept it.

"My birthday is in June," Quinn's amused voice rises from where she's crouched, refilling the pastry case. She nods at the gift bag, and I ignore the lingering question.

"Interesting place you've got here," I admit, taking a better look around. It reminds me of the spot Jackie dragged me to in Williamsburg when she was on one of her quests to find the perfect cup of coffee.

"Try a cortado and the cheesecake," she says. "They're the same as the fancy ones you have in New York."

I don't bother telling her I don't touch coffee or sweets.

"Coffee. Cream. To go. Throw in a hot chocolate and a blueberry muffin."

She nods, pursing her lips. "Hm. Exactly Eliza's sadness relief order. Isn't that something?"

I won't dignify her implication with an answer. Because it is. Eliza said something at one point in her continuous ramblings about it being her healing kit.

A too cheerful and trusting mail carrier accepted the untouched cup of coffee on my way to the car.

Eliza is home, hunkered in the armchair she dragged next to the window with a drawing notebook in her lap, erasing half of what I'm guessing are ideas for her tiny house.

"I ran into Quinn." My voice startles her. "She strong-armed me into delivering you this."

"Are we talking about the same blonde pixie who owns a coffee shop?"

"One and only. She's freakishly strong."

Confusion and suspicion dance along her features but she accepts the bag and pierces my eardrums with a delighted squeal after sniffing its content.

Sugar-filled and more alert, Eliza finally notices the large bag with the store logo on the front. She shifts on the armchair and stares at me, trying to read my mind. Usually, I'd let her stew and mess about, but she's still too fragile.

"I happened to park right next to the store. They're having a big sale. Today only." I place the box in her arms and the jitters keep me talking. "Clearing out the shop. They're retiring to Florida. It was practically free."

Eliza gawks between the box and me. "Ethan and his wife had a baby three months ago. They're in their thirties."

"Silly me." I run a hand over the back of my head. "I guess I've been bamboozled."

The wooden box opens with a soft click and her fingers caress the rows of pencils and ink pens, murmuring something to herself. I'm nervous like a kid handing out his first Valentine's Day cards.

She pierces me with those red-rimmed brown eyes and I'm afraid she'll see right through me and throw the heavy set at my head. Or worse. She'll start crying again.

Instead, the corners of her lips tug up for the first time in three days and my stomach flips over.

"Thank you," she says softly.

I'm still thinking about it that night when I lie awake and listen to the sounds of the pencils on the toothy drawing paper.

Boredom is wasted time. Successful people squeeze the most out of every second. It's something my father drilled into our heads from an early age.

It's time for the fence challenge. Eliza is not home. She's off pestering the construction crew for the next half a day. She showed me where she keeps the key to her precious shed and warned me not to touch her works in progress. Using the white paint for the fence did not fall under that category. I skimmed through a YouTube tutorial and got to it.

The problem with learning a new skill on fast forward is it gave me the false impression it would be a walk in the park. It's not. Especially since I didn't read the instructions on the lid and I can't lie to myself and pretend it looks OK.

Two hours down the drain and I have to start over. My muscles ache and the T-shirt clings to my back, when the gravel crunches under the large tires of her truck from hell.

Hiding the evidence of my stupidity as quickly as possible, I sense her coming to a halt around the corner. Sweat is dripping down my forehead and I get to my feet to wipe it with the shoulder of my T-shirt just in time to catch her shamelessly checking me out.

"It'll look better when I'm done." I crack a smile.

She looks excited but unsure. "You actually did it. You didn't have to bother. It's something I should take care of."

I never back away from a challenge and I'm not going to be defeated by a stupid fence.

"I'd like to finish it. If you don't mind. I've never painted a fence before. It's…calming."

"Then I'll get on with cooking. It's the least I can do."

"Please stop," I shout after her. "You don't owe me anything."

Yes, I did it because she said I couldn't, and I had nothing else to do. Never crossed my mind to gain something from her. It sounds so hypocritical to tell her not to suspect ulterior motives when I'm always on the lookout.

Bonus point, her surprise and delight warms my solar plexus again.

Sliding the brush over the last picket I sit up straight to admire the past few hours' worth of sweat and back pain. Working out is not the same thing as hard manual labor. I hate to agree with my mother but I'm not 100% recovered.

I have to drag myself to the back steps and rest my head back on the porch railing, sweat sliding down my neck. The blood is whooshing in my ears and my head's spinning.

"Are you OK?" The worry in her voice pokes at the nasty creature living in the back of my head who wants to yell at everybody to back off.

I wave her off and to my relief, the back door snaps shut.

Good. I don't want her to see me so weak.

But the door swings open again and a moment later, the scent of her lavender shower gel puts me on edge. I open my eyes to her bending over to place a cold cloth on my forehead.

Eliza dabs my forehead with the concentration and seriousness of a seasoned nurse. She slides the cloth over my temple and neck, lips slightly parted.

When our eyes meet her cheeks turn rosier and she wants to retreat but in a display of pure selfishness, I gently cover her wrist keeping her hand in place.

Her delicate throat moves in a hypnotic ripple with each nervous swallow.

"You looked overheated. I thought this might help," she says breathlessly.

"Thank you." I squeeze her arm lightly. "I feel much better now."

I should let go. The urge to bring her closer burns under my skin, a rippling wave of electricity. To set her in my lap and bury my head in the crook of her slender neck. Kiss the back of her ear, down her jaw and—

The direction of the fantasies snaps me out of the moment, and I drop my hand abruptly.

Eliza registers the change in my posture because she backs away, wrangling the wet cloth. She's getting too close for comfort. She might seem innocent, but I can't take that bet. I can't afford to.

"I brought you some cold lemonade with honey. It'll give you a boost." She's looking anywhere but at me.

I have to break this fragile connection before I cross the line.

"Thank you, Eliza," my father's voice speaks through me. The flattest master-of-the-manor tone I could manage to conjure. "I'd appreciate it if you stopped invading my personal space. We're far from that type of familiarity." She needs to stop looking at me like she wants me. "You can go now."

She draws back as if I've slapped her and that blush, making my fingers itch to touch her, spreads like wildfire.

The usual mantra of reasons I should stay away does nothing to temper the unease pulsing in the back of my ribs.

Chapter Fifteen

ELIZA

If he thanks or dismisses me one more time like I'm one of his employees, I'll end up on the evening news. In the moment, the onslaught of embarrassment swallowed any retort.

Then it faded away, leaving a bitter taste of sadness.

I overstepped with my blatant interest and it's the first time he has taken such an obvious step back.

"Thank you, Eliza," Carter says flatly while grabbing the plate I made for him on his way to the table outside, on the porch. He doesn't even look at me, I might as well be a Live, Laugh, Love sign on the wall.

He's been doing that every morning since the fence incident.

Things between us are back to being frosty, a throwback to the first week of living together and I have better things to do than embarrass myself further.

I'm tired of being humiliated. I won't allow Carter to root me back into that dark place I'm too painfully familiar with.

What am I doing anyway? Drooling over the first man I stumble upon when I'm still reeling, watching Jared and Caroline build the family I was begging him for.

The days pass with as little air exchanged between us as possible. In a stroke of luck, things start picking up at the little cabin and I'm out of the door at the crack of dawn, talking with Finn and his crew and driving to Thomas's store for missing materials. They're vaulting the ceilings this week and I'm more excited than a bear in a berry patch.

There are still things around the house I need to do for Carter and usually I don't have to check in with him, but I can't delay the inevitable today. He's been holed up in his bedroom for hours and I've reached my limit.

The first knock is polite because this is a business agreement, nothing more, and I'm the epitome of professionalism.

Silence.

I knock again, this time I put my wrist into it.

No answer. What the hell?! I know he's in there.

After the door rattles with my third knock, an irritated "Yes?" does nothing to bring my blood pressure down.

I try to control my voice. "Can I talk to you?"

"Is it urgent?"

Having this conversation through the door is embarrassing, but I grit my teeth. "I'll need to clean your room and change the sheets."

Carter doesn't say anything, but the light tap of bare feet on the hardwood floor is getting closer. He yanks the door open and scowls down at me, stone-faced.

"Do you have to do it right now?" he asks, annoyance glazing his every word.

Keep it together, Eliza. Just play nice. "No. I wanted to know whether I can do it tomorrow, if you plan to go out," I say, making a colossal effort to keep my face as neutral as possible.

Carter's jaw ticks. "There's no need for you to rummage through my room."

Rummage?! This asshole.

I answer him with a clenched smile. "It's my job, isn't it? I like to keep the house in good shape."

An uninterest grunt is all I get from him.

"So, what time? I need to schedule another appointment, so I'll work around you." My least favorite part of the last week was going to interviews for jobs I'm overqualified for. But beggars can't be choosers, and I have to keep on doing it until I land a job.

"Eleven is fine."

"O—" I don't get the chance to reply before the door slams in my face, leaving me to stare unblinking at the patterns in the wood until my vision goes blurry.

The fact that Carter ignores me completely when we're at the house doesn't stop him from texting his demands.

> CARTER: The light bulb in the bathroom might be busted.

Answering back that he's a spoiled man-child is not an option. I don't want to be sucked into the usual back-and-forth he enjoyed too much.

> ELIZA: Hallway closet. Fourth shelf.

> CARTER: You should come and check it out. For liability reasons.

> CARTER: I think I saw a bear behind the bushes in the back.

ELIZA: Don't pet it.

CARTER: My mother would be terribly unhappy if I got mauled.

ELIZA: Stay indoors.

CARTER: Your advice lacks the degree of worry required by the situation.

ELIZA: I'm sure the bear will survive a Carter sighting. I'll leave some berries out to make it up to him.

CARTER: Cold-blooded. Is this how you deal with your tenants' problems?

The three dots appear and disappear a few times.

I hate the disappointment bubbling in my stomach when they disappear for good, and he doesn't send another text. There are all the reasons in the world I shouldn't want to get back to that confusing sexual tension and dangerous banter.

If I could bash some sense into him with the frying pan without risking jail time I would.

Unfortunately, there's nothing to do in Silver Spring Falls after 8pm. Sometimes he's still in the living room, reading or working on his laptop, a crystal-clear sign to leave him alone. I make myself busy in the kitchen, as silently as possible, so that he doesn't snap at me again.

In my haste to put everything back, I manage to smack my head against an open cabinet door. "Oof!"

"Are you alright?" The edge of concern would usually be my cue to scramble and comfort.

"Happier than a clam at high tide." I do my best to act normal, rubbing the side of my head.

"What?" Carter crinkles his nose and it's so cute I have to leave the room in a rush.

Quinn's mustard armchair is a fluffy cloud, and I sink in and relax for the first time this week in her little sunroom filled with the most mismatched plants I've ever seen. Unfortunately for them, some look half-dead. She says they're being dramatic.

"Did you block him yet?" Quinn hands me a glass of fresh juice.

She's been asking the same question since they posted the engagement photo.

"I want to know," I mumble.

"Nothing good will come of it. You're only hurting yourself," she says with the conviction of someone who learned it through personal experience. "Do you miss him?"

"Oh, God, no. I just—" It's hard admitting the truth. "I wonder what I got wrong, you know? I thought it was going to be us, flaunting our happiness."

"What a pile of steaming bullshit." Quinn's got that look of determination that scares me a little.

The words I was too scared to say out loud come out pained, "Then tell me! Tell me why you'd build a life with someone for eight years but decide to marry and have a child with another woman the next day." All my shortcomings churn in my chest, almost choking me. "I wasn't good enough. I'll never be."

"No!"

I jump out of my skin when Quinn slams her palm on the coffee table between us.

"You listen and accept when the people in your life tell you that." Quinn bends to take my hand and I feel that all my broken parts are exposed. My first instinct is to run. But she keeps me rooted with her gentle grasp. "But what they're saying is a reflection of their faults. Not yours."

"You're too nice. I—"

"Unfortunately, you are. When it comes to others. You could start being nicer to yourself. See who you are through your own eyes."

Tears cloud my vision. "What do you mean?"

"OK." She perks up. "Tell me three things you're proud of."

"Um. I managed to finish college," I say, unsure, but she nods approvingly. "I'm fixing a house. I…don't know."

"You're smart. You're strong. You're creative. Say it."

I laugh at how silly she is, tears gathering on my eyelashes.

Quinn lunges for my face. "Say. It." She squishes my cheeks, leaning so close, the tip of her nose almost touching mine.

"OK. OK, you psycho," I gurgle through tears and the vise-like grip still pinning me in place. "I'm smart. I'm strong. I'm creative."

"That's my girl." Quinn beams and releases me from her impressive hold for a girl her size. "Say it three times whenever you doubt yourself."

I rub my cheeks in circles to restore the blood flow. "Your pep talks are a bit aggressive. Do you exercise with a hand gripper by any chance?"

"You can file a complaint with my Nana. Be prepared for a lot worse," she giggles but turns serious. "Speaking of which. Your phone."

The amusement drains away and a wave of panic crashes against me. I instinctively pull the phone closer.

"Why?" My voice is shaky and even I can spot the overreaction. "I promise I won't check their photos." Too often.

"Eliza." The outline of Quinn's face softens and she sighs. "It's not healthy."

"But—" I have no idea why I'm fighting her. It's enough that we live in the same small town. How do I stop wanting to know if he's happier with her? We weren't the happiest couple, but their blissfulness after the backstabbing irks me.

It burns too deep, and I don't wish him well. I hope he crashes and burns, and I get front-row seats to the show.

"You're right. I'll never focus on my life if I keep obsessing over theirs," I admit with a knot in my stomach. I give her the phone and silently plead with Quinn to help me.

"Promise you won't unblock them?" She peers at me sternly over the phone while typing and scrolling.

"I'll let you put parental controls on if I slip."

Quinn hands it back with a satisfied smirk. I guess she's happy I agreed to ignore Jared and Caroline, but then she says in the most deceptive, calm and casual tone, "You got a text, by the way."

CARTER: I made too many lobster rolls.

Damn it! Those are my favorite. It's a battle between my pride and the need to back away from him and my taste buds.

"Weren't you supposed to cook for him? Did you come up with a new arrangement?" she asks, laying it on a bit thick with the innuendo.

"He's a better cook, to be honest." I tell her the truth, veering past the fact that I want to avoid him.

Quinn tilts her head. "You don't look like a woman who has a gorgeous man in her kitchen cooking dinner."

"He's just bored. Don't overthink it." I'm going to skip it again. I only wish he didn't leave a plate out for me each time. It makes me feel guilty even though I did nothing wrong.

Quinn doesn't say anything but she's plotting something in her pretty blonde head. I can smell it on her.

When I get home there's dinner again on the island counter. A note in his elegant and even handwriting rests next to it.

Eat or I'm calling Martha.

Chapter Sixteen

CARTER

Joseph answers the phone with a sigh, wordlessly letting me know I'm a nuisance. It irritates me to no end.

"Pierre is poking around." I skip the pleasantries.

"Where did you hear that?" He doesn't sound alarmed.

"This is ridiculous and dangerous for the company. I should come back."

"It's interesting you called me and not Jackie or your mother." Joseph's baritone is laced with amusement.

"You're my right hand and are supposed to have my back."

"It's cute you don't want to hurt your sister's feelings. I didn't know you had it in you."

The old man is spot on. I don't want Jackie to think I'm fighting to get back because I don't trust her. Doing an abysmal job of hiding how proud he was of her, Adam told me she was the one to deliver the final blow to UniCore and land the government contract.

"You could persuade my mother." I try this angle again.

"Not a chance. I care for you as much as I do for Logan. But I'm not risking crossing her."

It's incomprehensible how she has Joseph wrapped around her little finger. A bitter divorcé, he had resisted all attempts to make him an honest man again.

None of the ladies auditioning for the role of Logan's stepmother managed to get him to change even the foyer table. But he folded like a chair for my mother.

"Have you seen her recently?"

"Yes."

"Care to be more specific?"

His voice is paternal. "Carter, your mother is allowed to have her own life."

"And I'm very interested in who she spends it with."

His answer is drowned by the cherry and white death trap coming to a stop on the small driveway.

In the most absurd development, since I decided to keep my distance, Eliza hadn't tried to pull me back in. I wasn't counting on it.

No. The distance is good.

But.

Mornings have a bland taste when one easily annoyed redhead isn't there to pester me with the most inane questions.

Following the same foraging trails she dragged me along felt less of an adventure and more like I'm rambling about with no purpose.

"We'll revisit this," I tell Joseph absent-mindedly and hang up over whatever his retort was.

I can't even have the satisfaction of scoffing at her overreaction. The cabin is always in order, a healthy breakfast waiting for me daily. She gracefully exchanged her warm and bubbly presence for a civil distance. She plasters on a polite smile, but her answers lack the usual abundance of detail. Eliza gave me exactly what I wanted.

The acute sense I'm missing something of vital importance corrodes my resolve with each passing hour. I don't even question it when my legs take me outside.

After keeping herself busy during the day, I know where she's going to avoid me.

The LED lantern hanging from the shed's beam carves a cold glow in the dark, white strips of light sneaking out through the wood plank walls. Eliza is kneeling on a tarp with a paintbrush in her hand, focused on a table leg. Some strands fall from her bun and tickle her face, but she just blows them away absentmindedly. Her moves are fluid, and her face lacks the tightness she tries to hide whenever we're in the same room.

A warm light I don't get to see any other time dances behind her eyes when she works. I don't want to spook her and I wait, mesmerized by this other side of her, leaning against the porch rails.

The icy light above her makes Eliza look like an eerily beautiful creature of the woods. It brings into sharp relief the delicate collarbones and the hollow of her cheeks. The movements of her hands resembles a ritual and I half expect her to say an incantation and turn the table sentient.

The moment she straightens, sitting on the heels of her boots, I step into the ring of light and the little forest fairy freezes. For a heartbeat, she's on the precipice of reaching back. Meeting me in the middle. But with a determined clench of her jaw, she refrains from crossing the line in the sand.

She gathers the chisels, hammers, putty knives, and pieces of sandpaper and puts them back in the shed.

"How can I help you?" she asks, her back to me, cleaning a metal brush with a rag.

That customer care politeness bothers me in a way it shouldn't and the persistent pressure in my chest returns. I had the same uncomfortable feeling when I saw she had moved the keys to the shed. I'm no longer one of the people she trusts with them.

But this frosty wall is doing its job. There have been zero incidents since the fence. The wandering dirty thoughts running through my head whenever she's too close are not something I want to explore, it's just pent-up sexual frustration built up over the months I've been focused on recovery.

"How's your tiny house going?"

She grimaces but turns it into a perfect fake smile. "Finn and the guys are working hard. Not much I can do to help them."

It's possible she won't move out any time soon and I find myself unbothered by it. But I'm not about to live like this for the next few weeks.

I'm locked in a staring contest with a tall graying woman wearing denim overalls when I open the front door. She's holding a small crate with plants I know nothing about. Can Eliza use them to poison me?

The woman in question rushes to my side, almost pushing me out of the way, and takes the wood box from our visitor.

"Thanks for these, can't wait to grow my own."

"Then I'll have to find another excuse to check on you," the woman chuckles. "I'm Martha." She peers at me with the expertise of a seasoned butcher planning to have her way with the fresh carcass in the freezer.

It might have intimidated lesser men, but I'm not about to cower under the scrutiny of a mild-looking New England grandma.

"Carter. Pleased to meet you."

She shakes my hand. "Don't rush to conclusions, young man." The grip of a reincarnated sailor and the shadow of a smirk curling her mouth are more ominous than friendly.

"Come on, I'll put the kettle on." Eliza catches the woman's attention before we have the chance to finish our wordless battle.

"What a great idea." I follow her tense back, knowing full well the invitation didn't extend to me.

In the small kitchen, a swirl of confusion and calculation in her eyes catches my interest before I'm sidetracked by the way she's worrying her lips. Eliza's too polite to say anything, especially in front of other people, but she's plotting to get rid of me.

"I saw on the news that the Opera Hall has a temporary Edward Hopper exhibition this month. You could check it out."

Nice try, kitten. "Already saw it in New York. It was at a fundraiser. I think I adopted a goat."

She grumbles and Martha chuckles in her palm.

"The satellite dish seems a bit crooked."

"Eliza's so thoughtful," I tell Martha. "Looking out for me since I came here."

I employ my most charming smile and get two very different reactions. Eliza rolls her eyes and with a resigned sag of her shoulders turns to the stove. Martha, on the other hand, has her poker face on, arms folded. A spark of amusement dances behind the green frames of her glasses as she looks from me to Eliza.

"So," she says, "are you one of those rich guys who did something illegal and now has to lay low?"

"No. Sorry to disappoint. Nothing that exciting."

"Running from a scorned woman?"

"Martha!" Eliza's outraged cry is barely audible over the burst of laughter I can't contain. I like this lady.

"Did you compile a list of questions?"

Martha's back is ramrod straight and she stares me down unapologetically. "Yes. It's extensive."

"By all means, do go on," I encourage her, curious to see where this is headed.

"That's not necessary," Eliza says, planting a hand over her friend's in an unspoken thank you.

It's one of the few times the needling doesn't bother me. Something about the way this elderly woman used her gaze to threaten me with bodily harm lets me know she's got Eliza's back.

"Fine," she sounds half-convinced. "How are you finding it?"

"The cabin is lovely. Eliza has good taste."

Cinnamon eyes grow big and she's looking straight at me for the first time. I file this moment under the highlight of my week, together with having her sit at the same table for the first time in days, because nobody will ever know. Other than peeping into my own company's yard from the outside and cataloging Eliza's movements, my days are pretty boring.

"I told her she's talented," Martha perks up. "And those pieces she saves—"

"No need to get into details. Carter here is not much of a talker. Let him finish his tea in peace."

I'm not ready to give up yet. "But I want to know more about—"

"No, you don't," Eliza snaps.

Her words rile me up. "Please don't tell me what I want."

She narrows her eyes and sharpens her claws. "Well, somebody has to because you clearly have no idea."

It's obvious even to the blue herons flying over the lake we're not talking about furniture anymore. She realizes we're back on the familiar thin ice between a civil teatime and making Martha clutch her pearls.

Eliza glowers at me but all I want is to get closer to those burning embers and warm myself under the heat of her rage.

I lean closer over the table, "I know exactly what I want, sweetheart."

She's rigid in her chair and that delicious vein on the side of her neck that pops when she's mad is fluttering with the intense thumping of her pulse.

A delicate cough breaks the invisible thread coiling around us.

"I'd better go or Sam's gonna burn the house reheating his lunch."

"I'm sorry," Eliza says but Martha leaps from the highchair and gives her a crushing hug.

Then she turns to me. "You missed it this week. Next time I expect you at our monthly catch-up dinner."

"He's not—" Eliza starts, panicked.

I cut her off. "I'd love to."

"Great. Carter!" Martha waves me to follow her. "Help me get the apples from the car. I'm a tired old lady."

I recognize a trap when I see one. I don't want to argue with the woman who could whisk Eliza away if she had any doubts about me.

Eliza's wringing her hands and I refrain from reaching out to trap her delicate wrist in my palm. I want to comfort her. "I'll behave."

"It's not you I'm worried about."

It makes no sense until I reach the open trunk and Martha's pinning me down with a drill-sergeant glare.

"You strike me as a smart man."

"Thank—"

"Don't interrupt me. I've read about you. You didn't turn your father's—God rests his soul—company to ashes. Quite the contrary according to the press. That's saying something."

I nearly open my mouth to stupidly thank her again, but I'm silenced by her cutting look.

"I also saw pictures of your dates and the kind of life you live."

A knot forms at the base of my throat.

"Eliza deserves to have fun. Carefree, young-blooded fun." She struggles with the next part. "Don't make promises you can't keep. Her life is already filled with people who let her down."

I finally find my voice and a new appreciation for the balls on this old lady.

"Do I detect an underlying threat?" Amusement curls my lips but it doesn't last long.

"I have enough metal knitting needles not to miss one if necessary." Martha rounds the car and opens the driver's door. "One of the old rusty ones."

She's gone with a wink, her tires projecting small stones from the driveway.

CHAPTER SEVENTEEN

ELIZA

Avoiding Carter is much easier this week between job hunting and daily trips to my future home. I check on the crew's progress and bring lunch and snacks. And an extra cookie for Sam, who camps there every day to boss poor Finn around.

Finn's never had a wingman as invested as dear old Sam. Yesterday he made the man blush with his over-the-top compliments about how Finn is *husband material* and *what a coincidence Eliza is single* and *you should get to know each other better.*

The dark-eyed blond is cute in the boy next door sense, with the body of a man pulling his weight on the construction site. It doesn't hurt that he's funny as hell, cracking me up every time I ask him a million questions about the renovation steps.

It's past midnight when I return to the cabin, dragging my feet, body aching. To my relief, the lights are off.

I close the front door and lean on it, taking a deep breath. My shoulders sag on an exhausted exhale. Today was rough.

The fishing shop near the docks is looking for a part-time inventory clerk. Stock and order management doesn't sound too exciting, but it's not like I can be picky. They offered me the job on the spot. Didn't need the extra time to think about it since my last paycheck is still being held hostage by Carl, who texts me daily.

I don't have much choice since the crew gave me a longer deadline than I hoped. It means even more money. I want to move out as soon as possible, but it'll take at least three extra weeks until I can start on the finishing touches and furniture.

Bottom line, it's another month at least sharing the space with Carter. And finding new ways to spend as little time as possible in the same room.

All I want is to crash on my bed and slip into unconsciousness.

A floor creak from the living room reverberates in the silence, pinning me in place. Dread creeps up my body and I break into cold sweats.

Carter's walking toward me, eyes focused, like a nocturnal predator. His fluid steps lock my limbs, my heart beating wildly.

That full mouth of his is a hard line. The only sign of his disposition. His movements are smooth and deceivingly relaxed like he's going on a nighttime stroll, not waiting to corner me in the dark.

"You're coming up short on our deal," he says, all business. I'm half expecting him to conjure up a contract.

Shit. He's kicking me out. I tried to stay out of his way, but it's not enough for him. He wants me out of the house and there's nothing I can do to stop it.

I'm not ready. The only solution short of camping is to swallow my pride and call the Duntons.

I clear my throat and stand tall. I'm not going to beg him. "What do you mean? I'm doing what we agreed to. Food and cleaning."

"My vocal cords are getting rusty," he says evenly.

Isn't he the one who said he didn't want my company? Mr. *I don't need nobody.*

"Go have a coffee in town. People here are friendly. You'd find somebody to talk to."

From the look on his face, you'd think I was sending him on a naked stroll along the main street, yodeling, rather than gently encouraging him to socialize.

"Per our agreement, you're supposed to show me around." He looks dead serious.

"It would mean spending time in the same place," I point out.

"I'm aware," he says in a low velvety voice.

There's no reason for bringing this up unless he's bored out of his mind. He can throw his money around to hire a personal guide instead of torturing me.

Carter comes closer and the intensity in those silvery eyes leaves me speechless. The air around us pulses with the tension pressing on my chest.

"I always get what I want. This won't be an exception," he says before walking away to his bedroom. "Good night, Eliza."

Chapter Eighteen

CARTER

The petrichor rising from the wet grass gives way to a new feeling of purpose this crisp morning. If I were honest with myself, I'd admit I've missed Eliza and didn't much care for the days she iced me out. Instead, I'll chalk it up to cabin fever.

The jitters dragged me out of bed before sunrise and I've been admiring the view from the back porch for a couple of hours.

A noise inside catches my attention and through the window, I spot Eliza tiptoeing and stealing furtive glances around like a first-time intruder.

The minx is sneaking out.

You're not getting rid of me that easily.

I give her no warning. "Where are we going?"

She gives a tiny yelp and scrambles to catch the shoes and bag clutched to her chest.

"We?" she chokes out, eyes wide.

"I made myself clear last night."

Eliza looks around, puffing her rosy lips. It's endearing. She's desperate for an out. Not this time, kitten.

"The library is hardly an exciting attraction."

"I'd beg to differ. The Internet informs me it's a historical landmark. One of the top ten must-see things in town."

Her mouth hangs open in the most adorable way.

"It's going to be boring and full of kids." She makes another valiant attempt to ditch me.

"Nonsense. I love kids." She doesn't have to know I always avoided the office on the days when teams were invited to bring their offspring to parties.

She levels me with a distrustful glare but steps outside while I bask in the sweet taste of victory.

"Get in," I tell her, heading for my car.

"I can't roll into town in that." She points to the Maserati with the grimace of someone stumbling on roadkill.

"Does this car offend your sensibilities?" I honestly don't see the problem. "You had no problem when I dropped you at work."

She takes a deep calming breath and struggles to give me a reason without offending me. "It was an emergency. It's too much for Silver Lake Falls. People will talk when I get out of your car." She falters, begging me to understand.

I pause to consider her situation. The recent scandal with the cheating boyfriend, no job. People see what they want. I don't care too much, but I'll leave this town and she'll stay here with gossip trailing her.

"How would you propose we get there? You can't possibly mean—"

Her grin is blood-curdling. "My truck!"

"No."

"It's perfect for these roads and going around town—"

"How old is it? When did you last have it checked?" Her mouth opens a few times to respond but I'm not done. "Does it have airbags? Air conditioning?"

"It's a fifteen-year-old, mint condition truck, last checked six months ago," she counts on her fingers. "And I don't plan on driving into a tree," she finishes, like a seasoned salesperson.

"If you don't feel safe, you can stay here and be one with nature." She has the audacity to smirk, thinking she won this round and I'll let her leave by herself.

Do I want to spend time around her that much? I can learn how to make wood carvings.

Who am I kidding?

"I hope you have good insurance," I tell her over my shoulder while yanking the door open for her to climb in. "My family won't be kind if something happens to me."

I catch the tail end of an exaggerated eye roll and prepare for a rough ride.

Sitting in the passenger seat while she's driving through town is the perfect opportunity to take in her tense posture, the delicate profile framed by an aura of windswept hair. I've come to terms with the fact I find her attractive, but in little glimpses, she's pure warmth making its way through my veins.

It's uncharacteristic sentimental drivel I hide under the pretense of admiring the shops opening or the view around the coastal road until we reach an old red-brick building with an angled roof, surrounded by shrubs and trees. It's a charming piece of architecture with large white framed windows looking over the harbor.

"Is this court-ordered community service?"

"Why do you always presume I'm in trouble with the law?" She does her best to hide her amusement.

"Because you look like trouble." In more ways than one.

"I do not." She lifts her nose in the air. "I'm a law-abiding citizen."

"Probably because you get away with everything by charming people's pants off." It's supposed to be a joke, covering the fact I'm thoroughly charmed. When her cheeks turn rosy, and she looks anywhere but at me I'm filled with a silly giddiness. I'll add *making her blush* next to *annoying her* on the list of things that make my day.

"I'll leave out the law-breaking part of your backhanded compliment," she chuckles.

A middle-aged woman wearing an eye-watering lime dress is waiting for us in the doorway, her hands clasped, grinning at Eliza. "The parents are so excited you came this week."

Eliza fidgets, uncomfortable with the woman's excitement. "I was hoping I could just read and dash, to be honest, Penelope."

"Don't be silly. The situation"—she air quotes the last word—"is taboo. I'll enforce a ban for life on anybody who dares open their mouth about the subject."

Penelope takes me on a tour of the place before we reach the children's colorful reading room. It's obvious it has seen better days.

"The library doesn't have enough resources to do more than keep our doors open," the woman says as I take in the rainbow carpet, floor-to-ceiling arched windows facing a little patio and garden. "But the families are happy to be here, they bring snacks and chat outside. It's a community gathering spot."

The people are enjoying the nice weather, laughing and glancing at the kids from time to time. I don't remember the last time I went to an event for fun.

A guy dressed head-to-toe in camo gear lingers too long around Eliza, even though she doesn't engage in the one-sided conversation. I'm about to check on her, but a little girl with braids beats me to it and pushes him toward the terrace, glaring at him until he chuckles awkwardly and puts his hands up in surrender.

Eliza, looking relieved, plops on a little yellow stool and claps animatedly.

"Kids, gather round. Let's find out what the little purple dragon is up to this time." She smiles at the hyper-excited group of kids who follow her siren call.

"Your kid in there?" a translucent woman, close to a hundred asks.

"No. I'm Eliza's bodyguard."

She guffaws, "You kids and your humor." The woman looks ready to pinch my cheek, so I sidestep the menace and find refuge behind a bookshelf with a prime view of Eliza.

The kids eat her up. Her eyes brighten as she gestures through the scenes. I was five the last time my mother was allowed to read me bedtime stories. My father said fairy tales were for toddlers.

My mind drifts to the soothing rhythm of her voice, to little feet slapping against the floor when I step through the door. Tiny arms rounding my neck and the smell of lavender and shaved wood telling me I'm home.

The vision bursts and reality comes into focus as sharp squeals hurry out to their parents on the patio. The sense of loss is so acute I wonder if I've lost my mind. How can I miss something that wasn't even real?

"You ready to face the firing squad?"

A small laugh escapes her and she bites her lip. "They'll be nice, but I'm not ready yet. Let's go home."

Home. The word is strangely comforting. But she'll find something to do as far away from me as possible.

"How about we get some fresh air? I want to cash in my tourist privileges until you decide to disappear off the face of the earth again."

She crosses her arms and tilts her chin up. "I'm busy. I have a life to get back on track, as you kindly pointed out."

Ouch. This Eliza, not afraid to call me out, is a shot of espresso to my system. The women around me let me get away with anything if it gets them closer to their goal. They'd agree mindlessly to any absurdity coming out of my mouth just for the chance to become Mrs. Rawlings.

"Do you have interviews on Saturdays?"

"No, but—" She ponders for a beat. "I could work on the house."

"Are you going to fix the roof by yourself?"

Eliza squints, confused. "How did you—"

I won't tell her I jog past the house, checking on the progress in a twisted countdown of how much time I still have with her. The roof is half-done, and she can't do anything until they put the drywall inside.

A frustrated "I can't believe this" trails behind me as we head for the car, and I smile to myself like a fool.

The wicked smirk she flashes once we leave is not a good sign, but at this point, I'd base jump into an active volcano just to spend more time with her. It all clicks when she grinds the old truck to a stop near a long dock. An old, weathered sea loft—Norman Boat Yard—looms over the boats swinging in the breeze.

I follow her to a small kiosk hiding behind the dark wood building. "Kayak Adventure" is painted in blue letters on a piece of wood you'd fish out of the water.

"Tandem please!" She bends over the counter to yell at the person in the back and it's impossible not to stare at her ass. It's the type you want to sink your teeth into.

Eliza throws me a life jacket and skips along with the man carrying the red kayak, chatting with an ease that makes me jealous. With us, there's always a push and pull, tiptoeing on shaky ground. As much as I want to get closer to her, there's an equal force holding me back.

"Do you have any idea what you're doing?"

"I worked as a guide during the summer in high school. I'll make sure you don't accidentally fall to the depths of the Atlantic Ocean," she answers breezily, with a suspicious stress on the word *accidentally*.

I enjoy her confidence too much to tell her I grew up kayaking at the yacht club. Maybe the only fun activity I was allowed to do.

I continue to play dumb as she explains how to climb in my seat. I prefer to listen to her voice and take in this unrestrained version of her. To let her fix my life jacket the right way so I can feel her hands on me.

Pathetic.

We glide smoothly away from the dock into the bay's waters.

"Focus on using your core muscles or your arms will get tired."

"Yes, ma'am," I say sarcastically.

She looks over her shoulder and the glint of mischief in her eyes flares before she swishes the paddle over the surface of the water and splashes me with a mouthful of chilly May water.

"I'm in charge here. There are strong currents out along the coast," she says sternly. "You're my responsibility and I want to get you back safely. Please…take it seriously."

It dawns on me she is really worried about me and it's my fault she thinks I'm useless in a kayak. I'm already on thin ice with her, I won't risk making her feel foolish for wasting so much time explaining things I already know.

I answer in earnest, "Tell me what to do."

She is satisfied with my cooperation, and we continue to paddle out of the harbor, gliding over the ocean waves toward the jagged outline of the Maine coastline. She tells me a well-practiced history of the old oceanfront buildings. I can imagine a younger, sun-kissed Eliza, excited to meet new people, telling them about the tidal lagoons, hidden passages, and secret inlets. Pointing to birds and sea creatures.

I ask her questions so I can hear her voice over the seagulls and the water lapping on the side of the kayak.

In the spring light, her eyes are golden, and she vibrates with energy. Her body moves with such precision and poise. She's breathtaking.

The fine hairs at the back of her neck pull my focus to the junction with her shoulder. It looks like the perfect spot to press my lips.

The list of reasons I shouldn't imagine how her skin would taste after hours spent on the open sea taunts me.

I don't know if I can trust her. She just ended an eight-year relationship. She's not the casual type.

It doesn't help I haven't had sex in a very long time and she is a fantasy come to life. A sweet small-town girl with a body I want to pin to the nearest flat surface. Her husky voice in the morning messing with my head.

She's also not the type of woman my father envisioned for me.

"You didn't need that Laura." He said her name with a disgusted curl of his lip. "When the time comes, we'll find a suitable wife for the Rawlings name."

"You mean for me. A suitable wife for me. One I'll spend the rest of my life with."

"Don't be dramatic, boy. You will marry a woman from a good family to give you an heir that will help our company grow."

For the first time in my life, I had the urge to punch my father.

If he was still alive I would've gone along with the arranged marriage, as I had with every decision he made. There was no point in fighting him, it did nothing. The thought feeds the festering pool of resentment bubbling inside ever since I realized I was a pawn in my father's plans. My happiness or wants never factored in. I had no expectations for a real marriage.

Am I free of that duty now that my father is dead? The idea never crossed my mind for the past three years. Until now.

"We'll rest here. You must be tired." She points to a small sandy beach.

Eliza stretches and a sliver of pale skin beckons me beneath the hem of her T-shirt. All this paddling is turning me into a hormonal teenager. Then she surprises me by opening the hatches in the bow and stern and taking out two dry bags. When did she sneak them in?

The first bag lands on my chest and it's softer than it looked.

"Put the blanket under that tree." Bossy Eliza is something else.

She then proceeds to take out water, dried fruits, beef jerky, and unsalted crackers.

"That's what he could spare," she said with an apologetic shrug. "I didn't imagine you'd care for it. Guessed we'd be back to the car in thirty minutes."

"You're so good at this I didn't even realize how long we've been out there," I tell her, and she tries to hide a satisfied grin.

"You didn't do too bad either. For a rookie." The proud wide smile imprints on my brain and travels down, flaring up my nervous system like fireworks.

We enjoy the well-earned snack, sitting so close I revel in the warmth of her skin, and she asks me about the places I've traveled. I ask her about her job at the paper factory and I find out her ex-boss is the human equivalent of a leech. We fight over the last bites, and I win when our fingers graze and she pulls back, blushing.

"The epitome of fine dining. The sand adds an interesting texture."

We laugh and forget who we are until the golden light of the sun setting covers the water in flickering stained glass.

In these moments I'm hit with an undeniable truth I'll have to leave behind, hidden between the rustle of the birch trees and the fizzing sound of the waves hitting the beach.

I savor the time spent with this woman who's too curious for her own good. I especially enjoy bringing out her feisty side and that she's not afraid to be herself around me. Such a peculiar feeling to be somebody's safe space.

Eliza keeps sneaking glances when our knees touch and I itch to take her hand and say the silliest things. Such as, *I love the smell of your shampoo.*

"Do I have a funny sunburn?"

"It's the first time I've seen you so relaxed. You're a different person."

"Equally handsome," I joke, to relieve the weight of her attention.

"I don't know about that." She pinches my chin and angles my head so she can have a better look and my heart is in my throat. Her eyes sparkle like amber in the golden glow when she traces the line of my jaw. The pink tip of her tongue slides over her lower lip when she zeroes in on my mouth and I hold my breath. To my disappointment, Eliza drops her hand and averts her gaze. "Your face has weird angles," she says.

It's such an innocent gesture but my insides twist and I wish she'd be bold enough and crash her lips on mine. Slim chance after I've been the one to pull back whenever we get too close.

Should I do it?

"It's time to go," she says, getting up.

The moment passes and I'm grateful I'm saved from complicating our peculiar arrangement.

"I've got a surprise for you," Eliza says as we leave the little island. Her nose is red from the sun and the wind, copper strands frame her face, and her smile is so bright it tugs at my heart.

We paddle until dark falls, and she guides us toward another enclave.

"Were you waiting for nightfall to throw me in the water undetected?"

She ignores me. "In this area, bioluminescent plants and little creatures get trapped between these little islands and they bloom and multiply."

She lifts her paddle, and we glide forward a few feet. "Give it a stroke."

I bypass the lame joke on the tip of my tongue and do as she tells me. The sea lights up beneath us and I'm stunned. We've fallen into the sky, surrounded by living stars.

The iridescent white light weaves strands of silver through her hair and sprinkles shards of stars in her eyes. She's out of this world.

I'm lost for words and overwhelmed when she smiles fondly at my awestruck expression.

"Beautiful, isn't it?" she says, swirling her paddle in the galactic soup.

"Magical," I say, looking at her. Saying it out loud for the first time.

Eliza reaches the front door before I bolt to check if it's her scumbag ex.

"I'm looking for a brooding big oaf," the hesitant voice I recognize instantly says from the porch. "I must have the wrong address."

"You'll find him in the living room. Can't miss the dark clouds and ravens circling his head," Eliza says, amused.

Adam laughs and I catch the glint of interest when he steps in. I'm familiar with it and I don't like it one bit.

Usually, Adam is one of the few people I'm always glad to talk to. It's been like that from the moment he sat next to me during our first class at Harvard. He hasn't left my side ever since. Even when Laura entered the picture, and it was obvious she couldn't stand him. The feeling was reciprocated, but Adam knew better than to say anything about her. I was too caught up in my first real relationship to care.

"What the hell are you doing here?"

He's tired and pale and I'm worried he's partying too much again. It's been a recurring cycle for the past seven years. It began when Jackie left for an MBA in London out of the blue and it got worse when our father died, and she came back. I never got the truth out of any of them.

"It's been over a month," Adam laughs and lunges for a hug. "I missed your pretty face and sunny disposition."

Eliza giggles and the sound goes straight to my dick.

"Carter, don't be rude, introduce me to this lovely lady." He turns back to Eliza, all charm, and a ball of possessiveness unfurls in the pit of my stomach.

"Why would I do that to her?" I play it off as a joke, but I'm not keen on letting her anywhere near Adam.

She scoffs. "Eliza. I'm renting Carter the cabin."

Adam holds her hand a moment too long and I find myself dragging the annoying idiot to the back porch. He sits and levels me with a questioning look.

"Anything new at the office?" Small talk is not part of our routine.

"Really. Are we doing this?"

I pretend not to notice the questioning look on his face. "That's what I'm interested in."

"It seemed to me your interests lie somewhere else," he says, tilting his head toward the cabin.

One reason Adam is so good at his job is he doesn't miss anything. I'm aware he's hunting for hints, so I decide to stay silent.

He doesn't push for now, but I know him too well to hope he'll drop it entirely.

"How are you?" His worry is genuine, and I tell him the truth.

"Honestly, better. If you say anything to my mother, I'll deny it, but she might have been onto something."

He snorts. "I'll take it to my grave."

"I'm still trying to find workarounds."

"I'd be worried if you weren't."

"My employees are too scared or ethical to go behind their backs. I'm relying on bits and pieces and what you've been finding out. It's frustrating, to say the least."

"Carter, besides some nosy reporters, nobody's making waves. Even Alicia is minding her own business."

"Never mind her. She doesn't know anything relevant for the press." I take a deep breath and relax. Adam is someone I can confide in. "After everything I've put into the company, it's hard not being—"

"In control and overworked?"

My cutting answer is interrupted by Eliza bringing out a tray with fresh lemonade.

"Sorry, I'll leave this here for you." She nods politely at Adam.

"Oh no, please sit with us. I bet you're better company than this old wet blanket."

She gives him a shy smile and looks at me for approval. Of course, she thinks I don't want her company after the way I've been acting, when all I want is to be in her orbit.

I pull out the chair for her and there's a fleeting hint of surprise on her face before she murmurs, "Thanks."

The traitor shamelessly flirts with her, and I grit my teeth to stop myself from going off on him. They talk about the cabin and she's wary at first, but Adam knows how to make people comfortable and open to sharing details about themselves.

It's the first time I'm jealous of Adam because nothing holds him back and Eliza shares with him more about her passion for design and reconditioning than she did with me. When he makes her laugh so hard her head snaps back, I have to remind myself my best friend was there for me during the darkest moments of my life.

When I'd been a wreck and my father wanted me to continue with his plan like nothing happened, Adam was the only one who understood what I was going through. The only person I could talk to about it. My father didn't allow wallowing. *It's not dignified for a Rawlings. It was for the best and in time you'll realize it.*

"You're entitled to compensation for putting up with his morning grumpiness." Adam brings me back to the discussion. "Morning classes with him were torture."

The cheeky vixen smirks. "I've learned to feed him first and let him play with his toys."

I huff. "Look who's talking. You have the grace of a bear out of hibernation when you stomp out of the bedroom."

She's wearing a loose pair of short shorts, and her skin looks so soft it's distracting. Her muscles flex when she crosses her legs and an image of having them wrapped around me takes shape, and I have to adjust myself discreetly.

"I'd have no problem waking up to her. I'd find a way to tame this wilding." Adam forgets he's not talking to one of his one-night-stands he comes on to in bars.

I see red.

"Watch your mouth. You don't speak to her like that." I squash his nonsense quickly.

He was a playboy in college, always talking about his hookups, dragging me to parties when Laura was working. The only reason I don't throw him out is because when I asked him, he's also the one who just hung out in my room, munching snacks and studying.

Adam grins and apologizes, nodding slowly like he's just confirmed something he already suspected.

"Old ways are hardwired."

I don't care he's my best friend; she deserves to be treated with respect and she should know it.

Eliza's hazel eyes are wide and that pretty blush, which I enjoy more than I should, caresses her cheekbones.

"He was kidding." Eliza puts her hand on my arm, and our surroundings fade away for a second.

I take Adam for lunch in the bay area so we can talk about the new governmental contracts, regulation changes, the shit our biggest competitor is up to, and the internal rumor mill. A twinge of guilt makes me regret leaving Eliza behind and I wonder if she ate this time. But finding her attractive and trusting her are two different things. I can't have her overhear sensitive information about my company.

"I should visit you more often," Adam says on the drive to the airport. I know he's baiting me, and I don't want to play his game.

"You do look like something dragged out of the Hudson. Need the fresh Maine air to put some color in your ashen post-bender glow?"

"Speaking about rosy cheeks—"

"Let's not."

"She's a lovely woman. I might call her. Maybe she wants to visit New York."

"If you so much as breath in her direction I'll bury you alive under the new headquarters in Midtown. We just broke ground. I still have time."

Adam doesn't say anything, and I don't have to look to know he got what he wanted. The smug bastard.

"You're an idiot."

"I don't need a lecture."

"No, you need someone to whack some sense into that thick skull."

"Is that a threat?"

"You know I don't get my hands dirty." He laughs. "I'll call Logan."

"She's…" I scramble for an argument that makes sense. "Too nice."

"Oh, the horror," Adam deadpans.

"I'll come back home in June. She's not the casual type."

"Did she tell you that?"

I refuse to entertain this conversation and talk with Adam about Eliza's sexual habits.

He heaves a long-suffering sigh, "I get the whole"— he waves his hand around to find a word for the subject we've been avoiding—"*scare* messed you up. But you won't die if you have sex. Enjoy life a little. You almost ran out of chances."

I mull over his words on the drive back. Thoughts about Eliza have plagued my brain for weeks and they've become more persistent, even when I did my best to distance myself. Lately, it's been worse.

Every time I catch a glimpse of her bare legs, I'm itching to press my fingertips along the backs of her knees and find out if her flesh is as soft as it looks. To fill my ears with the noises she'd make if I teased her until she was overcome with frustration.

Maybe I'd get over it if I surrendered to the pull. Just once.

At the last moment, I notice the yard sale in front of a dilapidated Victorian house and hit the brakes. She told Adam about going to auctions hoping to find a vintage light fixture.

"Excellent choice," a bespectacled teenager says. "It's an original mouth-blown glass lantern. The fern pattern is hand cut."

"How much?"

"My Gramps says fifty bucks, but you look like you could pay more," the girl says with confidence, despite her colorful braces.

"You're not supposed to say it out loud when you want to hustle money out of your mark," I tell her, handing over several large bills. Her eyes almost pop out and I can't help smiling.

My good mood gives way to doubts when I park outside the cabin.

"I thought you'd convinced Adam to smuggle you back to New York," Eliza says absentmindedly, typing at her laptop on the kitchen island.

"He's rather attached to his balls. Doesn't want to cross my mother."

"You make her sound scary." She shudders. "Tell me if she visits so I can find a hideout."

I laugh awkwardly because my mother is the last thing on my mind right now.

"I found this." I show her the light fixture. "It practically rolled into the road—"

"No way," Eliza shrieks, jumping off the barstool. "It's gorgeous. The glass is intact," she coos. "Where did—" Her mouth is agape and her eyes are shiny.

I have only a second to brace myself before she charges forward and envelops me in a bone-crushing hug. My free hand has a mind of its own and slides up her back, holding her tight to my chest. Plastered to my front I can feel her inhale, the pounding of her heart and the sweet pressure of her breasts.

Her arms around me confine me in the most delicious way.

Eliza, unaware of my turmoil, rises on the tips of her feet and plants her soft lips on my cheek.

It's quick and innocent but it dissolves the restraint I've been holding onto for dear life. It didn't matter. I can't stay away and deny the swell of longing when I'm this close to her.

I don't want to let go and when she finally looks at me the air around us becomes heavy with expectation. It pulses with desire and unspoken curiosity.

We stare at each other and her breathing becomes shallow, with dark eyes and a fucking sexy blush blooming over her cleavage. My mouth is dry and every part of her body touching mine is on fire. I want to thread my fingers through the light copper hair haunting my dreams, but she puts her palms on my chest and very gently pushes herself out of the embrace.

Disappointment sprouts in my gut, but I don't want to push too hard. "If it's not what you wanted I can take it somewhere else or—"

"No! We're not throwing this beauty away. Some polishing and wires and it will be as good as new."

The way she caresses the brass and checks the glasswork is so delicate.

Her eyes sparkle with joy now and she's talking to herself, planning the steps.

"Maybe I can help you," I clear my throat. "Or just watch," I fumble.

She smiles so brightly, like I gave her the biggest compliment.

"Sure, city boy. If you don't mind getting dirty."

The thought of getting dirty with her prompts another wave of inappropriate images. The lack of sex must be really getting to me if my dick is triggered this fast by an innocent comment.

CHAPTER NINETEEN

ELIZA

No matter how much I toss and turn there's no comfort from the frustrating ache wreaking havoc through my body. The sheets rub harshly against my flushed skin.

It's a restlessness that kept swelling to unbearable heights ever since I made the mistake of hugging Carter. The brief collision made a certain part of my body pulse and I'm close to breaking point. I need something. A release.

I throw the comforter away, irritated, and head for the kitchen. Maybe some water will help me cool down.

My body is throbbing from the warmth of his body against mine, the imprint of his hand on my back still burning, pooling lava in my belly. I want to scream and shed my skin.

I did my best to bury any attraction toward Carter. It's been extremely difficult this past week with all the time we spent together.

It was just a hug, Eliza! I don't even remember the last time I had sex with Jared, or more importantly, when I had an orgasm, but this is ridiculous. The heat of the moment was all in my head. Carter has made it more than clear he's not interested.

The creak of the floorboards startles me and I spin, grasping the kitchen counter in a death grip.

Carter is stock still, a statue in the semi-dark entry-way, his chest hardly moving. "I'm sorry, I didn't mean to wake you."

His stare is too intense, and my eyes drop to the floor. "I can't sleep."

Without a word, he steps closer. And closer. The intensity in his gaze is electric, a spark ready to ignite this charged air between us. I blink and we're standing toe to toe. The movement sucks the air out of the room, my lungs burning. I'm not imagining the hungry look in his eyes.

"Something bothering you, kitten?" His voice is low, but it fills the space around us. The dim light from the lantern lamp plays in his eyes and it's hypnotizing.

I swallow and he follows the movement, biting the inside of his lip. Carter rests a cool hand on the side of my neck, his thumb slowly pressing up and down. The touch is scorching, and it wouldn't surprise me if it left a mark on my skin.

"Maybe I can help you." He leans closer and his breath caresses my face. He smells of clean sheets and the honey soap I put in his room. I want to bury my face in the crook of his neck, but my knees are liquid. I'm afraid if I make a sound, the spell will break, and he will retreat again. I've yearned for his touch for so long. It's a moment I want to savor as much as I can until he puts his walls back up.

The muscles in his arms strain, holding back. "Are you going to let me?"

His question ignites me, heat rushing to my cheeks. I just nod, eagerness dripping down my bloodstream.

Carter's hand moves to my jaw and tips my head, forcing me to look straight into his molten silver eyes. A sharp surge of desire disconnects my brain's ability to work properly.

"I need you to say it," he says, almost pleading.

A shaky *yes* escapes my lips and it's enough for him to crowd me against the counter. The weight of his body is a delicious pressure, and my palms slide up his solid chest, clutching fistfuls of his T-shirt.

His face inches closer and I'm ready to taste his lips when he tilts my head slightly and grazes the sensitive skin under my ear. There's no time to feel disappointed because his nose slowly follows the line of my neck, and my strangled whimper fills the silence of the cabin when Carter's other hand slides to my waist. His thumb draws circles around my hip bone and with deliberate feathery touches, he trails the skin above the waistband of my shorts.

"I did my best to stay away," he says gruffly before dragging his lips over my shoulder. "It's been torture not to reach out and touch you."

His strained words are heavy with desire and anguish. I love the idea of being wanted to the point of making him break his rigid rules. It turns me on even more.

"Touch me now," I pant. This bold version of me is scary but any thoughts are dispersed into the wind when his fingers trail over the cotton panties while his tongue dips into the hollow between my collarbones.

The tips of his fingers ghost against the fabric between my legs and I shudder before a wave of warmth courses through my body. I'm acutely aware of everything.

The smell of tea herbs mixed in with his scent and the chilly breeze coming in through the cracked window.

Carter leans back, eyes wide, his breathing shallow. "You blush so prettily when you're turned on."

I want to feel more of him, and my hands roam the outline of his broad shoulders. I don't want to get lost in the swirling pool of his gaze, so I thread my fingers through his hair, pull gently, and skim my lips along his jaw. I'm rewarded with a deep noise in the back of his throat and the solid proof of his arousal pressing against my belly.

Tucking the seam of my panties to the side his fingers caress the bare skin, already coated in my need for him. The searing pleasure erases any trace of embarrassment I expected to feel.

A content hum echoes deep in his chest. "Were you thinking of me? That's what's been keeping you awake?" His breath over my lips makes me shiver.

When the pad of his thumb grazes the skin above my curls, my muscles strain with anticipation. He circles, teasing, not quite where I want him.

"Answer me, kitten," he rasps.

"Yes," I moan. "I couldn't stop thinking about you."

"Good girl." The low growl is intoxicating.

He slips a finger in and I clench around him, my back arching. His movements are slow, torturous.

"More," I beg in between incoherent mews. I don't recognize myself as I shamelessly rock against his hand, chasing my release.

Carter's lips find the tender spot behind my ear again and I squirm, overwhelmed.

"Be patient. I'll give you what you need." His breath is hot, gliding over my skin, and he increases the rhythm.

The edge of the counter digs into my backside with every thrust and my mouth pops open with silent murmurs of pleasure. Heavy exhales and the slap of his palm against my skin bounce off the wooden walls until a night bird's hoot pierces the sounds filling my ears.

"Oh, God damn it." He sucks in air through his teeth and pushes another finger in.

My eyes close. I'm lost in the cadence of his movements and the pulsing heat traveling through my nerves.

"Look at me," he says, curling his fingers inside me, and I choke back a whimper.

Waves of blinding arousal crash down at his touch. "I'm so close," I mouth into his chin.

"That's it. Let go for me." His expression is pure determination, beads of sweat wetting his hairline. His hold on the back of my head is firm and for the first time in my life, I quiet the noise in my brain and let go of any restraint.

I only feel the drag of his fingers, his minty breath on my face, and the drugging power of his body towering over me. With a firm swipe of his thumb over my clit, Carter lights a fire that sizzles like a match's head through my body.

My muscles are close to snapping from the strain and I wrap my arms around his neck, pulling him as close as I can, until my heart beats against his and I'm weightless, floating, and dazed.

The floor groans under him, snapping me back to myself and I lean back. Carter's eyes are almost black when he slowly slides his hand out of my shorts and without breaking eye contact, he wraps his lips around his wet fingers and licks them with a satisfied sound.

"Divine," he hums.

My mouth goes dry. I reach for the strings of his pajama pants, but he stills my attempt.

"Not now." His voice is raspy and velvety against my skin. Is there going to be a next time?

"I want to return the favor." I try to negotiate, hiding my frustration.

"You need to rest, come on." Next thing I know the floor disappears from under my feet and I'm cradled in Carter's arms.

My heart starts racing. He didn't want me to touch him. What did I just do? We're stuck together for at least another month. Different scenarios swirl inside my head, panic slowly creeping in.

He places me into the bed and crawls in behind me.

"Don't overthink it," Carters says into my temple.

His warmth and soothing smell relax my muscles. The steady rhythm of his heart and the strong arm holding me tight finally lull me to sleep and my mind drifts away, over gray clouds and rivers of honey.

The weight of what happened last night in the kitchen crashes down on me, alone in bed and mortified beyond words. Bold Eliza is a distant memory. Flashes of Carter's hands on me run through my brain and an ache deep in my belly gradually builds, adding to my anxiety.

What're my options?

Hide in the bedroom until he goes to sleep and make a run for it in the middle of the night? Pitch a tent under the half-finished roof of the tiny house?

Be a grown-up about it and admit the lapse in judgment. There's no other way to color it since he made it clear he regretted it and I'm supposed to focus on getting my life together and stop embarrassing myself in front of Carter.

God.

I remember the noises I made and how I completely unraveled over my kitchen countertop. I can never face the man again. An avalanche of thoughts floods my mind until a fully-formed headache and an exploding bladder push me out of the bed I hid in longer than necessary.

I'm not a coward! That's what I tell myself as I tiptoe down the hallway, an intruder in my own house, until I spot the back of his head. He's in his usual spot on the couch with his tablet, calmly reading the news.

Small mercies, I guess. I can grab a glass of lemonade undetected, and we can both pretend nothing happened. I'm ready to clap myself on the back for a good stealth job when his voice freezes me in front of the open cabinet.

"You slept in today." Carter's tone is even, still reading the article.

"Yes. Hi. Morning." I stumble through an attempt at playing it casual.

"Did you have a good sleep?"

The glass I'm holding clanks on the counter and I stare at it, still not able to look at him. "Yes, thank you." It comes out breathy and I want to curse myself for my lack of composure.

"You don't need to be embarrassed." There's a softness in his words, giving me the courage to lift my head.

As usual, he betrays no emotion, but I find relief in the lack of embarrassment or disgust. Instead, I'm thrown off-kilter by the comforting warmth of his eyes.

"I'm…not?"

"Come here." He pats the couch, his gaze never leaving me.

Dragging my feet to sit on the opposite side, I rest my chin on my knees, my stomach bubbling with uncertainty.

"We're two adults who enjoyed a moment of exploration," he says matter-of-factly. "I'm leaving, you're busy with the home. There's not much space for complications in either of our lives."

"Right. No complications," I answer flatly, stumbling along his line of thought.

"Nothing has to change. We can enjoy each other's company in the meantime."

"Ihm," is my less-than-articulate reply, until my brain catches up to his meaning. "Are you suggesting a roommates-with-benefits deal?" I squeak out.

"If it's something you'd be interested in." This time he smiles, and I'm thrown into a loop of self-doubt, shock, and interest.

I was never the casual type. Jared was my first real boyfriend. Maybe it's time I stopped obsessing over building my fantasy family and have some fun until I get my life on track.

"Consider it. If you're not comfortable with the idea, we can go back to business as usual."

His mask of nonchalance is firmly in place, but I catch the hopeful pitch of his suggestion. Despite the needles of anxiety prickling my fingertips, I still want to get more of Carter. Last night he didn't let me touch him and the want creeps back with every whiff of his expensive cologne and the way his muscles coil when he pivots in his seat.

"Do you have anywhere else to be?" He interrupts my fall into X-rated fantasies.

"No," I answer, unsure of his intentions. "I have to be at the shop after lunch." The small windowless office and the endless rows of orders and product series are mind-numbing. But there will be a check at the end of the week.

"Can we sit together for a while?"

His request catches me off guard. My body is tense and alert in the silence.

Carter hooks his palm behind my ankle and I nearly jump out of my skin. "What're you doing?"

"Relax." He's dragging his finger over my ankle in soothing circles.

The warmth of his hand seeps into my body with each stroke. I finally relax into the soft cushion and close my eyes. As crazy as it sounds, I trust Carter.

"Did you get this scar climbing trees like the wilding I imagine you were?"

My drowsiness evaporates and I realize what he's been looking at for the past five minutes. Most of the time I forget about it and I'm not too fond of remembering how I got it—another mark in the tally of Eliza's history of doing stupid things to be accepted and loved.

"I was a wilding on a bike. Kids' stuff." I brush it off.

His fingertips dig a little deeper around the red mark. Not enough to hurt, but it takes me back to last night and to the way he pressed his thumb between my legs. I have to swallow a small sigh.

"You could indulge me. My childhood was pretty sterile," Carter says, giving me a charming smile capable of altering my brain chemistry.

Why is he interested in stories about my crappy childhood?

"Fine. It was one summer when I was seven. The family had an older son and he used to pull the other kids on a rickety bike with his truck. One time he let me ride it and I crashed into the gate." That's the short and least sad version.

The older kids always messed with me, but I couldn't say anything.

Carter tilts his head and clasps my ankle. The heat of his palm squeezing goes straight to my core.

"You have a terrible poker face." He smirks when I gasp, offended. "I'd appreciate the whole story please."

How the hell does he know there's more to it? The way he pays such close attention unnerves me and the truth spills out.

"I wasn't usually invited to join in, so when he asked, I was so happy they'd finally warmed up to me. And it looked so fun." I focus on the hem of my shirt.

I remember how fast joy turned into pure terror when Terry kept going faster on the dirt road. "He didn't slow down this time, raced faster toward the farm's gate." I was so scared. I thought he was going to kill me. "He swerved before the old metal gate, and I crashed into it. I don't remember much because I hit my head and passed out."

I do remember the blinding pain. I was sure I'd lose my leg.

Carter is silent and I brace for the *poor Eliza* speech. His face has a gray sheen to it and he looks in pain.

"Tell me they didn't leave you with them after that," he says, placing his other hand on my foot.

"They didn't have to." I smile bitterly. "The first thing I heard when I woke up in the hospital was the father yelling at me for damaging the gate." I don't know why but I laugh. It's preposterous now, but Carter doesn't join in. "They were the ones who sent me way." Again.

Carter's frown deepens. I'm sorry for him. This isn't the funny childhood story he was looking for.

"Don't worry. It wasn't that bad." I laugh it off. "The sad thing is I was left with a crippling fear of riding bikes," I huff. "I can't get on one to save my life."

Such a shame. There are so many bike routes around the coast and the forest that it would be lovely to ride along during the off-season.

Carter opens his mouth when my phone vibrates on the coffee table. Carl is relentless. I slam the phone on the smooth wood. The more time passes the more aggressive he gets and he keeps calling and messaging.

A raised eyebrow prompts me to tell Carter the whole story. It's been exhausting stressing over it, especially since I can't find a solution.

"Why didn't you tell me? Are you going to go out with him?" His tone is sharp, and the implications slice me like a whip.

I yank my feet from his lap, anger surging through my veins.

"He's just a creep." I raise my voice. "Is that your first thought when you look at me? That I'm desperate, willing to do anything for money?"

His jaw twitches. The hard stare settles bitterly in my stomach.

"I see," I say in disbelief, stepping back. I never learn. Maybe I deserve to be taken for a ride since I keep falling for meaningless gestures.

"Call him," he says, a dangerous undertone to his request. "And give me the phone."

Chapter Twenty

CARTER

It barely rings before the man who has no idea he'll be unemployed for the rest of his life answers. I take a lungful of fresh air on the back porch to calm myself. I can't make things worse for Eliza.

"Sweet Eliza, you finally came to your senses?" He chuckles in a way that makes my skin crawl. "Tomorrow night at my place. Dress nice, but not too many layers, yeah?" He laughs. "What do you say?"

"Good evening. Carter Rawlings speaking. I'm representing Ms. Miller regarding her departure from Vista Pine. Am I speaking with Carl Davies, Ms. Miller's superior?"

"Yes," the piece of shit says in a confused voice.

When a man is in her corner, he's not so brave. The pig.

"It has come to my attention that there's an issue with Ms. Miller's final paycheck."

"Um…no. I'm not sure. I have to check with HR. I'm sure it'll sort itself out."

"Make sure you do work things out or I'll make things very difficult for you."

"Hey! Who're you to threaten me?" He suddenly finds the courage to speak up. "I don't appreciate what you're insinuating."

"Our conversation is being recorded. For legal purposes of course. It can easily find its way into your HR and CEO's inboxes, together with the texts you've been sending Ms. Miller."

A ragged breath is the only sound on the other end.

"Fix it today. Also. Another slimy text and you'll lose more than your job."

"I'll take care of her damn paycheck." Carl ends the call suddenly.

"How rude." I tut.

I send every text and the recording to my phone, then to Adam.

CARTER: Starting tomorrow this man is unemployable.

ADAM: Since you ask so nicely. The outdoors has done wonders for your people skills.

Eliza hovers in the doorway, clenching her fists in the soft cotton of her shorts. I recognize that look. This time I'm ready when she lunges and I welcome her with open arms, my anger at that piece of trash chased away by the tight grip and the weight of her body.

For a few seconds, I allow myself a moment of weakness and rest my chin on top of her head. We talked about casual and fun, but it feels more complicated when the need to protect and comfort her trumps those boundaries.

Eliza pushes back and beams. "You're so cool and sure of yourself. Teach me, please! Please! I want to be like you when I grow up."

She doesn't know what she's asking. My father's type of teaching came with a hefty dose of numbness and malice. *"Go for the soft spots, find the opponent's weakness."* It was his fatherly advice when my only friend in eighth grade finished top of our class, beating me by a slight margin. I won the following year, but we were no longer friends. Ruthlessness revs my engines whenever I come across a competitor. It's the reason Adam and Logan are my only friends.

"Don't wear your heart on your sleeve. You're so transparent. Easy prey."

Taking her chin in my hand, I'm not sure if I'm giving her business advice or warning her not to be so open. Whatever is going on between us has an end date.

"Got it." She swallows and I trace the movement, tensing when unmistakable desire burns in her eyes.

I brush the spot under her lower lip with my thumb. "I don't think you do."

I leave her behind, looking confused, unaware I'm one "please" away from fixing all her problems if she asks. Or bending her over the railing and fucking her senseless.

Whichever comes first.

Those minutes in the kitchen were the most erotic experience of my life. I could get addicted to the softness of her skin under my fingertips. I got off on her moans and the look in her eyes when she came. But I was ready to pretend nothing happened after reason slapped me in the face and stopped me from taking it further.

The problem is I haven't had nearly enough of her. Once the fantasy has formed it's impossible to ignore. It coils around my thoughts, mocking me.

She's not the casual type, no matter what she claims.

A deceptive calm has settled over our routine these last few days. The hunger is still there, simmering under the surface, and we're pretending not to notice the tension ready to snap any moment.

Talking to Robertson, I keep getting distracted by the shape of Eliza sitting at the end of the small deck. Evening light pierces through the clouds above her and hits the water around the wooden platform and her hair. She is a fire fairy toying at the edge of the water, a naughty creature tempting me.

"Call Adam off," Joseph says. "He's getting on my nerves, sticking his nose in everybody's business."

"He's worth his checks." My steps take me to her. The pull I can't resist scares me, but I don't want to fight it today.

"Damn it, Carter. Get a hobby. Try birdwatching or something," he huffs, aggravated. "Nobody wants to jeopardize your legacy, OK?" he says softly and I almost regret giving him a hard time.

Eliza's swirling her toes in the water in a state of serenity I have no idea how to achieve. I decide to join her anyway.

"Is this some sort of countryside Thai fish spa?"

Eliza's nose crinkles. "The call made you extra grumpy," she says.

I rest my palms on the weathered boards and lean back. "Grumpy implies a level of cuteness. I don't qualify."

"What do you mean? You're cute," she says and blushes.

"Please don't make this day worse for me," I groan. "Cute?"

"There's nothing wrong with cute, I'm cheering you up."

"Not being in the same category as a newborn calf would help," I grumble.

She heaves an exasperated sigh and looks at me with a quirky pout. "Are you going to make me say it?"

"Yep." It's childish but I want to hear it from her.

"This town has never seen so much hotness and smoldering in one person," she says in mock wonder. "They're talking about commissioning a bust. The lady who owns the souvenir shop said she's planning to sell cuddling pillows with your face on them. It will surely save her business," she finishes and her lips twitch.

"Sarcasm is the lowest form of wit, Eliza. I'm disappointed. I expected more from you."

"Stop fishing for compliments." Eliza shakes her head. "You even have sexy toes," she grumbles and it's so ridiculous it makes me laugh and she bursts into giggles.

The sound keeps carving at the hard scales around that soft tissue of vulnerability. Each day it's getting more difficult to stop her from etching her way in.

I'm more in tune with her than I've ever been with another human being. Sounds that have become so familiar tell me everything about her mood. The morning clattering in the kitchen, the frenzied scratching of the coloring pens against the drawing pad. If the sound of her favorite home improvement shows travels under my door past midnight, she had a bad day at the store. She's in a good mood if she works in her shed early Saturday morning.

It's odd how much comfort this tempo brings.

I've been using this cream for nearly half a year and the scar is still an eyesore. It stands out in stark contrast with my light skin.

Days in the hospital, weeks of recovery, and panic attacks. Those weeks come back every time I look at the jagged scar stretching down above my navel. A constant reminder of how weak I am. Of how close I was to leaving Jackie and my mother alone.

I have to shake these dark thoughts out of my head. I refuse to admit what I could have lost. Back at the office, I filled my time with work and it's what I wanted to do now.

Instead, I'm stuck in this confining silence, fighting off an unwise attraction toward the woman who invaded my space and mind.

A faint noise catches my attention and it's too late to pull my T-shirt on. I'm bare-chested, wearing only my pajama bottoms when the door swings open and a bleary-eyed Eliza stops in her tracks.

"Oh, sorry," she rasps. "I thought you were still—"

Her lips part on a gasp when her eyes catch the red line slicing my chest.

The blood rushes to my head and I'm overwhelmed with instant rage. "Get out!"

Eliza blinks slowly, her eyebrows arching. She's the first person who's seen it besides my medical staff. I don't want to hear what she wants to say. It's too much. My lungs turn to stone.

"I said get the hell out," I bellow, making her jump. I turn my back on her, clutching the sink, hiding my shame.

Her stricken face reflects in the mirror before she closes the door in a hurry.

It takes me a few minutes to get my breathing under control and compose myself. Guilt is already trickling down into my stomach.

I spend more time dressing and bracing myself. I can already hear her in the kitchen.

"Hey, Carter—"

"There is nothing to discuss." There's no way in hell I'm talking about it with her.

She comes closer, worry and confusion etched on her face. "But I—"

"Can you, for once, stop pestering me," I grit out, the blood rushing through my ears.

Her face hardens, eyes narrowed to slits.

I hate being exposed. Hate she saw it.

Eliza gently places the damn teacup in front of my chair on the little island. It's the blend she made for me, fixed the way I prefer.

Regret crushes me, but I don't know what to tell her. It's a subject I never talk about. If I could, I'd erase it from my memory.

"I'm going for a run. Don't wait up." I can't bear to look at her.

The run through the woods does little to calm the hailstorm raging within me. The house is mercifully empty when I return. The way she gives me space is a punch in the gut, the more I find out about her life. A girl who learned to avoid angry people. I don't want to be someone she is afraid of. She should feel safe. Always safe.

I decide to walk around Main Street, gaze unfocused on the colored storefronts and the people roaming the streets until night falls and the small town falls silent. Resting on a bench overlooking the harbor I pick apart my emotions, sorting through painful memories until the night's cold chills my bones.

The next day I'm surprised to find Eliza in her usual spot. Nothing in her demeanor gives away her state of mind, except for the glances she steals when I pretend to read.

She clears her throat and I instantly tense. "I want to address the elephant in the room."

"Must you?" My heart thunders between my ribs.

"I'm sorry I barged in," she says softly, locking eyes. "I know I'm meddlesome. But I'll never force you to talk about something you're not comfortable sharing."

Living with my father taught me to keep myself bottled up. He drilled into me the importance of not giving ammunition to others, of never being exposed because it can be used against you.

The sincerity in those warm eyes makes me want to tell her. To lay it down at her feet knowing she won't use it to hurt me. It's a certainty I can't shake. It's an undeniable truth and it scares me. Nobody has ever had this power over me.

She folds the kitchen towel with finality and continues. "That's all I wanted to say. I'll go to the site after work. Finn wants to talk to me about something." She grimaces. "I hope it's not another delay."

Before any words leave my mouth, she walks away with a soft smile and a wink that has me questioning what I thought I knew about myself when an unfamiliar heat rushes to my cheeks.

The day is a blur of heavy clouds of doubt and resolutions circling in and out of my head until the unmistakable metal grunt of her so-called truck pierces the silence. Every ounce of hesitation vanishes, and I let myself follow that invisible string leading me to Eliza.

This warmer night drew her out to the swing, where she's flipping through one of her DIY home improvement magazines.

The swing creaks under my weight and Eliza welcomes me with quiet amusement. I appreciate how she leaves me the space to talk if I want to. The light swing, the murmur of the forest, and her smell bring down my blood pressure.

"It was an ordinary day at the office." I focus on the tops of the trees swaying under the bright stars. "The usual argument with Joseph. I was tired, but it was nothing new with the long hours." I breathe in through my nose. "He was pestering me that I never took days off and saying I can't control all the aspects of the business because it will drive me insane."

The next part is the hardest. I only talked about it with my doctors.

"The pain didn't register at first, I was so riled up." I was overheating but I thought it was the anger directed at Joseph.

"The pressure became heavier until the tightness across my chest became unbearable. That's when the fear crept in." I knew something was very wrong and I had no control over it. Powerlessness choked me as the pain spread to my arms and clenched my jaw.

Eliza's cold palm slides over my fist. Her touch loosens the ropes of dread tightening around me in a death grip.

"The last thing I remember before it went dark was the panic of being helpless. Next time I was conscious was in the hospital, when I found out they had to cut me open."

The doctor had told me heart attacks in young people are not so uncommon. The workload, stress, and my family history were major factors. That's what killed my father, but I never thought it could happen to me.

Eliza keeps rubbing her thumb over my knuckles, but she's silent for a while and I don't have the courage to check if she's looking at me differently.

"How did you manage to keep this a secret?"

"Because I completely trust only five people in my life and my family makes generous donations to the hospital where I was treated. The rest signed an NDA."

I struggle to accept what happened and I hate talking about it. The weakness, the unshakable fear that it can happen again. The anti-anxiety medication helps, but it's still difficult and it's the main reason I don't want people to know. The stress and fear of another one has haunted me ever since I came back to life. I can't abandon my mother and sister. I have to be there for them and the family business.

Eliza's brows scrunch. "Why not tell everyone?"

"What does a heart attack at thirty-two say about me? About the future of the company?"

"That you're human. Is that so awful?" There's no judgment or reproach in her tone, but she's too naive.

A small sad smile is all I can give her. "It might be if people start thinking less of me. They can take what our family has built."

"I don't think less of you. You're still a giant unbearable arrogant prick," she says with a smirk.

The laughter bubbling out breaks the tension and my lungs finally function properly.

"Oh, shoot. And I tried to kill you with breakfast the first morning!" She slaps her hand over her lips, eyes going wide.

Another burst of laughter makes her face crumple. "I fixated on what I thought was healthy. I'm sorry. So, that's the reason I've been exiled here."

Eliza's mouth quirks. "You don't strike me as the kind of man who does things he doesn't want to. Your mom and sister are lucky you love them so much."

"They told me I had to be careful." It made me paranoid. "I'm sorry for being an asshole. You've been nothing but kind and I'm an ungrateful twit."

"It's OK."

My fingers thread through hers and I rest our hands on my chest. "No. Far from it. I'm sorry I yelled at you. I'm—" The words jam into a lump in my throat. "I'm ashamed of it. The scar."

"Is that why you," she hesitates, shy. "Wouldn't let me touch you?" she says quietly.

There's a rawness in the silence surrounding us. It's unfamiliar and daunting but she was so brave to show me who she is. Eyes sparkling in the moonlight, she raises her other hand and hesitates over my shirt. My lips part, but I don't stop her.

We could both feel it. The threshold we crossed into uncharted territory. But no one backs down and we stand together in this new space we've carved out of our fears and insecurities, filling it with fragile trust and something warm I can't define.

CHAPTER TWENTY-ONE

ELIZA

Carter's face is priceless when we pull up outside Thomas's old hardware store. I promised to show him my favorite spot in Silver Lake Falls and take him for walk around the town because it's part of the deal.

It also might have something to do with the constant guilt gnawing on my insides. He's usually uncomfortable any time he lets slip anything personal, but he looked in pain letting go of this big secret. Carter wouldn't have shared the story if I hadn't stumbled on him shirtless.

Tension lines the curve of his shoulders. He acts like I now have ammunition to hurt him, and it stings.

"You and I have very different views on sightseeing," he says in that dry and detached tone he uses as a shield.

"The entire town knows what happened with Jared. If I have to swallow the embarrassment of facing a ton of people who pity me, you can bear to spend five minutes here." Quinn is right, I'm hiding. I can't avoid meeting people who know me forever.

The old man is at his usual place, smoking and reading his paper.

"Morning, Thomas!"

He doesn't bother with pleasantries. Usually, he lets me roam around and pick what I need. "Check out the back for new colors," he grumbles behind the newspaper.

The shop has all kinds of supplies for fixing furniture, plus construction materials and an owner with a heart of gold. More than once, I was short for change and he'd write it in a notebook for next time. I always made sure to bake an extra pie for him on Thanksgiving.

"This time I'll need your help."

Thomas looks over his newspaper and I flash him my most charming grin.

"Finn gave me a list. Can you call me when you pack the materials?"

"So, you two get along?" he grunts, getting up.

"Yeah, he's been great. Helped me a lot."

"He's a good boy, that one. An' no wife," he says, cheerier than ever on his way to the counter. "Maybe bake him one of your pies."

I burst out laughing at his surprising and relentless meddling.

"It's no laughing matter, young lady. He's one hard-working man and you're not bad on the eyes. He can build you a house and fill it with babies."

"Thomas, you're an excellent wingman," I coo, playing along.

"Can we get on with it?" Carter's icy voice wipes the smile off my face. I hadn't even noticed he'd followed me into the store. He's tense. A deep vertical crease on his forehead darkening his gaze. We haven't been here too long. So impatient.

Thomas gives him a once-over and winks at me. What's that about? I give him my list and scurry outside, Carter following me closely.

"I'm done, you needn't be so rude. I come here often," I say, irritation lacing my words.

"Why is he pushing the foreman on you?"

He sounds angry but he schools his features when his palm wraps around my arm and turns me around. The energy surrounding him is different, something new.

"He's just being funny."

"What's so funny about pawning you off to a middle-aged man? He probably has kids."

"Finn?" I ask, distracted by the fact my back is now pressed against the truck, Carter's chest a hairbreadth away from mine. "He's my age, what're you talking about? No kids and single, as Sam constantly points out."

Carter's silence presses hard on my eardrums. His eyes swirl with a darker shade of silver and his jaw ticks.

"Sam said they worked together. I thought he was a guy in his fifties, with a beer belly and three kids at home." His tone is sharp, and I'd jump back if I had the space.

"No—"

He moves closer, the warmth of his body and the way he presses into me leaving me breathless. "And you've been alone with him all this time?"

"And his crew," I squeak. "What's gotten into you?" I ask, confused. Carter's eyes drop to my lips, his Adam's apple bobbing. It throws me off balance. He refused to kiss me the handful of times we were this close. It might be for the best, but it doesn't mean I don't crave it.

In my Carter-addled daze, a thought pops out of nowhere.

"Wait." It can't be. "Are you jealous?"

"Of course not," he scoffs, drawing back. "I'm a concerned roommate. Does this guy know what he's doing?"

"Yes, he's very good"—I grin at him—"with his hands."

I cackle and even his annoyed growl doesn't dampen my mood. Who knew Carter's jealousy was a boost of serotonin?

Dragging him along is more fun than I thought.

"That lady behind the counter is the gift shop owner." I point to a dark-haired hippie, draped in a sheer purple shawl. "She makes her business decisions after consulting her tarot cards. She's also one of the two tree wardens in Silver Lake Falls."

"Now I'm sure you're making fun of me…Is this something you read in a fantasy book?"

"You're such a city boy," I tease. "Next door is a martial arts studio run by an ex-marine. He's from away, but people love him. He also teaches the kids for free, even if he can't afford it."

"From away where?" Carter's upper lip curls in confusion.

"Oh, I mean he wasn't born here."

I show him some more places, giving a short introduction before taking him in to meet the locals.

As I feared, most come out from behind their counters and it's weird introducing Carter as a tourist renting the cabin. Roommates with benefits doesn't exactly cover it, since he's yet to cash in on his benefits, and casual is too soft a word for what's been going on lately, but I refuse to dwell on that.

Most of them bring up Jared.

"Lara's husband was at the bar, and he told my Jim. Then the baby announcement, oh, you poor thing."

"Yep."

"You're young. Still time to pop out some babies."

"Oh, thanks?"

"I'd be so embarrassed. Oh, my dear, I'd move to the West Coast. You're so brave."

I know they mean well, but after a few stops it's getting harder not to let the mask slip. I brace for another round at the art gallery when Carter steps in.

"Who curates the collections?" he asks the owner.

The woman basks in his attention and preens. "I'm an art major. Didn't Eliza tell you? She always asks for my opinion when she finishes a piece."

That's slightly inaccurate. She compulsively comments on them whenever she visits someone in town who has pieces I reconditioned. She's been relentlessly pushing me to rent one of her rooms and display a selection of refurbished antiques.

"Aren't they great?" Carter looks sideways at me, a ghost of a smile curving his lip.

"I keep telling her!" She waves excitedly. "I know a lot of people with deep pockets who love this kind of stuff."

I drift away, letting them chat, grateful for the change in the Jared topic. Having Carter as a buffer is not so bad.

By the time we reach the ocean-side boardwalk lined with seafood restaurants, I'm overwhelmed by the number of people stopping to talk to us. They're not only after the hot gossip about me. They're curious about Carter. It doesn't surprise me. He *is* striking. A quiet type of sophistication, built on money and power.

"The restaurant over there has the best view of the bay. If the owner walks in after 6pm with his shades on you can bet all your money he's high as a kite." He shared more about his personal life than was necessary the summer I worked there as a hostess. "After his divorce, he kept telling anyone who'd listen that marriage disrupted his timeline. He's going back to his youth to give it another go. Now he's living the life he should have. Or so he says."

"You know a lot about these people."

"I've lived here most of my life and when you're not important, almost invisible, people tend to get loose-tongued."

A strange shadow flashes over his features. "I'm not sure that's it," he says quietly.

"This guide gig is exhausting." I change the subject. "Let's visit Quinn, I need a pick-me-up."

The coffee shop is bustling at this hour with the growing wave of tourists. We're lucky to find a small table. A murmur of whispers catches my attention after Carter pulls the chair out for me. Women mostly sneak glances and talk in hushed voices. Is this the kind of attention Carter gets back in New York? Does he bask in it? Bringing home different women?

I don't know why it stirs an unpleasant urge to keep him hidden. I don't exist in his real life and never will. It doesn't stop the images forming in my mind until a firm hand slides down my spine, resting on the small of my back.

"It's coffee for two after all," Quinn grins, looming over me like a wicked princess doll, with her blonde waves and flowery dress.

I fumble something about being friendly and Carter chuckles.

When she returns with our orders a spark brightens her eyes. I know it means trouble.

"Since you're not in hiding anymore," she says casually, "we should have a girls' night out. It's time." Quinn looks pointedly at me. "Maybe meet some guys."

The shit-stirrer stares directly at Carter and asks sweetly, "Don't you think so?"

Carter's hand goes very still on my back.

I'm going to kill her.

Chapter Twenty-Two

Carter

Eliza is slumped in the chair across from me, tossing around the pieces in her stew.

"Order something else if you can't eat it."

The restaurant is not the kind of place I'd go for dinner back home, but the food is delicious. The stops and chats today made me wonder if I could ever live in a small town like Silver Lake Falls. It's a stupid thought.

The heart attack was a bump in the road. My place is back in New York, without copper-haired women complications. *No, Quinn. I don't think she should be going out and meeting men.* She's been quieter after her friend yanked a promise out of her for Saturday night. Is she considering it's time to move on from her ex? She's free to try again. Find her white-picket-fence guy.

Why does that idea taste like charred pickled herring?

"How come you're not married?"

The question catches me off guard, and my first instinct is to go on the offensive. But the morose air about her tempers my response.

"Want to fix me up with the tarot lady?" I smirk to hide the uncomfortable hold on my insides.

Eliza rolls her eyes and groans. "Forget I asked."

"What's this about?" I reach for her hand with the most natural ease.

"Do you believe in real love?"

Her questions trigger my fight-or-flight response, so I do the obvious thing.

"Nobody forced you to stay with a walking red flag."

She yanks her hand away. "Hi pot, meet kettle. What's her name? Alisa?"

Unfortunately, my ex is trying her old tactics, involving the press and rehashing old photos of us. It was all over social media last week so I had to give Eliza the short version of the story.

"Alicia. Not the point. It's easier for you to search until you find real love because your name doesn't send the media into a frenzy."

"Ouch." She grimaces. "Make a girl feel special, won't you?"

"I don't have to. This is my point. Somebody will love you just for yourself, not because you can give them something." And there's plenty to love about her. She is resilient and sees the best in people. Radiates a warmth that paints the world in sunny colors.

"Tone it down with the compliments or I'll combust," she says flatly.

The look on her face makes me uneasy. I didn't mean to insult her.

She waves a dismissive hand, chasing away the comment. "Either way, being nobody and having nothing to *bring to the table*"—she air quotes the phrase—"didn't quite work for me either."

When she says it like that it sounds harsher and meaner than I thought.

"I didn't mean to offend you."

"And yet you do it so effortlessly." She tries to crack a smile, but my careless comment cut deep and I hate myself for it. I'm not used to sugarcoating what I tell people.

We stare at our plates in silence, the murmur of voices and clank of cutlery against porcelain morphing into white noise around us.

"I did, once." The confession slips out.

She's quiet. Giving me the chance to choose to tell her more. She wouldn't force it out of me, even if she could.

"Believe in real love." The words grate the inside of my throat. "I grew out of it."

Eliza follows the swirl of the remaining lemonade in her glass, as she plays with the stem, deep in thought.

Outside the restaurant, the boardwalk is deserted, streetlamps casting a golden glow along the old wooden planks.

"Take a walk with me?" I want to clear the air before we return. This day has been too surprisingly lovely to let it end on a sour note. "I've never seen a lighthouse up close before."

Eliza glances at the building in the distance. A gust of wind blows through and plays in her hair, swirling it around her face. It takes her by surprise, and she bursts into giggles after trying with no success to tame her long hair. My mouth is dry and I'm overwhelmed by this woman.

"You're beautiful," I blurt out and she stills, blushing prettily.

I can't resist and close the distance between us, stroking the wild hair from her face, taking in every little detail. Burning it in my memory for the cold New York nights. My hands rest on the sides of her head, holding the soft hair trapped and I angle her head, urging her to lock eyes with me.

"You don't need a famous last name to draw people in. That's what I meant earlier. Some can't handle what you can bring. Weak, dull, small people are scared by how bright you shine. I want you never to hold back."

Her lips part, delicate and inviting.

"I'd gladly let you burn me if necessary."

We're so close the chocolate on her breath fills my lungs with her taste. Breathing her in until it hurts, because I want to selfishly keep any part of her I can.

"Show me?" she pants into my mouth.

Emotions run unchecked and I don't stop to consider the way she unleashes the fire I keep sealed.

The rise and fall of her breasts grazing my shirt draws out a low groan and I'm a whisper away from crashing against those sinful lips when a high-pitched whistle jolts us apart.

A group of tipsy giggling girls hollers at us before diving into the next bar. "Go get it, hon!"

"That man's a whole snack," one of them warbles while giving a thumbs up.

Eliza's eyes are dark chocolate, burning with the same desire. I regret not being behind a closed door, far away from rowdy drunks.

The spell is broken, but every cell in my body vibrates with awareness. I'm not the type to slow down and smell the flowers but my senses are on high alert. My skin prickles against the fabric of my clothes. The taste of the salty water. The soft breeze. The smell of seafood and the ocean. Small bits of life I could have lost if I didn't survive that day.

We walk in silence, holding her hand to ground myself. Old dark thoughts have begun to resurface since I told her about the heart attack.

"It's inactive," she says while crouching near a regular-looking stone at the base of the lighthouse. She fishes out an old key from a box buried under the rock and grins at my obvious confusion. "It's a small town. It's no secret where Grayson keeps the spare key."

"Are you sure? It looks ancient," I say, peeking inside the dark space.

"You're safe with me," she says, holding out her hand. Her words burrow deep in my soul and I'm afraid of how much I want them to be true.

The interior is an empty circular brick tower with a metal spiral staircase climbing to the top. With each step, more distorted shadows sewn out of hidden fears fly out through the crack, clouding my mind. Death would have erased me. All I owned and did. Irrelevant. Scattered ashes. In between the ticks of a clock, I would've been gone. Leaving what behind?

On the lantern deck, the wind blows harsher, waves crashing on the rocks, filling the air with a salty spray.

Holding the railing with sweaty palms, unable to keep the panic at bay, I screw my eyes shut.

I was on the brink of death. I refused to accept it. To absorb the enormous significance of it. Same with my whole history with Laura. I have the habit of extracting these thoughts with surgical precision and sealing them tight.

"I almost died." It's the first time I've said it aloud.

Now that I've allowed the thought to slither out of its vault, it grows as dangerous as a fire fueled by oxygen.

Walking my sister down the aisle. Adam. Logan. My mother. The doctors and my family urged me to go to therapy. I refused. I wanted to leave it behind, not relive it.

My head drops between my shoulders. Panic loops around my neck, a tight noose, cutting my air.

A small weight presses against my back. Eliza's arms circle my chest and she locks her fingers tightly over my sternum.

"Breathe with me." Her voice is soft, soothing. "I'm here with you." She rests her cheek on my jacket and takes a deep breath. Her chest expands and I fall in sync with her, my head clearing with each exhale.

Bright stars pierce the vast darkness around us and glimmer on the crest of rippling inky waves. It feels like we're drifting inside a painted glass globe, separated from the rest of the world, with the salty wind rushing past our little island.

I'm here. At the top of a small-town lighthouse.
I am alive.

I'm rattled and ungrounded. An urgent instinct to retreat into myself takes over after being so exposed. I've reached my limit of talking about it and Eliza can sense that. When she's not at the fish shop getting bored out of her mind or doing a quick check on the site progress, she keeps me quiet company.

It says so much about her, when I know she always has questions. She gives me enough space and comforts me with light touches, good food, and foraging trips. Lets me watch her while she works in the shed.

When Saturday night rolls around I'm more or less back to my composed self by the time Eliza waltzes into the living room and my stomach does a peculiar flip.

She's nervously pressing the fabric of the dress to her sides, and I can't tear my eyes away from her bare legs. It's stupid of me to want her to stay. Not that kind of relationship, I have to remind myself. She needs this. To do something fun.

"You look lovely." It's an understatement.

The compliment earns me a bashful smile, making her rosy cheeks pop. "I wasn't sure. I left with few clothes."

"I can come with you and get the rest if you want."

"Nah." She shakes her head. "Most of the dresses were Jared-approved. When my life is back on track, I'll let Quinn drag me on an Eliza-approved dress shopping spree." The idea lights a spark behind her eyes, and I take an unspoken vow to put my card down in her name at every clothing store in a thirty-mile radius when that happens.

Twirling in her cute yellow dress that wraps against her curves makes my heart ache for trivial moments I never knew I wanted. Carefree Friday evenings with a pretty girl. A hot summer night in a pub garden, laughing with my friends while she burrows herself under my arm and I hold on a little tighter because she is so sweet and mine, and her eyes sparkle when she looks at me.

"Don't wait up," she says giggling. It's the nervous laugh that's meant to hide her anxiety.

"I'm looking over some business proposals. I'll turn in late." I give her my best impression of casual. "Give me the address. If you need a ride text me."

Please text me to pick you up and don't go to another man's house is what I mean. I've not entirely lost my mind, so I keep the silent plea to myself.

Eliza hits me square in the chest with her cutest smile. "My personal driver. I dig the idea." She sinks her teeth into her lower lip, and it takes every bit of willpower not to jump from the couch and press her against the nearest wall.

It's a dangerous rush of possessiveness, out of the realm of casual. It's not what I promised Eliza and certainly not what I need.

CHAPTER TWENTY-THREE

ELIZA

The exterior is a real English pub front at the corner of an old red-brick brewery. I'm not surprised Quinn knows this place. The weathered wood bar in the corner is lined with taps of local craft beers more to her taste.

I'm happy and nervous being out. The bar is packed with people who don't look familiar. Taking a sip of white wine, I notice Quinn winking at a blond guy leaning on the other side of the bar.

"Give me a sec." She hands me her drink and I watch the scene unfold before me in awe. Quinn's confidence is counter-proportional to her height and that guy has no chance against her charm. His phone is out in less than sixty seconds and she's back at my side with a wicked grin before her glass started sweating from the cold beer.

"Cute," I grin, nodding in the guy's direction.

"We'll see," she says. "Lucky for me, Mike is new in town and badly needs a friend," she giggles. The man in question abandons his empty glass on the bar over some crumpled bills and heads for the exit, eyes glued to Quinn. With a tip of his head and a crooked smile, he disappears into the crowd and I'm thinking of taking some notes from her playbook.

Quinn leans in. "Anybody catch your eye?"

All I can think about is Carter as I left and how silly I am for wishing he was here. I know we agreed to no strings attached, but my cheeks are still flushed from the way he was looking at me.

"I wouldn't know where to start." I didn't date much before Jared. "I'm kinda rusty after eight years," I say, a bitter taste filling my mouth.

"Let's find a seat." She motions to the red leather capitone upholstery benches along the wall. We talk and laugh. A couple of guys offer to buy us drinks, but sensing my hesitation she shoos them away.

Quinn is so much fun, the type who makes you belly laugh. The night is going great, and I break my rule by getting a second glass of wine which makes me warm and giddy. My head is a colorful merry-go-round of moving bodies reflected in the large, gilded mirror on the other side of the room.

We're so engrossed in our little bubble of girly fun that the four men dressed in leather suddenly circling our table rattle us.

"You two look like you need company," the older one says.

Quinn's smile drops. "We're good."

"Don't play coy. We're just talkin'." He plops on the bench, too close for comfort. I can smell the beers on him.

"Then pay attention," Quinn starts, but another one drops his bottle on the table and sits next to her. "We're not interested."

All four snicker, the others blocking us from the rest of the crowd in the bar.

Quinn is close to smashing her beer bottle and jumping over the table at them.

Nobody else notices the uncomfortable exchange.

A bad feeling blooms in my chest and I send Carter an SOS text with trembling fingers, under the table.

Panic claws its way up my body, and I don't know how long passes with them getting more beers and talking about taking us to another bar where "we'll have real fun", the one next to me says with a slimy grin, looking down my dress.

"We're not going anywhere with you," Quinn seethes. God, this woman is fearless.

"Ladies, your ride is here," Carter's voice booms over the music and the pub's chatter.

Relief pours through my limbs.

"Fuck off. We're having fun. Aren't you, ladies?" one of them says, laughing. "We'll give you a ride later."

"They'll be taken for a ride, alright." They laugh.

Carter steps closer. "I advise you to back off."

"Or what, pretty boy? You gonna take us all?"

Carter's jaw ticks and he's looking ready to go for the kill.

Another voice breaks through the tension. It's not hard to recognize him even without the uniform and badge. Our new Sheriff might be the youngest in the history of the town to get the job, but you'd have to be insane to cross him. He's a tall, bearded man, with tattoos all over his brawny arms. And right now, he's sporting a murderous glare, knuckles white from gripping a baseball bat.

Sheriff Walker looms over the table. "Get out now," he snarls, glaring at the men surrounding us.

The men snicker but one of them spots something through the large windows. Two officers in uniform stare back with their hands on their holsters.

"Whatever, you can have these frigid bitches," the older one says, pushing his way through the crowd and I go slack with relief. The officers outside trace their movements until loud revving and backfire roars reach us.

Quinn shakes herself. "What're you doing here?" Her tone is cold, glowering at the Sheriff with pure contempt. He might be close to our age but her tone stuns me.

"You know I find out when you get yourself in trouble," he says softly, not in the least offended. I'm taken aback by the worry creasing his features and the subtle way his body leans toward my friend.

Confusion and trembling legs keep me glued to the bench until Carter touches my elbow lightly and he takes us to his car.

He shakes hands with Sheriff Walker and the two officers while we're huddled together in the backseat. Quinn has her arms around me, and I realize I'm shaking when she squeezes harder.

"What's the deal with hunky Sheriff over there?" I ask her, trying to fill the silence.

She nearly bit his head off when he offered to take her home.

Quinn's face goes blank. "Nothing important."

If my oversharing friend wants to put a lid on the subject, I'll let her. Who knows what would've happened if she wasn't with me? Or Carter, who's driving silently. I catch his eyes checking on us in the rear-view mirror.

He opens the door to the passenger side once we drop off Quinn. "Come on. Keep me company."

In the silence, a knot of shame tightens in my stomach. He had to come all the way to save me because I couldn't handle some drunks on a night out.

"I'm sorry. I panicked and texted you. I never drink more than a glass of wine, but…" Guilt amplifies. I wanted to relax and have some carefree fun. "I'm so embarrassed."

He takes my hand, tracing my knuckles with his thumb. "I'm glad you did. You don't have to be ashamed to call for help."

"Yeah, but you're not…" What did I want to say? Responsible for me? You're not somebody who cares?

"I would have hated it more if you didn't text and something happened to you."

Back in the safety of the cabin, the wave of sadness is overwhelming, and I dive into the soft couch. Can't I have anything nice?

Instead of going to his bedroom, Carter looms over me and sighs deeply before cocooning me in the fluffy throw blanket resting on the back of the couch. He's nicer than he should be considering the trouble I'm causing him.

The couch dips under his weight.

"You don't have to stay with me." My voice comes out muffled. "I'll drag my ass to bed as soon as I finish feeling sorry for myself."

"Your ass looks comfortable here," he chuckles, patting my bottom then sliding his hand over my back in calming circles. Exhaustion drags me down; I can barely keep my eyes open.

"How did you get to the pub so fast?" The question slips out through the sleepy daze.

Silence. Maybe he didn't hear me.

"I was getting some ingredients for a new recipe. Was on my way to the store," he says without a trace of hesitation, still rubbing my back.

My heart swells with a dangerous emotion. There's no 24/7 store in Silver Lake Falls.

Chapter Twenty-Four

ELIZA

The wheels are turning behind his squinting eyes. He's absolutely adorable and I have the urge to hug him.

"I thought it came easy to you." I can't help but tease him, because somebody has to take him down a notch or two.

He scowls at me.

"It's taking you double the time you usually take to finish."

Carter's eyes widen and a slow smile creases the skin around his eyes. Damn it, I walked right into it.

"I'm flattered you keep close tabs on me."

"I just want to know how long I have to suffer through breakfast with you."

"Is that so?" He's alight with amusement. "I know it's your favorite part of the day, since I'm at your mercy. You can chat my ear off."

"You can always take your breakfast on the porch again. It's warmer now."

Carter's attention is set on me. "I could."

His focused gaze washes over me like an electric wave of apprehension.

"But you don't."

I don't know how to interpret the look that crosses his face.

"Why?" I don't know what I hope to achieve with this question.

He's a storm of indecision. But he settles on an answer that has my heart thundering.

"Maybe I enjoy being cornered by a chatty forest woman."

I can't hide the delighted grin making Carter roll his eyes.

"Get dressed," he orders.

"I'm not sure I'm fond of you bossing me around," I say, digging my fists into my sides.

It's the wrong thing to say. Next thing I know he's sitting too close, one hand shooting to my waist. Painfully slow, he brings our bodies together. "I think you get off on it." Carter drags his nose along my jaw, his gritty voice traveling down my body, dissolving into a hot pool between my legs.

"Put the yellow dress on." He presses his thumb under my belly button, and I almost lose the ability to stand straight. "I'll get the car. We're not going into town," Carter finally says, a thick gruffness coating his words.

"You have to get me back by six."

He arches an eyebrow. "Oh. Do you have a date?"

"Yes, with Quinn. That disastrous night at the pub she met a guy called Mike. As a good friend, I need to be filled in with all the details. She sounded excited about him."

Driving in the opposite direction to Silver Lake Falls, he's quieter than usual. I always remind myself Carter's not Jared and his silences are not meant to punish me because I did something to upset him. It still makes me uncomfortable, but it's manageable.

Until the silence stretches for too long.

I take in his stern profile, the faraway glaze of his eyes, and a taste of unease springs under my tongue. His hands are relaxed on the steering wheel, but the set line of his mouth might give way to a scowl.

This time anxiety expands to a threatening crest that triggers my fight-or-flight response. Since I've never been one to fight, I consider jumping out of the moving car rather than taking the silence for a second longer.

"Does it hurt?" he asks, pointing to the mark I'm rubbing without realizing again. When people ask, I pass off the small jagged white line crossing the tail of my left eyebrow as another childhood shenanigan.

Talking about it is the last thing I want, but Carter told me about his. I know it was a difficult moment for him that should be repaid in kind.

"The foster father I had at fifteen was a drunk. One day he got mad because I didn't get up fast enough to get him a beer. Smacked me with an ashtray." I ended up in the hospital ready to run away and live on the street. Maybe catch a bus to Portland or Boston, anywhere but another foster family that treated me like trash.

Carter is grinding his teeth. The vein on his neck is protruding as an angry blush spreads up his face. Is he sick? His heart?

"Are you OK? Do you want me to drive?" I ask, slightly panicky.

Carter looks at me with warmth and swallows. "What happened next?"

"Carter your—"

"Please tell me."

"Oh, OK." I'm a bit overwhelmed by his intensity. "The Millers showed up at the hospital before I could leave."

They were in their seventies, enjoying retirement, after having kids of their own and fostering for decades. The social worker on my case called them asking for a favor. Grams and Gramps didn't hesitate. Literally saved me. I heard stories about other kids living on the streets.

"So yeah, it's a reflex, I guess. Stress and fear take me back there."

Alcohol is another issue. But I keep that to myself.

"Are you afraid now?" he asks, a hint of hurt in his voice.

"No, just anxious, I guess. You're too silent." I shrug.

"People are capable of sitting with their thoughts."

"I know." Silence means danger. Not knowing if it's just the silent treatment or the calm before the storm. Can I be honest and tell him I'm so weak silence scares me? "It puts me on edge. Because I can't read your mood and I don't know what comes after the silence."

The lines on his face soften and he looks at me too closely.

It unnerves me. Nobody has ever paid me so much attention.

"Nothing bad, I promise. Never something bad." Carter unglues his hand from the leather steering wheel and engulfs mine in a steady hold. He's pensive for a beat. "Did you know the first general-purpose electronic digital computer was developed in the forties, during World War II? It was huge. It filled an entire room."

What's he talking about? Is he having a stroke?

"This one was used only by the military. It wasn't until the fifties that they built the first commercial-use one," he continues with the energy of an excited kid talking about his dinosaurs.

Oh.

"I didn't know." I encourage him, melting like a toasty marshmallow.

"Computer predicted the outcome of the 1952 presidential election on live television. The invention of the microprocessor in the seventies changed everything."

He keeps talking, my fears left behind in pieces on the twisting road until we reach a bay with a long white dock and the sign "Boat Rentals" pinned to a pole.

"Do you know how to drive this?" I look between his outstretched hand and the Wellcraft swaying along the water ripples.

Carter scoffs. "If your family aren't members of *the* yacht club, you don't matter." He pulls me into the boat and is careful to fasten my seatbelt.

My intention is not to prove further that we're from such different words, but I can only look at him with a straight face for so long. My cheeks burn from the strain, but it's a losing battle. I burst out laughing. It's so absurd I can't stop, holding my stomach.

"Do you even hear yourself?" I ask, wiping the tears out of the corner of my eyes.

He grins and smoothly guides the boat out of the dock. We glide out, the wind tousling his hair and playing with my skirts. Because in a moment of temporary insanity, I did put on the dress he wanted. It was impossible to think straight when he was so close, touching me.

"My father insisted I join the New York Yacht Club. *Nos agimur tumidis velis.*"

"Speak like the commoners, please," I bite out.

"*We go with swelling sails.* I had zero interest in the old-time rules and the constant history lessons. But the rest of his business partners' kids were members. It was another way to keep them close."

My face falls and I can't hide the rushing wave of sadness that engulfs me.

"What?"

"Nothing." I can't tell him my opinion of his father. Nobody wants to hear strangers criticizing their parents.

He navigates with precision, steering the boat along the coast. "Spit it out."

"Not my place to say anything."

"I want to hear it either way." He pauses and flashes a dangerous smile. "If I don't like it, I can throw you overboard."

"Hey! You said you wouldn't kill me."

"I said I wouldn't kill you in your sleep."

We stare at each other for several seconds, the wind and the waves lapping on the side of the boat the only sounds around us while Carter continues to look at me expectantly.

"It just sounds so manipulative," I finally burst out. "Did you even like to sail?"

"It didn't matter. I had to."

Words come out of my mouth before I realize the overstep. "I'm sorry he used you."

He's rigid, a statue blown by the wind, eyes hard, hands gripping the steering wheel. I want to catch him before he retreats into himself completely, but I'm too scared to unbuckle. I grip the material of his trousers and bunch it in my fist behind his knee. I want to anchor him to me and this beautiful moment out on the water.

Carter drops back to me, slightly confused until I smile at him, tugging gently on the rough fabric and he beams.

"Hold on, kitten," he says before the boat picks up speed and I can barely hear my own squeals and giggles over the wind.

What I do hear is the wild drumming of my heart singing with pure joy fueled by adrenaline and the feeling I get when Carter looks at me and lets go, laughing, living the moment with me.

People have the constitutional right to water their gardens in peace. Not being pestered by their annoying roommate. No matter how good-looking he is or how deliciously the muscles of his arms twist when he folds them over his chest.

"You're telling me you've never been to New York."

This again. "Obviously not," I grumble.

"Were you never curious? To go beyond Silver Lake Falls?"

His condescending tone is slowly raising my blood pressure. "Your privilege is showing." I take a large gulp of air to stop the string of names pushing to be unleashed on him. "For your information, I've been places. For work. And Jared took me to Ohio once. On our anniversary."

Carter chuckles and it raises my hackles instantly. "Oh, kitten. That's unbelievably…sad. Depressing actually. I don't think the man liked you."

Blood whooshes violently in my ears. As if I didn't come to realize it. "Oh, shut up! His aunt gave him the ticket to visit her."

"That's even worse," he says, too amused by my pathetic travel history.

"You pompous—" I'm so angry words fail me. My body vibrates with frustration, and I yank on the hose to do something with the unrest coursing through the tips of my fingers. My palms stop itching. The unfortunate side effect is I end up spraying Carter with cold water from head to toe.

He's stock-still, water dripping from his hair, the top of his nose, and the hem of his T-shirt into a puddle around his boots.

My hand flies to my mouth and I gasp. "Shit."

A flex of his forearms and the murderous fire in his eyes have me bolting over the rows of herbs and bee balm, around the shed, shooting for the back door. Heart pounding, I skid on the fresh grass rounding the side of the house and almost fall face first. I have the door in my field of vision. A couple of yards before I reach the steps and can slide through…

Strong arms wrap around my middle and the proper and polished Carter tackles me to the ground, rolling on the grass, his back taking the brunt of the fall. He holds on tight until I'm pinned under his weight, both panting.

"OK! OK! Sorry," I gasp, out of breath.

He looks feral. With his coffee hair disheveled, streaks of mud on his face, nostrils flaring. The cells in my body are on alert. I'm not scared. Not with Carter. I'm strung with anticipation.

Then his eyes turn playful, taking me in.

"You can let me go." I give him an out. We've hardly touched each other since he had me pinned against the kitchen cabinets. I'm not sure he still wants to keep pushing boundaries.

The playfulness shifts into something more primal. "Are you sure?"

He pins my wrists over my head with one hand. His lips are dangerously close, but he avoids kissing me again. It wouldn't be good for me anyway.

"You either overestimated your ability to outrun me or wanted me to chase and catch you. Tell me, Eliza." His nose drags along my collarbone when the tip of his tongue traces the swells of my breasts. His lips caressing the hollow of my throat. "Is this a game?" He presses down on me and I swallow my moan.

A growl echoes in the back of his throat. "Do I get to play now?"

"Please," I pant out, too turned on to care I'm begging him to touch me.

"Good kitten," his fingers drag along my ribs, sending bolts of electricity between my thighs. "Do I win if I make you come all over my hand?"

"Ihmm. Whatever you want. Just, please…I need you."

The grass prickles my back, but I'm too consumed by the trail of his warm palms and the hungry flash in his eyes. My gasps swirl up, getting lost in the rustle of the trees, and caution flies out the window. It's scary how often this happens when it comes to Carter.

"I'm fond of this game." His breath is hot over my neck, his fingers moving boldly under my waistband.

Carter peppers scorching kisses between my breasts, and I catch on fire, wishing I could vanish the flimsy tank top so I could get closer to him. Holding me in place with his taut frame, he has the same idea and bites down on the seam of the cleavage, dragging the fabric down with his teeth.

Exposed to the breeze and the brush of his lips, I writhe under him, mumbling pleas and promises of a slow painful death if he continues to torture me.

"My impatient, pretty girl," he chuckles roughly, drawing lazy circles around my clit. "I'll take my time with you." Carter slowly pushes two fingers between my legs, and I feel my airways closing with the tension pressing down my belly, traveling up.

He grunts in frustration. "These are in my way." Carter pulls back on his knees and yanks down my shorts and panties together.

A shocked gasp catches in my throat and my skin burns. I can't tell if it's from the way he takes me in or the embarrassment of being so naked outside my bedroom.

"We're out in the open," I mumble, scrambling to cover myself, but Carter's not having it.

He grabs my wrists again and bends to kiss my jaw, one of his hands sliding against my leg until he reaches between my thighs. "I've got you," he says between nips and licks, pushing his fingers inside me. "It's just the two of us here."

The unfamiliar sensation of fresh air on my bottom and the way his movements increase in pace coil my insides like a spring, ready to snap. "I'm so close," I pant raggedly.

The earthy smell of the lake's shore fills my lungs, together with Carter's expensive scent, in an unreal sense of euphoria.

With each push, Carter's back and arm muscles tense, a low rumble roiling in his chest. "Break for me, kitten."

It doesn't take much to make me fall apart. I've lived in a constant state of arousal around him for the past few weeks.

The wind cools my flushed skin, and I come back to earth. "You win," I sigh.

His features are a mixture of awe and uncertainty, but a smug purse of his lips quickly covers it. "If you keep stroking my competitive nerve, I'll have to prove I can win each time."

I tilt my head to the side, eyeing his pants. "Speaking of stroking."

His head dips and he hides his smile in kisses on my nose and under my ear. "I'm in no rush. Plus," he says, lifting us both, "I was promised we'd go skinny dipping."

"Cliff jumping. Not skinny dipping."

"Mmm. We'll see about that."

His charming air is disarming, and I pray to all the things above I won't become a cliché, falling for the first guy I meet after Jared. Time is running out on his stay, and it won't have the rom-com finale where he miraculously finds the meaning of life and love and starts wearing flannel shirts.

This time I won't make the same mistake. The deadline gives me a sort of liberty I never had. It's a lack of that pressure I never lived without and I'm going to enjoy the hell out of it.

Chapter Twenty-Five

CARTER

A branch nearly takes my eye out because Eliza's ass is hypnotic in those very short tight pants. I do my best to pay more attention to the path.

"Aren't you afraid of the bear stalking you?"

Oh, yes. The lame attempts to make her talk to me. I have no remorse for those. "It'll take more than an ugly bear to scare me out of these woods."

"Don't hurt its feelings, it might be lurking around," she chides, giggling, and I nearly trip on a root because she turns me into a fumbling idiot.

"Leave your stuff here." She points to a large flat rock when we reach the shore. The freshwater smell and moss covering the water's edge send a shudder through my limbs. I tell myself that's why I keep my T-shirt on while Eliza undresses.

I'm about to make a snarky comment about dangerous creatures lurking in the lake but words catch in my throat. It is happening again. I'm certain I'm on the brink of another heart attack when Eliza slides her shorts off. Those bikinis are a safety hazard.

She dips her toes in the lake. "The water's not bad," she says.

The dark green two-piece makes her creamy skin look delicious. Something I would taste and graze my teeth against.

I start questioning my sanity for resisting going further with her. A rational adult, with a cleared-for-physical-activity note from his doctor wouldn't hesitate. *I don't know if I can trust her. She just ended an eight-year relationship. She's not the casual type.* The mantra gave me valid reasons to keep my distance before she showed me I was overthinking it. But in the back of my head, a small seed of doubt sprouted the first time I made her come.

What if the heart attack makes me unable to—

Eliza threads her finger through mine before I finish the horrifying thought and drags me to a cliff towering above a darker spot in the lake. A large pine tree towers over the ledge, with a rough, thick rope dangling from a solid branch.

"Let's do this before you lose your nerve," she jokes, but I'm still reeling.

What if I can't satisfy her?

"Want me to jump first? So you can see it's not a carefully crafted plan to kill you?"

"Do you think I'm scared?" I ask, affronted.

She shrugs and waves her hands around, making a point of emphasizing I'm the one to say it.

I step forward, scowling at her audacity, ignoring the epiphany hitting me over the head. I am indeed scared of having sex because I might make a fool of myself. Preposterous.

The rope is harsh against my palm as I tug a few times, making sure it can hold my weight. I'm doing this. Breaking into a run, my feet leave the cold stone and I'm hurled into the air. One moment I'm suspended, feeling weightless. The next, my grip slips and I splash unceremoniously and painfully on the surface of the lake.

My lungs burn in the cold water until I swim up and gulp in a few mouthfuls of air.

Eliza's at the edge of the cliff, a bright smile on her lips, palms pressed against her chest.

"So graceful," she hollers.

I beam back at her. "A solid 9.5 jump."

She skips to the rope and lunges, dropping near me. Her face breaks the surface of the clear water, and she starts laughing. All giddy and unguarded joy. It's contagious. The light filtered by trees fans around her, and she looks like a divine gift. I'm not a religious man, but this woman makes me repent for everything I might have done wrong.

The image barrels through my chest with the force of a tsunami. The impact cracks something inside and lets her light and warmth in.

Shit.

I'm completely in over my head and it's too late to retreat to shallow waters.

The explosion of adrenaline and energy makes me restless. I want to touch her, bring her closer.

Her ember eyes burn. Waiting. Curious. She's silent as we balance, chest to chest, on the round rocks littering the bottom. Her hand travels up my arm and rests on the center of my chest.

Under the water, I cup her ass firmly and press her against me. Eliza gasps when she feels how hard I am for her. She blushes that adorable pink and I wait for her to put some distance between us when she shocks me. Her palm slides over my trunks with a boldness I didn't expect, gripping me gently.

Eliza's raspy voice runs straight to my cock. "We need to even the score, Mr. Rawlings."

She slips into my swim trunks, and I tense, my fingers digging deeper into her soft flesh. It's slow and torturous. The feel of her hand on me, stroking and tracing my tip with her thumb, is better than anything I could've imagined. There's no rush in the way she gently kisses and licks the side of my neck. I get lost in her rhythm, every fiber coiling with the urge to let go. Her other hand fists the hair at the back of my head.

Fuck.

Who knew I was into rougher touches? She increases the pressure and her strokes are faster. The heat coming off me could warm the entire lake.

I'm going to snap from the pressure building at the base of my spine until she presses my face to her breasts. I wrap my lips around her cold pebbled nipple. I'd spend hours devouring this woman.

Eliza twists her fist and grinds against me until the hot ball of energy unfurls and travels through my body with such force, it nearly knocks me off my feet.

My arms move to hold her securely and she wraps her legs tightly around me. We're still, my face buried in the crook of her neck, lost in time until our lips are purple.

Something in the water must have rotted my brain because two days later I end up taking her to ride a tandem bike on a paved, smooth, straight path along the shoreline.

"I look ridiculous," she says, after I make sure her helmet, elbow, and knee protection are properly fastened.

"You look like I'll be less worried about you and be more focused on riding the bike."

"Aww, does the ice-cold city boy care about me?" Her laugh is cut short when I start peddling.

"We'll go slow. I promise."

My mother's eyes narrow and she leans forward as if she can see me better through the tablet camera.

"You're…" She pauses and blinks at me, taken aback. "Energized?"

"Must be the ocean air. I went cliff diving the other day."

"Cliff—" The satisfaction I get from the shock on my mother's face is priceless. "Wonderful, son. I'm glad you're having fun. Just, please. Find the kind of fun that gets you home in one piece, alright?"

"I don't know, mother, I saw some people skydiving. It got me thinking."

"Carter Rawlings," my mother snaps.

"Relax, you won't have to come down here and scrape me off Route 1."

"If this is your way of twisting my arm, it might work." She smiles affectionately. "But only because you look good. Let's talk about it next month."

The news adds to my excitement about the little secret project I have been mulling over since Eliza told me about her passion and how little faith she has in making it work. She's willing to let her brain cells die working on the stock and orders at the fish shops because she desperately wants to be employed.

Eliza's on the couch, sketching a large chalet bathroom with the box of colors I got. It makes me irrationally happy.

"Why don't you put your designs out there? You hate it at the store." I perch next to her, admiring her work while I play with the strands escaping her ponytail.

"I don't know where to start. I never thought I could make a living out of it. Jared and my friends never… Anyway." She corrects herself. "I'll look for another office job after I move out."

"There's no hurry." My answer comes fast. A visceral reaction to her leaving. A feeling of immediate loss. I tap the tablet and Eliza's Interior Design website fills the screen. It's a mix of her sketches, pictures of this cabin, and pieces she refurbished.

Eliza's confused as she takes in the colors, the pictures, and the sections I created after looking at other websites. I pride myself on doing a good job, but she's frozen and silent.

"You don't have to be a tech whiz to make one," I backtrack.

I could have asked any of my junior developers to handle it, but I didn't want people in the company to ask questions. If I were honest with myself, I wanted to give her something I made. Did I overstep, is it too much?

"You did this."

I nod.

"For me?" she chokes out. The gratitude and disbelief burn in her eyes and the blood under my skin runs hotter.

She leaps and straddles me, grabbing my face. "The woman you decide to give the whole relationship thing a try with will be a very lucky lady."

"It will be like winning the lottery," I joke, because the way she sees me is staggering.

"A man who sticks around when I'm puking my guts out and remembers my favorite drinks. Phew. I'm sold!"

"Your standards are abysmal."

She doesn't bite. "You're a kind man."

Her words settle over me like a weighted blanket.

She holds my head steady so she can peer into my soul. "You put in time and effort because you think I have a shot."

"You do."

"This means a lot to me." She leans in and my pulse is erratic, but she kisses the corner of my mouth.

I'm disappointed. And in awe of her.

This might be my new addiction. Seeing the light shine bright in Eliza's eyes when her wishes come true. I turn into a fucking genie. Otherwise, I can't explain why I make sure she has another girls' night with Quinn. A safe and fun one.

I get them a table at an exclusive bar in the next town over with an open tab in my name. One of my security guys poses as a driver to escort them and keep them safe. I haven't brought up the fact that my team is close by, and it's a little too late now to spring it on her.

I wanted to smack my head against the wall after she left, looking excruciatingly beautiful. She was so happy, I pretended I didn't wait up until her high heels click-clacked past my door.

The itch to go to her, touch her, let her tell me about her night was spiking under my skin. But I didn't want her to think I expected something in return.

CHAPTER TWENTY-SIX

CARTER

"You've never met this uncle before?" Eliza asks me from the passenger seat.

"Nope."

"He lives so close, isn't that a weird coincidence?"

It might be one. If you didn't know my mother. "Unlikely."

"I'm worried. You've reverted to single-word answers."

"Sorry. I don't know what to expect."

"And you brought me along as a human shield?"

"You'd make for a lousy one." I laugh at her offended expression. "But you'd be perfect for distracting them."

The Ashmore Farm sign over the pebbled road leading up to the main farmhouse is familiar, but I can't put my finger on it. We pass large greenhouses, three smaller houses, a small yellow barn, and pastures stretching over the hill that hides the rest of my uncle's fifty-acre farm.

Eliza's awestruck gasp is followed by a mini meltdown at the sight of the family house. A large white classic New England home with a pitched roof and clapboard siding.

The red front door opens and a tall, grizzled man in overalls struts across the wraparound porch, throwing his arms to the side. He's ready to hug us and I consider putting the car in reverse, but Eliza is already out.

"Your home is—"

I yank the door open and get a better look at the man I assume is my uncle. He has something of my mother around his eyes. The rest of him is too rough to have anything in common with the woman who wouldn't be caught dead in rubber shoes.

The deep lines of this sunburnt face bend around a large grin and the inevitable happens. He wraps his large arms around me in a bear hug. I don't remember being this uncomfortable in my life.

"I'm…We're so happy you came. I've been waiting for this day for so long," he says gruffly in my ear, patting my back. The sincerity of his words hits me under the solar plexus. My parents never talked about him. I only found out he existed after my father died.

My uncle steps back, taking me in, palm firmly on my shoulder like he's afraid I'll disappear. He doesn't wait for my reply and turns to Eliza, who is looking at us with misty eyes. My heart drops. This is probably something she's dreamed of. Some lost family members coming for her and giving her a loving home.

"Kenneth Ashmore, glad you joined us. You came by at the perfect time."

I swallow the painful ball of emotions and focus on Kenneth. "Why?"

"Didn't your ma tell you?"

Of course she didn't. Clara Rawlings moves us all like chess pieces on her board.

A loud group of boys and girls of all ages overflows from the front door, laughing and giggling until a tall, kind-looking blonde woman narrows her eyes at them and it gets quiet. I instinctively reach for Eliza's hand as she stands there smiling politely, drinking in my newfound relatives. She's quiet. I'm afraid it's too much for her.

"Linda!" My uncle calls over his wife. "We've got more guests for the party tonight."

It's the man's fiftieth birthday and he's invited his neighbors and friends for a barn dance.

"We don't want to intrude—"

"No bother, dear." Linda greets us. "The more, the merrier. We haven't had new people over in ages."

My uncle hooks an arm around her middle and drags her closer for a loud kiss on the cheek, making her blush. "This is going to be the best birthday in years."

"Your uncle is easily excited. Come meet your cousins. Don't worry if you can't remember their names. Sometimes I mix them up too." She winks at me, and I gulp through the dryness in my throat. This family dynamic is uncharted territory.

Eliza's hand squeezes mine in quiet support.

It takes me a minute to get used to the smell. New York is not exactly a freshly bloomed magnolia, but my eyes water when my uncle takes us into the barns with cows and sheep. Eliza doesn't seem to mind, as she stops and talks with the animals, petting them gently.

"You have to see the horses." My uncle beckons us along the weathered fences separating the pastures and the paddocks. The mountains blanketed by thick forests rise in the distance, solid against the clear blue sky.

At the end of the tour when I suspect Eliza is plotting to take one of the foals back to the cabin, my uncle guides us back to the main house by a shabby barn. "We keep old stuff in here, nothing interesting."

"Eliza would love to see it," I find myself saying.

Her eyes widen and her lower lip drops. For a few beats, I get the feeling she's peering into my soul again. Then she focuses her doe eyes on Kenneth. "Can we?"

Being unable to tell her no runs in the family because a second later I lose sight of her behind mismatched sets, light fixtures, benches, chairs, and tools.

"Eliza reconditions vintage pieces for fun. She is very talented," I tell him, sounding too much like a proud husband.

"Isn't that something?" My uncle eyes me knowingly and then shouts over the mess, "Pick anything you want and have a go."

"Oh, I couldn't just take it," she says, shaking her head. "Tell me a price. I'll get what I can afford."

When Hell freezes over. I'll buy her the whole damn barn if she wants.

"My wife would love you forever if you'd take some of the stuff off her hands. She's been bugging me for ages. I might be paying you for the favor." He belly laughs. "Let's get ready for the party. You can choose afterward."

"I…What do you want to do?" she asks timidly, a tiny spark of hope flashing behind her beautiful eyes.

For you? Anything. Barn party, square dancing, sign me up.

"I just met my uncle. We have to stay."

Her reaction is instant, sinking her teeth into her lower lip.

"Is there a motel around?"

"Don't be silly, son. You can take one of the guesthouses. You passed them on your way here."

Eliza clears her throat and looks at me intently. "I didn't pack anything for overnight."

Sleeping naked sounds like a great idea. "I have an emergency bag with some clothes in the trunk."

"Problem solved," Kenneth says. "Come on, the girls are excited to get ready with you, I'll show you more tomorrow."

The guesthouse has one bedroom. I drop the bag on the floor and rush outside before I get lost in fantasies revolving around sharing a bed with a sweet redhead riding my cock until we're both spent.

"They're gonna keep your girl," Kenneth says, leading me to the larger, red and black barn.

My girl?

"They're squeaking and giggling like teenagers up there."

My heart warms for her. Being in the middle of a big loving family is something she craves. It's not the worst feeling in the world, but it doesn't come naturally to me. It's uncomfortable like a new pair of dress shoes and I'll need some time to get used to this type of family life.

"She's not my girl. We just—" Why am I explaining this to him? "It's nothing serious."

"It never is in the beginning." My uncle laughs heartily.

"I have to return home soon." Why do I keep talking? "It can't go anywhere. The company needs me."

"Does it?" At my confused expression, he continues, "You don't run a family bodega. It's an empire. At this size it's self-sustaining."

"I can't leave everything behind. My mother, Jackie—"

"I can't tell you what to do, son. I've missed so much not seeing you grow." He shakes his head and puts his arm around me, this time I don't tense as much. "This farm is the biggest supplier for restaurants and shops in the state," he says, brimming with pride. "Been through bad times. But I always had Linda by my side. You can build a business without being buried by it. We built it together. This beautiful family and the farm. It would mean nothing without them."

The uncomplicated logic of this man disarms me. "It doesn't work for everybody."

Kenneth huffs, amused. "I saw the way you were looking at her. I'm willing to bet all my goats you had no intention of spending too much time around us."

My mother sent me here with zero context. "I didn't know—"

"It's alright, son. I can't refuse my Linda anything either."

The family is bringing food into the barn, the long table heavy with mouth-watering dishes. My aunt prides herself on the farm-grown ingredients. A pile of familiar sweets catches my eye. The two chocolate-cake-like round sponges with white cream filling in my parents' fridge pop to the front of my mind.

"I remember these." I know why the sign is familiar. It was the logo on the white cardboard box I always found in the fridge around my birthday.

My aunt's blue eyes sparkle with unshed tears. "I wish I could have shared them with you then."

Bitter resentment floods my insides. I've been robbed of my family's love and care and I didn't even know it.

I find Eliza talking with my cousins and other guests who arrived at the party. She stands out with the grace of a water lily in a clear pond. It's not the flowery dress or the way my cousin styled her hair. It's that smile and the twinkle in her eyes when they joke around.

My girl is beautiful.

Despite the alarm bells going off in the back of my head, I relax and have some fun while Linda and Kenneth introduce me to an entire branch of the extended family. They welcome me without judgment and share stories about my mom growing up in the area. I wonder how my father managed to erase every tie to her family. Did she miss them?

While my uncle is surrounded by his loving family and friends, Angus Rawlings would have turned it into a business opportunity. I can't help but imagine the type of person I would've been if I had the chance to spend my summers here, surrounded by rowdy cousins and benevolent relatives.

Eliza is in and out of my line of vision, but I never lose track of her. She's laughing and dancing, a vision vibrating with life, a beacon of light drawing me in.

Joy is pouring out of her like radio waves, and it gives me such a rush seeing her so relaxed in the middle of my family. It's a taste of what if. Could this be my life?

I scowl at my second glass of Maine-made rum. A knot lodges deep in my airways and I ditch the glass on the first flat surface I find. Where's that mint lemonade my aunt is raving about?

"Is this seat taken?" Eliza asks playfully, nodding toward the bench.

"Didn't think I'd talk to you again tonight," I tease her.

Her head whips around, strawberry blonde strands grazing my jaw. "I'm sorry. You were getting to know your relatives." She sounds remorseful. "I wanted to give you privacy."

The band slows down to a mellow tune and my body acts on its own.

"You can make it up to me." I hold my hand out, hoping and dreading that she'll say yes.

Eliza smiles, bright-eyed, her warm hold tight as we make our way between other couples. Dusty floorboards creak under our weight as I pull her closer, the sway of her body calling to every fiber of my being.

She lowers her voice. "You fit in here more than you realize."

"I don't know how to feel about it." I let the truth slide out. But I wouldn't mind finding out.

The singer's twang vibrates with emotion, pouring out a soulful nostalgia about a small-town, lost love, and the smell of pines.

I'm caught in her gaze, unable to tear my eyes away. Diving into pools of warm caramel, my awareness zoomed in on the spots our bodies touch. The pulse thrumming in her wrists gives the rhythm to my heartbeat.

The barn and party become a fading watercolor of people, wood beams, and dry hay.

"Did you also take dancing lessons?"

"Yes, but not this type." My grip grows tighter, an unfamiliar possessiveness rushing through my veins. "It's considered highly improper."

Her lips part, their softness inviting me to taste them. "We wouldn't want to damage your reputation and ruin your prospects." She laughs lightly.

"You can ruin me all you want, Eliza." I know I'm on the precipice, toeing the point of no return, the momentum unstoppable.

The fairy lights above us cast a golden gleam waving through hazel and gold specks. The colors in her irises shift, unfurling like silky petals. Blooming dark peonies so delicate and beautiful, drawing me in with their mesmerizing dance.

I want to tell her how beautiful she is, but my tongue is too heavy for words. I dip my head, nudging the tip of her nose and she goes still, holding in a breath. Her lavender scent mixed with fresh grass and ginger ale makes me dizzy.

The strong gravitational pull toward her lips feels natural and I close the gap between us, softly brushing our lips. The connection is effortless and floods me with warmth while my stomach does a concerning flip. I don't lean back, breathing in her shuttered exhale, but I do give her the chance to push me away, even though the urge to taste her again is overwhelming. I want to chase the thread linking us. It's like nothing I've experienced before, and I'm being pulled to opposite sides by curiosity and fear.

Eliza fists my shirt, rises on her tiptoes, and pushes closer, sealing the microscopic space between us. It spurs me on, and my hands cradle her head, the kiss morphing with eagerness and lust. It goes from tentative pecks to liquid strokes, pushing and demanding.

The unsteady sensation of stepping into the void has my pulse racing.

When we part, we're sucked back into a too bright and loud world. We hadn't noticed the song changed, guests clapping and dancing to an upbeat song around us.

She looks up at me, dazed and flushed. Her panting warms my neck before she steps back.

Without a word Eliza turns on her heels, heading out of the barn. The look she throws me over her shoulder is pure heat and leaves no room for interpretation.

An enormous bonfire my cousins were so excited to start roars tall behind us as we walk toward the guesthouse, our shadows searching for each other on the uneven dirt road. The unpaved path around one of the greenhouses leaves the sounds of the party behind, the silence stretching over green hills into a clear night sky. It adds to the pressure of everything unspoken, growing the closer we get to the guesthouse.

When the backs of our hands touch, my skin warms up and I question my sanity for this reaction. But our eyes meet, and I recognize the same awe coated in apprehension in Eliza and my fingers wrap around her dainty ones like it's the most natural thing in the world.

She takes in the utilitarian interior while I close the door and lean on it, admiring her. There's only a small couch and a living room set in the single room where the metal farmhouse bed is pushed under the window.

I rub the back of my neck when she twists, looking unsure. "I can take the couch."

It's a last attempt to give her an out. The brain-altering kiss changed nothing. She's still not the type of woman comfortable with casual sex and I'm still leaving.

Eliza smirks and threads her fingers through mine, a spark of determination lighting her eyes in the moonlit room. "No," she says, leading me to the bed and giving me a little push. "Wait here."

I swallow and give her a nervous nod.

My mouth is dry, tension tightening my chest. Left alone with my thoughts, it doesn't take long for doubt to rear its ugly head. I don't want to disappoint Eliza. Maybe this isn't the best idea.

I'm overheating, tugging at my collar.

When the bathroom door opens and she appears in the doorway wearing one of my shirts I can bet all my assets the universe is working against me, because she is fucking irresistible. Leaning against the doorframe, the shirt's hem barely covers her. She wets her lip, not moving an inch. She's waiting for me. It takes me a moment to decipher her hesitancy.

I've been the one pulling back. Not asking for more.

Electricity surges through my body and I bite the inside of my cheek to stop myself from sounding too desperate. "Come here."

She steps between my legs and I take her in, my gaze traveling from the scar on her ankle, up her slender legs, the shy sliver of skin between her breasts peeking between the unfastened top buttons, to her rosy cheekbones and burning eyes. I touch the back of her calves, caressing my way to the sensitive skin behind her knee and she twitches under my palms when I dig my fingers into her flesh.

"Are you real?" I whisper reverently.

The moonlight filtering into the room draws the curtains' lace pattern on her skin. My fingers trail the delicate shadow tattoos under the shirt until I reach the soft fabric of her panties and she sucks in a breath.

"As real as you want me to be." Eliza's voice wobbles and she nicks the edge of her lip.

I follow the seam of the fabric, a map to the spot between her legs while she watches me with parted lips. Teasing her drains the patience I still possess, because all I want is to fuck her senseless. But my curiosity over everything Eliza is and does wins over and I press my thumb against the wet fabric of her panties and she gasps, the blush I've come to adore spreading up her skin.

I clear my throat. "Is this what you want?" I fucking hate how vulnerable I sound.

She strokes my cheek, lowering her head until our foreheads touch. Her lips skim mine, sending a wave of pleasure down to my toes.

That tender fucking kiss cracks me open and the hunger I've been keeping at bay swells out. I pour it into the next kiss, crashing my lips against hers, tugging and grazing, tasting until we're both breathless.

"I want you," she moans into my mouth and the words glide between my lungs like gasoline on fire. "Please let me feel you."

People have asked a lot of things of me. Money, favors, expensive presents. Eliza only wants me to bare myself to her. Does she realize that after the surgery, it's the hardest thing to give?

Her hands travel over my back, grabbing my shirt, but I don't stop her, even though my heart is in my throat. She presses another heated kiss to my lips and leans back to tug the fabric, leaving me exposed, bracing for her reaction. Eyes wide and lips swollen, she drops the shirt to the floor. It's not pity I see in her eyes. It's appreciation and a hunger mirroring my own.

I give in a little more, tired of fighting the confusion she unleashes with her laugh, and the tightness under my navel from her firm and warm touches.

Weeks of flirting, teasing, and undeniable attraction have led to this exact moment and I want to make it unforgettable for her. I want to be burnt into a part of her brain and have her trembling long after I'm back in New York.

There's too much space between us, my skin aching for her softness, and I pull her into my lap. Hands sneaking under the shirt, I drag my fingers up her inner thighs seeking her warmth, knuckles grazing the wet spot at her center. A tremor goes through her and I clasp one palm around her ass to steady her.

As much as it boosts my possessive streak seeing her in my shirt, I unbutton it slowly, grazing her skin as I go until a gentle tug unveils the beautiful woman straddling me.

"You're torturing me," Eliza says, the unmistakable tinge of frustration tugging at the corners of her mouth.

The sweet braid is next, silk through my fingers when I release her hair, letting the wavy copper curtain drape over her shoulders and chest. "I'm admiring the view. Can't really blame me, when you look like this."

She's an absolute vision, flushed, eyes glazed, clad in the simple blue cotton panties.

My hands roam the delicate slope of her neck and she loses her patience with me, rolling her hips, rubbing over me in slow, torturous motions.

"Easy, kitten," I growl.

She does it again, pressing my head between her breasts, and I bite her gently.

"If you keep doing that, I'll never be able to look you in the eye again." It might come off as a joke, but she doesn't get how close I am to embarrassing myself.

"I don't care." Her voice is huskier.

"Eliza, it's been more than six months—"

"There's more than one way to make me come," she says, making her point with another sway of her hips. "I need to feel you inside of me."

Is she trying to kill me?

The house is quiet and I can hear her every breath.

My hand slides up her spine into her hair and I buck my hips.

She moans against my mouth, her tongue sliding past my lips and the most delicious taste of chocolate floods me. I'll never be able to look at chocolate again without getting hard.

With a surprised shriek, Eliza finds herself flat on her back while I stare at her. Mapping out her body, burning every part of her into my brain. Every soft exhale, every shiver, and the silky texture of her skin. Her muscles bunch under my touch when I drag my nose past her navel, peppering her with kisses.

"Fuck, Carter."

The way she moans my name, breathless. It's a firestorm burning the fragile threads of my restraint.

The light wind outside fills the room with the perfume of wildflowers through the cracked window, but

I'm lost in the smell of her skin and the unmistakable tang of arousal bringing me closer to losing my mind.

Splayed out for me, hair disheveled around her and panting, completely letting go, she's a goddess.

"You look like a fucking dream," I murmur into the taut skin over her hipbone, and she twitches when I slowly bite the spot.

"Please," she murmurs, like she wants more but doesn't know how to ask.

I lean back and she looks panicked.

"I'll take care of you, kitten." I prop my hands on her knees and slowly slide my fingers down, on the inside of her tights until they tease the edge of her soaked panties.

"I know you will," she says softly, scorching my skin with the heat in her eyes. Four simple words that change my brain chemistry.

I capture her lips again and revel in the feel of her breasts on my skin. I travel down, trailing kisses over her chest, teasing her nipples and lower, on her stomach, her nails dragging across my back. When I reach the panty line and hook my fingers around the fabric, her nails dig into my shoulders, a shiver running through her body.

"You don't have to." It comes out strained.

"I've been thinking about how you taste for a while now." I pull the cotton down and take her in, my mouth watering. "Please don't let me die of disappointment."

"Don't be drama—" A throaty moan cuts off her argument when I flatten my tongue against her.

The needy noise hidden in the back of her throat sets me on fire. An acute sense of purpose drives me. I want her to release it. Loudly. Until I can't hear anything else but her cries and moans.

I brush my thumb over her soft flesh. "I might get addicted to your taste."

Eliza's eyes are glassy, an angry red trail swallowing her neck and cheeks. "Don't make fun of me," she says meekly, and I choose my words carefully.

"Oh, sweetheart. Have I ever given you the impression I like to joke around?" I put my lips around her clit and gently suck on it until I have to hold her still against the mattress. "I never do anything I don't want. And right now, I want you to come all over my mouth." I gather her moisture on my finger and tease her entrance. "Do you understand?"

"OK," she manages to breathe out when I push my finger inside her, her head falling back. She's hot and wet.

"Look at me, Eliza." I add another finger and when our eyes meet, I continue to lick and taste her until her body vibrates with tension. It takes a few strokes of my curled fingers for her back to arch off the mattress, going completely still before her high-pitched moan fills my chest with satisfaction, and my cock strains against the zipper of my pants.

Pushed forward by need, but held back by doubt, I'm rooted in place, admiring Eliza's body as she relaxes.

"Talk to me, Carter." It's hard to wrap my head around the ease with which she reads me.

I rub my jaw, pushing the words out. "Considering calling it a night while I'm ahead."

A flicker of hurt glosses over her dazed eyes before she says, "Don't you want me?"

I'm messing this up for both of us. I prop my knees on the edge of the mattress, making my way above her, until my lips find the sweet spot on the side of her neck. "There's nothing I crave more at this moment," I confess into her skin. This next part hurts to say, but she deserves the truth. "I don't know if I can. If you end up disappointed, it will kill my ego."

I expect her to make fun of me, but I should know better by now.

She outlines the edges of my jaw with her thumbs, forcing me to look at her. "You have enough ego to spare," she smirks. "I don't want to push if you're not ready, but—" Her legs wrap around me and she presses me into her, the small roll of her hips bringing us so close, rubbing against me. My vision goes black for a second.

"This ache I have," Eliza moans. "It's painful. Only you can soothe it," she says, reaching for the button of my trousers. What a gift she gives out freely. Her trust and want crumble my insecurities to dust. Whatever happens, she won't judge me.

I answer with a deep kiss, threading my fingers through her hair, and angling her mouth so I can have more of her.

Her delicate fingers wrap around me and she whispers in my ear, "I'm on birth control."

I'm so lost in the thought of feeling her bare, using a condom doesn't even cross my mind. Layers of resistance peel back until I take what I thought I couldn't. The rest of our clothes are thrown somewhere in the corner, and I let this hunger for her consume me, surrounded by Eliza's scent and the smell of starch from the crisp sheets. Her soft curves are welcoming when I press down on her.

Eliza's heated sighs urge me on. With one hand I shackle her wrists over her head and with the other I slide myself over her center until a string of incoherent pleases leave her wet mouth.

The first thrust leaves me euphoric. I pull out and slide in again, slow and steady until her breath quickens.

I want to pace myself; it's been so long, and she is perfect, but she opens her legs wider and digs her heels in my backside, asking for more.

"You're so fucking perfect," I murmur between her lips. Her exhale is my inhale, and it clouds my brain like a drug.

My name comes out in pieces, broken by little moans. Ember eyes shine under the silvery light coming through the window. "You feel so good," Eliza croaks.

We find a rhythm of push and resistance set by the need to be closer, to match the furious thumping of our hearts. She thrashes under my hold, harsh wails of pleasure she fights to hold trapped behind pressed lips.

I slow my movements to catch her attention. "None of that, kitten. Don't hide it from me." I bottom out with a sharp thrust, and she clenches her jaw. "I want to hear you." Another slow drag, making her back arch. I repeat the motion and she finally gives me what I want. A loud moan which shoots through my spine and increases the pressure in my lower abdomen.

"That's my good girl." I slide my arm under her back and pull her to my chest, swallowing her gasp. With her wrapped around me, I move to the end of the bed, propping her against the metal headboard.

"Hold on to the rail," the words scratch the inside of my throat. I'm so close, but I want more of her.

Her arms stretch along the bar and her palms wrap around the chipped-painted frame, which puts her breasts on full display for me. Still on my lap, I spread her wider and push back in, the old bed creaking under us.

Her walls are pulsing around me, and I'm deliriously lost in the feeling, surrounded by her sweet smell and whimpers. It consumes me, pulling at every nerve ending.

"Touch me," she moans as I press her into the bedrail with a steady cadence, sliding my hand between us.

I reach the spot where our bodies meet and draw lazy circles, adding more pressure with each swipe until she cries out. Her messy hair, head thrown back, the melody of our bodies coming together. It's too much. My muscles strain until the tension in my body snaps with a hoarse shout and I have to steady myself against the headboard.

Her arms clasp around me and we're both panting, my pulse erratic.

Eliza's words are muffled against my chest. "If that was you afraid to disappoint me," she exhales, spent, "I don't know if I could handle confident Carter."

I let out a sharp laugh. I should be worried I'm in no rush to roll over and leave. Maybe it's the fact it's the first time I've had sex since ending up in the hospital, but it felt different. Not just a way to relieve tension.

Coming down from our high, she's sober and apprehensive, although I haven't moved, and her walls still pulse around me.

It's supposed to be a reassuring peck, but our lips start moving together. Without urgency but unwilling to let the thread connecting us snap.

We exchanged touches and secrets in the dark. When she asks me about my life the words come easy. She is a fragile wisp of light I want to push against my sternum until it warms me from the inside.

Eliza's breathes even and she falls asleep clutching my hand.

Close to drifting off, a bolt of panic strikes me out of nowhere and I stiffen.

I didn't use a condom.

CHAPTER TWENTY-SEVEN

ELIZA

Carter is gone, his side of the bed crumpled and cold. Old insecurities come barreling in. Does he think it was a mistake sleeping together? Does he regret it?

The front door opens and I slide out of the bed. He's in the middle of the small living room, with an unreadable expression. Before I say anything, he pulls a paper bag out of his jacket and hands it to me.

"Hi, what—" Words fail me when a small box falls in my palm. Plan B.

I told him I was on the pill. Jared kept postponing having kids, so I was always careful. I look at him, but he gives me nothing.

With shaking fingers, I take the pill out and stare at it in my palm.

"Swallow it." His tone does not invite argument.

It goes down smoothly as shards of glass. Shock morphs into annoyance and I straighten my back and pull my shoulders back. "Do you want me to stick out my tongue?"

He's struggling with his decision, so I drink the rest of the water he brought me.

Carter's frame drops an inch and I try not to be offended by his request. Some fresh air will help. Some distance. Last night was a lot and this is not what I expected to happen the second I opened my eyes.

"I needed to be sure," he says evenly, no trace of the tender man who touched me last night.

"Yeah, I get it. Poor girl, rich boy. Why would you trust me when I told you I'm on the pill?" I fumble through the drawers, rummaging for the clothes I came with. "You don't want to be baby-trapped, or blackmailed, or whatever."

I want to get away from him fast and keep my composure while I pull on jeans and shove my feet into my sneakers.

"Let me know when you're ready to leave," I tell him and nearly trip at the look on his face. This is a man in distress. Anguish and regret darken his features.

I'm too hurt to comfort him, and I close the door behind me without another word.

Linda wouldn't let us leave before breakfast with the family and the scattered few who also stayed the night.

Carter materializes behind me and draws out my chair, his hand lingering over the back of my neck when I sit. A weird energy passes between us. Carter is stealing glances and I'm putting on a good front.

Everybody's in good spirits and I focus on their conversations, doing my best to claw my way out of the barrel of old memories. Voices and faces from foster homes. *Waste of space. You're nothing. Nobody wants you.*

Why did Carter's Plan B bother me so much? It makes sense. It's safest. He wanted to be sure. There's a lot at stake for him. It still rubbed me the wrong way.

Carter must have noticed I spaced out because he brushes the inside of my arm, leaning closer. "Where'd you go?" he asks, trying to sound casual, but the crease in his forehead gives him away.

I don't intend to make a scene or embarrass him in any way, so I blurt out the first thing I can come up with. "Oh, imagining having a puppy like your uncle's." My smile is tight, hoping he'll leave it at that. It's so easy to step into my old role. Pretending nothing is wrong.

His brows furrow, but instead of pressing on, he places another slice of French toast on my plate and refills my glass with fresh juice, making his family chuckle and my cheeks bright red.

"Please come back for the Harvest Festival." The youngest girl of the family bats her lashes at me. "We have a booth and a petting zoo and games," she prattles on. I nod politely, not making promises. Carter's going to be long gone by then.

Linda reaches over and takes my hand in a motherly gesture that rattles my heart. "Even if Carter is too busy in New York, we'd be happy to have you."

It takes everything in me not to cry and she doesn't comment on my teary eyes.

We spend two more hours with them, mostly them filling in Carter on thirty years' worth of family lore. Kenneth insists I pick more than one thing from his barn, promising to drop them off at the cabin on one of his deliveries.

It's a struggle to pretend I'm OK. It's just fun, I tell myself. Relax and enjoy this. Don't make it awkward. I turn to my usual silence-filling tactic and bombard him with questions.

"Do you do this every time?" He interrupts me.

"Do what? Be adorable and sociable?"

"Not tell people what you really feel or think."

The deep inhale fueling my tirade gets lodged in my throat because he doesn't give me the chance to defend myself.

"You told my aunt you loved the scrapple. I saw you giving it to the dog under the table."

"I wasn't going to upset the woman in her own house. It's called being polite."

"You let your so-called friends talk you into forgiving your cheating ex for an hour when they should have been thrown out the door after five minutes."

"You heard—"

"You were ready to live in a dingy cabin not fit to house a stray dog, so you wouldn't inconvenience me—"

I defend myself. "Well, you didn't opt for a roommate when—"

"—or Martha and Sam," he looks at me pointedly.

"How do you know about that?"

"Martha is very chatty when she threatens people with bodily harm. They care about you. Still, you'd rather sleep in their abandoned cabin than accept their help."

We don't speak for several minutes.

"Technically it's *my* abandoned cabin now."

He shoots me a very unimpressed glare. "What're you afraid of? That people won't like you because you're honest?"

Yes. Living in constant fear of disappointing people close to me and turning them away with too much neediness is my reality.

"What's your point?" I ask, even though I'm not keen on hearing any more from him.

"What happened this morning upset you."

"I don't know what you mean." Why am I reacting so childishly? It's irrational, but I can't shake the idea that it's a rejection of everything I am.

"It might have been a little harsh. Making you take the pill." His tone is softer. Apologetic. "Are you angry with me?"

"I don't do angry. I told you before."

"You do, you just don't want to admit it. You showed me once."

"It doesn't matter. It's nothing."

He's relentless, poking and prodding. I'm not used to people looking so closely.

"It matters."

"Why? Why do you keep bringing it up?"

"Because I don't want to upset you. I had to do it."

"I don't know about *had to*," I mumble. "I get it. I told you already. It was a little extreme and it caught me off guard. That's all."

An unconvinced scoff vibrates in his throat. "Is it?"

"Look. You didn't foil my plan to baby-trap you. I'm allowed to be annoyed about some things without sharing them with you."

"Why don't you want to talk to me about it?" He sounds genuinely hurt.

Is he for real? Mr. brooding and monosyllabic.

"Because you don't need this intel about me to have sex." My head is starting to throb, and I press my thumbs to my temples, hoping to soothe the pressure.

He's contemplating, and I think he'll drop it, but instead he decides to send me spiraling. "You make me curious. I want to know more."

"You were supposed to be fun and casual," I remind him. "Don't go back on your word."

The phone chimes and Quinn's face flashes on the screen.

"It's time," she squeals before I even get a hello in.

"I love it when you're mysterious and excited, but can you elaborate?"

"You, me, Mike, and some chicken wings. Wednesday after work?"

My mood instantly lifts. Quinn's been testing the waters, and I haven't seen Mike since that night at the pub when she gave him her number. "Yeah, I'd love to go out with you guys."

Carter glances at me sideways but doesn't say anything. His brows scrunch together, but I'm still too sour about what happened this morning to waste my time trying to decipher him.

"Wear the dress you know I love. Prepare to dazzle him and then hit him with the hard questions. I'm counting on you to vet him."

"Yes, yes. I'll wear the pretty dress. I don't know about the rest," I tell her and take in a very confused and frowning Carter. "I have a terrible track record."

Chapter Twenty-Eight

CARTER

I'm in the kitchen getting breakfast ready when my tablet rings.

"What on earth are you doing? Cooking?" Alicia's voice stops me in my tracks. I didn't even bother to check who it was. Only my family video calls me.

She's flawless, as usual, her shiny black hair falling in perfect waves around her sharp features. The tomes in the antique library of her family home behind her deserve an eye roll. I know for a fact she never uses the room for anything other than photo ops and sex.

"Very astute observation."

The cutting tone doesn't deter her. She's not one to give up easily.

"Where have you disappeared to?" She narrows her blue eyes at the screen, pursing her glossy lips. "Are you…on a holiday? Come back, I'll take care of you," she says seductively.

"Don't—"

"Who's she?!" Alicia shrieks and my hand flies to the red button on the screen, realising Eliza just walked into the frame.

She freezes.

"Do you have someone?" Eliza's crestfallen and I rush to reassure her, but she takes a step back. I'm not Jared, damn it.

"She's in the past. I thought it was my mom and I answered."

Eliza shakes her head, pulling away. "She said she'll take care of you."

"Something she certainly can't do. I know that for sure. She didn't know much about what happened when I had the heart attack. From the way my sister reacted, she must have thought I was dying so she just cut her losses."

Eliza looks at me with a slightly nauseated expression. "Tell me she didn't."

"She found out I haven't kicked the bucket and wants back in on the Rawlings money." It surely wasn't for me.

"Do you want to get back together?" she asks in a voice so small it twists my insides.

"It would have ended anyway. She knew it wasn't serious."

Eliza nods but a dark cloud passes over her face. "Even if you'd have ended things at some point, it's still not OK for her to ditch you when you were at your worst."

Her righteous anger on my behalf is amusing. What would she say if I told her about the rest of my dating history? Would she look at me the same or as the stupidest man to walk this earth?

My focus is solely on Eliza. After I found out what it feels like to have her, I'm obsessed.

"Everything is a mess," she mumbles into the pillow after another day of rotting in front of the computer for hours at the shop.

"I know how to make you relax. I saw these in the drawer the first night I arrived." I fish out a box of condoms from my pocket.

"Go and buy some yourself. Just in case I poked holes in those."

So, she's still angry about how I reacted. I know I screwed up, but I couldn't sleep as a wave of panic washed away any rational thought. The nagging paranoia tortured me until I jumped out of bed and called one of my security men to find the nearest pharmacy.

Eliza pinches the bridge of her nose. "I'm sorry. That was unnecessarily mean. But seriously, you should. For your peace of mind."

How can she be so kind and considerate? I'm certain I offended her on so many levels.

"I didn't mean to hurt you."

"It's the truth." She takes a deep breath and decides to let me see another hidden part of her. "I don't want somebody to be stuck with me. I want to have a family with somebody who chooses me," she says, her small palm pressing on the middle of her chest.

The admission weighs heavy in the air between us. I cup her jaw and kiss apologies into her skin. Touch her until she's panting, and I get drunk on the small noises coming out in heated breaths.

I cram her into the small shower and show her the filthy things I imagined doing to her.

The red marker crosses out another day with an annoying scratch I hadn't noticed before. Six more weeks to go. It occurs to me I've thought less and less about returning to the office.

"If you keep glaring, it might catch fire."

"I was just checking—"

"How much longer you have to stay here." She gives me that small smile I've come to recognize. The one putting people at ease. The one that covers her sadness or worry. What she's not saying out loud is I'm using her and running at the first chance. Am I? Isn't this what we agreed on?

I told myself I wouldn't stay the night in her bed. There needs to be a clear line in the sand.

Eliza never says anything. She watches me go, all spent, wrapped in crumpled sheets, cheeks flushed, and lips swollen.

I find it harder and harder to leave.

These mornings with Eliza are something I'll take to the grave with me. I pack and store for old age the sounds in the kitchen, the smells, Eliza telling me stories about the town, little snippets from her childhood, the endless teasing and kissing her against the pantry door.

I never intended to cross this line, but now the urge to taste her lips is all-consuming. The push and pull, the nips and licks, her soft tongue tracing my sensitive inner lip until want is all consuming and my skin burns too hot.

The cold shower comes in the form of my little sister dropping by unannounced. The crunch of tires in the driveway brings me to the front door in a flash, geared up for a confrontation in case it's one of the people Eliza doesn't want to see.

My steps falter when I spot a dark SUV and one of the Rawlings guards I recognize moves to the back of the car and opens the door.

My sister steps gingerly out of the backseat and smiles brightly when she notices me in the doorway, sprinting to launch herself in my arms.

"I gave you space for weeks so you wouldn't bite my head off. I see I was worried for nothing." She pirouettes and takes in the place. "You seem to have settled well enough. It's cozy." Jackie walks into the kitchen and spots Eliza. "Oh, hello!"

"She's"—I hurry to say, in case my sister starts rambling about very inappropriate things—"the host."

Eliza's greeting smile freezes on her face. "Yes, Eliza, just the host." Her laugh has a fake ring to it. "Pleasure to meet you."

"Jackie, this grump's sister. You have a lovely home. I love cottage chic."

"Yes. Thanks." Eliza's shoulders are tense, a small blush dusting her cheekbones. "I'll go" —she gestures toward the door—"check how work is going at the house."

Jackie deflates. "Don't leave on my account."

"I'll give you some privacy," Eliza says, grabbing her keys and jacket. She doesn't spare me a glance and it hits me square in the chest when the door closes behind her.

"Well, if you were getting some—which, good job, she is stunning—you blew that up."

"What?" I focus back on my sister.

"Dear brother," she tuts. "You look like a lost puppy right now."

"You always had a hyperactive imagination."

"Yeah, right. I suggest you find a way to mend things with your *just the host* lady friend. Or your hand will get splinters."

"Don't be gross."

She ignores me. "This breakfast looks nice. Is that tea?"

My scowl doesn't stop her.

"But you hate tea."

"Apparently, nobody else knows how to make a good cup."

Jackie has our mother's soft exterior. Sweet blonde with blue eyes. She never played the cutthroat businesswoman card. She didn't need to scare people into submission. She is too smart. She has instinct and flair.

I hit low, changing the subject. "Adam stopped by three weeks ago."

Jackie stills for a nanosecond but composes herself quickly. We spent so much time together when Adam hovered relentlessly after the Harvard mess. I was glad the two of them got along and I suspected it was more than that. I still don't know what went down, but the shift in dynamic right before she left for London was sharp.

"I haven't seen much of him." She walks along the wall lined with bookshelves and picks up a heavy vintage paperweight, examining it. "He keeps himself busy."

It's an elegant way of saying he's on a binge again after his last breakup. Parties and women. Somehow worse than in our college years. It's self-destructive, an endless cycle over the past seven years.

Jackie has to return to New York, but only after squeezing every detail about Eliza out of me. I make the critical error of showing her the website and unsuccessfully try to keep Jackie from following her social media page.

"Try not to mess this up more than you already have," she tells me when we walk to her car.

"There's nothing to mess up. We're…" Fuck buddies? Friends with benefits? Nothing sounds right. "Temporary."

"God, you're dense sometimes," Jackie scoffs and slams the door in my face.

I keep turning the past few weeks in my head. The moments between us since I arrived here.

An apology is necessary. I know she didn't ask for more, but I don't want her to think I'm ashamed to introduce her to my sister. So I cook dinner and wait until it gets cold. I begin to worry until she texts.

> ELIZA: I haven't been eaten by a bear. I'll stay the night with a friend.

Disappointment drags my mood down even more. I hope her friend is Martha or Quinn because the possibility of it being another man makes my blood boil.

Chapter Twenty-Nine

ELIZA

He's leaving in just over a month, I have a life to set back on track, but I'm playing house with a stranger. What's wrong with me?

When his sister walked in, so beautiful and graceful, the difference between us couldn't have been more obvious. I wasn't expecting to be introduced as a girlfriend, but he seemed ashamed. Ashamed to be associated with me. An orphaned girl working at a fish shop, hiding in the woods. My face never burned so hot from humiliation.

The problem is I never craved somebody's presence with an intensity that scares me. I'm afraid it will consume me and leave me a husk of a person after he leaves.

Finn has to wrap it up faster. I don't care if I sleep on a mattress on the floor. I need to move out before I get too attached to Carter.

"Oh, you brought Quinn's rhubarb tart," Martha says when she lets me in. I feel bad for showing up at her door unannounced, but she must sense I'm off because she doesn't pry when I ask her if I can stay the night.

Martha and Sam Dunton are the parents I wish I had and it's easy telling them about my plan.

"Design courses." Martha stops mid-chew. "That's great. Oh, dear. How exciting!"

"These are online, I thought…" I hesitate, but they both look at me with such pride and excitement, I feed off their encouragement. "I should learn more about it. If I want to make a living out of it."

Sam's grin is infectious. "I might come out of retirement for you. Nobody knows how to work wood like I do." His trust in me is a shot of adrenaline, boosting my spirit.

"Let's see." I temper my enthusiasm. "It'd be good to go to some showroom events in Boston and Portland. Maybe New York. Might learn more about materials and trends. I don't know."

"Hey, don't back out now," Martha says with a resolute set of her brows. "You have a good eye for it and already learned a lot on your own."

She takes Sam's hand and they share a glance, having the sort of conversation married people carry out wordlessly.

"We'll be your first clients. The kitchen is older than our marriage."

I'm speechless and my lower lip wobbles.

"And I heard Mrs. Benson wants to do something about the lake cabin she inherited from her aunt. Spruce it up and rent it," Sam continues, and the dam breaks.

I jump from the chair into their arms and hug them tight. I don't know yet if I can rise up to their hopes, but their faith in me strengthens the decision to follow my passion.

Fat drops of water pelt the window of the Duntons' guest bedroom. I trace them and let my mind drift. I can't sleep when the air is so heavy with dark clouds and loud thunder.

The electricity traveling along the wet molecules in the air settles on my skin, making me fidgety. Thoughts of Carter circle my mind. I can't afford to be reckless with my life and my heart, but I want to enjoy the four weeks we have left.

The ticking clock pushes us closer to the end with each red mark on that annoying calendar. I'll have to be able to be on my own and not let him leave with what little is left of me.

@Jackie_Rawlings started following you.

The notification is soon followed by a series of pings. Carter's sister is a stream-of-one-liners type of texter.

> I'm sorry we didn't get to chat more the other day.
> Love your style.
> Carter showed me your sketches.
> I need you in my cold corporate life.
> I have a mood board.
> Your pieces are adorable and amazing.
> Adorazing? Amarable?
> Anyway.
> My office desperately needs your touch.
> Please don't judge me based on my brother.
> I promise I'm nice.
> Text me if you're interested.

My fingers hover over the keyboard. It's what I set out to do, but she's Carter's sister. What if he thinks I want to weasel myself into his life? What if I'm not that good and—I can't keep thinking like this.

A moment later I hit send.

ELIZA: You had me at mood board.

We launch into conversations about styles and colors. She sends me a lot of pictures from her office and it's a glimpse into Carter's world. That's the building where he goes every day. His office is probably similar. He doesn't want to talk about his job or anything Rawlings Enterprise related and I feel like I'm peeping into something private, but I chase the thought away.

The morning gets better when I meet Quinn and Mike at his place. She's so smitten with him that it makes everything around her brighter.

We're lounging outside in Mike's dingy fishing chairs, telling him about the dos and don'ts of Silver Lake Falls.

"Never go to Joe's barbershop with a pic of some haircut from the internet. It offends his artistic sensibilities, and you'll go home with a bowl cut," I warn him. Jared made this mistake once.

Mike laughs, not taking my advice as seriously as he should. "I've got my trusted clippers. Never been a fan of pampering."

"My rugged woodsman." Quinn looks at him appreciatively. "You're sexy as hell, but you might wanna do something about that air mattress," she says, pointing her thumb toward the house over her shoulder.

"Don't bring the air mattress into this. It's comfortable," Mike huffs in mock outrage.

"Maybe you could give Mike a hand," she tells me sweetly. "His place is more hideout-chic than a home," Quinn teases her boyfriend, who has recently moved to the area.

"Don't be so tough on him." I laugh as he shakes his head, clearly amused. "He must have some good taste." I point to his car. "I love the sky blue color."

"1952 Studebaker," he puffs proudly. "Worked on it with my dad," he says, a bit pensive, and my heart aches for him. He must miss his family.

"I wish I had the time and money to give my ol' gal a makeover," I sigh. On my list of priorities, having a shiny, refurbished car is somewhere second to last.

"I know my way around a car." Mike fidgets with his beer bottle before looking from his girlfriend to me. "I could work on it a bit when I have time. I'm on the road a lot, but I don't know." His voice becomes smaller, and it tugs at my heartstrings. "We could patch it up."

Quinn leans in to take his hand, all starry-eyed, and I have to swallow the knot of emotion.

Back at the site, the team is working on the finishing touches inside. Vaulted ceiling, freshly sanded wood flooring, repainted windows. My little home.

I want to fix the front door myself, so I spend the better part of the day sanding it down and replacing the broken window. Going through the motions relaxes me and also gives me an excuse to stay away from Carter for a bit longer.

The lights are off, and the cabin is quiet when I get back. My insides constrict with guilt when I spot the leftover plate in the fridge. It has a note with my name on it.

I can sense him even before he says anything. "You better practice cooking for one because soon you won't have to bear my presence." I laugh but the joke falls flat in the dimly lit kitchen.

"What do you mean?" I must imagine the hint of panic in his voice.

I'm fussing in the kitchen, avoiding him, filling the teapot and getting the bags of fresh herbs Martha gave me.

"The house is almost ready. I'll be out of your hair in no time." I still avoid looking at him.

"If it's about what I said yesterday…"

I open the oven and spread the herbs on the metal tray.

"You'll have the place to yourself. I'll throw in a month's bonus, if you want, my treat, for intruding on your holiday. You can use the other bedroom if your sister visits or you want to have other people over."

"That wouldn't be a problem if we slept in the same bed."

I take in the tall frame leaning against the kitchen island. Those broad shoulders I love digging my nails into when he presses me into the mattress. The way his clothes hug his taut body. He looks delicious and he pulls me toward him like a magnet. It takes everything in me to stand my ground.

"You know it's not a good idea." I give him a tight smile. I won't let myself be consumed by this fantasy. "I can't keep hiding here. It's not healthy."

The violent whistle of the teapot jolts me out of staring at him and we spend the next five minutes in tense silence while I fix us two cups. I place the teacup in front of him, lingering a second too long in his gravitational pull, and his hand circles my wrist.

"Asking you to stay was one of the best decisions I ever made."

My heart thumps harder, warmth spreading through my limbs. I clamp my mouth shut to keep anything stupid from coming out. *I want to stay. I feel too much around you. This is more than sex.*

Instead, I murmur a soft good night and will my legs to move away.

Chapter Thirty

CARTER

Eliza laughs and throws her head back while one of the construction workers touches her arm, giving her a carefree smile. It's completely unprofessional of him to touch her so casually. The guy looks about her age, a bit rugged around the edges. He's well-built, but I have no doubt I could take him down if he touches her again.

It's the second night in a row she's missed dinner. The way she spoke sounded like a goodbye and I'm not ready. I want more of her until it's time to leave.

That's what I came here to tell her. But the sight of them together unearths something ugly and poisonous from the pit of my soul.

They don't notice me until I stop next to Eliza and wrap my arm around her middle, pulling her flush.

"Hey, kitten. Are you done for today?" I completely ignore the man staring at me.

Eliza recovers faster and slides her palm up my back, confusion marring her features.

"Carter. This is Finn, my foreman. We're talking about the size of the bed in the upstairs loft."

Oh, I remember. The one who's *not* a middle-aged man with three kids. The one Sam keeps trying to set up Eliza with.

"Big enough to fit me," I say, looking at the confused man for the first time. His brows lower and he corrects his posture, unsuccessfully trying to reach my height.

"Carter!" Eliza pinches my side.

"Can I have a word with you?" I don't wait for her answer and pull her toward the tree line.

"Hey, Eliza, are you OK going with him?"

This man is braver or stupider than I thought, but Eliza cuts me off before I show Mr. Foreman he's the one who should be very afraid.

"It's alright. His manners are down for maintenance today," she shouts.

We stop behind a large oak and I step in front of her without touching her, close enough to distinguish the drops of color in her irises. Eliza is waiting, swallowing me whole with her honey eyes.

"You've been avoiding me." I break the silence.

She dismisses me with a bored roll of her eyes. There's my feisty kitten.

"I'm busy. I wish you wouldn't interrupt me so I could get it done faster."

I lean forward and she backs up against the bark. A flash of uncertainty rips through her mask of indifference and her lips open in surprise, wet, inviting. My hands find her hips and I stop before I take her mouth, and press the tip of my nose on her cheek, sliding against the smooth skin until I reach her ear.

"I'm not fond of the jealousy game." My voice comes out coarse. "But if you want to play…" Her lips part to speak and I pull on the lobe of her ear with my teeth because I can't help myself.

"Jealousy?" It comes out half a moan. "Why would you be—"

"Play games again and I'll tie you to the bed and tease you until you lose the ability to speak." I pull her hips forward and Eliza's eyes widen. Everything about her gets me hard and I want to spin her around and slip those tight jeans around her knees. Slide inside her and make her scream. Her pupils are blown wide and the quick warm exhales down my neck make me think she wants it too.

"Eliza, we're done with the shiplap." That guy's voice is too close. He doesn't have any self-preservation instincts.

"Dinner is at seven. Don't be late." I kiss the corner of her mouth and Eliza leans in, searching for more. "Mr. Foreman better be keeping his hands to himself. While I'm still here, I don't share. Understood?"

Eliza pulls out of her lust-induced daze and when my words settle, she snaps the mask back on, squaring her shoulders. She pushes me and slips away, stomping the ground, shaking her head.

The satisfaction I get from staking my claim is as new to me as acting like a possessive boyfriend.

Rationally, I know I shouldn't. I might return home before the three months are up. My mother is pleased with my progress and as much as I trust Jackie, I don't want to leave all the pressure on her.

This complicated tapestry of intimacy and lust we're threading is ill-advised. I'm drawn to her and crave her presence. I'm a normal person around her. Her touch makes me feel alive. Present. Makes me want things I have no business imagining.

Even considering accepting the extra month is proof she is messing with my head. I never hesitate when it comes to my duty. And yet, I keep staring at the flowers she drew on the calendar, at the end of the bonus month.

Eliza comes home in the evening and changes before she sits next to me at the kitchen counter. What I said today swarms in my head, but she doesn't push me to talk while we cook together. The tension is a floating ball of energy between us. The spark ignited a month ago is now too big to be ignored. We don't mention it because it leads to questions without answers.

We move around each other with the naturalness of long-term partners and this familiarity puts my mind at ease in a way that makes my heart tremble with fear.

When dinner is done, she threads her fingers through mine and leads me to the bedroom. In the dark room, she strips herself and then peels the clothes off me without a word, her eyes unwavering.

She kisses me tenderly until I let myself melt under her lips. Then her palm envelops me, and I let her stroke me until she pushes me onto the bed and guides me against the headboard then she slowly begins to roll her hips, coating me in her arousal. Eliza lifts her hips and without hesitation takes me in a swift move that leaves me breathless.

"Fuck, you feel so good." I bring her down, pressing her against my chest.

Her forehead pushes against mine.

"More, please," she moans.

Her movements pick up speed and I anchor myself to her hips, digging my fingers into her. I chase the sensation bubbling in my lower back and press her against me so I can control the rhythm. Closer. Deeper, as her walls squeeze me.

Eliza screams my name and shudders, fingers clenched in my hair. I hold her tighter.

It's more intimate, the air charged with what we both don't want to admit out loud. Her pants drive me wild, and my thrusts become erratic until I fall into the void, murmuring words of praise in her hair, tattooing the imprint of her body on my nerve endings.

Eliza is soft and malleable on top of me, only the rustle of the trees and the night crawlers breaking the heavy silence.

She slowly lifts her head from the crook of my neck and her hot breath slides above my collarbone, over my pecs, and rests at the top of my scar, the tips of her fingers tracing the line. This is not the clinical touch of my doctor. I tense. Nobody else has touched the scar. Warm lips brush against it and it shakes me to my soul. I can't wrap my head around the way her touch brings the sort of pleasure that resonates to my core.

"I hate it," I find myself confessing. "It reminds me how weak I am." I feel exposed, even in the pitch-dark room, but her next words lack any judgment or pity.

"It makes you look like somebody who went to hell and back and survived to tell the story." She traces the scar with her finger and it warms my entire chest, coating my heart in a cocoon. "If anything, it makes you look like a warrior."

A strangled laugh rushes out of me, and I say the stupidest thing without using any brain cells. "Then stay here. I need a princess to protect."

I know it's a mistake even before she stiffens in my arms.

"This is not a fairy tale, Carter," she says softly, without reproach, but the distance she keeps slices through me, even if I know she's right.

The night rushes past faster than I wanted. I don't leave her bed. Why torture myself?

It's just temporary.

The next morning the bed is empty, and it leaves this hollow feeling in my chest.

The foiled breakfast plate on the kitchen island is such a bittersweet reminder of something so quintessentially Eliza. There's also a note with a ridiculous sketch of a female stick figure, with what I guess is a painting brush in hand, near a toddler-level drawing of a house. The silly note makes me smile, imagining her hunched over the island, the tip of her tongue peeking out.

"I'm so screwed," I mutter to myself, digging the heels of my palms into my eyes, hoping for a reset.

The walk to her cabin clears my head, so I won't put a damper on her enthusiasm. Even though I know helping her brings the day she'll move closer, I'm compelled to support her.

I find her surrounded by different sizes of deconstructed pieces of wood, paint cans, and tools.

"Should I be worried you could hammer a coffin out of that?"

"I had this idea in my sleep." She beams at me and my chest hurts. This is bad. Horrible. Can't be happening to me. "It was too early; I didn't want to wake you."

"The brilliant idea was to dumpster dive for all the broken cabinets and shelves in town?"

She laughs and the way it affects me almost has me running into the wilderness surrounding us.

"I saw this tutorial on YouTube about building a corner office by the window with different storage spaces. I dreamed about how I wanted to build mine. It's going to be perfect!"

"YouTube," I repeat, shaking my head. Eliza confidently watches a tutorial on any DIY project and has zero doubt she can do it. She's amazing. I heave a long-suffering sigh. "Show me."

She gives me her phone and I watch a blonde in overalls being too chipper about measuring the walls and taking apart some old study, when the phone vibrates and a message pops up.

> FINN: You can take me out to lunch as a thank you. It would be a win-win for me 😉

My hand tightens on the phone. The device barely escapes the sledgehammer resting near the other tools.

"Mr. Foreman keeps being inappropriate."

"Stop calling him that. It's weird." She rips the phone from my hand and starts texting. "Finn's just being a nice guy."

"With an agenda."

"That's rich coming from you. Aren't you going back to *your* home in a few weeks? What more do you want from me?"

To live in this bubble a little longer. To take you with me.

"I don't want anything bad to happen to you. That's all."

She huffs. "Thanks for the concern but our arrangement has given me a taste for casual flings. It's not the worst idea."

I'm going to murder Finn the fucking foreman.

The next days blend together with an unsettling speed. I'm not ready to let her leave, but she is either working at the shop or putting the finishing touches on her new home. I hold on tight to the silly conversations during breakfast, to her smell as she kisses me on the cheek before leaving, to her content sight whenever she finds the perfect spot for one of her pieces, or the soft moans coming out in breathy waves when we spend the night together and pleasure overwhelms her.

I end up doing something against my nature. I almost beg when it's time to move her tools from the shed.

"Are you sure you want to move out?" I scramble for any reason to make her stay. "Your new shed is a lot smaller. Where are you going to put these?" I shake the box in my hand to make my point.

"I can put some of them inside," she says. "This time no one will tell me they smell bad or that it's a junkyard. I'll use the storage space under the kitchen."

"Is there really a rush to move? I thought you liked it here."

She smiles at me with warmth, and I can see the determination shining bright in her eyes.

"I've never lived alone. Deciding for myself as an adult. I carried the abandoned child's fear for too long. At this age, I shouldn't rely on somebody to take care of me."

"There's nothing wrong with receiving help."

"Says the man who was forced to take a break after almost dying."

"Fair point. But I shouldn't be the standard for normal behavior." I try to lighten the mood and make her smile.

"I don't want to be afraid to be on my own anymore. It's holding me back."

"Don't downplay what you achieved by yourself so far. That's all you. Nobody can take it away."

The way she gazes at me makes me think I said too much.

I desperately want her to stay. I know I can convince her if I outright beg. But I can't be another obstacle in her way.

"It's better if I go by myself. I'll be too tempted to make you stay over." She grins at me, but her nerves are showing in the way she fiddles with the handles of a worn-out duffel bag.

The silence of her absence pierces my ears.

CHAPTER THIRTY-ONE

ELIZA

It's surreal. I'm lounging on a chair on *my* extended porch admiring the sunset. The evening is cool, and the skies changed into beautiful shades of orange and pink, but the gray clouds rolling in worry me.

The first hour of living here I wander around, admiring *my* tiny home. From the bright white wood siding to the Victorian lamp Carter got me lighting the porch above the deep green door, I can't wrap my head around the fact that it's mine.

When I eventually crawl into bed, the adrenaline rush and excitement fade away and it leaves too much room for the sounds of a home with only one inhabitant. The creaks from the walls, leaves rustling outside as the gentle whistle of the wind moves the trees. A June storm is in the air. Did I close the windows? Turn off the oven? I stare at the ceiling wondering why I thought moving in alone was a good idea.

The phone rattles on the nightstand and I lunge for it, answering a bit breathlessly, "Yeah?"

Carter's laugh travels through the speaker, a comforting sound in the middle of the storm of doubt brewing in my head.

The stir of the forest echoes in my ear. "Are you out?"

"Just wanted to take a stroll," he says like it's no big deal he's not from around here and it's pitch-black outside.

"At this hour? Don't get lost."

"Don't worry, I know my way between your house and the cabin with my eyes closed."

My heartbeat spikes. "Where exactly are you?"

It's stupid but I want to know, even if it's a dangerous territory we've been both thoughtlessly toeing.

"Nearby if you need me."

I'm close to flying down the stairs out onto the dirt path connecting us. I fist the sheets and draw my knees under my chin to stop myself.

"Can you tell me more about those satellites of yours?"

He chuckles and I know he's smiling.

"I was a teenager when my father stood in the middle of the command center, and we launched the first satellites." Carter's deep and even voice lulls me to sleep and I close my eyes, a strange feeling of safety relaxing my muscles. I don't know how long he's on the phone with me talking about broadband, Earth's orbit, spot beams, and bent-pipe architecture, but in the morning, I'm still clutching the phone to my chest.

Quinn made me promise to stop by for coffee after I moved and now I'm staring at a house-shaped cake with pink icing that says, *Congrats! You're a big girl.* 🩶 I'm doing my best not to cry and hug her to death.

"There, there." She pats my head, "it's just a cake."

"You're awesome," I snivel. "Does Mike know how lucky he is?" The man seemed crazy about Quinn.

"It's dawning on him." She plays coy. "He's been sending me flowers and planning dates."

"That gets him bonus points in my book. I always had to beg Jared to take some initiative. Not flowers and presents, but the little things to show I was on his mind, you know?"

"You don't have to teach somebody to think about you. They either do or don't," she says with a frown, and I get the impression she's not talking about Jared. "I'll come over for lunch someday." She abruptly changes the subject. "Break the house in for visits. I'll bring food."

"Don't close the coffee shop for me."

"Ah, don't worry. My landlord miraculously lowered my rent. By a lot. I don't know what got into him. I can pay a part-time employee now. I hired him three days ago."

"Look at you! Does he call you ma'am or boss?"

"Neither. Quinn Supreme." She laughs. "I expect nothing less." She worries her lip. "I would've asked you, but you made it pretty clear you don't want to mix things again."

"Yeah, after the friends-at-the-office fiasco, I'm not doing that again, don't worry," I assure her, and I mean it. "Do you want to expand beyond coffee and pastries now that you have help?"

"Yeah, but I'd need a lot more investment money I don't have. For more space, a bigger kitchen, staff. Who knows? Maybe one day I can cater for small events."

"Yo, Quinny!" a scrawny teenager calls from the kitchen door. "The fruit guy is here."

She groans and I mutter a *Quinn Supreme, my ass,* under my breath, earning a finger salute from her.

"Excuse me, are you from around here?"

An out-of-towner smiles at me from the other side of the small table. It's obvious he's a tourist and his shy smile and the wedding ring on his finger put me at ease.

We strike up a conversation and I find out he's on an anniversary trip with his wife. He's so sweet I give him a full list of the best restaurants in the area for a romantic date and places they could visit. I love Silver Lake Falls and I'm so happy to share my little town with the tourists who want to discover its little hidden gems.

Carter sways leisurely through my home, a small smile tugging at the corner of his lips.

"What's so funny?"

"This place is so you. Sunny, cozy."

I don't know why his comment makes me all warm and gooey.

His hair is overgrown after two months, giving him a boyish air. The strands fall over his eyes when he bends to peer at the sketches in the best spot in the house: the little workspace under the window, facing the lake.

"I like this look on you," I say.

"Maybe I'll keep it and shock everybody in the office."

The subject of his departure is sobering. We have an expiration date.

We fall into a rhythm. He comes in the evenings with dinner I learned to accept without giving myself an aneurysm.

Most of the time we don't make it to bed. There's a hunger and a rush to feel one another as much as possible.

He takes me slow and hard.

The power he has over me scares me. Whenever we're close this version of me tentatively makes her way to the surface. The more time I spend with him, the bolder she gets, demanding more and more. Demands to shine, to try, to say more. Picks at the hard shell until she makes space to hatch. Until it expands to the very tips of my toes and the ends of my hair.

I get lost in his eyes, shining with unspoken feelings. Maybe if I told him first.

"Carter, I—"

"Don't. Please." He kisses my forehead, my nose, and a deep kiss robs me of any words I wanted to say.

It hurts, but he has a point. That's not what we agreed to. I'll keep it to myself for the few weeks he'll be here. My little treasure.

"Will you stay tonight?" I refused to let him stay over in an attempt to prove I could do it on my own, but all it did was waste the precious time I had left with him.

He doesn't answer but kisses my neck and murmurs, so softly into my hair, the secret we won't talk about. "I'd never leave."

The sight of a shirtless Carter cooking breakfast in my kitchen is the newest item on the list of things he does to turn me on. Even after I stumbled into the bathroom and saw his scar, he's not usually comfortable exposing it except when we have sex.

Carter's ease in this unguarded moment scorches me, a molted stream, flowing through my veins.

I stare at him without any restraint. I've gotten past the point of being ashamed to appreciate his body, but the faint pink on the tips of his ears when he sees me tugs at my heartstrings with a dangerous force.

Carter scratches the back of his head, looking unsure. "I can put something on if it bothers you."

"Don't you dare." I walk closer, overpowered by the urgency to feel his skin under my palms. "This kitchen hasn't seen something so hot since Sam nearly burnt it to a crisp frying clams."

"Your compliments could use some work."

"Maybe I can show my appreciation another way."

Carter's lips twitch. "Are you going to bake me some cookies?"

"Not quite. Since you're so fond of games," I challenge him, fueled by that unfamiliar boldness, "grab the counter."

Carter leans against the kitchen cabinets, smiling down on me with a mixture of amusement and intrigue playing in his eyes. In the daylight, I admire the ripples of his muscles as his hands hook over the wood top. My core tightens, but I have to be patient. To get him as mad with want as I am whenever he touches me.

The tips of my fingers reach for his jaw and travel down his neck, over his bobbing Adam's apple, skimming his scar, and resting on his taut abdomen when he takes a sharp intake of air.

"If you touch me, I'll stop," I warn him.

In a flash, his eyes become almost black. "What?" He grits out.

My fingers slide lower, need pulsing between my legs. When my fingers hover over the waistband, Carter almost stops breathing, staring at me, his gaze a roaring fire. I pull him out and when I lick my palm a low growl rumbles in his chest, spurring me on.

Being in control sparks a surge of power, pushing me to make him lose his mind with every stroke and twist of my wrist. He gets harder in my palm, his knuckles white from gripping the counter.

"I have to touch you."

"Patience, Mr. Rawlings. I'm having too much fun."

"I bet you are," he says through his teeth. "Driving me mad—" A deep moan cuts him off and his head falls back. "Fuck…I want to spread those beautiful legs of yours and bury myself so deep, you'll never forget the consequences of teasing me."

"Oh," I whisper teasingly in his ear and nip his earlobe, earning a shudder. "I've just gotten started."

"You're playing with fire, kitten."

My knees hit the floor and I scrape his inner thighs with my nails. Carter looks in pain.

"Then we'll both go up in flames."

He opens his mouth to say something, but the words melt away on an exhale when I take him in my mouth and his hand shoots to the back of my skull.

I let him guide me, drunk on his pleasure.

Breaking Carter's composure brings a high I never want to come down from.

Chapter Thirty-Two

Carter

An array of annoying pings yanks me from a fitful sleep. Getting used to sleeping next to Eliza makes the lonely nights pass in excruciating restlessness.

I grab the phone, an impending sense of doom looming over me. After my mother and Jackie froze me out there was little reason for it to ring this much. The message on the screen makes my blood freeze. It's a media alert on my name.

Dozens of articles fill the screen.

Is Carter Rawlings Dead? Shocking Revelation Rocks Rawlings Enterprise!

Carter Rawlings' Heart Attack Sparks Uncertainty at Rawlings Enterprise!

CEO Crisis: Rawlings Enterprise Braces for Turmoil Amid Carter Rawlings' Health Scare!

Panic twists my insides as I go through the articles filled with details only a handful of people know. And Eliza.

My phone pings again with a message from an unknown number. It's a picture taken from outside Quinn's coffee shop. Fuck. This can't be.

Eliza is at the coffee shop with— I slam the phone on the bed and bend over in pain, clutching my head. I couldn't have been this stupid. The only man who hates me more than my business rivals is chatting with her, taking notes. Fred Pierson, the reporter hunting for any scrap to write shit about me.

I leap out the door, anger filling me. With every step, something cracks in me.

"Hi—" She jumps back when I burst through the unlocked door of her tiny home.

"You sold me out!" I yell, chest heaving with rage.

Her forehead creases. "What're you—"

"I was an idiot for believing your sweet girl act." Pacing through the small living room, like a cornered animal. "I have to admit it. You were pretty good, I'll give you that."

"Carter!" Eliza stomps her feet, eyes big with worry.

"I'm talking about this." I shove the phone in her face, and she pales as she scans the headlines.

"How? Wait." Her eyebrows scrunch and understanding dawns on her. "You suspect it was me?"

Without a word, I show her the incriminating picture.

She squints at the screen and a flicker of recognition flashes in her eyes. "He's the guy I met a few days ago."

"Yes, you met with Fred Pierson. A fucking reporter."

Her mouth hangs open. "I had no idea who he was. We chatted for five minutes and then he left," she says feebly, wringing her hands.

"Chatted. That's what you call spilling my biggest secret?"

"I'd never tell anyone about—" she stammers. "He said he was on holiday and asked about a good restaurant."

"And I'm supposed to believe it's a coincidence?"

"Have you had any reason to doubt me so far?"

"I—" I swipe a hand through my hair in frustration. "I don't know, Eliza. OK? When you're me—"

"Oh, poor rich guy, everybody is out to get him." She slashes the air with her palm, looking at me with pure anger. "Me sleeping with you was a long con? So I can spill your secrets to the press?" She paces, agitated, furious.

"I—"

"We have this thing. 'Casual', as you put it," she says, slashing the air with her palm. "Yet you don't act it."

I want to defend myself. I never intended to lead her on in any way.

"You're the one who does these sweet and thoughtful things, who touches me like there's not going to be another woman, who wants to share secrets and truths and *you* accuse *me* of being deceitful?" Her tone is shrill, pointing a finger toward me.

This conversation took a turn I wasn't expecting, and my reply sounds feeble even to me. All anger drains away, leaving too much room for doubt.

"Eliza, you know I have to leave."

"Yeah, I know." She exhales loudly, trying to expel her emotions. "And still I'm falling for you like a fool," she says, looking straight into my eyes.

My brain refuses to have any reaction and my muscles are rigid. Her cheeks turn redder and her lovely hazel eyes are shiny. Eliza's throat contracts and her hand flies to grab the truck keys from the table.

She swiftly maneuvers around me, leaving plenty of space so she doesn't have to touch me, while I can't find my voice or ability to move from where I'm rooted in place.

Her footsteps falter behind me and I'm both hopeful and terrified she might turn back.

"I would never do that to you." It's the last thing she says, her small voice barely audible, before the door slams shut.

The phone keeps vibrating in my pocket. It rang from the moment I left the cabin, but my rage kept me focused on the person I wanted to find and punish.

"Finally!" Jackie exhales on the other end. "We've been trying to reach you all morning. Joe is on the line."

"I saw the news," I tell her before she starts her rant.

"I'm sorry, Carter," she says, and the worry and stress in her voice are unmistakable. "It was one of the nurses at the rehabilitation center."

The ground runs from under my feet and I slump on Eliza's couch, a different kind of ache spreading its tendrils around my chest.

"I can't believe this," I croak out.

"Our investigator traced the source to one of the temporary nurses."

Fuck. I screwed up.

"But she was not the only source." This time disgust laces Jackie's words. "Pierre gave Fred Pierson the bits he needed to start digging."

Adam warned me. "She didn't know anything. What—"

"Your little girlfriend put two and two together. She's not stupid."

"I've never had anything to do with her outside the office!" I defend myself.

Jackie sights, exhaustion bleeding into her voice. "Either way, she was worried about you and thought sharing notes with Fred would give her some answers. The fucker duped her like a first grader."

"We'll handle things. Don't do anything stupid in the meantime." Joseph's voice comes down like a hammer.

"Too late for that," I sigh.

"What did you do?" Jackie asks.

I tell her and she snaps, Joseph's groans in the background not helping. "How convenient. You received an anonymous photo exactly when the news broke."

"It made sense," I defend myself.

"For an idiot, maybe!" she yells, and I don't think I've ever heard her so agitated in my life. "Send Derrick the number and the data with the photo." Jackie pauses and takes a deep breath. "Although I wouldn't get my hopes up."

Silence fills the house and my thoughts spiral out of control until Joseph's voice reminds me he's also on the call.

"Who's Eliza?"

I crash back on the comfortable couch, the memories of nights spent with Eliza in the same spot filling me with regret.

"A wonderful woman who might want me dead."

"Ah, so your future wife." He chuckles but it does nothing to ease the increasing pressure against my ribs.

"Let's not. I'm not in the mood for your jokes."

"Who said I'm joking?"

This is not the time to dive into it with him, so I change the subject. "How's my mother? I didn't get to call her."

"Of course, because you were too busy accusing an innocent woman of selling the story to the press. I'm more interested in the fact you told her." Before I can say anything, he continues. "She's fine. Worried about how you'll react. Blaming herself for not convincing you to release a statement after it happened."

The ball of guilt grows bigger, clogging my airways. It's my fault. I refused to let anyone know. My pride disguised as the company's interest meant more to me than her peace of mind.

"I'll come back tonight."

"Stay put, son. Let us figure things out for once."

"But—"

"I'll call you later with an update."

I'm glued in the same spot until the sun is high in the sky, processing the situation.

JACKIE: Burner phone, I'm afraid.

Shit. What we have will come to an end soon. There's no point in dwelling on it, but she still deserves an apology.

My body aches from sitting for so long, unmoving, mulling things over. Cooking dinner would be more productive. The beginning of an apology. Some steps and motions to keep me from going back on my decision to come clean. At this point, I've already given up so many long-kept secrets I'm starting to think she puts truth serum in that tea.

It's late when she comes back and seems none too pleased to find me still lingering in her home.

"What're you still doing here? Did you go through my drawers checking for a fat wad of cash? Or do you want to see my pathetic bank statement?" She's seething and I'm just happy she's not freezing me out.

She doesn't move away from the door, and I don't make any hasty moves. I don't want her bolting until we've talked.

"I owe you an apology," I say cautiously.

Eliza crosses her arms, shredding me with unrestrained annoyance. "Let's hear it."

God, I love it when she's no longer hiding, standing up for herself, even if it's at my expense. I fully deserve it.

"I'm sorry I accused you." It's strange how easily I can utter these words when apologies were a foreign concept in my vocabulary until I came here. "I didn't have all the facts and I overacted."

My father is probably rolling in his grave.

"Overreacted? You barged in here yelling! You didn't even ask me anything, just pointed fingers and accused me of…of tricking you. Selling your story like…like…" She's so flustered words fail her, but then she composes herself and pierces me with watery eyes.

Her tears are a knife twisting in my heart. I want to reach her, but she puts her palm up.

"People have called me a lot of names. But hearing you accuse me of selling you out? Nothing ever hurt so bad."

"Eliza—" I whisper, gutted by her admission.

"Why do you even bother? You'll be gone anyway, and it couldn't be more obvious you don't trust me."

"I have a hard time trusting people. I've been burnt before."

"If it's the Alicia story again, I got the gist." She drops her hands and her shoulders slump, finally moving closer to the pots on the cooker.

I want to wrap my hands around her and hold her tight, but I've got one chance to make this right with her and won't risk it.

"Unfortunately, no. Let's sit. Please."

Eliza tilts her head, pinning me to the spot with her searching eyes. After a few seconds, she comes to a conclusion and motions us to the porch with a heavy sigh and we plop on the front steps. She's looking out, her face devoid of any emotion, having already decided there's nothing I can tell her worth her forgiveness.

Chapter Thirty-Three

Carter

"My father was very controlling. What I've told you were just the little things. He kept me on a short leash all my life."

She gives a noncommittal hum and I swallow my shame to keep going.

"When I finally went to Harvard, I thought I'd be free and live a little. I met Laura at a campus bar. She was so interesting, and I couldn't care less she went to a community college nearby. It made it better. She was different. We dated for four years."

The information piques Eliza's interest and she finally turns to look at me.

"It ended badly? Considering she's not in the picture?"

"I went home after graduation planning on telling my parents I wanted to propose and move her to New York. The moment I stepped off the plane she ghosted me. She didn't answer my calls, texts. Nothing. I was frantic and thought something had happened to her. I was about to call the police."

The next part still makes bile rise in my throat. It's a visceral reaction I can't shake.

"That's when my dear father told me I shouldn't get so worked up over Laura because it was over."

"Did he have anything to do with her disappearing?" she asks, horrified.

"Worse. He had a hand in her coming into my life. He paid her to be with me and disappear once I graduated."

Eliza's eyes widen, a disgusted grimace twisting her face. "No."

"I didn't believe him and went back, desperate to prove it was a lie. Our apartment was empty, her things gone as if she didn't exist." I went to the cafeteria on campus where she worked and found out she quit the day I left. *I love you. Can't wait to start a family.* The last thing she told me before I got in the car.

"Why would anyone do that? It's sick!"

Here's why I might be falling for this woman too. After being a gigantic dick to her this morning she's still angry on my behalf.

"For my own good apparently. To avoid being baby-trapped or getting too distracted with girls and failing school." In hindsight, she always pushed me to study, claimed to hate parties. I was so naive and grateful for her interest after years of being starved for any meaningful connection. "His puppet was supposed to behave and come back to be his obedient heir."

Something broke in me after Laura. The certainty that there is nothing else to love about me besides my money rooted itself deep in my soul. "I could never trust my feelings after being so wrong, or trust anyone else to be genuine."

She was my first everything and while it meant the world to me, she was pretending.

The notion of love was tainted. Every memory, every word muddied by the knowledge it was not only fake, but bought with a lot of money. There was no room for doubt or the feeble hope she might have loved me. After four years I couldn't even have that. The gray area of ignorance. It was a painful void. It was only business.

"How can somebody just give years of their life away?"

"For the right amount, some people would consider it." For a long time I tried to figure out what motivated Laura for four years to lend her life to my father. "I'm sure she had a dream she needed money for."

Eliza's pensive. She's so transparent with her emotions, they're dancing like a kaleidoscope on her features. "I wonder if it was worth it."

"What? Spending time with me in exchange for money?" I scoff.

"No, to pay for her dreams with pieces of a man's broken heart."

The unexpected rush of emotion tightens my throat and leaves me speechless. Ever since it was clear I'd been played, I've never let myself feel the hurt and disappointment. Angus Rawlings didn't want a weak son.

Eliza shakes her head, looking shell-shocked. "That's horrible. Nobody deserves to be crushed with so little regard." Then she bends her knee, shuffling closer until she can lightly squeeze my leg with her delicate hands and it's such a bliss to be warmed by her bright light again. "That's an awfully lonely way to live your life. But I'm not her. Other people in your life won't be her. You can't keep hurting everybody, yourself included. You're a smart man. Find a way."

She leans forward, sliding her arms around me, and holds tight, just like the night at the top of the lighthouse, fusing some of the broken parts with the sheer force of her care. "I'm still mad at you."

"I'll make it up to you until I leave."

It's supposed to be a joke, but the reality douses us in cold water. We embrace in silence until we need to reheat the food. Neither of us brings up her confession from this morning. She might regret it and I'm too confused and drained from rehashing the most humiliating and heartbreaking moment of my life.

Articles keep pouring out, a few mentioning Jackie's statement. The sharks smell blood in the water and they're circling, sinking their teeth into my life. Questioning my fit as the company's CEO after my father's death, dissecting my personal affairs, painting me as a playboy.

Even one of the biggest financial newspapers publishes a damning piece that affects the price of our shares. It's the first big drop in thirty years. And it's my fault. I should be back doing damage control, not having a heart-to-heart with a woman I'll never see again after my exile is finished.

Exposing my past to her only reminded me of what my life is supposed to be. There is no place for her and no point in considering it. The feelings I might have are irrelevant. My life and work are in New York.

The next days are spent in never-ending video calls and crisis meetings. It's bad enough that my mother and

Jackie finally relent and let me back in, even if I'd prefer to be in the boardroom, not pacing the floors of the cabin. It helps me feel in control and distance myself from Eliza. Put some much-needed space between us. She doesn't press and I don't know why I'm not happier about it.

Until Martha calls. "It's time I cashed in your promise to join us for dinner."

"It's not a great time."

"Even more reason to take the night off and relax." Eliza must have told her. "You can't leave before you taste my famous moose roast."

"That sounds…" Appalling. I wonder if she hunted it herself; she would be the type. "Intriguing."

"We're expecting you both tomorrow. Don't be late, Sam's been fretting with his computer, but he's too proud to ask for help."

When did I become the IT guy?

The conversation forces the thought of Eliza back to the front of my mind. Why did I tell her the whole story? She manages to peel off the layers of protection my father built with terrifying ease; the shields woven into my being to the point I can't tell the difference.

Solitude is preferable to finding out I'm worth nothing more than my name and fortune. I'm in control when I don't let people get too close and allowing her to hold this power over me is not a gamble I'm willing to take.

A clear sign this is a mistake is that I spent too much time thinking about her instead of focusing on what's important and real. I must have lost my mind.

The small section of wine is not something to write home about. I've been stuck in this aisle for far too long picking a bottle. And stalling. I dread seeing Eliza for the first time in days.

The laughter of two women in the next row distracts me and my ears perk up at the mention of Eliza's name.

"Greta saw them at Mark's restaurant. She says it looked like a very romantic dinner. She was all over the boy."

I peer through the gap in the shelves and one of them is leaning over the shopping cart, hungry for gossip.

"I would be too if he was my meal ticket. The fact that he's a hunk doesn't hurt."

They cackle and I'm livid. The seed of doubt sprouts and unease slides up my backbone. Is the way she gives herself to me and the intensity of it fake? She didn't strike me as that kind of a person. But neither did Laura and she had me fooled for four years.

My mood sours as I keep turning over the facts in my head on my way to Eliza's. I'd reluctantly agreed to leave together. Each news alert is a drop of gas on my foul disposition. They've been relentless.

I'm shaking my head by the time I finish the last report and she opens the door.

"Can I help with anything?" Genuine concern pinches her features.

"I wasted my time here," I scoff, waltzing into her house. "It's all going to shit and I'm making social calls."

Her steps falter on the way to get her bag. "You don't have to come. I guess you have more important things to take care of." There's no hint of reproach in her voice. She doesn't look at me, and I hate she's so considerate.

"What's two more wasted hours?" I dismiss her. It's petty and a cheap shot. I don't attempt to contain the frustration eating me alive while I write a rebuttal in the company crises group chat.

The front door slams behind her and a wave of guilt washes over me before I remind myself I have more pressing issues in my life than cradling her ego.

During dinner, Sam keeps trying to engage me in conversation, but my mind keeps drifting to the list of tasks to delegate.

"How is it going with the courses?" Martha asks and I don't know who she's talking to until I lift my eyes from the plate.

"Not bad. Mostly they show me I've got a long way to go before I can call myself an interior designer," Eliza says with a self-deprecating laugh.

"You're taking classes?" The question spills out before I can temper the incredulity marring my words.

Eliza recoils but looks at the Duntons and shrugs. "It's just some online course from a school in New York." The way she minimizes her efforts doesn't sit well with me. "Who knows if anything will come of it?"

"You already have talent and a website. It's a start." I try to soothe the defensiveness in her stance.

"What website?" Martha asks, frowning at me.

"Oh, Carter made one for me. In case I want to start a business. I haven't got around to—"

The way Martha lights up, you'd think I saved all the kids from a burning building, and it makes me uncomfortable. It's no big deal.

Who am I kidding? I'm more invested in Eliza's life than I should be. The traitorous warmth on my face gives them the wrong impression because Sam flashes me a huge grin and pats my shoulder.

"There's no shame in doin' what we can for our special ladies, son."

What's going on between us is growing into something too real. Emotional touches too hot for my liking. I preferred my clinical spreadsheets and clean reports.

How did she trick me into wanting to make her dreams come true? That tendril of doubt grows larger, curling around my brain, blinding me to anything but the pressing urge to get out.

We drive back in silence after Eliza stops trying to pull anything but monosyllabic answers out of me. I'm so wound up, my skin vibrates with the force of the storm brewing inside of me. Doubts about her, the dread of going back, worry and frustration over the company and the scandal. It's all churning in my solar plexus.

I follow Eliza inside her little home out of habit and while she talks about her classes, I stare aimlessly out the window, into the dark forest.

What am I still staying here for? My sister did a great job calming the investors and the public but today UniCore posted an attack piece causing another drop. Their CEO and perpetual thorn in my side is saying my disappearance left the company adrift and an inside source claimed the investors are still worried despite Jackie's reassurances.

"During our last class, the teacher mentioned the school has these events in their auditorium. They bring out successful people in the industry and students can ask them questions."

She's excited and I finally turn to look at her. "You plan on going?"

"I'd love to check it out," she says with more enthusiasm now that I've tuned in to the conversation. "I could visit you after you go back. Crash your place in the middle of the night, scare you to death, and then force you to be my roommate for three months."

She laughs, but I see red.

There's no stopping the aftermath of the worries colliding inside my head. The torture of having thoughts of a life with her and ruining my future because I want too much to stay here with her. Everything I worked for, my father worked for. My mother and Jackie left without protection.

"Don't think I'll be your golden ticket out of here. You're nice but there's nothing more."

All the joy drains from her face, her lips parting. Her wide eyes swim with confusion and hurt.

Fuck, this does not feel better.

"Get over yourself, Carter. I'm perfectly happy here!" She bites her lip, hands-on hips, piercing me with a cutting gaze. "OK, not perfectly." She pinches the ends of her hair and twirls the strand deep in thought. Then with a resolute exhale, she continues. "I'll be happy. I'll make it happen."

"Who're you trying to convince?" I scoff.

"At least I'm not afraid to try."

"To what end? We're not—"

"I made the jump." She cuts me off. "Even with an end date I still let myself fall. It scared the hell out of me. I never took risks, but you know what? It feels wonderful. Even with the hurt waiting around the corner. I'd rather get burned than not live at all. Can you say the same?"

"You're too naive," I bite.

"Aren't you tired of pretending you feel nothing? How long are you going to lie to yourself?"

It stings. Calling me out like that.

"Just because we fucked around for a few weeks doesn't mean you know me."

Eliza gasps and steps back, holding a hand to her collarbone.

"Please, save me your self-righteous pity. This whole simple and happy act. You all want the money and the glamor. The man with the fat pockets." I serve a quote direct from my father. "I can't pretend we're something when my future is crumbling while I waste time here with you."

She squares her shoulders and nods, her lips two hard lines.

"I'm sorry for you if that is what you think." Her voice is thick, and the sound lodges painfully in my heart.

She's shutting the door on her feelings for me before the hurt bleeds out of her. What we have is more than casual hookups, but I can't shut up and temper the unstoppable advance of venom in my system.

"Bullshit. Tell me you don't look at me and see my position, the money. How it could fix your problems."

"You want to know what I see when I look at you? I see a boy who is hurt. Who wasn't told he is enough. I recognize him."

"We're nothing alike."

The compassion softening her features reduces me to that boy—the lonely, miserable boy who couldn't get his father to care for him. I feel unsafe and helpless.

"I'm doing my best to heal from the past. Some days I'm afraid I'll never fix it. But I'm trudging on. I deserve the effort. I hope you get to see you're worth that too."

She doesn't expect a reply and slides into the yellow chair in her creative corner.

I'm deflated now.

"Eliza…" What do I even have to say?

"I'll be working late tonight. I have to sketch a home office for school." She pulls out her black drawing notebook and the box of art supplies I got her. A physical reminder of when I began falling for her.

It guts me and the fog starts to lift, leaving a quiet desperation in its wake.

She lets me decide, again. To stay or leave. It's the first time I realize she does this constantly. Gives me a choice.

And I make the worst possible one.

Chapter Thirty-Four

ELIZA

The grip of a claw clenching my insides intensifies until I can no longer pretend it's a usual morning. Dread suffocates me and I jump into my jeans, without worrying about the messy hair or brushing my teeth. An invisible ticking smashes against my eardrums, forcing me toward Carter's cabin.

The cold morning air hurts my lungs, but I push through and break into a sprint. A coppery taste fills my mouth but it's nothing compared to the slicing pain between my ribs. Something is wrong. I can feel it in my bones.

His car is not here. With trembling hands, I swing open the unlocked door. I don't need to check the bedroom. The cabin is devoid of his overwhelming presence. It's the quiet of a house empty of his crisp shirts arranged by color in the dresser. No expensive boots under the small entryway bench. I know he's gone even before I spot the key on the table over a folded piece of paper.

Miss Miller,
Urgent business needs my attention sooner than I expected.

The financial agreement with my mother still stands.
Thank you for your hospitality.
Best regards,
Carter Rawlings

Is this a sick joke? This is all he has to say? Anger slowly trickles down my veins and the paper crumples in my tight fist.

Carter was supposed to be a summer fling. Something easy because I'd had enough of hard.

I accepted the kind of love Jared showed me, thinking it was what I deserved. But whatever this was with Carter, I won't beg. I'll never again reduce myself to something so small I don't even recognize myself.

The message was clear and this time I'll listen. With Jared, I filled in the blank spaces and the silence with my own version of reality, instead of paying attention.

After the article came out, I didn't press. My heart bled for the man who expected to be betrayed. Who thought he couldn't experience genuine love. I wanted to hold him tighter when he pulled away. It's my nature. To dig my heels in the ground. But there was nothing to save. Nothing to hold close. I sensed he was already halfway back.

Deep inside I expected him to leave sooner, just not like this.

The jar of blend I made for him glints on the counter and I grab it. I'm not sure what I'm going to do with it, but it feels wrong to leave it for other guests.

Curled into a ball on my bed, I let myself wallow for exactly three days.

One for the way he left.

One for how hard I fell for him.
One for a future we can never have.

The small dark oak cabinet with leaded glass doors mocks me from the center of the tarp. I've been debating letting it be, but I won't sweep things under the rug anymore.

"Isn't this supposed to be your happy place?" Quinn says, approaching with a pitcher of iced tea and two glasses. She's worried and I understand why. I probably look a bit insane scrubbing the old wood on the verge of tears.

"Carter's uncle wanted me to have it." A week after he left, I broke down and confided in Quinn. I was so tired of holding my sadness inside and I took a chance on our friendship. It was like pulling teeth during our first girls' night in, cuddled on my couch, drowsy from the food she made me try. She was patient, letting me spill the entire story before asking if I wanted to send him a pie with laxative filling.

"Wouldn't you feel better if we made a nice toasty campfire out of it?" She places the drink in the grass and plops in a fishing chair out of the sun.

"No! This beautiful woodwork has done nothing wrong. After I sand and oil it, it will be perfect for the living room."

"Why? If it makes you think about him?"

"I'm tired of pretending I can easily forget him." It's confusing to grieve something that never was. "It's part of the process, you know. Of moving on. He helped me question some of the things that were holding me back.

For that, I'll be forever grateful. And let's not forget the best sex of my life." I grin at Quinn when she coughs into her glass.

"Whoa. Did not expect that. I adore this oversharing version of you." She taps her chest after regaining her voice. "Then we'll only hate him a little."

I love this woman. She came to the rescue forcing me to move forward and be more open.

What Carter said about being afraid to lose the ones close to me if I'm raw and honest stuck with me. I should trust these people to truly care for me. And have faith in them and our bond. This brings me to Martha's garden after work and I tell her everything.

Martha's eyes widen for a second at my voluntary word-vomit.

"Emotionally, I'm in a worse place after the whole Carter complication than three months ago when I saw Jared cheat on live TV."

The first weeks of July had gone by in a blur. I caught my breath every so often, sketching under the shade of the white pine in my yard. My heart only cracked half the times I opened the box Carter gave me.

"Finding love is not a complication."

"Love?!" I splutter. Falling for him was as inevitable as the Nor'easters. But love?

A couple of days ago I was added to a group chat. *Besties reunited.* What a joke. The lack of any apology should have tipped me off. At least I had the common sense to meet them at another coffee shop. Quinn doesn't deserve a run-in with the police. Although I'd love to see another face-off with the hot Sheriff. There has to be a story there.

"When did you start wearing makeup?" Jenna tilts her head, her eyebrows furrowed. "You didn't care for your appearance much before."

I thought I looked cute when I left this morning, but I'm starting to feel self-conscious under their scrutiny. "It's not much."

"Is this your revenge glow-up?" Amy guffaws. "Better late than never, right?"

"I just wanted to try something new," I say, sinking in the chair another inch.

"Give the girl a break," Jenna says, smiling sweetly. "For somebody so plain she must have some secret talents if she got her hunky tenant to bang her."

Shame creeps up my chest and neck and I'm thrown back into the uncomfortable nights out when they would all gang up on me.

Amy slaps her palm on the table, eyes wide. "Maybe it's services included in the rental agreement," she barely manages to get out between bursts of laughter.

They both laugh so hard, wiping tears from under their eyes, and I just stare into space, wondering why I am still sitting here with them.

"We miss your cooking at Sunday barbecues," Amy tells me when they manage to calm down.

"Oh, so you're still doing that." They nod, without any idea of how much it hurts. "You're all getting together, just without me." I busted my ass the last five summers to make the cookouts special. They went on as if I never existed.

"It would have been a little weird. Don't you think?" Jenna asks, hinting I might be daft.

"I think it's weirder you accepted two cheaters and excluded me."

Amy rolls her eyes dismissively. "Hey, now. Don't be dramatic."

They're not real friends. They're the type to tell you to stop embarrassing yourself if you have fun or call you dramatic if you show a backbone.

"Yeah, besides, we can get together again now that everybody knows you managed to land that moneybag. Jared and Caroline would love to see you."

"The baby shower is coming soon," Jenna chirps.

"Can you imagine the presents he'd buy?" They look eagerly at one another. "Maybe they can do the baby shower at her cabin."

They chat excitedly, making plans, ignoring me.

I should trust my gut more. Watching these two act like they didn't lie to me for two years and constantly belittle me, I wonder what's wrong with me. I'm so desperate to go back to my pre-Carter life I convinced myself I could still be friends with Jenna and Amy.

"So." My tone alerts them and they finally pay attention. "You imagine I might bag the wealthy hottie and you want to be friends so you can benefit from it."

"We want to be friends, and spend time together, and of course he's gonna take care of the expenses. He's rich, right?"

"I'm sorry, I—" It comes out reflexively and I pull myself together. "Wait. No."

They look puzzled, like I've grown a second head. It's hard being a recovering people pleaser, but I'm done with apologizing for not agreeing with them, for being myself.

"I'm not sorry. You're vile human beings." They both gasp and I stand too fast, sending the chair scraping back.

I fish out some bills and throw them on the table. "We're done. You only care about yourselves and taking advantage of people."

"Eliza, how dare—"

"I'm not finished. Never call or message me again. If you see me on the street, cross to the other side. I don't want to know if your grandma turns one hundred or your cat dies. If you get dumped again by one of your truck drivers or if your horoscope tells you that you're going to break your leg."

The bell above the door chimes behind me when I leave the two of them with their mouths hanging open.

Jackie texts and calls even after Carter left and I don't know what to make of it. She never brings him up, although she has an inkling something happened between us. We chat about my classes and her ideas for the office.

She's lovely and I adore talking her ear off, but I don't want Jackie to do it out of pity or obligation.

"You don't have to keep tabs on me. I'm sure you have more important things to do and I promise I won't spill your family's secrets," I tell her.

"Do you think I'm doing damage control with you? Because my brother can't get his head out of his ass?"

"Jackie," I chuckle. "You're a high-profile business baddie. Really, I don't mind if—"

"I'm going to stop you right there. I have a meeting in two minutes and can't dissect this right now. I'll talk to you tomorrow."

And that was that. I knew it. Once I gave her permission not to feel guilty, she'd disappear.

But on Saturday I almost spill hot tea on my lap when loud bangs rattle my front door. My heart is in my throat while I tiptoe to the front windows, hands shaking on the rolling pin I grabbed on my way to the door.

"I know you're in there," Jackie's voice booms from the porch.

Rattled to the bone, I swing the door open and gape wordlessly at Jackie, who's very proud of herself and breezes past me into the house.

"Come on. Let's get some coffee and continue our conversation. I have the weekend off."

She's so casual for somebody who dropped in unannounced. Jackie pirouettes through the small living room and nods, touching the kitchen cabinets while I follow her moves like a marionette on a string.

When the paralyzing thrum in my chest simmers down, all the fear bursts out into a shrill "What's with the Rawlings siblings and your gift of making me think I'll be murdered?"

Jackie grins. "A family quality?"

I splutter with a lack of grace that turns the corner of her lips up.

"Make yourself presentable. My mother is waiting for us in the car," she says in a tone too upbeat for the kind of terrifying news she just dropped on me.

"What? Your…" I can't breathe. "Carter's…. I don't want to meet his mother!" I wail, exasperated. "No offense," I continue more quietly.

Jackie plops in the armchair and closes her legs at the knee, brushing invisible lint from her jeans.

"She's here. I can't send the woman back, can I? It would be rude. Are you rude, Eliza? Will you send her packing after she traveled all this way?"

"You took the private jet, didn't you?" I deadpan, but the emotional blackmail is chipping away at my resolve.

"Yeah, but the traffic to the airport was horrendous. We deserve, at least, some good coffee."

My insides are torn apart by contradicting emotions. Annoyed Jackie has learned so quickly how to read me. Touched she jumped on a plane to visit me.

His mother is here. Why? I can't shake the feeling I'm walking into a trap.

"At least take her on the back porch. Enjoy the view while I get myself together," I grumble. "There's fresh tea in the kitchen."

Jackie's smile is worrisome, and she skips out of the house while I retreat to the bedroom. What does one wear for meeting the mother of the man she fell hard for, only to be left with an aching hole in her chest?

It's shocking how much Jackie resembles her mother. They're sipping tea and gazing over the lake reflecting the clear blue skies and the forest around it and I get a few seconds to take in the older woman.

Straight back, blonde hair pulled back into an elegant bun, she oozes quiet luxury. Nothing she wears is flashy, but I know her shoes cost more than my old truck. I can't read her from this distance, her face doesn't betray anything.

"I'm ready," I say stepping out, chin held high, pretending this is normal.

"Eliza. My mother, Clara Rawlings. Mother. Eliza Miller," Jackie introduces us with a flourish that eases the tension in my shoulders.

The woman nods, scanning me with unreadable blue eyes. The shadow of a smile is so faint that I almost miss it. Now I know where Carter got his unnerving analytical gaze. I'm being audited and the worst part is, I want to make a good impression.

"Welcome to Silver Lake Falls, Mrs. Rawlings."

"Clara is fine." She waves an elegant hand. "It's not my first time in the area. Didn't Carter tell you I grew up around here?"

"He might have mentioned it was the reason you chose my cabin."

Clara tilts her head. "It looked charming. Warm. I'd hoped he'd find some peace," she says wistfully and places the empty cup on the porch railing. "But it seems he also found something else." Clara looks at me meaningfully and Jackie finds a sudden interest in birdwatching.

I know better than to comment, even if the back of my neck is warming up. His mother is testing the waters. It makes me wonder if they're worried about the family's privacy and she wants to make sure I don't talk about his time here.

Clara doesn't wait for a reply and changes the course of the conversation completely, throwing me for a loop.

"When Carter returned from college, his father made a list of potential wives. Suitable young ladies from good families." Clara admires her nails. "Our son could only have the best. And the best was what suited the company in the long run."

The muscle in my jaw strains under the pressure of keeping my mouth shut.

"Doesn't sound like you, Miss Miller." Carter's mom slides her gaze to me, throwing down a challenge she knows I'll never be able to overcome.

Straight for the kill. She fooled me with her affable country-club-wife act. So she's worried I'd tarnish her precious son's future with my less-than-stellar background.

"No. It doesn't."

"Doesn't that bother you?"

I won't let her intimidate me. "I can only be the best version of myself. That's going to be enough for someone one day," I whisper the last part to myself, mostly as encouragement.

Clara peers at me with a steady gaze, peeling off layers, curious to find if there is something worthy hidden.

"Kenneth's waiting for us." Her demeanor changes again. "We're having a family breakfast."

I look at Jackie for help, but she loops her arm through mine and drags me to their car. "Let's loot Quinn's kitchen. I'm starving."

She wasn't kidding. The largest table in the coffee shop is filled with pancakes, bagels with smoked salmon, a large plate of Lobster Benedict, biscuits, monkey bread, and crullers. Luckily, Kenneth has an equally large appetite in the morning, or else I'd be concerned for Jackie.

Quinn tried her best to take our order with a straight face but the moment she rounded the counter and caught my eyes she mouthed, "Kidnapped?"

I have to stifle a laugh, which brings Jackie's uncle's attention back to me.

"I was kinda hoping Carter would stay a little longer," he says.

Me too, Kenneth. Me too. I press my lips together to stop anything stupid from coming out and nod understandingly.

He takes a large gulp of his coffee and decides to throw me to the wolves. "The boy looked ready to drop to one knee if you ask me."

"Oh, no—" I jump at the same time Clara cuts in, "Let's not get ahead of ourselves."

He laughs heartily, enjoying our reactions. "The girls were asking about you." He smiles at me. "They're babbling about ideas for the guesthouse they wanna run past you at a"—he slides his hands through the air—"just ladies, no dads, brothers or boyfriends allowed cocktails-based sleepover."

"That'd be lovely," I manage to say.

"You staying for longer this time?" Kenneth asks with the first hint of reproach toward his sister.

"No, the three of us are expected at the Portland Women's Club luncheon."

I realize I'm one of the three when she turns to me and says, "I'm sure you don't have anything suitable in your wardrobe, so Jackie brought an extra dress."

"Don't worry. It's approved by my stylist. He nearly fainted when I showed him a picture of you."

"I'm going to faint right now," I grind out the words. "I can't go with you. Thank you for the invitation, but—"

Jackie dabs at her lips with the napkin. "Nonsense. It's a networking event. You need to put yourself out there and mother is invited all the time." She reaches out and takes my hand in hers. "Plus, we have unfinished issues to settle," she says with finality.

"This is a rather casual affair," Clara tells me in the car, on our way to Portland. "Don't stress about hair and makeup."

I *am* stressed now she's mentioned it. Clara and Jackie look effortlessly chic and put together. Even with this blush pink summer dress, I'm a far cry from the polished Rawlings women.

The winding pathway through the lush garden takes us to a private corner of the oceanfront estate. The sheer size of the main house and the land around it are enough to make me feel out of place.

We approach the groups of women already enjoying their drinks and the appetizers sliding around on silvery plates. Clara and Jackie are swarmed the next second with greetings, over-the-top thank yous, and compliments on their appearance. I'm stranded at the fringe of this cloud of soft fabrics and expensive perfumes, stiff as a poker, hands clasped in front of me.

"Ladies, this is Eliza Miller," Clara interrupts them, reaching out to bring me closer, and the group instantly splits, drawing me in. "The up-and-coming interior designer I told you about."

Blood freezes in my veins. It's one thing to daydream in my creative corner, sketching, or talking to people I've known for a long time. Coming up with ideas for places I'm familiar with. It's why I'm taking the classes.

I was not ready for the onslaught of questions that follow for the whole excruciating two hours I spend there. Endless discussions about trends I have no clue about.

"Where did you study design?"

"Did you see the Roche Bobois Spring collection? Oh, my. I want to redo my living room all over again."

"I heard Gladstone has a secret Serra painting, stashed away. Do you know anything about it?"

A drop of sweat slides down my back. I'm embarrassed. Stressed. Holding my hands tightly behind my back to keep them from trembling. Clara knew exactly what she was doing when she brought me here.

Jackie is no help as she's being dragged from one group to another, and I can't follow her around like a lost puppy. So, I suck it up, deflect what I can. Encourage them to talk more about themselves, which is not difficult.

I hold on with everything I have, following Jackie and Clara's lead, and wave politely. The frozen smile melts away when the car door closes, and my lower lip starts quivering.

"If your purpose was to show me I don't belong in your world, you made your point. And you." I point at Jackie. "I thought you were the nice Rawlings."

Jackie's face is pinched, but her mother speaks before she can open her mouth.

"No, dear." Clara is calm in the face of my meltdown. "It's to show you what to expect."

"When? It's not my scene. As you wanted to point out, I'm a small-town nobody with zero qualifications for design."

Clara looks straight at me and after a heartbeat of hesitation, she says something that makes my brain malfunction. "When you're dating my son, you'll have to attend these events frequently."

"I'm not—"

"I know him too well." Clara steamrolls me. "I couldn't change his mind even if I wanted to. If you want him, stop being so naive. It's not enough to be charming and talented. If you're not equals it will never work." She pauses. "And wouldn't that be a shame?"

"You've been misinformed. Jackie, please explain to your mother there is no dating. No relationship. Carter is in New York, living his life." It's painful to lay out the truth. "And I'm home in Silver Lake Falls." I thought it would hurt less as weeks passed but saying it out loud still pierces my heart with a hot iron.

For the rest of the two-hour drive Clara and her daughter go through their schedules. They avoid any further mention of Carter and I stare out of the window, drowning in confusion, hope, disbelief, and fear.

"Jackie. Thank you for this, um, interesting day. Let's not do it again, OK?" I tell her when we get out of the car in front of my house.

She makes that graceful sound when she laughs, and I have to wonder if it's something you're born with or if it comes when the zeros in your bank are more than six.

"It's not funny. I'm struggling with enough self-doubt and your mom doesn't think much of me."

"Take it from somebody who grew up with the woman. If that was true, my mother wouldn't give you the time of day. She did her homework," Jackie says with a wink.

"I should be happy she's pointing out my flaws?"

Jackie cups my shoulders. "They're not flaws, Eliza. It's the little things in our world which might be your undoing. Most of the people will be ruthless, the newspapers even worse. My brother claims he doesn't care what anybody says about him, but do you want to put him and yourself in that position? Being with my brother involves a lot more than what's going on between you two in your bubble. He can't protect you forever."

"Somewhere there's a clog in our communication," I say, frustration mounting. "Why do you keep insisting? We're. Not. Together." My voice trembles with each word and Jackie lunges for a tight hug. "I saw the pictures with Alicia anyway," I say defeated into her smooth hair.

As much as I wanted to, there was no escaping Carter once he left. The media went wild when he called the press conference. They followed him relentlessly. Pictures and pictures of his painfully handsome face darkened by a deep frown. Always in a hurry.

Until a month later when my heart dropped into my stomach.

It hurt to read his goodbye note. But the pictures from the charity ball gutted me. The woman he told me there was no chance of getting back together with was everywhere on the Internet at his arm, smiling adoringly. She went on about how scared she was when he was in the hospital, in interviews. Did he lie about that too?

Jackie leans back, smiles, and says, "Just sleep on it, OK? Whether you want it all when it comes to him. I don't want to see you hurt."

Too late.

Chapter Thirty-Five

CARTER

The loud thump of the music and flashing lights pierce my brain like rusty nails. If Adam wasn't close to a brother, I wouldn't step foot in this club. Even less for a double date. But I'm worried about him. This time his downward spiral isn't showing signs of giving up.

I swirl the amber liquid in the untouched glass. The color reminds me of Eliza's eyes when she looked at me sometimes, thinking I wasn't paying attention. Velvety and smooth. And warm. At this hour Eliza is probably nestled in her comfy chair drawing. Or she's out with Quinn. Meeting people. My stomach churns as Alexa, who's supposed to be my date, leans closer to whisper something about her dress in my ear. She's been trying to get me to talk, but my mind keeps drifting off to memories of going out in the canoe, and lazy afternoons reading with Eliza napping on my chest.

Adam and the two women are on the second bottle of whiskey, and I barely touch my glass. They're blitzed and in the mood to dance. I'm not, but the daggers Adam throws my way have me getting up with a groan to Alexa's giggly excitement.

She does nothing for me. No desire to end the night at my place. No stirring whatsoever, no matter how much she tries to rub against me.

"Why are you so weird," Adam slurs, pulling me aside.

"We should leave."

"You're a handsome devil, but I'd prefer to spend the rest of the night with…um—"

"Shelly."

"Yeah, yeah. Shelly. And maybe her friend. Since you're a prude after your countryside escapade."

I take a deep breath and decide to leave my bodyguard to babysit Adam.

"Call for a car for those two ladies. Then haul Adam's ass to his place."

"Yes, sir."

Testing the theory that I craved Eliza's touch because I hadn't had sex in a long time was unnecessary. I knew already. I was only lying to myself.

I wanted to call her the moment I landed in New York but what could I say? I wrote and deleted texts dozens of times.

I'm sorry I left earlier.

I'm sorry I shoved my insecurities on you.

Sorry for leaving like a dick.

Nothing sounded right. How can I text her about the regret patched to my soul from the first moment I stepped back into my penthouse? And how I miss her. Do I have any right?

Sleep doesn't come easy anymore in this large bed. In my house mornings are too quiet. I fill my dinner calendar with meetings because eating at home alone is nerve-wracking. The silence is loud.

"I'd love working directly with you," the director of Sintex says, smiling wider than appropriate for a business discussion.

Tonight's meeting with the director of the research lab we plan to acquire is taking an unpleasant turn and her tone made me take a closer look at the woman. Her cheeks are flushed, leaning over to give me a prime view of her cleavage.

"You'll be dealing mostly with Jackie. She's still in charge of R&D," I say, skimming over their financial reports from last year, completely shutting down her advances.

"But you're back now. I don't mind a bit of micro-managing from the famous Carter Rawlings," the woman says seductively.

I stare at her unimpressed, my jaw tight. "Are you telling me how to run my company?"

"Oh, no," she stammers, scooting back in her chair, flustered by my dismissal.

She doesn't know it yet, but the acquisition won't protect her job. Her father is the great mind behind Sintex and their leaps in artificial intelligence development. He's the one I'm interested in.

And this young woman tonight is only a pale shadow of the woman haunting my dreams.

As the weeks go by, I'm still a stranger in my own life. The things I was so eager to get back to seem hollow. This is what I wanted, I just need to get in the right head space.

"How was the meeting last night?" Jackie comes into my office daily now. She fills me in on what I've been missing, we discuss strategy. "When do I take over?" she asks, sifting through the final proposal.

She's in full business mode and I smile for the first time in a while. My little sister is so much smarter and more capable than our father ever gave her credit for. Her focus and unwavering support kept operations going smoothly after my heart attack and I couldn't be prouder.

"Wow," she says, her eyes on me. "It's the first time I've seen you smile since—"

The problem with my sister is she doesn't let go of uncomfortable subjects. She'll hound me about my health or worse, about Eliza, and I do everything I can to stop her before she goes into full therapist mode.

"I never thanked you. For taking over while I was recovering."

"Mm," she hums, biting the inside of her cheek. "You might consider going back for some more *recovery*." Jackie air quotes. "You look—" She waves her hand up and down my face with a grimace and I know what she means.

She doesn't need to worry about me. "After I readjust to my schedule, things will get back to how they were, don't worry."

Jackie stops mid coffee sip and I swear her eye twitches.

"How they were?!" She slams the coffee cup on my desk, dark drops messing the scattered documents.

Her reaction takes me aback. I can count on one hand the times she's raised her voice at me. Her nostrils flair and her eyes have a glossy shine to them.

"Jackie, what's—"

"You want to go on as if nothing happened?" she yells. "Go back to how things were before?"

Jackie shoots up with a force that topples the chair over and dread burns my insides like acid as I watch her pace back and forth in my office, her hands in her hair.

I don't want to have this conversation again. But my sister is on a war path. There's no escaping her wrath. She's ready to let it out and leans in, throwing the documents on the floor with a swipe of her hand. Tears fall down her cheeks.

"You almost died," she whispers in a strangled voice that twists my lungs. "Do you understand?" she asks, this time with more punch to her question. "It wasn't a minor inconvenience ruining your schedule. You. Could. Have. Died." She punctuates every word with a slap on the desk, and something in me cracks. "I can't lose you. You're my big brother. You can't—" She falters.

After the breakdown at the lighthouse, I didn't want to think about it anymore. It scared me. But my little sister had to see me taken by the ambulance unconscious and intubated after the surgery. Terrified I could leave her. We never talked about what it meant for her.

Two strides and I reach Jackie, crushing her against me. Her head falls on my shoulder and I gently rock us as she lets out the tears she's been hiding from me.

"I'm sorry," I say. For scaring you. For being selfish. "I won't leave you. I promise."

Every muscle in my body screams with pain. I forgot how brutal Logan's training is. I thought I was ready after months of jogging in the woods. Instead, my body is punishing me as if I've lounged on the couch for the past six months.

"Do you know why Joseph is so chipper lately? It's unnerving." I try to preserve my dignity and talk in a normal voice, but my question comes out between harsh inhales.

Logan has always stayed out of his father's business. Growing up he told me he wasn't interested in Joseph's dealings. His successful private contracting firm after he left the military proves he either was a bullshitter or maybe some things are just in your blood.

"It's that vapid charity ball. He's on the board." Logan stops and takes deep breaths, stretching his arms above his head. Two women running past us almost trip on each other looking over their shoulders at him.

I huff a laugh at how things have changed since we were little. Short, scrawny Logan hiding during breaks because the other kids were making fun of him. I wish I could have done more than keep him company back then.

He was halfway through his one-year contract when I had the heart attack. Flew back home without hesitation and only left after he was sure I wouldn't die.

"Why are you saying it like he joined a cult? He did this sort of stuff before."

Logan stops his post-run stretches and tips his head back, taking calming breaths.

"I suspect he's trying to trick me into a date with one of those insipid socialites," he grunts, crinkling his nose in disgust.

That is the funniest thing I've heard in a long time. I bark out a laugh. West Point graduate, ten years of active duty. The only time Logan Robertson is worried is because his father wants to set him up with a woman who is probably his polar opposite.

"I'm happy to see you laugh. Even if it's at my expense."

I haven't been the best company since I returned. The constant state of misery bleeds out in all my interactions. But even if my employees and business partners don't dare mention it, the few people close to me have no problem pointing it out. Incessantly.

I miss that fucking tea and the smile Eliza tried to hide whenever I gave her the empty cup. She always said a good brew is a balm for the soul. But it was her all along, and I don't know how to move on knowing how those months with her felt.

"Therapy did wonders for me after I left the army." Always on alert, Logan's gaze sweeps the area before landing back on me. "It's the best decision I ever made."

He might have a point. I remember how tortured he looked after the last tour and I'm willing to try anything to get back to something resembling a normal life. A life where the smell of lavender doesn't make me want to jump on the plane to Eliza.

CHAPTER THIRTY-SIX

CARTER

The pressure in my skull increases while I swipe through the hundreds of links with pictures from last night. My irritation is mounting with each article framing Alicia and me as a loving couple reunited after a health scare.

The ring of the front door camera saves my phone from taking a dive from the 21st floor.

"A parcel for you, sir." My doorman hands me a small package. "Security vetted it."

"Thank you, Ivan."

It's a small box wrapped in brown paper and bound with string. Weird. I twirl it around, something heavy shifting the weight inside, and the return address is in Maine. My heart tumbles out of sync. I place it on the marble table in the lobby, equal parts excited and fearful. What if it's a hateful letter and bear dung?

Between crumpled pieces of newspaper, the jar gleams in the sunlight flooding the hallway through the floor-to-ceiling windows. A slow disbelieving exhale escapes my lips. It's the tea blend she made for me for more energy after I mentioned in passing that I didn't drink coffee anymore. I cup it in my hands like it's the most precious possession and inhale the memory of mornings with Eliza. Peppermint, cedarwood, pine, and rosemary. She'd fix it with a teaspoon of raw sugar and three drops of lemon.

The longing rips my chest open—the care she had for me. I'm holding tangible proof of Eliza's existence. I never thought a jar of herbs could bring tears to my eyes. I want to hear her voice so badly my finger is hovering over her name. How would that conversation go?

Hey, thanks for the tea, I almost burst into tears thinking about you.

The little jar weighs heavy on my mind for hours. I keep circling back to it and I'm torn between guilt and the selfish instinct to reach out for the thread of hope.

Striding, lost in my thoughts, through the office lobby to my private elevator, it's too late when I notice Alicia squeezing between the closing doors.

She's out of breath, leaning against me, sliding a palm over my chest. "I'm so glad I caught you. The Forbes party is next week, how about we make it a longer stay and enjoy a hotel room for the weekend?"

"Who the fuck keeps letting you into the building?" The entire security firm will be fired for this. I specifically banned her from the company building.

"Don't be silly." She laughs. "We're back together now, why wouldn't I visit you?"

The smell of her perfume makes me nauseous. "Where did that idea come from?" I peel her off me.

"Carter," she chides playfully, and it curdles my blood. "The media loved us at the ball. And you love the perks of spending time together," Alicia purrs suggestively.

Anger flairs back into my muscles when I remember how she ambushed me, and how I couldn't shake her off without causing a scene.

"There was no us, and there won't be. Ever."

"You're better now. Everything can go back to normal."

Jackie is right. The old normal is not a good place for me.

"Do I have to remind you that you abandoned Jackie when you thought I had one foot in the grave?"

"She's a big girl and she'll get over it. I know you won't hold a grudge." Alicia's pout is not as cute as she intends. "I just hate hospitals."

"I don't feel any way about you. Are we clear now?"

"What, don't tell me you spoiled your taste with a bit of small-town girl who stabbed you in the back for a few dollars. You're better than that, Carter."

The weight of her slip-up leaves me stunned. Alicia set Eliza up for the picture. She's more devious than I gave her credit for. I step closer but the look in my eyes tells her she messed up.

"I'm giving you only one warning. It's more than you deserve. I don't want to be associated with you. Don't come near me at events. Keep my name out of your mouth. If you still want to be allowed in this world you're so desperate to slither into, forget about me and my family or I'll make it my mission to make you regret ever crossing my path."

When I reach my floor, I don't even bother looking back. "Security will escort you out," I say, nodding to the guards posted outside my door.

I feel the softness of the leather chair, the smooth rich wood of the meeting room table, and a part of my brain registers the words and answers them on autopilot.

The rest of me is 400 miles away, on one evening in June, watching Eliza sitting on the little dock, feet dangling above the water, her toe grazing the surface of the lake. She lets herself just be for ten minutes, ignoring the stress and her fears. I wanted to sit behind her and pull her tight. But I thought it was too much then. Too intimate.

Now I regret not taking every opportunity to hold her and smell her skin.

The team closes their files and my body knows I have to leave this room and get to the next meeting. My feet are doing all the work when Joseph's voice pulls me out of the memory into my own skin.

"I'm amazed at your talent of appearing like you're fully here, with us." His voice is heavy with concern and understanding.

"I am. Right here." The bitterness in my tone is new and it alerts Joseph, who sits back in the leather chair.

"Should you be?" he asks cautiously.

"I am healthy, my brain is intact," I snap. "I'm taking care of myself, why wouldn't I be?"

Out of everyone, I didn't expect him to doubt me.

"That's not what I mean," he placates me, and the burst of anger cools off. "Your mind seems to be somewhere else." Joseph taps his index on the table, hesitating. "With someone else."

My eyes cut sharply to his. My first instinct is to protect her. Keep her away from this world, but Joseph is not one to do anything that would hurt me or the family.

"Did you talk to my mother?"

His small smile is confirmation enough. He always does that when somebody mentions her. Something he keeps only for himself. His precious little secret. I don't know how I didn't figure this out earlier. I wonder how long he has been harboring these feelings. Does she know? Does she love him too?

"She wants you to be happy and have the future you deserve."

"My future is this company," I parrot my father for the thousandth time.

"Your future is not written in stone because you're Angus Rawlings' son." He clasps his fingers over his knee. "The only way to know what's in store for you is by making your own choices."

I let Joseph see my weak spot. "I can't abandon Jackie and my mother."

After my father died, the thought of letting somebody else step in didn't even cross my mind. It became my life, my duty, afraid I would disappoint him even beyond the grave.

"I know you feel responsible, but you're working under the assumption that these women can't hold their own. Your sister would be disappointed to hear you doubting her after over half a year of running the company in your place."

I falter. "I didn't mean—"

"Do you trust them?"

"Yes, of course."

"Then stop obsessing over protecting them. They're financially secure. Jackie could start her own successful business if you don't allow her to thrive here. The reason she hasn't done it by now is because she sees you putting in sweat and blood here and doesn't want to leave you drowning."

"I know what she did these months. She handled some situations better than I would have. But I don't want to leave this burden on her just because she can handle it."

"Did you talk to Jackie about it?"

I groan and throw him a look.

"You young people see things too much in black and white. Do I have to spell it out for you or are you just finding excuses to hide in your tower?"

"I'm not hiding." I bristle.

Joseph waves a large hand, his expensive watch shining in the evening's warm light. "When we were young, our office was the command center. Now?" He pulls out his foldable last-generation smartphone and brandishes it at me. "It's ridiculous that we're even having this conversation. So, yes. You're hiding from real life and using the office as a fortress."

He lets the words slowly sink in through the wall that protects my rationalization process. His eyes soften and he rests his forearms on the table, asking his question with caution. "What would you want to do? If you managed to free yourself from this glass cage you've built?"

"I haven't let my mind wander too far from this place," I confess, since from the moment I was born there were no other options for me.

Until now.

"Your father's ghost is not haunting you. You're the one chasing it."

On his way to the door, his heavy hand lands on my shoulder but this fatherly gesture and support are too much.

"Dead men don't have opinions, son."

373

Chapter Thirty-Seven

CARTER

The clack of that atrocious-looking ancient clock on the wall disperses my thoughts every time I come close to condensing them into coherent sentences.

"You're pensive today," Dr. Daivari says in that soft monotone that used to drive me crazy during our first sessions.

Ticktock.

Tick.

Tock.

The ticking is irregular, I can't even plan my answers around it.

"I think I'm a coward," I blurt out.

"How so?" he asks, his face betraying nothing about what's going on behind those round glasses.

I called her a coward for seeking refuge at the cabin. But for her, it was always going to be temporary. Because she's fucking tough as nails and knows how to pick up the pieces and move forward through the pain.

Me? I'm hiding in plain sight by standing still. Not daring. Letting my father control me even now.

I stay silent for too long, so he follows up with another question. "What would it mean to be brave, for you?"

Eliza is so resilient in the face of obstacles and drama in her life. She rebuilds over and over again, hopeful in a way that comes across as naive.

Meanwhile, I hold tight to my past, not growing, not living.

The next day I stare at the Sudoku grid until my vision blurs. This used to help me focus, shut out any distractions. Now it takes me back to the mornings she'd ask me about it and I'd hop her on my leg so she could see better and I'd have an excuse to hold her a little longer. And her little gasp of wonder, when I completed the puzzle very fast, gave me a stupid sense of pride.

If the doctor hadn't assured me I was fine after the last checkup, the increasing pressure on my solar plexus would have worried me.

Her absence is a physical ache. It's followed me around ever since I crossed the town's borders, driving as fast as I could away from the woman who turned my world upside down. I kept rubbing my fist against it absentmindedly until I gave up trying to soothe the pain. I deserve it. I embrace the discomfort as proof that it was real, and I am to blame for the way I left things.

An iron tang floods my mouth and I've never felt more ashamed of something I've said.

Every morning when I come into the kitchen I smell the blend. Imagining her fills me with joy and aching nostalgia, but it's better than nothing.

I took the advice of the doctor and the therapist and stopped organizing my day so strictly. Today it ends up being a bad idea when Jackie and my mother ambush me.

"Is this an intervention?" I wave them in, bracing myself for another lecture.

"Don't be absurd. Can't we have a family chat over some tea?" My mother follows me and picks up the jar of blends.

"Not that one!" I say too quickly. "I might run out of it. It's hard to procure."

My mother's eyes follow me around the kitchen. "I'm sure you can get some more."

"It's not the same thing," I grumble. She made this before I hurt her. When she cared about me.

"You remind me so much of your father when he was young."

I stiffen.

"Not because you're a carbon copy of him. He too held on tight."

I narrow my eyes at her, not appreciating the comparison.

"That's not the worst thing. He was not always as bad as you remember him. He wanted what was best for his family."

"Did he know what that meant?" I ask bitterly.

"He thought he did. I know you resent him, but he had his reasons," my mother says cryptically. "I'm only sorry I didn't protect you more."

She sniffs and dabs her nose when her phone rings in her purse and her face changes, a strange smile lighting her up.

"I'm going to take this on the terrace," she chirps and glides outside.

I watch her retreating figure with confusion. "Do you know anything about that?"

"It's none of our business," Jackie says and moves to sit next to me on the couch. "You work so hard to protect and care for us, but who cares for you, Carter?" My sister looks at me, pleading. "You have to let us in. You know I'm good at this."

"I never doubted it. I'm so proud of you." When it comes to business, she has that natural hunger, the instinct of a predator.

"Then let me. So you can stop using it as an excuse to run away from your feelings."

"When did you get your degree in psychology?"

"I know you inside out, Carter. You think being alone is safe and you let Dad turn you into an island."

"You know that would have happened eventually."

"No! You don't get to defend him. He stole a part of you I never thought I'd see again." She is teary and it breaks my heart. "But I saw it clearly at the cabin. It's painful to watch two people so in love fighting so hard to hide it."

"You met her for two minutes, you have no idea—"

"I went to visit her," Jackie says sheepishly.

I'm in shock. "When?"

"In August. After the charity ball."

"What? Why would you do that?"

"Because she is my friend and she's sweet and caring. Just because you still haven't figured out what's best for you, it doesn't mean I have to cut contact with her."

I'm lost for words. And jealous of the time Jackie got to spend with her. Or that my sister can knock on her door without risking bodily harm. I wouldn't blame Eliza if she wanted to chase me around with that ax of hers.

"Are you happy here?" Jackie's voice softens.

"You're here. I promised not to leave you."

"I meant don't die on me, not *stay glued to my hip*, you idiot!" she shrieks. "We can live our lives at opposite corners of the earth, and I'll be OK if I know you're happy."

I stare into my glass of water, processing her words.

"Please stop punishing yourself for Dad's mistakes. You deserve to be loved and happy."

Since it's the first time we've broached the subject of love in a very long time, I have to ask her, "What about you and Adam?"

Jackie reels back, waves of shock and anguish crossing her features. I'll never forget how they were clinging to each other for support in my hospital room. I was fighting through my grogginess, struggling to open my eyes, but the strength she found in Adam was obvious.

"I know it's your life but is there anything I can do?"

Jackie shakes her head. "Unlike me with Adam, you know where Eliza stands. That woman loves you so much and lets you be your exasperating self. She doesn't tell you because she doesn't think you feel the same way. Maybe when you finally catch up, she'll give you a chance." She ends her tirade, leaning back on the couch, eyebrow raised. "If it's not too late."

"What do you mean?"

"Nothing." She shrugs.

"Jackie—"

"Girl code! You can't make me tell you. I will not break the girl code!" She pouts, crossing her arms.

I'm gobsmacked, mouth hanging open. I've never seen Jackie so protective. I love it because it's for Eliza. But the undertone of her comment has the same effect as swallowing a fistful of nails.

"Is she seeing somebody?"

Jackie avoids looking at me.

"J," I growl.

"I love you, but you won't make me a bad friend," she says, admiring the tips of her shoes. "But she saw the pictures with Alicia," she drawls reproachfully. "That I can tell you."

Cold sweat prickles the back of my head and I'm stunned speechless until the door to the terrace slides open.

"You two are to blame," I tell Jackie and my mother, half joking. "I could have gone to a luxury rehabilitation center."

"You're young, honey." My mother saunters in and sits next to me. "Don't pretend your life ended with Laura. Or that you're supposed to take care of us. We're big girls."

"It makes me feel in control."

"Are you really in control of your life? Or are you keeping yourself lonely?" My mother cups my cheek the same way she did when I was little. "Try something new, give yourself the chance to build a dream from scratch even if it fails. Regret will be worse when it's too late to take that risk."

For someone trained to spot any vulnerability, I missed the biggest hidden risk of getting to know Eliza. The risk of not leaving as the same man who walked in that first night. The risk of finding out what love tastes like directly from her lips.

I tiptoed around the feeling, not recognizing it.

"I'm stupid for not seeing it sooner," I finally confess.

"Love has different faces," my mother says. "When you're ready to let it in it will be as familiar as your own heartbeat."

"Am I worthy of it? I ran away like a coward."

"We all make mistakes. What matters is how far are we willing to go to atone for them."

It has taken me months to come to terms with the truth. I miss Eliza because she saw me, and I got to know her better than myself. I love her. And for the first time, I want to choose the direction of my life.

"As far as I need to." A new sense of purpose ignites within me. "I do have a private jet."

My mother smiles. "You do."

Chapter Thirty-Eight

ELIZA

I'd rather chew on broken glass than admit the Rawlings women might be right. They're certifiably insane, but some of the things they said made sense.

I don't know what they were on about when it comes to Carter. There's nothing to prepare for. The thought twists my heart when I let my mind drift for a second, imagining a life where I wake next to him or watch him cook every evening—silly, bittersweet fantasies.

After the Portland luncheon blitz attack, I pulled myself together, brushed off the humiliation, and looked at the bigger picture. It's not enough to rely on my intuition. Going against the caution encoded in my DNA, I quit the fishing shop job to fast-track my online classes. That day I threw up four times.

Then I asked Quinn for some pointers about promoting my designs, since she has the experience. She's a one-woman show at her coffee shop.

"Oh. My. God. I was waiting for this moment! I'm so happy you finally asked."

"I'm working on that." I laugh. "You know I hate bothering people."

"I'm sure Quinn won't mind," Mike—who's around most of the time lately—says, making Quinn glitch with his dazzling smile.

"It's going to be so fun. Give me a list of the people who have your pieces. We need a photo shoot, including the Miller's cabin. Then we'll sketch out a marketing plan."

She keeps at it with a contagious enthusiasm, and I feel the tiniest flicker of hope that I'll be OK.

Once we upload more of my restored works on the website and post more on social media, my phone starts ringing more often. They're mostly small projects, some rooms, or beloved pieces of furniture that are destined for a new life.

My big break came recently when Valerie invited me to view one of the houses on the other side of the lake in a few weeks. It's a big deal and the nerves get to me even before I've set foot in that house.

Since the day I quit, I've chased every workshop, free event, and product presentation around Maine and places close enough to drive. A month into this routine, Clara summons me to another brunch that, what a surprise, is in the city where I'm spending this weekend. I could call the first two times after Portland coincidences, but the strings she's pulling are starting to show.

"They're expecting us at the League of Women Voter Brunch tomorrow in Montpelier. My car will pick you up at nine. I'll be at the salon."

Sometimes she spices things up and drags me to do our hair and makeup together where she drones on and on about who'll be there and what everybody's deal is. When I stopped blocking her out, I found that her insights are actually useful and made my life easier.

There's no point in arguing.

"How did you know I'm in Vermont?"

Clara chuckles in that elegant way of hers. "Our security team keeps tabs on people close to the family," she says before hanging up, leaving me to scowl at the floral roll of wallpaper I'm using for inspiration.

The woman drives me insane with her entitled demands and general high-brow attitude. The fact that I adore her daughter is her saving grace. And that I'm still stupidly in love with Carter. And maybe the fact that I did pick up some useful mannerisms after I paid more attention. At least the hypervigilance I developed in foster care is good for something. I mirror everything, from the way they hold their glasses, to how they eat and sit in their chairs. Conversations don't feel the same as interrogational torture anymore.

After the first hour of networking my stomach sounds like an angry goose and Clara gives me a disapproving side-eye.

"It's not my fault I didn't have time to eat before the car came," I mumble and spot the basket with the small loaves of bread and the butter you could swear is soap.

Clara gently taps my elbow before I use the large metallic plate in front of me. That's rude. Can't I even eat? The waiter brings in the appetizer a split second later and sets a small pink plate on the larger silver one already on the table.

"That's called a charger plate," she bends slightly and whispers in my ear. "It's decorative."

I sigh, a little disappointed in myself. Impressing these ladies is my chance to get them as clients, but sometimes the gap between our upbringings feels more of a canyon.

My eyes shut and I do my best to regroup. *I'm smart. I'm strong. I'm creative.* The phantom grip of Quinn's strong hold still pulses in my cheeks, lifting my spirits.

"I don't understand why you want me to come to these events," I say, genuinely curious and a little deflated. I'm not even mad about it anymore. I've got a lot more out of them than I could've ever imagined a month ago.

"I've always hated to attend these things alone," she says, a little crease appearing between her perfect eyebrows, a hint of worry in her blue eyes.

"Why not take Jackie?"

Clara smiles. "She only attends the big ones now. But she had her proper introduction when she was younger."

"Not to sound unappreciative, but why *me*?" I don't know how else to stress how absurd I find her focus on me.

"Why not?" She shrugs, dainty and feminine. "You're not such bad company."

Great. I'm having brunch with the Riddler. This woman is infuriating.

"My friend Irma wants to talk to you." She waves over a short platinum-haired older lady wearing a hemp dress. "Beware. She's obsessed with fuchsia and fiberglass."

Mike's house is the very definition of *A roof over my head and the hinges on my front door make for a livable home.* I grew fond of him after all the time Quinn made us spend together this summer. I don't know if it's for his benefit, because he doesn't know many people around here, or because she's afraid I'd become one with my couch and let nature swallow up the house with me in it.

"Come here," Mike beckons, grabbing Quinn by the middle. He's a simple man, happy with a rough-looking couch and the things left behind by the former owner. There's something comforting about the way he carries himself and I'm over the moon for the goofy smile on Quinn's face, so I don't mind third wheeling most of the time.

"Don't creep her out. She spooks easily." Quinn laughs and swats him, shaking her head.

We're sitting on the lake shore, on a large driftwood trunk, chatting and soaking up September's mild warmth.

"Are your folks from here?" Mike asks, taking a swig of his beer.

Quinn, bless her heart, kept her word and didn't tell him the sad truth, because he seems clueless about my past.

The phone buzzes in my bag, saving me from giving him another vague answer.

I step away, giving Mike and Quinn some space, and take the call.

"Next week. The weather's great." Jackie forgets to switch off the bossy tone. I let it slide. I know how busy she is.

"I want to come but, honestly, I don't want to see Carter. I know he's your brother and it's not fair of me—"

"One second." I hear her typing. "A week from now his calendar says he's away for a few days."

I exhale deeply. A visit to New York is long overdue.

"You promised to help me with the final orders." She reverts to normal-voice Jackie. "I'll ask Michelle to book us a private viewing, whenever you're up for it."

Sometimes I forget the weight this family can throw around. The thought of having the showroom to ourselves has my skin humming with excitement. "I did promise."

I can't believe how much my life has changed in half a year. Some days are hard because it's so easy to slip back into my comfort zone. But the end game is so enticing I keep working hard. And I remember a pair of soft gray eyes looking at me like I could conquer the world.

That's why, even if I'm tired to the bone from driving to Portland and taking the train for over seven hours, I have so much energy I could run a marathon.

I meet Jackie at the showroom and the city already smells funny by noon. The changing season is late to reach the hot concrete, but I take it in and almost lose track of time gawking at the shop's windows.

"How's living alone working for you?" Jackie asks while we peruse the store.

"It's something I didn't know I needed. The peace that comes with being on my own and doing what I love." I sift through a pile of soft carpet samples. "I needed the wake-up call to figure out how codependent I was."

"You can't blame yourself for your ex's mistakes."

"It's more of a realization. It was unhealthy and if it didn't happen that way I might have carried on for years." Got married, started a family with Jared. What a terrifying thought.

Jackie picks up some brass ornaments for the hundredth time. Michelle, her assistant, takes notes of everything Jackie touches.

"How do you even have time for this? You know I could have come here and sent you pictures."

"Unlike my brother, I don't think killing myself over work is what's best." She plops on different leather chairs, testing them. "He might not think it either anymore though," she says, looking at me strangely.

I don't want to ask. I shouldn't. "What do you mean?"

"Let's take these samples to the office," she tells the alert salesperson, who's been hovering ten steps behind us the entire visit. Then she turns back to me. "His therapist is making him try something new."

I'm speechless. The man guarding his secrets and pain with the determination of a cornered badger is going to therapy. The part of me that still loves him is so proud of him. He deserves to be happy and find his peace.

The office building stretches upwards in a flawless display of glass and steelwork, almost blinding.

"Yeah, I know. Our father valued appearances above all else."

When we reach the top floor, Jackie takes me through the open space, pointing out different people who smile politely at us. I nearly pass through the large glass door to her office when my gaze catches on the golden letters.

CHIEF EXECUTIVE OFFICER

I'm confused. "Isn't Carter the CEO?"

"Oh, yes. He gave that up," she tells me casually.

"Why? Is he OK? Is it his heart again?"

A devious smile blooms on her face. "It's his heart for sure," she says, peering over my shoulder.

Oh, no.

I can sense the intense gaze on the back of my head before I slowly turn, imagining all the ways I can murder Jackie and get away with it.

He's in the doorway. Carter is here. Scowling in his pristine tailor-made suit. The dark blue fabric changes his eyes into liquid silver dripping on my skin.

Panic bubbles between my lungs. He's going to think I'm a stalker and a clinger.

"What're you doing here?" I stupidly ask.

"As far as I remember I still own part of the shares." If Carter's as rattled as I am, he's hiding it better.

The sight of him makes my heart jolt against my ribcage, fighting to escape his heavy gaze. My palms are clammy and my face heats up. I hate that he'll know how much he still affects me.

The color swatches are the most interesting things in the world for Jackie and she's as helpful as a mouse-nibbled umbrella during the rainy season.

"I was told you were away on business." I straighten my back, smoothing my expression. "Of course, you can be wherever you want. I'm just helping Jackie." The words come out harsh and sandy.

Seeing him for the first time after three months leaves me breathless, scrambling to act normal. The way his suit fits him flawlessly and the confidence he exudes in his natural element, don't help matters much.

I need to get out of here.

Chapter Thirty-Nine

CARTER

Michelle storms into the room, laser-focused on my sister, tapping at her company-issued tablet.

"Don't forget about your five o'clock. Wrap it up as fast as possible if you want to make your dinner reservation with—" She clams her mouth shut, suddenly aware there are other people in the room.

"I forgot about this meeting completely," Jackie groans, rolling her eyes dramatically.

Subtlety is not her forte when she meddles in situations she shouldn't.

"I'm so, so sorry, Eliza. Do you mind if we cut this short? This is important." Jackie hugs her unmoving figure.

"Make sure she gets home safe." She breezes past me, wordlessly threatening me in a thousand ways not to screw this up.

Jackie leaves with Michelle on her heels and the air in the room becomes dense with tension. We stare at each other like two fighters in a ring. She's wearing a tight black dress and heels, a real work of art, but I miss her casual outfits. The relaxed look, the easy smiles. Now she's tense and cold—a beautiful marble statue.

I want to reach out and pull her into my arms, hold her tight until her heartbeat syncs with mine. But it would be a stupid thing to do when her eyes are shards of glass cutting into me.

When I open my mouth to say something she cuts me off. "I should be going. I leave at seven."

"You came only for a day?" The disappointment in my voice is palpable but it doesn't affect her.

She shrugs. "It was nice visiting New York, even just for a few hours."

"You can always stay." I want to beg her, but I have no right. "I—We have plenty of space."

"I'm sure you do. But I have other plans," she says flatly, moving toward the door, and a surge of panic runs under my skin.

"At least let me drive you to the airport." She looks ready to refuse me. "Please."

"You must be busy," Eliza says, analyzing the artwork in the office. "I'm sure you have more important things on your schedule." She rolls her lips, glancing at the view. I almost cave and run to her to press my thumb on her lower lip and release it.

"Not as important as this."

The woman who has my heart finally turns those beautiful amber eyes in my direction. Doubt and hesitation cloud them until she sighs and puts me out of my misery.

"Honestly, I'm too tired to refuse you on principle."

The walk to the underground garage where I keep the cars I prefer to drive myself is silent. My driver is tolerable, but once in a while, I want to get behind the wheel. Eliza is nervous, looking over her shoulder at the two security guards following us.

"Don't mind them. They'll be in another car." My security chief might hate it, but I'm not sharing my alone time with Eliza with anybody else.

Her forehead creases and she rubs her arm. "Do they follow you everywhere?"

"Most of the time," I say cautiously. I don't want to rattle her.

"Back home—I mean, when you stayed at the cabin," she corrects herself, "they weren't with you."

"They hovered in the area."

She flinches and now I hate myself for not coming clean sooner. "Not around the house, don't worry. Just close enough to drop in in less than two minutes."

"That sounds very close," she bites. "I wish you'd have told me I had eyes on me all that time."

I round the car and get the door for her, holding my hand out. She eyes it like I'm handing her a hot poker, but the Porsche is too low for her to sit in that tight dress and high heels without help.

Her soft hand lands in mine and I hold on to the lifeline, soaking in the surge of electricity going up my arm. When she wants to pull it away, I don't let go. "I never let them come too close. The team only knew my location."

Relief softens the lines of her face, and she nods. "OK."

"Which airport?" I ask her as we climb the ramp that leads outside the building.

Eliza clears her throat and folds her hands over her lap. "Penn Station, please."

I'm confused, why would she…? The answer hits me in the head with the bluntness of a brick. She traveled all this way only to help my sister for a few hours. "I'm getting you on a plane. It's too far."

"Don't waste your money on me. I don't want it." She bristles. "I left my truck in Portland anyway."

"I'd spend as much as it takes to know you're safe."

Eliza gulps and shakes her head. "I can handle it."

After some back and forth I comply. She's getting annoyed and she hates me enough as it is.

So much time thinking about Eliza since I returned, and I have no idea where to start. "Thank you for the tea." I go for a safer topic.

Eliza doesn't say anything, looking straight ahead at the cars dragging along us.

"I love it. It reminds me of Silver Lake Falls, of the dock," I admit. "Of you."

Pain flashes across her light brown eyes and I know I can't keep beating around the bush and let Eliza go without telling her that nothing I said that night was true.

"I'm sorry", I tell her, voice thick with emotion. "The things that came out of my mouth had nothing to do with you and everything to do with my messed-up head. I regret saying that to you as much as I regret having to leave."

Eliza sits straighter, her jaw set. "I bet Alicia was happy to have you back sooner," she replies evenly, unaffected by my apology.

"What?" The goddamn pictures from the gala. "Don't believe what you see in the news. She is nothing to me."

She peers out the window, not meeting my eyes, and it's a struggle to keep my hands to myself.

"I panicked and got tunnel vision. It was hard to get out of that state."

"Not even for a goodbye?" The hurt in her voice is raw.

I tighten my grip on the steering wheel. "I was a mess."

"I thought Mr. Calm and Collected was a pro at playing it cool. Hiding his feelings," she mocks me.

"It doesn't apply when it comes to you, apparently."

She inhales through her nose and her chest rises, her shoulders dropping with the exhale.

"I knew I'd be heartbroken when you left, but not humiliated. Used. Disposable. Thought you'd at least be a gentleman about it." She's not angry. Her voice is distant, reaching me through a thick protective layer. She has her walls up.

"Eliza, I handled it wrong." Therapy helped me sort through my feelings and recognize what I want. I barely have one shot at this. "If I wanted to return to Silver Lake Falls. Would you want me there?"

Her brows furrow and Eliza opens her mouth ready to tear into me, but instead sucks a breath in, reeling everything she wants to say back in.

"Doesn't even matter," she finally says with a blank face. "You don't have to deal with me anymore. Valerie has it covered and there are plenty of other cabins."

The distance she puts between us is a fist to the stomach. I've never been so unsure.

"But would you give me the time of day? Can I show you how sorry I am?"

Eliza's icy stare slits through me. "I used to think I deserved the way Jared treated me. That he was the only one who would want somebody broken. I won't be treated like that anymore. I can do better. I don't want to be just tolerated or taken advantage of."

The words dislodge from my soul, racing to tumble out of my mouth. I want to tell her I love her. That she consumes my days and nights. That I desperately want a life with her.

Not now. Not when she hasn't forgiven me.

We're thirty minutes early and she strides straight to the platform, head held high. I step into her space carefully, in case she knees me. Eliza's breath shudders and she wraps her arms around herself protectively. It reminds me of the first time she opened up to me. Trusted me with her vulnerability. The guilt and the urge to comfort her bring me closer and I give in, wrapping my hand around the back of her head, I draw her closer and brush my lips against her temple. The faint trace of lavender goes through my system, loosening my muscles, and I close my eyes, wishing we were alone in her garden and not in a noisy train station.

Eliza leans in for a brief second, a soft whimper landing painfully on my chest. Much too soon she remembers herself and pushes me away with her palm. Her lower lip is quivering, and she presses them together until they turn white.

My strong girl. Not giving an inch. That's exactly what I deserve and I won't stop, even if she makes me grovel on my knees.

I bend until my mouth is close to the shell of her ear. "This is not goodbye," I tell her, grazing the sensitive silky skin. Her entire body trembles but the warmth that shone in her eyes back in Silver Lake Falls is now a dull emptiness and I force myself to move away and call Jackie out of earshot.

"You let her spend all night on a train?" I bellow at my sister the moment she answers.

"I'd appreciate less yelling and more context." Her tone tells me she is only half paying attention.

"My future wife spent over seven hours on a train, at night, to come help you choose a fucking carpet," I grunt through gritted teeth.

Complete silence on the other end. My harsh breath is the only sound traveling between us.

"I'm too shocked to go into the first part of your statement," Jackie says tentatively, and I realize what came out of my mouth. Surprisingly, I don't regret it. She takes a deep breath and groans. "She didn't say anything. I didn't ask…I dragged her around for hours," she sounds remorseful. A loud thud rattles the coffee cup Jackie usually has on her desk. "You know what? I asked her to stay so we could spend more time together, but she refused. *Didn't want to be an imposition.*" My sister's Eliza impression is completely off the mark. "It broke my heart and it's all your fault for making her think she'd be taking advantage of anyone."

Sometimes I regret confessing my stupid outburst to my sister. Because she has the aggravating habit of being right.

Jackie is silent for a beat, and I know she's coming up with a plan. "I can put Dixie on a plane. She can pick Eliza up on the way and drive her home."

Flying my sister's driver down to help Eliza would be the sensible solution.

"Don't bother, I got it covered."

CHAPTER FORTY

ELIZA

The train's small jerk forward loosens the knots around my lungs. The sooner I put some distance between Carter and me, the better. Meeting him rattled me to the core and I've been tightly wound, doing my best to keep it together from the moment he materialized in Jackie's office.

It's hard to be mad at him when he's so open and unguarded in his apology, those gray eyes reflecting my own hurt. When those hands that know me so well drag along my skin, cutting off all brain functions. It's better to go back home, focus on what I have to do, and move on. This is my version of a pep talk while I sink in the window seat.

My pulse slowly drops back to normal. Being so close to him, I was hanging by a thread. Ready to give in. To kiss him one last time. I wanted to smooth over the guilt etched on every line of his face. He probably felt bad meeting me face-to-face after what he said. Why would he come back? It's nonsense.

People are milling along the aisle, looking for their seats. One of them reaches for the spot opposite mine and a flash of familiar expensive fabric catches my eye. My jaw drops when the man takes his seat, sucking the air out of the coach.

"You can't be here," I stutter.

"I sensed you needed some company." He smirks and there's no trace of the sorrowful man apologizing from earlier. The man sitting in front of me is determined and confident in whatever crazy plan he's hatched in the last half an hour.

The dark blue pants stretch over his thighs when he moves his legs to trap me. With an elegant swirl of his fingers he unbuttons his jacket, giving me a mouth-watering view of the white shirt hugging his wide torso. Hard flesh under expensive linen, so tempting I want to reach out and perch in his lap like a cat.

"Hey, man. That's my seat." The bubble bursts when a guy who looks tired to the bone looms over us, unaware of the emotional turbulence I'm going through.

Without batting an eye Carter fishes out an alarming number of one-hundred-dollar bills and a ticket from his wallet. "This is your seat."

Life pours into the haggard man, and he stands straighter. "Definitely! Must've mixed it up with this one," the guy says, handing Carter his ticket, leaving the two of us in a heavy silence.

The shadows of the changing landscape are dancing on Carter's face, who's enjoying my shock.

"Are you insane? It's going to be midnight when we get to Portland!"

"It's been a while since I admired the view from a train seat."

My eyebrow arches. "Have you ever?"

He smiles and my insides melt. "No."

I stare at him, unsure what to think. "What's in the bag? A tiny laptop and a mini satellite dish?"

His lopsided grin and the way he tilts his head to study me heat my chest and the flame travels up to my neck and ears.

"No. I don't want anything distracting me from the view," he says while raking his eyes over my body. It's heavy as a physical caress and my belly clenches.

He takes out something wrapped in white paper. "You didn't have time to eat." His outstretched hand is unwavering and it's a battle between my pride and my growling stomach that decides to settle the matter with a loud grumble.

This man. Neatly wrapped in crisp parchment paper I stare at my favorite ciabatta beef sandwich. No onions.

I peek at Carter under my eyelashes and the hopeful roundness of his eyes convinced me to take the first bite. Of course, it's the best I've ever eaten. Carter Rawlings doesn't do anything half-assed. Unless it's saying goodbye to the woman who fell for him like an idiot.

"Thank you," I tell him from behind the napkin I use to dab my mouth. "It was delicious."

"I'll let the weird Michelin star chef know," he teases, his smooth voice sliding around me like velvet. "Try to get some sleep. I'm here."

Belly full, the long night on the train and the full day in New York catch up to me. I can't fight off the exhaustion and there's also the two-hour drive from Portland I have to consider.

"Wake me up if you decide to hop off in Boston." I give him an out, so he's not stuck here with me out of a misplaced sense of obligation.

"I promise I'll stay by your side all the way," he says and leans back, relaxing in his seat.

Are we still talking about the train ride?

The truth is I do feel safer with him here than sleeping alone, so I let my heavy eyelids drop and drift off, rocked by the moving train.

When I wake up stiff and groggy his jacket keeps me warm and my legs are propped on his knees, his large hand holding my ankles in place. Scorching heat goes up my leg and it nests between my thighs, pulsing, calling for his touch. His smell is intoxicating, but I reluctantly hand his jacket back. Carter's watching me with an expression I've seen before. One I can't bring myself to trust again.

We don't talk much on the short walk to Congress Street, where I parked my truck, but his nearness scratches at the healing wound in my heart. Carter smiles down at me and it's like looking into the sun. When he reaches for my hand, I'm unable to step away and I'm hypnotized as he lifts it until his lips press over the pulse point in my wrist. I nearly implode.

His touch is a warm bath after being stranded in cold weather for too long.

"Give me the keys," he murmurs against my skin.

The temporary daze clouds my brain, and I can't make sense of what he's saying.

Confusion scrambles the words in my head and I come up short for an answer, but that doesn't deter him.

"We're going for a ride, sweetheart. And you're going to sit your pretty ass in the passenger seat, like a princess."

"Do I have any say in this?" I ask, a bit amused, a lot more suspicious.

He blinds me with the most arrogant grin. "No," Carter says and turns his palm up, motioning me to give up the car keys.

"You said my car was a death trap," I remind him, feeling out of place in the passenger seat of my car.

Carter laughs. "If you still haven't figured it out, I'm inclined to choose against self-preservation when it comes to you." He takes the exit toward the Coastal route. "Also, I'll take any chance I can to be around you." He taps his fingers on the steering wheel and sneaks a peek at me. "Even if it's two hours of death stares."

Which I dutifully deliver because I don't know what else to do besides filling the silence with the local radio stations. His actions tell a different story than the one I've made myself believe after he left.

A company car's waiting for him when we reach my home.

"The jet is ready for you, sir," the man in a dark suit tells Carter after opening the back door of the SUV.

Carter nods and turns back to me, smiling.

"Um, thanks for the ride," I say, clearing my throat. "And for the company."

"Any time, kitten." He winks and turns on his heels, leaving me disoriented and obsessing over what happened for the next few days.

The living room space that opens into a large deck through sliding glass doors is breathtaking. I've been bursting with excitement since I stepped over the threshold of this impressive house. The floor plan is generous and well-divided. The rich, hardwood floorboards almost make me weep.

Valerie's call came at the right moment since I was driving myself mad over Carter and his behavior.

"As you can see," Valerie says, waving her hand toward the kitchen, "the place was remodeled last year. It paid off. The sellers got more than they ever dreamed."

The dark granite countertop beckons me closer. I want to run my palm over its cool surface. "Do you think they'll let me repaint the cabinets? This kitchen deserves more than beige doors." A dark dusty-green finish for the lower cabinets would go great with a light wood island after I strip the paint off. Brass lights above.

"You're free to do whatever you please." She winks. "Blank check and all."

"That's not very specific."

"Look. They don't want a cookie-cutter type of house. Something out of a magazine."

"They must have some idea of what they want. If I meet them, we can talk some options over."

"Unfortunately, it's not possible. They're extremely busy between the move and their overseas business. The best I can do is a video call." She walks us through the master bedroom with a walk-in closet larger than my living room on the right side and a light blue and marble bathroom on the opposite side. Natural light floods the wide bathtub and bounces off the floor.

"They loved your portfolio and since you've been in the area for so long, they trust you to make it fit the Silver Lake Falls story." She rounds a corner to a camouflaged double shower. "Think of it like this. What would make this the perfect home for you, if you could live here?"

I laugh at the absurdity. "A girl can dream, right? At least tell me if they're young or retirees. Do they have a large family? Pets?" I scramble for any hint.

"They're young. They want a place to raise their family," she says, opening the door to what could be the linen closet.

My mind is spinning. OK. Family-friendly. Got it. I can work with that.

"Oh, and they want to move in by the end of October."

"I have a month to do this?" Panic floods my veins and my ideas scatter in the wind.

"As I said." She turns on her heels and looks me over, concerned by my shrill tone. "You have endless resources at your disposal. I'll help you with logistics." Valerie smiles. "We can do this."

This is my chance. I just have to imagine having a family and kids without curling into a ball and crying my eyes out. Sounds easy enough.

CHAPTER FORTY-ONE

ELIZA

Of all the places in this universe, the sidewalk of a run-down brick building is the last place I imagined running into Carter Rawlings. Or maybe my brain is playing tricks on me after he's been on my mind for weeks.

But then the mayor, who I hadn't noticed, playfully slaps his shoulder and they burst out laughing like they went to the same preschool. The rich timbre of Carter's laugh is unmistakable, and it flares up my temper. I was going to the pizza place next door, but my appetite just disappeared.

Two steps back to my truck he spots me.

"Eliza!" The insufferable burr stuck to my heart is grinning, strolling toward me, too sure of himself. "I was just thinking about you."

"Highly doubt it," I bite.

His eyes light up. "I've missed you."

I blink owlishly, rage simmering to a boiling point. His audacity leaves me speechless. He doesn't get to waltz back into Silver Lake Falls and say things like that.

"You might be wondering what I'm doing here." His tone is annoyingly casual. The fact that I don't say anything doesn't stop him from continuing the conversation.

"Something was nagging at me ever since I left." He rubs his jaw, looking nervous for the first time. "Turns out last summer was the happiest time in my life and I was an idiot for leaving."

"I'm glad you managed to sort through your feelings. Now excuse me." My heart is thundering with the flow of emotions flooding my chest. I can't be near him.

I continue my power walk toward the car, but he falls in step with me, enveloping me in his imposing presence. Thankfully he doesn't reach for me and I'm grateful for that because I don't know what my reaction would be. Punch him or kiss him until my lungs burn.

"I'm planning on a longer stay. Hope you don't mind I'm monopolizing your cabin until I find something more permanent."

That traitorous smooth-talking realtor! Valerie said somebody booked the place but didn't bother telling me it was Carter.

"I'm fine, thanks for asking," he continues, amused.

Steam is probably coming out of my ears. "I didn't—"

"It'd be even better if we started over."

That stops me in my tracks. "What is that supposed to mean?"

Carter invades my personal space, ignoring the people giving us weird looks. "I know I have to work for your forgiveness and trust. It was torture without you. I'm willing to do anything to have you back," he says without a hint of hesitation.

A part of me desperately wants to believe Carter and his pleading eyes. What's left of my rational side can't trust his change of heart will last and he'll never flee again. He'll get swept up in the fantasy until boredom shifts his mind back to New York. When he sees I'm holding him back from greatness and starts missing the rush of high-stakes business deals, the glamour of the city, and the important people he used to rub elbows with.

"I don't want to be your little experiment. Who knows how long your city boy awakening will last until you realize you want your life back? The one you *worked so hard for*," I quote, and he flinches.

When Jared constantly criticized me, I didn't stop loving him. But loved myself a little less every time. I don't want that to happen again.

I have to put a stop to whatever this is. "I'm just a nobody you met one summer. You'll get over it."

"You're not…"

Throwing his words back at him is petty, but so satisfying.

"You're everything to me."

Nothing that comes out of his mouth makes sense. I'm dizzy.

"Don't say things you don't mean," I spit out. "I'm not a toy you can play with and discard whenever you get bored. People have underestimated me all my life. And I let them. I believed them. Not anymore. I deserve better than that."

Carter narrows the gap between us, a delicious temptation. His face is grave. "You're right. I underestimated you. How much you changed my life. How lasting your touch is. How addictive your smile is. I was a fool for thinking leaving you behind would erase my feelings for you." He reaches for my chin and gently caresses the skin under my lower lip. "Let me show you."

I can't take any more of this conversation. The cool fall air presses down on my skin and the sense of peace I carefully designed after he left is a sandcastle crashing down in a storm. I jerk my head away and turn on my heels, fleeing to the truck.

The next morning a handwritten note is stuck in the windowpane of the front door. If I didn't recognize his distinct, tidy strokes in black ink, the thick smooth paper would be a dead giveaway.

I miss your good mornings.

I remember his sleepy face and the feelings I've pushed back since June work their way up.

Today the note delivers another blow to my decision to stay as far away from him as humanly possible.

I love the tea you make for me.

Change of plan. I need Quinn to slap some sense into me.

"And then he pops out of nowhere and says he wants to—" I stammer, outraged. "I don't know what to call it. We were never together for real." The lukewarm chocolate swirls in the cup I keep fidgeting with.

Quinn is unaffected by my agitated state and is unhelpfully silent.

"You said we'd hate him. Nothing to say now?"

"To be fair, I said we'd hate him a little bit." She's bouncing her leg under the table.

I leave my indignation aside for a moment and pay closer attention.

She's chewing her lip, eyes shifting to the side.

"What's up?"

"Promise you won't get mad," she says, eyeing me nervously.

"That doesn't sound ominous at all," I deadpan, but an uncomfortable sense of déjà vu pokes at my insides.

Quinn takes a deep breath and knocks me back into my chair. "Carter's hub offered me a grant to expand the coffee shop." She gulps and I keep staring at her. "I can do the expansion we've talked about. It would be a game-changer. His only condition is I get a booth at the fall and spring fairs and donate the money to a local charity of my choice."

"Oh." My mind is struggling to keep up with her news. Carter's hub?

"I know," she says, deflated. "I know. I can turn it down—"

"Don't you dare!" I cut her off. No matter my issues with Carter I'd never rob Quinn of her dream. She's been nothing but supportive. "It's great news. I volunteer to help you at the booth. Anything you want. If anyone deserves this chance, it's you."

Her lower lip wobbles and she jumps off the chair to crush me in a hug that whooshes the air out of my lungs.

"I won't take his side just because he's funding me with a truckload of money," she promises, talking rapidly. "On that note. What're you wearing for your date tomorrow?"

Oh, crap. With Carter storming back into town I forgot about Matt.

"Don't make that face," she scolds me. "You're not bailing on this one." That's what I get for last-minute canceling every one of her most recent efforts to set me up on coffee dates.

We don't need to have a repeat of the discussion about Finn. Her notepad almost didn't survive when I told her there was no spark. My blood doesn't warm my cheeks when he's near and I don't want to settle anymore if it's not something I can feel deep in my bones.

I like him as a friend, and he seems to be OK with that. We even talked about doing some projects together.

When a guy I knew from the library asked for my number while I was waiting for my order, I almost turned him down, but Quinn's eyes were bulging menacingly. A wordless reminder of her incessant push to start dating. She waved away my excuse of being buried in work and the fact I was still reeling after seeing Carter last month.

"Stuff will always happen. Perfect timing is an illusion," she said with the attitude of an experienced life coach. She could have pulled it off if not for the flour dusting half her face and most of her hair.

I gave in and now I'm on a coffee date with a nice enough, well-mannered Matt who's brought his niece a couple of times to reading time at the library. It seems he didn't want to give up his signature camouflage vest even for our date. I picked the coffee shop so Quinn could bail me out in case it goes south, since she's the reason I'm wearing uncomfortable heels on a Thursday afternoon while Matt looks like he's going hunting for boars straight after.

After he orders the "healthiest" smoothie on the menu for me, because he knows what I need, according to him, Matt proceeds to give me a ten-point lecture on how sugar affects female fertility. I can barely get a word in. Keeping my mouth busy with the drink turns out to be a bad idea. The swamp green concoction is the grossest thing I ever tasted.

"I love kids. I'd like to have at least five. What do you think, Miss Cherry Pepper?"

Oh, God. "That's ambitious," I mumble into my glass. But I remember the smoothie tastes like mold and I gingerly place it back on the table.

He preens and I'm doing my best to stay focused on the conversation. I've had job interviews more pleasant than this.

"My last girlfriends didn't understand that this was their role. It's not that difficult," he scoffs. "Men are born to spread their seed and women should be grateful to be chosen to bear our offspring and take care of the house. Why would you need a job anyway, right?" He must take my shocked silence as agreement because he keeps going. "My wife will have her hands full, that's for sure." He laughs and I want to ninja-star throw my spoon at Quinn, who's pretending to ignore us behind the counter.

I have a mile-long list of things I should be doing rather than wasting my time here. The clock is ticking on my first big project. Valerie's clients squeezed me into their busy schedule for two grainy video calls. They appeared to be somewhere in Asia. The nice couple is around my age and were overly excited about my proposals for their lake house, which tempered some of the doubts I had.

The screech of a chair nearby startles us both and I'm equal parts relieved and frustrated to see Carter leisurely sitting at our table, pinning me with his gaze, two glinting silvery bullets piercing my flushed skin.

"Who's your friend, kitten?" Carter asks, the muscle in his jaw popping.

"I'm her date," Matt bristles.

"You're confused." Carter talks at him with that posh tone that drives me up the wall. He levels my poor date with a cool glare, oozing the confidence of a man who knows Matt has zero chances against him.

I forgot what a turn-on it is. I narrow my eyes at him. "How did you find me?"

Carter smiles cheekily at Quinn over Matt's shoulder. The double-crossing hag! My eyes snap to my supposed friend who finds a pesky stain on her counter that requires all her focus.

His intrusion in my life is outrageous, but the sight of him, so mischievous, carefree, smiling—it's a heart-stopper.

"Excuse me, we were in the middle of something," Matt's raised tone turns some heads.

Please don't make a scene.

"If you're searching for a breeding mare, you're at the wrong table." Carter leaves no room for debate. "You can go now."

Matt's looking at me, but I don't have the heart to stop him. "I'm sorry," I mouth and Matt storms off in a huff.

With a resigned sigh, I switch my attention back to Carter. "What *are* you wearing?" That flannel shirt looks too good on him.

"I'm trying my hand at casual. Don't worry, it's designer," he grins. "I want to blend in."

Blend in? He could be the cover model for a fancy men's magazine for the outdoorsy. I don't want to make his head bigger so I don't say anything, but my exhale snags on its way out when he leans closer and whispers.

"What do you say, Miss Cherry Pepper?" His nose slides over the shell of my ear. "Want to go out on a proper date? We got a bit ahead of ourselves last time."

His touch and unmistakable scent make me dizzy and I can't deny I still want him. The smug bastard knows it, but I won't allow him to use it against me.

"Call me that again and they'll never find your body."

"Are you sure you want that? You look flustered, Eliza."

I want to slap that impertinent smile off his face.

"Tell me. Did you touch yourself thinking of me while I was gone?" He comes closer and the carnal darkness of his eyes sets off a blast of hormones through my system. "I did. I have an archive of moments of you burned into my brain. When I made you come. The sweet sounds you make while I fuck you. That same fire in your eyes I see now, that tells me you want me to devour you."

I want him desperately, there's no two ways about it. I miss spending time with him.

The message scribbled on the thick paper made me tear up this morning. Both from laughing and crying.

I'd go anywhere with you. Even in your deathmobile.

I felt seen and cherished in a way nobody made me feel before. He also showed me I can't keep him for long. So why am I contemplating saying yes?

Because I can't help it. Basking in his attention is addictive.

CHAPTER FORTY-TWO

CARTER

The front door bursts open and Eliza's stomps echo through the house.

"Carter Rawlings!" Eliza yells. My name never sounded better.

She comes to a halt in the bedroom doorway, fists clenched. God, she looks beautiful when she's mad.

"Do you think you can buy your way back?" she snarls, barging in, pointing her finger at me. "Meddling with Quinn's shop and the library?!"

It seems Miss Penelope forgot about the anonymous part of the donation.

"Don't you like it?" I ask cautiously.

"I love it!" she yells. "The kids are over the moon. And put a shirt on, I can't be mad at you when… when…" She waves her hand around my torso. She's flustered and I love it. "You flaunt your body in my face."

"Flaunt—" I bark out a laugh and it only pisses her off more. "The problem is that you miss me too," I say quietly and take her fingers, drawing her closer. She doesn't resist when I press her palm on my chest and Eliza's eyes soften when they lower to my scar. The one she turned into one of my strengths.

Goose bumps blossom all over my skin in the wake of the soft brush of her thumb over the red mark. "It doesn't make you weak to admit it. That you've thought of me as much as my mind has wandered through memories of you, every day since I left."

"I know," she whispers, surrounded by a cloud of sadness.

"Then what's the problem? I wanted to help. Don't reject it because it came from me, and you haven't still forgiven me."

"Your idea of forgiveness is to throw money at things that would make me happy."

"No." I cup her face with my other hand and sigh in relief when she doesn't flinch away. How the tips of my fingers missed her. The rounded edge of her jaw and the soft skin over her cheekbones. "I want to be a part of your life any way I can. I won't apologize for having the means to support your dreams. Don't let your pride get in the way of helping the people you care about."

Eliza sighs, leaning into my touch, and my heart soars, pulling me closer to her inviting lips.

"I did forgive you," she murmurs into my palm. An absolution for my mistakes, sweet words that will bring her back. She pushes me lightly, her gaze reaching the very abyss of my soul.

"We both had issues we needed to fix." She shrugs. "I moved on. You should too."

I'm brought back down from the high of my raised hopes, but I'm not ready to give up.

"I can't go back to that night and unsay the words. Can you give me a chance to prove I didn't mean it?"

There is no pride in my begging. There is no room for it in the way I love this woman.

She smiles at me as if indulging a rambling child. Eliza doesn't believe me. I ran away once, she's got the right not to trust me and it hurts. I never wanted to be another person she couldn't rely on. Who disappointed her.

"What if what I want is for you to leave?" Her question is soft but it tears me to pieces.

"Do you?" The words are painful coming out. "If you do it would break my heart but…I'd never want to cause you harm again."

Silence stretches into an eternity with my heart balancing precariously on the edge of her next words.

"I wish I could tell you to leave," she huffs humorlessly. "It'd be easier than stopping myself from saying yes every time you ask."

"Then say it," I urge her, a hand snaking around her waist. I press her into me, relief flooding my veins at the weight of her body against mine.

Her lips pop open, eyes darkening.

My head drops to her ear. "Say yes." I can't help dragging my lip along the shell. "Please."

Our date is going better than expected. Eliza talks about her summer with ease, the food is great, and I'm loving every moment of it. Until she takes out her wallet.

"I know you're working on your independence and you don't spend time with me for my money. But hell will freeze over before you pay for anything on our dates. I will spoil you and treat you as you deserve, and you will accept it."

Walking to the historic district to catch the play that starts in thirty minutes, Eliza's pensive. She was surprised

I wanted to take her on such a public outing and that I'd planned the entire date. I don't know what hurts more. That she thought I wanted to see her in secret or that she was surprised I'd do anything for her.

"Dare I ask what you were doing with the mayor?"

"You can ask me anything." I thread my fingers through hers, loving the way she grounds me. "I bought the old post office."

She turns to me, eyebrow raised. "Why do you need an abandoned building? It's been out of use for years."

"You of all people should know the power of giving new life to things." I grin, enjoying her aggravated groan.

"Stop using my own words against me. It still doesn't explain why *you* bought it."

"Ouch. Believe it or not, I want to try something new."

"But your company—"

"I'm still on the board and own almost half of it. I let Jackie handle the hard part. Our father overlooked her, but I didn't do her any favors either by being overprotective."

"Look at you being reasonable." Laughter bubbles out of her and it's the loveliest sound I've ever heard.

"You inspired me."

The way she blushes makes the work I've done in therapy worth it.

"You followed your dream even if it scared you." I understood her search for independence. It's a desire that faintly echoed in the back of my head, always silenced by the pressure of my family's legacy. It's time I created a legacy of my own.

"Are you making calendars, Carter? I know you're fond of those."

"Not exactly." I laugh. "It's a hub. For local business owners. Maybe some business consultancy is better than tarot reading. The pilot stage will take place here. If it works, I'll extend the program nation-wide."

I've forgiven myself for choosing a different challenge and letting go of my father's obsession with the company. It's safe between Jackie and Joseph.

All the time spent in Silver Lake Falls has opened my eyes to a different type of challenge when it comes to business strategy. Getting to know some of the mom-and-pop places and their stories planted a seed of curiosity and creativity I didn't know I could grow.

"So that's your spark," she says thoughtfully.

"Pardon me?"

"Your spark. I see it now." She looks up at me with soft eyes, swirling shades of brown and gold, twinkling in the streetlamp's light.

"You mean my manly roaring fire?"

She ignores my awkward attempt at being funny. "What about your life in New York? Your responsibilities and work."

"I'm right where I'm supposed to be," I tell her while I open the heavy carved door that leads into the marbled foyer.

I'm glad she doesn't ask me anything about the play during the drive back. While Eliza's attention was focused on the stage, mine was firmly set on her, holding back the impulse to reach out and touch her.

"You never called," she says after a long stretch of silence. "All these months."

"I wanted to. Even eavesdropped on one of Jackie's calls, so I came to the showroom opening in Boston, a month before I found you in Jackie's office. I was outside when I saw you talking with some people."

She was beaming, chatting animatedly. Pride swelled in my chest seeing her explore her passion. Growing and feeling at ease. My wonderful Eliza.

"Why didn't you say something?"

"I decided not to ruin your evening, even though I burned with the need to be near you and apologize on my knees."

She doesn't say anything, and the rest of the ride is silent.

I walk Eliza to her dark-green front door. She's looking at her hands and I wait patiently until she finds the words, even though my instinct is to hold her and tell her she's allowed to miss me too.

"We can't just pick up where we left off," she says abruptly. "I know it wasn't part of the neighbors-with-benefits deal, but it became more for me. I can't pretend you didn't hurt me." Her jaw is set, and a determined frown creases her forehead. "The no-strings-attached hookups are off the table," she says, her tone unwavering.

"Good," I tell her.

"What?" Eliza's taken aback.

"Why do you think I came back? What do you think I left New York for? A hookup?"

I take her hands in mine. "I was drowning in denial before I came here. You showed me I wasn't living. You, Eliza, are pure light warming every corner of my heart. I'd be the luckiest man in the world to be allowed in your orbit."

Tear-filled eyes search me, looking for any sign of deception. She's still hesitant and it kills me when she nods and wordlessly walks inside, leaving me a mess on her doorstep.

CHAPTER FORTY-THREE

ELIZA

Six months ago, I would have never imagined I could take on this challenge. The budget opened the door to a world of luxury, but I still sprinkled in some pieces I found at the antiques fair. They gave the place a distinct personality.

Even with the nerves and excitement, this morning's note circles my mind on the last walk-through of the finished lake house.

You taught me the true meaning of being strong.

The things he said on my doorstep cracked my heart open. All the feelings furiously bursting its banks, too strong for words, too consuming to trust my judgment in that moment. I left him looking crestfallen, his pain haunting me.

"You did an amazing job, Eliza," Valerie says as I take another picture for my portfolio.

"I hope they love living here." The light pouring in through the large windows makes the rooms warm and homely.

To be honest, it'd be my dream home if I had the money for such a large piece of real estate. I could see

419

myself baking in the large kitchen, sketching in the hidden corner around the living room, or cuddling on the fluffy couch, reading while the kids run around the backyard that slopes into the lake.

Kids, a family. A want etched so deep in my soul, a never-healed wound that will keep bleeding until I meet the man I can see myself spending my life with. Or until I trust Carter when he says he wants to be that person for me.

"They adore it." She beams, looking around.

"How do you know?"

"I sent them some videos," Valerie says sheepishly. "Sorry I didn't tell you, I didn't want to add to the pressure."

The large ball of stress weighing on my shoulders lightens and I sit a little bit straighter.

"No problem. I'm a little relieved actually. I wish I could meet them in person and thank them for the opportunity."

"You'll have your chance." She pirouettes around the dining room, swiping invisible dust off the windowsill. "There will be a housewarming party next week and they insisted you join them."

When Valerie mentioned they'd invited some townsfolk, I expected it to be neighbors and close friends, but the deck and backyard are bustling with quite a crowd. On my way to find the hosts I spot Quinn hugging Mike and giving him an innocent peck. Although the sheriff is glaring at them from the opposite side of the garden, like they're having sex in the middle of the party.

Martha and Sam are near the dock, gesturing to the house and nodding.

"Happy to see familiar faces." I laugh, feeling relieved.

"We were surprised Valerie reached out," Sam says. He's wearing his best sweater and shirt, glancing around, as confused as I am.

"I guess the owners want to make nice with everybody in Silver Lake Falls." I can't wait to meet them. Even if they've already seen the place in videos there's still the nagging doubt. It would make a world of difference if they loved it and recommended me to other people. "Did you take a look inside?"

"We just got here. Want to show us around?" Martha nods toward the house.

From the corner of my eye, a flash of perfectly coiffed blonde hair grabs my attention. "You go ahead, I'll be right with you," I say, managing to plaster on a smile. My heart is picking up speed, but I don't know why.

Clara is sitting on the antique iron bench I found at the last minute to complete the garden area. She's talking with Kenneth and his wife, looking relaxed and not at all like the last person I expected to see here.

"What are you doing here?" Surprise laces my voice, any trace of manners flying out into the lake.

Clara chuckles. "Glad to see you too."

"Sorry," I mumble. "I mean, do you know the people who bought the house?"

Kenneth chokes on his drink, his eyes turning red.

His wife pats him on the back, rolling her eyes. "Hi, sweetheart," Linda greets me with a warm smile.

Carter's mom ignores my question and rises to take my hands in hers, a look in her eyes I've never seen before. "I'm so proud of what you've done here," Clara says, beaming at me with a motherly pride that robs the air from my lungs.

All my questions about her being here are forgotten. "But…you were so harsh."

"I only wanted to help you. I was once a simple girl who had to make my way up and there was no one to guide me." A sad little smile curves her lips. "Those people used to look down on me, but they had to tolerate me after my husband became one of the richest men in the world."

It dawns on me that she's been training me. What I learned in the last few months is partly thanks to her. Every dig was a push in the right direction so I could improve myself. Those events felt less daunting, I made some connections and caught on to the way their world works. She made it happen.

"Why? I—"

The words die on my lips when I spot him. Handsome and confident, his energy blurs everything around him, bringing the man I'm afraid to love into sharper focus.

Carter's walking over to the patio, champagne glass in hand, smiling at me. And I just know—the truth landing with a final thud at my feet.

This is his house.

CHAPTER FORTY-FOUR

CARTER

It wasn't my plan to linger in the shadows for so long, but I'm in awe of Eliza. Some might consider this light stalking. What can I say? I enjoy seeing her getting praised for the house. She looks so good walking around our home. Eliza made it ours without even knowing it and she belongs here. Next to me.

My fierce kitten thinks she's invisible. But she shines brighter than anybody. I'd spot her in Times Square on New Year's Eve. And I'd pick her out of every woman there.

"Are you done being creepy yet?" Jackie snickers.

"I don't want to scare her."

"Oh, no. God forbid. You just bought a ten-million-dollar house, tricked her into decorating it, and are planning on asking her to move in."

"Accurate. If marrying someone means moving in, for you."

Jackie's eyes go wide as saucers.

"I'll suggest a pretty peach for the bridesmaids. You *do* love it." I wink at her. Jackie will put me six feet under if anything resembling that color comes near her.

"Quit stalling." She shoves me lightly toward the deck. "Lucky for me, Eliza has better taste than you."

She's in my line of vision as soon as I step outside. Our gazes clash and realization blossoms on her face. She's still, then turns on her heel and leaves.

Oh no you don't. I catch up to her when she reaches the tree line hugging the lake.

"Why did you give me the project?" She whips around, close enough to the shore that a wrong step would land her in the clear October water. Her chest is heaving, her eyes a blaze of fury.

"Because I trust you. I wanted you to create the house of your dreams. For us."

She's pacing and muttering. It's better if I let her go through the process.

"I can't with you anymore," Eliza mutters. "What does it mean? Nothing for the Rawlings." She stops and scowls. "I bet you have at least ten houses all over the world."

"Yeah. I do. Over twenty. But none have you in it. I told you I'm here to stay. I am here for you." My feet take me closer to her, I can't take this distance any longer. "If you want to move, pick any of them." Wide eyes swim with disbelief, her soft lips parting in wonder. My girl is getting it. "But I must warn you none of them feel as welcoming as this one. You can redo them too. You can do whatever—"

She cuts me off with a brush of her lips. A feather-light, tentative kiss that has me soaring. It's over too soon.

My hands fly to her waist and I pull her against me, dipping my head.

"Do you understand now?" I caress her cheekbones, murmuring into her lips. "There's no future without you. I'm completely yours. I love you, Eliza."

She leans back, a look of wonder lighting up her face. "It's starting to sink in." The breathy edge of her voice goes straight to my groin, watery chocolate eyes swallowing me whole.

I pull her closer and kiss her hungrily. I can't get enough of her now I have her in my arms and relief floods me. I kiss her until my lungs burn. Until I'm dizzy with her taste and my palms slide under the blue dress I want to rip off her so I can touch every inch of her skin.

"Let's get back to your guests," Eliza pants, resting her head on my chest. "Someone might come looking for you."

"I'll kick them out," I breathe into her hair, and she laughs.

"Not if you really plan on living here."

An annoyed sigh blows out some of her strands and I tuck her hair back behind her ear. "You're right. But I want to show you something first."

Eliza cocks a brow and tilts her head, but follows me to the edge of the estate, without barraging me with questions.

"Who the hell did I have the video calls with, if it was you all along?"

I laugh, remembering the utter confusion on their faces when I explained what I needed from them. "Some old friends from Harvard. They married right after college and moved to Thailand." I brush the small of her back, desperate to touch her. "We owe them a visit."

Eliza cocks a brow. "Sure, I want to congratulate them on their acting skills," she huffs.

I stop in front of the large wooden outbuilding. "Did you wonder why this shed was off limits?"

She puffs. "More of a barn. I thought *the owners*" — she stresses the words with mock reproach—"already brought some personal stuff and didn't want it lying around the house while people were in and out…"

I open the doors and I hear her behind me sucking in a breath.

"Oh." It comes out strangled. "Are these…?" Her hand covers her trembling lips and I give her a gentle push to go in.

This is her space. The one I built the second I signed the papers for the house. It's filled with workbenches and tools and materials for her projects."

She walks through the full-staked studio gingerly touching the worktables, hesitant, afraid they're going to disappear in front of her eyes. Her face morphs and a playful spark lights up her eyes. "Weren't you a tad overconfident?"

"I've had an epiphany, kitten. Not a personality transplant."

"That would've been a tragedy." Eliza melts my insides with a blinding smile and wraps her arms around me in a fierce embrace, welding the last pieces of me that were drifting aimlessly before I met her. She's been putting me back together ever since and it took me almost losing her to realize it.

We make it back, hand in hand. I leave her to chat with Martha and offer to bring the old woman something to drink to give them some privacy.

"A yard so large begs for some kids." Martha nods wistfully, looking out, not noticing my return. I know they don't have any children and her words have no ill intent, but Eliza's answer twists my stomach.

"Please don't say things like that," she whispers with an edge of panic in her voice. "We're nowhere near that point. If he hears you, he might freak out again. I couldn't come back from it if he accused me of wanting to baby-trap him."

"Here's your lemonade." I hand Martha the glass.

"Um, thanks—" She jolts. "I better go find Sam."

It's the first time I've seen this woman unsure of something, so I lean closer. "Better be ready to babysit."

The smile she throws me over her shoulder can only be described as smug. All is right in the world again. Except for the woman I'm madly in love with.

"Kitten."

She's tense, holding on to the handrail, refusing to look at me.

I never wanted to make her afraid of saying something, walking on eggshells around me.

I slide my arms around her, trapping Eliza between my body and the banister.

"I'd want two. When you're ready," I whisper into her hair. "The total number is up to you."

She twists her neck to shoot me a scowl. "Don't even joke about children."

"I wouldn't. I'm all in. In case you were wondering." My lips graze the tender spot behind her ear. "I want at least two red-headed kids with their mother's heart." I press my cheek on her head, relishing her sweet smell I missed so much. "And my impeccable style, of course."

I want her to imagine a future with me. I want her to wonder how our kids would look and dream about reconditioning old cribs for them. I want to love them so much there is no chance they'll end up as miserable as I was.

Eliza's eyes brim with restrained excitement. "What about your freedom?"

"It's just agony if I can't be near you. I'm bound to you. I want a future with you built on hope, not fear. What do you say?"

CHAPTER FORTY-FIVE

ELIZA

The house is finally quiet after all the guests leave and I have the chance to tell Carter what's been on my mind all evening. Pacing the wooden floor under the porch's warm lights I brace myself for this conversation.

"Your family has different expectations for you. A…" The words are sour in my mouth, but it's important I get them out. "A suitable wife. I'm not saying—" I fumble, but he silences me with a fiery kiss.

"It's my choice. You're my choice." His resolution is set in the firm line of his jaw, determination blazing in his eyes. "Besides, I have an inkling my mother's been rooting for you."

"Maybe you should consider the implications."

"That's what I've been doing for the past four months."

"Oh." I lean on the porch column.

"I'll give you time to catch up," he says, pressing into me, his fingers tenderly grazing my legs.

It's enough to set me on fire and I don't stop his bolder touch, climbing under my dress until he reaches my panties. Without warning he rips them off me and he swallows my protest with his lips.

We're both hungry after the time we've been apart. Carter is rushed and possessive, his greedy mouth and hands branding me.

The wooden column digs into my back and the fresh wind brushes the chill from the lake against my heated skin. I anchor myself tighter, a hand fisted in his hair, my legs wrapped around him.

"I…Oh, my. I missed you," I mumble incoherently into his neck.

"Louder," Carter growls, his pace punishing. "I want them to hear you across the lake so everybody knows you're mine."

In the in-between moment I shatter in his arms, the truth breaks free. "I love you," I whisper into his mouth.

"Say it again," he pleads, forehead pressed into mine.

"I love you."

Carter's toasty death grip around my waist is safe and strong, the warmth of his skin working as a heating pad on my aching soul. It's difficult to wrap my head around the idea of him moving to Silver Lake Falls. All the hard work I put into letting go of the memory of him and the love I thought was one-sided was blown in the wind when he showed me he was here to stay. For me.

As much as I want to smother him with kisses and wrap my fingers around his morning wood, I slide out of his embrace as quietly as possible.

"I'll be back in time to have my way with your lovely kitchen," I promise him with a short kiss between his shoulder blades, and head to my place.

As I run around my perfect tiny home gathering supplies, I think back on my conversation with Carter yesterday and what it all means for us. I hope he's willing to spend some time here too. I know it's ridiculous but it's my very first home, and I want more of me before it becomes all about us.

The knock on the door pulls me out of my own head.

"Hi, you're early." I open the door wider and move to grab the box with the materials I had prepared.

He comes in without a word and the second I turn around I feel a wet cloth over my mouth. I'm kicking and screaming but his hold is too tight. The living room starts swimming around me, my limbs become heavy and I'm powerless to struggle any longer.

My mind is void, paralyzed by fear before my living room dissolves into darkness.

Chapter Forty-Six

CARTER

Eliza might not be sure yet, but I know damn well I am. Leaving a half-cold bed after everything we shared is not enough to push me away. I told her I'm not giving up easily and I meant it. I'd be an idiot to let her slip through my fingers and lose the woman who taught me love doesn't have to hurt.

Her front door is slightly ajar, and dread takes hold of my insides like a sharp claw.

"Eliza," I call out, hopeful, but my gut feeling is sounding the alarm.

The bag she had at the party is on the floor, its contents spread under the living room coffee table. A wave of nausea washes over me and I act at the speed of light.

"Code red. Somebody took Eliza," I bark into the phone. "Send the tactical unit here." The air is thick, moving sluggishly in and out of my lungs. "Put the rescue team on the helicopter to sweep the area. I'll give you details as soon as I know more."

"On it. Are you in any danger, boss?" Derrick's voice is the epitome of cool professionalism.

"No." I wish I was the one taken, instead of her. She knew so many people and Derrick's team did a background check on all of them. There were no red flags. "Send me the sheriff's contact. ASAP."

My mind scrambles to go through all the scenarios. Jared? He's an asshole, but his record is clean. Would he want to hurt Eliza just because he's a jealous bastard?

My security chief is still on the line, a flurry of activity in the background. "Somebody you pissed off, boss?"

The thought makes me sick. I'll never forgive myself if I've put her in danger with my carelessness. There have always been people with an ax to grind against big tech companies. They were loud, but never made any moves to actually pose a threat.

The competition is fierce in our field. I've met many shady people wanting to use our tech for less than honorable or legal purposes. I've always blacklisted them. Did one of them plan to force my hand by taking Eliza?

"Walker." The brusque baritone of the sheriff bellows in my ear and I fill him in. "Stay put," he orders.

The next call is to the only other person I'd trust in this situation besides Derrick.

"I need your help." I let my panic bleed through.

Logan doesn't miss a beat and speaks over the sound of his fingers flying over the keyboard. "How bad is it?"

"It's Eliza. Get your trackers on her. Somebody has her."

"Shit," he grunts and yells at somebody in his office. "Get Patel and the squad on the plane. Fire up the tank in Boston and send it to meet them when they land."

"You own a tank?" I ask stupidly. As far as I'm concerned, he can send a full-fledged military fleet to Eliza's rescue. I'll pay whatever it takes to find her.

"Yes, but *The Tank* is our surveillance and forensic armed vehicle. You still have the tracker on you?"

"Yes." My thumb instinctively rubs over the small bump near my wrist. I thought it was excessive at the time, but Logan's paranoia proves to be well-founded.

"Pinned you. They'll be there in forty minutes. Give me access to your satellites."

"Thank you," I breathe out in a short-lived sense of relief.

"Save it for when we find her." He hangs up just as the police car skids to a stop. A man built like a bear climbs out. His face is familiar, but I don't have time to dwell on it.

"Sheriff Walker." He frowns and scans me as if I've done something to Eliza. "You're Eliza's guy from New York."

He makes it sound like I'm somebody you'd call for shady permits. "I moved here. She spent the night at my place. Something happened here. Look inside. I didn't move anything."

The sheriff doesn't take long to assess the interior. "I need a list of people she's been in contact with recently."

Fuck. I've been gone for more than three months. Who knows who she met? Her business is also taking off so there were even more people who could have taken her.

"Better talk to Quinn. She knows everything going on in Eliza's life."

The sheriff's eyes flash and he nods toward his aid who is hovering near the patrol car with his forensic kit.

"I'm going to need you to accompany me to her."

"I can't follow you around, I have people to talk to, to help find her. I can't waste time."

"There won't be time wasted if we get Quinn to talk faster. Trust me. Let's take your car. I don't want to tip off the guys if they're stupid enough to still be in the area."

In the car, Walker barks orders into his phone. "Put out a BOLO for Eliza Miller, a Caucasian female, red hair, brown eyes, last seen last night. She might be wearing a blue dress. I just sent you a picture. She's missing. Possible kidnapping. Report any sightings and canvas the area along the access road. Set up checkpoints on all exits."

At least he's not a mumbling small-town sheriff.

"I should call in the FBI," he says after he jots some notes.

"No. I don't want them messing this up. Our rescue team is better trained than anyone. They'll coordinate with Logan's security contractors. I trust them with my life."

The bell above the coffee shop door gets Quinn's attention and she greets us with a deep frown, scowling at the sheriff and crossing her arms. "Out where you came from."

Now I know where to place him. He's the guy with the baseball bat who came to the pub with his police friends when the girls were in trouble.

"Official matters, I'm afraid."

"That's some bullshit excuse," her voice is shrill, but she spots me and her eyes go wide.

"Eliza's missing. Time is running out."

Quinn falls into a chair, trembling fingers pressed to her lips.

"We don't know much right now." I bend over to place a hand on her shoulder, to make her pay attention as her eyes follow Walker taking a call a few feet from us. "You need to think hard about anybody she met lately who might seem suspicious."

The sheriff rushes back to us. "Somebody saw a light blue vintage truck speeding up the road. Do you know any friends of hers who drive one? Or somebody she didn't get along with?"

Quinn's face becomes ashen. "No…can't be. Maybe they had to run an errand together…" she says to herself, unlocking her phone with shaky hands.

"Her things are scattered all over the floor. Including her phone," I point out. There's no way she left willingly.

Quinn gulps. "Straight to voicemail."

"Who?" Walker gets in her face until she's plastered to the support beam behind her.

"My b-boyfriend. Mike. He drives a 1952 Studebaker," she whimpers. "It's his pride and joy."

"Full name and plates. Now."

The floor caves in under my feet when both Derrick and the police records come up empty.

"He gave you a false name."

This is not a random kidnap.

The sheriff nods grimly. "We'll set up the command center in my office. Call your people."

I don't miss a second and alert Derrick and Logan. "Done."

"You're coming with us," Walker tells Quinn, who's shivering, looking close to fainting. He sighs and puts an arm around her middle, taking her to the car.

The harsh fluorescent light in the cramped interrogation room burns my brain as my grip on the metal chair turns my knuckles white. My patience is running on fumes. I'd rather scour the wilderness for Eliza than listen to the hollow sound of Quinn's frantic back and forth on the worn linoleum.

She's pale as a sheet, wringing her hands.

"She told me she kept misplacing stuff in her house," she says hoarsely. "The last time it happened, she noticed the paint was chipped near the doorknob. She thought she'd ruined it when she left in a hurry with her tools. So many projects popped up in the last month, she couldn't remember where she'd put things."

"Why the hell didn't she tell me this?" My fist slams on the scuffed table, making Quinn flinch. She was in danger all this time and never said a word. Rage and worry burn through me.

"Watch it, Rawlings." The sheriff gives me a death stare before returning his gaze to her.

"What if…" Her eyes fill with tears, and she bites hard on her lower lip to stop it from trembling.

Walker stares at her and does a weird half-reach to comfort her, then slides the tissue box nearer.

"How didn't I see it?" She lowers her face into her palms, slowly shaking her head. "I brought him into our life."

I was so happy to be back near Eliza, doing my best to convince her to give me another chance, that I failed to ask my team to do a background check on the new people in her life.

I should have protected her. She didn't tell me about feeling paranoid. She wanted to be independent and self-reliant so badly it put her in danger.

Logan's name on my phone screen launches me out of the door into the secure room behind the one-way mirror.

"We have a short list of people who own that type of truck. Something interesting jumped out in connection to one of the names. You'll want to see this."

I put him on speaker to check what he sent me. Dread drops to the pit of my stomach.

Eliza's sealed file.

"She might be in more danger than we thought. Tell your sheriff to round up his CIs while we comb the group's known whereabouts."

My heart sinks reading her file. It's the painfully detailed story of her childhood after she was abandoned. What Eliza already told me is only the tip of the iceberg of what she went through.

The faded note from her mother, written hastily on the back of an envelope, is an eye-opener. Now it all makes sense.

CHAPTER FORTY-SEVEN

ELIZA

My lids are heavy as I struggle to clear my head. Slowly I regain my senses but pulling out of the darkness in my mind is like getting out of a pit of quicksand. With my eyes cracked open I notice the room is unlit, scattered rays of light coming through ripped strips of newspaper covering the windows.

Tremors run through my body while I fight off the need to spill the contents of my stomach on the concrete floor. My head is pounding. When I try to rub my temples to soothe the pain, I realize my hands are tied behind my back and my legs are bound to the rickety chair.

What does he want from me? My heart is beating furiously behind my ribcage, almost breaking its way out of my body. Carter sleeping peacefully and his safe embrace are a distant memory, and I cling to it so I won't fall apart.

The screech of a rusty door behind me freezes the blood in my veins. Several steps echo in the empty room and when a pair of dirty boots stops in front of my chair, I'm afraid to look up.

"Hello, little fox. I've been waiting a very long time to find you."

I screw my eyes shut in a useless attempt to shut reality out, but a rough hand clasps my chin.

"Open your eyes, girl. I'm not gonna hurt you."

Terror blazes through me and my nose stings with unshed tears. I've watched enough TV to know that seeing your kidnapper's face is close to a death sentence.

I yelp in pain as he digs his fingers harder into my flesh.

"Don't make me ask twice!" His yell warms my face. The smell of cigarettes makes my skin crawl, but I don't want to anger him more.

Tears slide down my face when I peer at the rough-looking man with graying blond hair beneath a stained baseball cap.

He tilts his head, examining me in silence. Terror pours through my limbs, unable to shake the grisly scenarios flashing through my mind. He takes a slow step back and flicks his faded army-style jacket back to plant his fists at his sides.

The motion exposes the unmistakable shape of a gun's handle peeking above the waist of his pants.

His grin is terrifying. "You look just like your mother," he says with a strange wistfulness. "Too bad she didn't know what was best for her."

Shock leaves me breathless. Does this man know my mother?

"My mom." My voice quivers. "Where is she?"

"Better off cuz I can't get my hands on her," he says, displeased.

Shaking against my restraints is useless, the old chair scraping the floor, but I struggle until I'm out of breath.

My captor shakes his head. "Nice try, little fox. But that won't get you anywhere." He tuts patronizingly.

Years of hurt win against my fear of this man. "What do you know about my mom?!"

"The crackhead who told me about you said she's dead," he says, unaffected, scratching his stubble. "I'll give it to her. She disappeared with your mom and kept her mouth shut for twenty-five years. But the woman's so far gone now it only took some cash." His laugh is grating, trickling ice down my spine. "In the end, I always get what I want."

Nausea creeps back up my throat. As soon as I turned eighteen, I tried to find out who my parents were, but it was a closed adoption. She's dead and I'll never get to meet her. The flimsy shred of hope I was holding on to shrivels like burnt paper. What about my father? Looking into the brown eyes of the man before me, my mouth dries and it's difficult to get the question out.

"Who…Who're you?"

The man puffs out his chest with an unsettling smile, and I spot Mike behind him, arms folded, too comfortable with his surroundings.

"What the hell?" I pant. He knocked me unconscious this morning. "What is this? Untie me! Why would you do this?"

"Relax, sister, we only want to chat," he chuckles.

The word lands like an atomic bomb in my chest. My mouth falls open, my mind frantically going through all the times I've spoken to him since he started dating Quinn. His questions about my childhood…I thought he wanted to be friendly.

"No," I whisper hoarsely.

"Isn't this a fun family reunion, *daughter*?" The older man says mockingly, confirming my fears. "We can all live happily ever after. Josh here could need some help with our operation," this stranger who claims to be my father says in the casual drawl of a dinner table conversation.

"Josh? Even your name was fake?" I screech. "Oh, Quinn! I swear if you hurt her—"

The blond man raises his hand. "Your mother was fierce too, when she was young," he snickers. "Your little friend is safe."

Relief floods through me.

"We needed Josh to get closer to you since you slipped through our fingers that night at the pub," he says with a disappointed tsk, tapping his chin. "Your knight in shining armor won't be able to find you here." His brown eyes are sharp as razors. "This compound's been out of the feds' reach for thirty years."

"What's going to happen to me?" I gulp, another tremor running through me.

CHAPTER FORTY-EIGHT

CARTER

The cramped room at the station reeks of cheap coffee and heat coming off the people looking intently at the corkboard. The team Logan sent, together with my security chief Derrick and his rescue unit, are all sandwiched between a handful of the sheriff's officers.

Sheriff Walker points to the satellite map pinned in the center. "This place is a maze. It's an abandoned logging camp from the 1920s. We can't go in guns blazing through the main gate. It'll give them time to move her and gear up at the armory that's in one of the new, reinforced buildings." He taps along a row of dark gray rectangles.

"Our surveillance showed us two vulnerable points," Patel, Logan's task force leader, interjects. He points his laser at the map. "The tree line here is closest to the fence. It gives us good cover to cut through the barbwire fence. The old ramp to the river is the other one. We'll approach from upstream, in the water."

Restlessness itches under my skin with every minute we spend here, instead of going after Eliza, but I know we'll put her in danger if we don't prepare. "What about their security?" I ask.

"My CIs say they have heavily armed guards and attack dogs," Sheriff Walker tells us.

"The Tank picked up signals from over twenty security cameras around the place. We won't see them under the leaves, so Spike"—Patel points his chin to one of his men tinkering with his tactical command kit—"will freeze them for ten minutes."

Walker's brows knit together and he crosses his arms over his chest. "Is this enough time?"

"It has to be. More time and they'll figure out somebody messed with them."

"What's the next step after your men enter the premises?" I ask impatiently, ready to bolt.

Patel narrows his eyes, assessing me, but has the good sense not to comment on my involvement. "We'll deactivate the guards in the towers—"

"That better mean immobilize," Sheriff Walker cuts him off. "This is already an unsanctioned mission. The higher-ups will have my head if it ends in a bloodbath."

"Then maybe you and your men can step aside and leave it to the big boys. I don't mind getting my hands dirty," Patel grits.

"This is my backyard; I won't let a bunch of war dogs blow shit—"

"Enough!" The bang of my fist against the metal table rattles around the walls of the small room. "We don't have time for this nonsense. Let's move fast. They won't hold her in the same place for long." The thought of Eliza alone with them makes me sick. She's probably terrified. If they've laid a hand on her, I'll raze the place to the ground.

Patel and Sheriff Walker continue to throw daggers at each other but don't say anything else, while the officers exchange weary looks.

Derrick clears his throat, getting everybody's attention. "They must have more than cameras to alert them. We should expect traps and movement sensors. I'll have my boys clear the area before you reach the compound's border."

Patel nods, looking at his team. "The second we deactivate their eyes above ground, you come in and extract the target. The sheriff can waltz in after we secure the armory. Wait for our signal and fire up the sirens. The noise will draw them to the entrance."

I bristle at the term for Eliza. "I'll come with you," I tell my security chief.

Derrick looks at me with unease. "No offense, boss. But this mission is extremely dangerous."

"I wasn't asking for your opinion. I'm telling you. Eliza needs me."

One of the younger officers raises a timid hand like she's at school. "'Scuse me, sir. What happens if they spot us and raise the alarm?"

Patel, Sheriff Walker, and Derrick seem to reach an unspoken consensus. "Prepare for the worst. Our contingency plan involves explosives," Patel answers, a little too pleased with this option.

"That's right. I'm not leaving before she's out of their hands, even if it's the last thing I do," I tell my security chief. "Now, gear me up."

The tension and weight of the stakes follow us outside, the overcast weather hanging heavy over our group. The forty-minute drive into the forest stretches into eternity while Derrick briefs his team one more time.

Shoulder to shoulder with Derrick in the muddy pit, we're all crouched along the linked fence that Patel's men went through two minutes ago. They'd better move fast because time is running out.

Seconds go by in complete silence, interrupted only by the occasional bark and the voices of the guards roaming the compound.

I'm not sure I'm even breathing when Patel's voice cracks in our headsets. "The heat scanner shows her with two individuals in the long barn at four o'clock."

Peering over the thick roots above us, I spot the building. She's so close.

"Don't even think about it," Derrick hisses in my ear. "Stick to the plan!" He shakes his head, regret written all over his face. "Oh my God, Jackie's going to kill me."

I ignore him and check the timer, my stomach in knots. The ten minutes of video jam are almost up, and I feel like we're sitting ducks if they spot us.

"The armory is secured." One of Patel's men barks. "I repeat. The armory is secured." The static slices through my brain. "Sheriff, light the sirens at the next signal."

Sixty seconds to go, and every strain of my muscles wants to push me out of this hole, headfirst into the barn holding my heart.

Finally, Patel's voice explodes in my ear. "Move out now! Go! Go! Go!"

CHAPTER FORTY-NINE

ELIZA

My father pulls out a buzzing rugged-looking black phone with an antenna from the inside pocket of his jacket and taps a few keys before he answers.

"We're rolling out at 1800 hours," he says. "Yeah, I have the coordinates for the drop-off."

He looks at me with a worrisome smirk while nodding along to what the person at the other end is telling him.

"Yeah, she's here," he answers. His tone rattles me to the bone, but his next words are even more ominous. "She'll behave. I know how to keep people in line."

The man claiming to be my brother sits on his haunches, lips pursed, and eyebrows drawn together. He sighs like hurting me was the last thing he wanted to do.

"I'm sorry, sis." He looks hurt when I recoil. "I didn't mean for the whole thing with Quinn to get so out of hand."

"I hope she hunts you down and puts you through the meat grinder," I spit out. I can't believe I fell for his act.

My father places a hand on Josh's shoulder and looks at the both of us like this is a cute little family reunion.

"Are you going to hurt me?"

"No," he drags out the sound, lifting his index finger. "*If* you play nice."

I swallow my unease. "What does that mean?"

"All I want is my kids together. I wanna pass on the Hall legacy to my bloodline. Your mother didn't get it." His nose crinkles in disgust. "In the end, she was too weak."

I have to keep him talking. Maybe if I buy some time, someone will find me, before they take me to God knows where. "What legacy?"

I've played this game before. Get the heat off me by letting proud angry men talk about themselves. I scan the dusty room for any way out but the door behind me seems to be the only exit.

The two men share a knowing grin.

"You'll see soon enough." He tilts his head and a vicious smirk curls his lips. "I wouldn't think about doing anything stupid, if I were you." He pulls another phone out and shows me the screen. To my horror, it's a video of Carter. He's talking with the sheriff in front of my house. The threatening message is clear. With all the security Carter has, they still got close enough. I'd never do anything to put him in danger and this asshole knows it.

"I won't," I grit through my teeth.

My father's expression is softer when he continues. "You're a tough cookie. Josh got his hands on your file." He looks at me, expecting me to wear my miserable childhood as a badge of honor. Anger boils inside of me.

"You had no right to dig through my life!"

His jaw ticks and I get a glimpse of a scary man, his fatherly facade crumbling in an instant. "I had every right!" Spit flies out of his mouth, his face turning red. "I'm your father and your place is next to me. Your mother wasted enough time, I could have taught you how to—"

The sound of breaking glass sucks the air out of the room and cuts his rant short. Through the window closest to me a metal cylinder flies and rolls to a stop at Josh's feet. They both jump back as the can hisses out dark green smoke spreading around the room like a misshapen snake.

"Fuck," my father spits. "Go! Go!" He pushes my brother to the opposite corner. I make out a pile of cardboard boxes he throws to the side, bending to the floor.

The taste of chemicals burns my mouth and eyes. Tears fall uncontrollably as I gasp for air, coughing and spluttering, pulling on the zip ties around my wrists. They only cut into my skin, warm blood coating my palms and dripping from my fingertips.

"This isn't over, little fox. I'll come back for you," a dark shadow half-buried in the floor yells through the thick smoke.

The claws of darkness slowly close over my eyes. My heart is in my throat, tired and slow. Through the haze in my mind, voices and shouts pierce the murkiness. I don't have the energy to keep my head straight and it lolls from side to side. Blue and red lights paint the room and loud bangs echo rhythmically behind me. I never thought dying would be similar to a poorly ventilated rave.

Loud thuds rattle the metal door behind me, over and over again until it flies open and smashes against the wall and the sound of heavy boots reaches my ears.

"Rawlings, stand back!" A booming voice travels through the smoke. "Are you insane?!" The voice bellows again. "Don't go in!"

"Eliza!"

I must be hallucinating from the lack of air. Hearing his voice for the last time is not a bad way to go. Then I hear my name again. It's distorted through the white noise in my ears.

"Damn it, Rawlings, the room might be rigged. Stand back!"

Big firm hands cup my face and my favorite mirage holds my head up, looking beautiful in a haunted sort of way, eyes filled with fear.

"I got you." Carter's voice is muffled, like I'm hearing him through water.

He's here for me.

The zip ties pull for a moment before my wrists are released and I cry out from pain as a million needles prick my skin.

He slides his palms up and down my arms. "You're going to be OK." I'm a rag doll in his arms, my head falling on his chest when my eyes roll back into my head, and it all goes black.

Chapter Fifty

CARTER

Eliza sits through the doctor's check-up and police interviews in the back of the ambulance with unfocused eyes, her shoulders slumped. Her steady hold on my hand is the only sign she's anchored to the present. I don't leave her side through the overwhelming hours, guilt and pain churning in my stomach when I glance at her wounds.

Sheriff Walker asks again if Hall said where he was going to take her, but she looks like she's going to collapse at the slightest breeze.

"Enough." I tighten the blanket around her and face Walker. "Eliza needs to rest. She's given you enough details for now."

"He's one of the biggest gun movers in the state," he says through his teeth.

"Then do your job and catch him," I spit out, sheltering Eliza behind me completely. I step closer to him and drop my voice. "My men will send you the intel they find."

He's about to argue when a fleet of government cars pulls up around the scene and Walker slides a hand over his mouth. "The FBI and the ATF are here." He rolls his shoulders, preparing for a confrontation. "You owe me, Rawlings. They should have been notified the moment Hall's name popped up. I'll probably get my ass chewed."

This man has been as crucial to finding Eliza as Logan and Derrick. My hand clasps his shoulder. "I won't let you take the fall. We'll sort this out and find the motherfucker."

The sheriff raises a skeptical brow but has no idea of the influence our business has within law enforcement. He'll find out what it means to be under Rawlings Enterprise protection. Walker turns on his heel to face some angry-looking suits while I text Adam to work his magic.

Eliza is cradling her bandaged wrists, peering out the window the entire ride to our home. She might not realize it yet, but there's no chance in hell I'll let her spend another second alone in her unsafe house. I want to comfort her and get her to talk incessantly again, but she needs some time. She's too rattled.

The guards are already at their posts when we reach the gates. If she's confused by their presence she doesn't say anything, just silently takes my hand and follows me inside.

"You have some clothes upstairs," I tell her when I notice she's fidgeting, unsure of what to do next. My heart constricts and I close my eyes and take a deep breath. I want to tear those two limb from limb for what they did to her.

Without a second thought, I slide my arm under her knees, and I'm rewarded with a squeak before I climb the stairs to the master bedroom.

"You carried me enough today," she says faintly, and I tighten my hold on her.

"I'll never get tired of it. Plus, I don't want to take any chances. What if you trip and sue me for damages? Can't have that."

My arms refuse to let her go when I reach the softly lit room. Feeling her weight against my chest is the only thing keeping my heart rate down. The prospect of losing Eliza forever still looms over me like a dark-winged creature. She's looking for the same comfort, pushing her nose under my chin. My girl takes a deep breath and her muscles loosen. The thought that my scent relaxes her fills me with booming happiness.

Eliza presses her lips to the juncture of my jaw, sending a wave of peace and comfort through my veins, and pushes herself back gingerly, but I don't let go.

"You can put me down," she says, amused.

"I'm not ready yet," I confess into her hair. "Let me hold you a little longer."

"I'm not going anywhere." She cups my face, giving me a reassuring smile. "But my clothes smell like I spent my day burning tires in the junkyard."

She eyes the small bag at the foot of the bed.

"Quinn brought some of your stuff, so you don't have to go back there any time soon. Anything else, I'll get the goddamn store for you, OK?" I reluctantly lower her to the floor, my hand glued to the back of her neck, unable to let her go completely.

"You're doing it again," she says with a roll of her eyes. "Being over the top."

My unapologetic shrug amuses her and she crouches next to the bag. "I want to call her. How is she holding up? Poor Quinn."

"She was very scared for you. Now she's mad. She might track your brother faster than the FBI."

"Could you—" She bites her lip, unsure.

"Tell me."

"I don't want you to think I'm taking advantage, but…could you spare one of your security guards to check on her?"

My knees hit the soft carpet and drag her onto my lap. "Ask me for the world, kitten, and I'll bring it to your feet in an instant."

Her eyes widen and get misty.

"Her home is already secured, and she'll have a tail on her 24/7. I won't let anything happen to your friend."

Eliza closes the small space between us with one of her bone-crushing hugs and exhales deeply. My relief mirrors her. Twelve hours ago, I didn't know if I'd be able to hold her again.

"How did you find me?" Her question is faint, into my chest.

"Do you want to talk about it now?" I run my fingers through her hair. "A hot shower would be better."

"There are too many gaps in my memory. Not knowing what happened while I was out of it is an itch I can't scratch."

It should be no surprise I'm incapable of refusing her anything. I love this reality where she can ask me for anything, and my only purpose is to make her happy.

I release a long sigh. "Logan's surveillance drone picked up the truck parked inside the compound."

She makes a "Hmm" in the back of her throat. "Remind me to name our firstborn son after him," Eliza says, dead serious.

I rock her in silence to the sound of my singing heart. She'd never say that as a joke.

After a couple more stolen seconds her mood shifts. "I don't think he wanted to harm me," she says tentatively.

I close my eyes and reign in the rage aimed at her father. "You're giving him too much grace, Eliza. What would have happened if you'd said no? Would he have just let you go?" The thought leaves me sick and desperate to protect her from now on.

Eliza shivers in my arms, burying her head deeper into my shirt.

"This house has the best security system there is. A team is guarding the perimeter. You're safe here."

"Is it necessary?"

"Until they get the bastards, yes."

"But—"

"He's very dangerous, kitten." I lean back and cup her shoulders. "How much did he tell you?"

She looks at her trembling fingers. "I didn't catch much. Something about a family operation."

"He was an army firearms instructor. Dishonorably discharged." I wouldn't burden her with this, but she has to know who we're dealing with. "He started with petty crimes when your brother was born and graduated to gun trafficking. He's been smart enough to avoid capture. This time he slithered his way out of the compound through secret tunnels the CIs knew nothing about."

She's pale, nodding with a faraway look. "Do you think they'll catch him soon?"

"I'll make sure they do," I say resolutely.

To my surprise, we both end up in the shower after she sagely points out I also smell like a dumpster fire. We let the hot water soak us and take turns cleaning one another in complete silence. It's pure intimacy and trust bonding our souls together. Even though my body reacts in the most obvious way to having her hands all over me, this is not the time.

She lets me dry her with the towel and put on the fluffiest socks I can find. This permission to take care of her is a gift that puts a knot in my throat. Eliza doesn't say anything while I pull one of my sweatshirts over her head, just watches me with an intensity running hot over my skin.

"Get in," I tell her, lifting the covers.

She's running on fumes, her eyelids heavy with exhaustion. "Will you hold me?"

The crisp linen rustles as I slide in next to her. "Always."

Her breath evens out in a matter of seconds but I'm too anxious to sleep. There's something else weighing heavy on my mind, but she's in no state to deal with it. So I stare out the window over the swaying treetops and the still lake, mulling over how I'm going to break the news to her until the sun is up.

I let her sleep until it's almost noon, she needs her strength for what's next, and gather my nerves while Eliza finishes her late breakfast.

"You're quieter than usual."

"I want to talk to you about something." I pull her out of the breakfast nook, and we settle on the large comfy outdoor couch.

"Oh, no," she gasps when she sees the cup of hot chocolate Quinn dropped off. "How bad is it?"

I half turn toward her in my seat and tuck her beautiful hair behind her ear.

"Walker told you how we found out who your father is," I say slowly. This is going to be difficult.

Eliza's eyes drop to a thread in the blanket, and she twists it. "You unsealed my adoption file." Her voice is small, and I hate that she's ashamed of what's written inside. That I would see it.

"And made the connection. Your parents were never married, but it wasn't hard to find out they were dating before you were born."

I pull out the weathered photo that's been burning a hole in my back pocket all morning and hand it to her. Eliza gasps and chokes on a sob, her hand trembling on the old portrait.

A pregnant young woman in denim overalls beams at the camera, holding her dark copper hair against the wind.

"You have her smile," I say gently.

Eliza's hazel eyes fill with tears. "Where did you get this?" she asks with a trembling voice.

"My team found some of her old friends."

"It's true she died?"

I bite the inside of my cheek. I hate this. "I'm sorry." I rub her arms. "Ten years ago, she got diagnosed with cancer. It was too late."

Her eyes screw shut and she takes a shuddering breath.

"Does…Did she—" Eliza can't finish the question. It's difficult for her to even show a little hope.

"Her family is still in Maine. Her parents…Your grandparents are still alive, and three aunts."

Tears roll down her cheeks and her lower lip trembles.

"They don't have any affiliation with your…with Hall's illegal activities," I tell her, running my thumb under her wet eyelashes.

She's in pain, gently swaying. It kills me, but I have to let her go through it and decide what she wants.

"Do you think they'd want to meet me?" she finally asks.

"All you have to do is reach out. They had no idea. Were a bit shell-shocked when I talked to them." I clear my throat. "There's something else."

"I'm not sure I can take more," she says hoarsely, resting her head back on the couch.

"There was a note in the file. From your mother." I clasp her hand. "It's your choice if you want to read it."

Eliza takes a big fortifying breath, tears streaming down into her hair. "You read it, I can't."

The envelope crinkles in my hands.

To the wonderful people who want to adopt,
Giving my baby up is the hardest thing I've ever had to do,
but Eliza is not safe with me. I pray you'll welcome her into
your family with open arms because she's a blessing. The
sweetest baby girl and a ray of joy from the moment I first
held her in my arms.
It breaks my heart to let her go, but I hope she has a safe
and wonderful home with you.

Eliza pulls her knees up and wraps her arms around her legs, her soft whimpers falling over us like heavy snow.

"Do you want me to stop?" I'm worried it's too soon. Maybe I should have waited a few days.

"What else?" Her gruff question is barely a whisper.

The last lines of the note I've memorized by now are lodged in my throat and my voice is thick.

"It might be too late for me,
but my daughter deserves a better life."

My nose is itchy, and the air scratches the inside of my airway remembering what Eliza's been through since she was adopted.

"Please take care of her. She's my light in the dark."

The dam breaks and Eliza lets go and crumples in my arms, wailing. She shakes from the force of her sobs and I'm useless in helping her, in taking the pain away, so I just hold her as tight as I can, whispering comforting words in her hair and rubbing circles on her back, the way she once did for me last spring.

"She loved you so much." I rock her small body through her tears and cries. "Your mother wanted you safe."

We stay locked in a tight embrace until the sun sets over the mountain peaks, Eliza lost in her thoughts and emotions. I don't interrupt her, she's got a lot to process. From the fact that her biological father is an arms dealer who kidnapped her, to having a brother who stalked her for months, to finding out she was loved, and her mother protected her the best way she could.

I remember what my therapist told me about coming to terms with a new reality after holding on to another truth your whole life.

Her breath evens out eventually and I carry her upstairs to our bedroom. She doesn't protest.

"I bet you regret stumbling into my cabin that night," she sniffles, a sad smile curving her lips.

"I never stumble," I say half offended, half amused, placing her on the edge of the bed and kneeling in front of her. My palms run up behind her legs until they're trapped between her warm skin and the mattress. "But it was the luckiest night of my life because otherwise, I would have never known how it feels to be whole. To be so incredibly, stupidly happy and in love, I almost forget the pain I felt before you decided to blow my heart to pieces and put it back the way it's supposed to be."

Red-rimmed brown eyes swim with emotion until her eyebrows knit and she gnaws at her lip. "I'm sorry you didn't get to meet a version of me that is not broken, with so much baggage. You deserve so much better."

Silly girl. My silly girl.

If she thinks there's anything about her that would scare me away, she's in for a big surprise. I caress her cheekbones, threading my fingers into her silky hair. I tilt her chin so she can read the truth in my eyes. "This is the version I love. My soul calls to you and I would've found you in any version, in any circumstance. And I would fall for you every time."

"Even when I'm hard to love sometimes?" she says in awe, eyes round and bright.

"Especially then. Weren't you the one who said broken treasures just need a bit of love? I'll give you all the love, I'll carry the baggage for you, no matter how heavy." I kiss her forehead, her teary eyes, and the tip of her nose. "Will you let me?" I ask into her scorching lips.

CHAPTER FIFTY-ONE

ELIZA

"I'm only going to Thomas's shop!" I say exasperatedly.

Carter gives me an unimpressed look over his Sudoku. "I'm not taking chances while they're still out there."

After all these months of living together and receiving the Rawlings security treatment, I'm still uncomfortable. We'd compromised that they'd stay out of sight and travel in different cars. It's not fooling anyone in Silver Lake Falls, but it makes me feel better.

No matter how annoyed I get at the whole situation, the random messages sent from burner phones starting with *My little fox* serve as a harsh reminder that I'm not safe. I know it drives Carter crazy, but he keeps it together for my sake. I didn't want to admit it, but it made sense once I started traveling a lot more between construction sites and the events Clara wouldn't let me weasel out of.

"Are you meeting Lexi today?"

A fresh burst of joy warms my heart when I think about my new tenant. It makes me less sad to know my little house I worked so hard to fix up will help others.

"Meeting her at noon. Poor soul is still skeptical. I can't wait to see the look on her face when I hand her the keys," I tell Carter giddily.

I decided to put the much-loved house to good use after I moved in with Carter. Lexi will be the first kid out of foster care I'm going to help with a place to stay until she's able to stand on her own two feet. The deal is I won't charge her rent for the first three months until she gets a job and saves up a bit. After that, she'll pay a symbolic sum for the next year. Valerie will help her find a decent place and the next kid out of foster care will take Lexi's place.

"Don't forget about dinner with the Duntons." Carter heaves a sigh and closes the distance between us, sliding an arm around my waist. "The old menace hustled an expensive dinner out of me. And I suspect you were in on it." He bites my neck lightly.

"Whatever do you mean?" I play dumb but the next bite is around my ticklish spot, and I explode into fits of giggles.

"You could have mentioned he's been playing poker since he arrived on the Mayflower."

"Don't be a sore loser. He's not that old!"

I leave him to get ready for his meeting with the town council. It's amazing how much fun he's having with the business community here. It balances the high stakes and stress of the Rawlings board meetings or late-night calls with Jackie.

The fresh spring air hits my face as I close the door behind me, and I know I wouldn't want to live anywhere else. At least not now. It's still a safe haven, close to the people I love.

Sometimes when I'm alone the anxiety creeps back, sadness piling up, but I remind myself constantly how strong I am. How loved and cherished Carter and the people around me make me feel.

The truth about my mother is a bittersweet pill to swallow. Finding out she loved me hurt in a different kind of way. It's difficult to come to terms with the fact that I can't talk to her about it and that even with her best intentions, I went through so much growing up.

I catch a glimpse of the security guards in the black sedan trailing behind me as I drive my fully reconditioned cream and cherry truck. It was a Christmas gift from Carter. It says a lot about how well he knows me that he didn't take the easy way out and buy a new car.

"It's you again." Thomas's grumpy old man routine doesn't scare me. I know he's a big softy at heart.

"Wouldn't want you to miss me too much." I grin. "Are the samples here?"

The new projects keep me pretty busy. Even though now I can afford to shop at bigger stores, I get as much as I can from Thomas first. Without his help, I don't know if I would've kept on trying my hand. Now it's my chance to return his kindness.

I'm almost late to dinner because I make a quick stop at Quinn's that turns into a mediation session between her and our sheriff. I found them glaring at each other, at a standstill over the decorations for a child's birthday cake.

It's dark already and fairy lights hang around the heated deck. I can see Martha and Sam from the parking lot. They're laughing over wine at a table. Carter's not with them.

"Argh!" I yelp when the concrete flies from under my feet and I'm unceremoniously thrown over a broad shoulder. "Are you insane? Put me down!" I slap Carter's butt as he leisurely strolls away from the restaurant.

Martha looks up from her plate and smiles, waving at me.

"Why are they eating without us?" is the next burning question out of my mouth. I've passed up one of Quinn's quiches to save my appetite for this dinner.

"The food will still be there for you in half an hour."

"Why do I even have security if they're useless when I'm being manhandled like this?"

Carter barks out a laugh but ignores my question.

When he finally releases me, I'm confused. "Are we going for a drive?" I take in the equipment and the small boat waiting for us. "I don't need to work up an appetite, you know?"

"I'm feeling nostalgic." He takes one of the life vests and pulls it over my head.

"I'm wearing a dress. And heels."

Carter smirks and kisses my temple while he ties a waterproof cover around my middle. "We'll be out just a bit."

What's come over him? We've gone out on the water a couple more times until it got too cold, but I didn't think he'd be so excited to do it again that he's willing to endure Martha's wrath for being late.

He fires up the engine and we slowly drift out.

"Do you remember when you showed me the disco algae last May?"

How could I forget? It was torture being so close to him and not kissing him. So much has happened in the last year.

"It's called bioluminescent," I correct him, although I know he's joking. "I remember someone stole the last cracker. It wasn't very gentlemanly of him."

He looks over his shoulder and raises an eyebrow. "It was earned fair and square."

We drive in silence, the wind rushing past my ears. When he takes a turn toward the small cluster of islands my heart picks up speed.

Carter kills the engine and sits facing me and throws the anchor over just as the water lights up beneath us. The ripples shimmer around us, casting a soft magical glow.

He takes my trembling hands, love sparkling in his eyes brighter than the glimmering water, setting my entire body on fire. "Last time we were here my life changed. I didn't know how, but it was powerful enough to scare me."

The air catches in my throat.

"I'm not afraid now. I'm grateful for that change and for the chance you've given me."

"Carter—" I whisper feebly, emotion choking all other words.

"You came into my life when I thought I'd never meet a person who could pull me out of my shell. It was dark and miserable, but you burst it wide open and filled it with light and love. I don't know how I got to be so lucky," he says and kisses my knuckles.

Tears prickle the back of my eyes and I squeeze his hands tighter. "Because you deserve it." I swallow back the overwhelming emotion threatening to suffocate me. "There's nobody else I'd feel safe enough to trust with my heart."

Carter's given me the most precious gift of being free to be myself, of loving me unconditionally.

"And I swear to protect it for as long as I live." His Adam's apple bobs, and he's breathtaking in the eerie light. "Eliza." My name comes out heavy with the weight of his adoration. "I can't imagine ever walking this earth without you by my side. Every part of my being is bound to you. I'm hopelessly in love with all of you. Would you do me the honor of going down this road with me?"

Carter drops to his knees and slides a small black velvet box out of his pocket. I can hardly see him through my tears and jump into his arms, making the boat rock dangerously.

"Yes," I say into his lips. "Yes." I press my mouth to his. "Yes to everything," I laugh through my tears, his tender fingers cupping my face, wiping the drops.

Rays of light brighter than the living galaxy underneath us burst through the seams of my heart. It pours through me, bringing with it peace and sheer happiness.

THE END

* * *

About the Author

Khris Andrews is a literature major living in Bucharest with her husband and two boys. She writes slow-burn contemporary romance novels with characters who grow and make you fall in love with them.

When she's not daydreaming about her stories, you can find her devouring true crime documentaries and home improvement shows. Khris loves traveling with her family and finding hidden corners in every place she visits.

Thank you!

If you enjoyed A Place for Love, please consider leaving a review!

Don't miss Jackie and Adam's second chance story coming out in 2025.

Follow Khris for sneak peeks and exciting news about the next releases.

Website:khrisandrews.com

Facebook:@khrisandrewsauthor

Instagram:@khrisandrewsauthor

TikTok:@khrisandrewsauthor

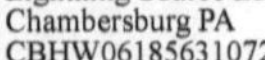

9 798991 607612